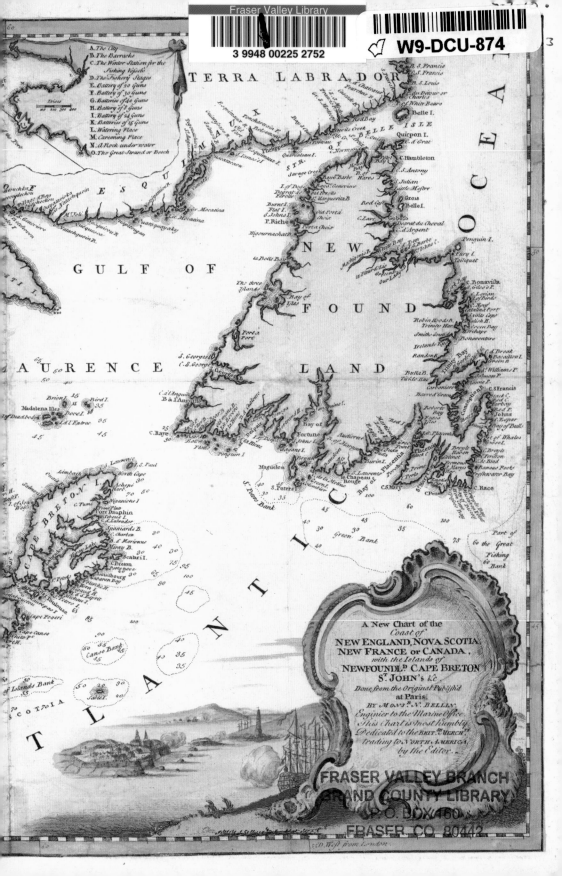

Evangeline

EVANGELINE

Ben Farmer

THE OVERLOOK PRESS
New York

This edition first published in hardcover in the United States in 2010 by

The Overlook Press, Peter Mayer Publishers, Inc.
141 Wooster Street
New York, NY 10012

Cataloging-in-Publication Data is available from the Library of Congress

Book *design and typeformatting by Bernard Schleifer*
Manufactured in the United States of America
FIRST EDITION
2 4 6 8 10 9 7 5 3 1
ISBN 978-1-59020-043-8

for Alison

KITH AND KIN

THANK YOU TO THOSE WHO HELPED WITH VALUABLE INFORMATION AND logistical support in Nova Scotia and Louisiana, and in particular, to my traveling companions—Alison, Aaron, Sam and Thomas— who helped make the research for this book a pleasure.

Particular thanks are due Peter Mayer, who thought that Longfellow's poem would suit as a novel, and was enthusiastic and generous in his encouragement. My gratitude goes to him for the idea, and to my editor, Aaron Schlechter, who advanced me for it and has remained excited about my work over the years.

As those men were fundamental to this novel's existence, so were my brother and father to its quality. Thoughtful readers and penetrating writers, their humor and insight made revising a joy that it could not have been without their enlightened participation.

I could not have attempted this without the unwavering support of Alison Michel. Alison cheerfully supported me through a process that stretched longer than I told her it might, and was the second set of eyes on every word that I wrote. And thanks to my mother, who always took my phone calls. Thank you all.

EVANGELINE

A Cast of Nations 1755

⌖

THE KINGDOM OF GREAT BRITAIN
(His Majesty George II, r. 1727-60)

Colonies—Acadia, Newfoundland and Labrador, Massachusetts, New Hampshire, Rhode Island, Connecticut, New York, New Jersey, Pennsylvania, Delaware, Maryland, Virginia, North Carolina, South Carolina, Georgia, Rupert's Land, and numerous Caribbean islands

North American Allies—Iroquois Confederacy (Cayuga, Mohawk, Oneida, Onondaga, Seneca and Tuscarora), Cherokee, and Catawba

FRANCE
(King Louis XV, the Beloved, r. 1715-74)

Colonies—New France, Ile Royale (Cape Breton), Ile Saint Jean (Prince Edward Island), Louisiana, and several Caribbean islands

North American Allies—Abenaki, Algonquin, Mi'kmaq, Lenape (or Delaware), Huron (later Wyandot), Ojibwe, Ottawa, and Shawnee among others

Other Allies—The Kingdom of Spain, with colonies including Cuba, Florida, Hispaniola (Dominican Republic), and Mexico

A Note on Acadia

⌘

ACADIA WAS AMONG THE FIRST EUROPEAN COLONIES founded in the New World. Its history began in 1604, when Sieur de Biencourt led forty Frenchmen ashore to establish Port Royal for Henri IV. It concludes in 1755, with the dawn of the fourth and greatest of the Indian Wars fought between England and France in North America, and the onset of this story.

Acadia (a vaguely defined territory which in colonial times included Nova Scotia, Cape Breton, Prince Edward Island, and a disputed stretch of New Brunswick inland from the Bay of Fundy) was the first French settlement in North America, but it was abandoned shortly after its founding in favor of the uniquely defensible cliffs of the Saint Lawrence valley around Quebec. Biencourt returned with more settlers in 1610, but was overwhelmed three years later by Captain Samuel Argall, who commanded a ship out of England's fledgling North American colony, Jamestown. Only three years removed from a winter where starvation, disease and exposure had reduced the English colony from hundreds to 60 (an occurrence not unusual, but rather indicative of the 'seasoning' suffered by first-generation Europeans), Jamestown teetered near extinction, yet was motivated enough by the rumor of French colonization to dispatch

Argall, who burned the first Jesuit mission in New France on Mount Desert Island (now part of Maine) before successfully laying siege to the new fort at Port Royal on the peninsula.

Biencourt and several dozen followers escaped into the woods, where they were sheltered by the Mi'kmaq, an Algonquin tribe that controlled the Acadian peninsula and surrounding islands. Already partners in the fur trade, widespread intermarriage between Acadians and the Mi'kmaq over the ensuing decades strengthened these relations (like many settlers of the New World, the early Acadian colonists' ranks held few women).

France regained control of the colony in 1632, when the Treaty of Saint-Germain-en-Laye returned Acadia (and Quebec, which England had captured in 1628), in exchange for the unpaid dowry of England's Queen, Henrietta Maria. More than two decades of renewed immigration from France—which resulted in clashes between the newcomers and the existing French population—ended when a large force of Massachusetts volunteers conquered the colony. Despite the fact that England and France had not been at war during the hostilities (the militia had been raised to fight a quickly concluded war with the Dutch), England retained control of Acadia until the Treaty of Breda formally resolved the matter in 1667.

Far from having their growth blighted, the Acadians thrived under English rule, engineering dikes that created arable land from the tidal rivers around Port Royal. Families and neighbors labored together to shape the earthen walls, which were supported by logs sunk in the mud, and punctured by aboiteaux—valves that closed with the incoming tide, and opened with its ebb to expel rainwater that slowly desalinated the fields. Though this efficient practice allowed the Mi'kmaq to retain traditional hunting grounds even as the Acadian population swelled, the two peoples drifted apart as the eighteenth century approached and farming replaced the fur trade as the Acadians' principal means of subsistence. The fracture was deepened further by consistently hostile relations between the Mi'kmaq and the English, whose legal authority the Acadians were increasingly forced to recognize.

This was a quarrel in which the Acadians refused to intervene—their posture in all disputes regardless of the belligerents—as their unenviable positioning on the shifting border between imperial powers forced the decentralized farmers to avoid direct involvement in the incessant conflicts to avoid reprisal. Each time the colony was exchanged between negotiating empires, Acadia was left further isolated from its neighbors—English colonists in Massachusetts, their French counterparts in present-day New Brunswick and Cape Breton, and the Mi'kmaq who still controlled the interior of the Acadian peninsula. Ideologically separate but economically tied to the English colonies, the Acadians were a people distinguished by their French language and Catholicism, but also by their necessary and unique status as noncombatants in wartime. They were referred to as 'French neutrals' by their neighbors, but the prosperous peasants increasingly viewed themselves as distinctly Acadian.

The most peaceful period of French rule over Acadia began in 1667, when the colony was returned to France following the Treaty of Breda. The Acadians continued to multiply, illicitly trade with Massachusetts, and spread their homesteads around the margins of the Bay of Fundy—settling Grand Pre in 1682.

King William's War—the first of four wars between England and France that saw major battles fought in the New World—broke out in 1689. English forces under Sir William Phips captured Port Royal the next year, and Acadia reverted to

English control. The Treaty of Ryswick in 1697 restored all captured territory, and Acadia was handed back to France. Queen Anne's War followed hard upon in 1702. In 1710, after a week-long siege, Port Royal fell to an overwhelming force of 3500 mixed English and colonial soldiers (overwhelming by colonial standards, as hundreds of thousands were killed in the related battles of the War of Spanish Succession back in Europe). Under the terms of the Treaty of Utrecht in 1713, France ceded Acadia, Newfoundland and Labrador to England, though Cape Breton and Prince Edward Island remained under French control. This marked the seventh time in a century that the Acadian colony was traded between France and England, but though it could hardly have seemed likely in the moment, this time, Anglican rule was to endure.

King George's War lasted from 1744 to 1748 with Acadia remaining an English possession, and the undisturbed Acadians continued to thrive. Nearly without aid of immigration after 1713, the population grew from about 500 in 1670 to more than 7500 in a 1737 census, and that number had doubled by the outbreak of war in 1755. This prodigious increase can be traced to interrelated benevolent factors including: a rich and varied diet, abundant productivity from both mothers and fields (it was said that Acadians devoted themselves only to raising crops, cattle and children), low infant mortality, a rural population which discouraged widespread disease outbreaks, and a lack of direct involvement in war thanks to their unbroken neutrality. This proclivity for fecundity greatly unsettled several of their English governors, and it—along with their nearly insubordinate stubbornness regarding personal freedoms, and their presumed untrustworthiness as French Catholics—prompted the English crown to formulate a systematic plan for their removal.

Evangeline

It is a cruel circumstance, but one frequently echoed in history, that insists this tale of deportation and wandering be told, as it was a century and a half ago, in the language of the conqueror.

"This country from a thousand vexing cares has set them free . . ."

—SIEUR DE DIEREVILLE, *French surgeon and historian, on the Acadians in 1708*

Gaspereau River 1755

From the mountain's top the rainy mists of the morning roll away,
and afar we behold the landscape below us.

*T*HE TORCH FLASHED ACROSS THE RIVER'S SURFACE AND
drew the dark-eyed, shimmering prey, their instinctive
bodies twisting and darting toward the luminous
deceit. Evangeline leaned toward Gabriel, her free hand outstretched for balance, the pine pitch hissing as it cast its halo
around his feet. They balanced on posts, surplus from a past season's dike building that had been sunk beyond the barriers so
fisherman could tie off their small boats. After several years, the
moorings jutted at rude angles from the soft bottom, but they
had chosen these tenuous perches to show off for each other. If
they did misstep, the water was only knee-deep.

Gabriel thrust, and withdrew the spear. The scales of the
small salmon glistened like metal as he freed it from the iron
point and flipped it to shore where it lay, silently gasping on the
dark riverbank. After he added several more, Evangeline let their
torch slip into the Gaspereau, and they sat beside their catch,

talking quietly and watching the few other torches flicker until the sky softened into dawn.

Home for Evangeline was the top of the hill, but Gabriel had a long walk back to the Habitant, where he might still arrive in time for the day's work at his father's smithy. There would be no sleep for Gabriel, but she could expect a few restful hours.

Grand Pre woke early and noisily on summer mornings. The spear fishermen trudging home passed farmers headed toward the water to check on stock left overnight to graze. The cattle were unmarked, but each man knew his own and his neighbor's. Children hurried through milking and wood gathering to free themselves to spend the afternoon on a river. A skiff was beached on the gray mudflat of the Minas, landlocked by the ebb tide. A man sat in the boat, sewing a linen patch onto the canvas sail. As he worked, the man looked out to sea, worried over what he might find there.

"Evangeline," Benedict said that morning. "When did you get in last night?"

Benedict had been leaning against the doorjamb, prodding her awake with his cane, but he pretended innocence when she sat up.

"Just a little before dawn. "

"My neglect has reached new limits. Your mother and I were never allowed to stay out so late before we married."

"Well, I brought home fish for lunch."

"That's my girl. How is Gabriel?"

"He's doing wonderfully."

"I'm sure that he is. Let's get a taste of your cooking before you start wasting it on someone else."

Evangeline had waited half the summer to model her wedding dress for Sofia, but, tired as she was that afternoon, quickly lost patience with the older woman's careful measurements and was anxious to be finished by the time the heavy silk settled about her shoulders.

"Your mother's dress deserves a bit more respect than that," Sofia protested. "I certainly didn't have anything so fine to wear when I married Jacques."

Evangeline smoothed the long stomacher and took a deep breath before explaining herself.

"I was fishing with Gabriel last night." And, in response to Sofia's disapproving look, "I only held the torch, he did the spearing."

"They'll just be the grilse now."

"Yes, they were. But it was fine. I hadn't seen him for days."

"You're going to see plenty of him soon enough."

"Not for months yet, Sofia. And I'm not sure that I ever love Gabriel more than when I see his face by torchlight."

The older woman's brows wrinkled. "You'd be better served following that branch to the trunk."

Evangeline considered Basil, Gabriel's father, and the little hairs that grew off the tops of his ears, and bushed out of his meaty nostrils. She realized that she did not consider Basil Lajeunesse to be an attractive man.

"That doesn't matter," Evangeline said, gaining force as she continued. "When Gabriel gets old and fat and hairy, we'll just douse the lights."

Sofia grunted quietly as she eyed the intricate knotwork around the neckline. "It's a bit more skin than is currently the fashion," she said with a disapproving glance at Evangeline's bare shoulders.

"I'll be lucky if I can just keep it on," Evangeline said.

"Yes, I imagine a full-figured woman once looked good in

this dress." Sofia fingered the stitches running the length of the embroidered corset. "These could have been for your mother. I met her when she was wearing this dress," Sofia said familiarly. "You've heard me say it before, but you're fortunate to have taken after her so."

"You leave my poor father alone," Evangeline retorted cheerfully, but Sofia continued her fiddling in silence.

"Do you know why wedding dresses are white?" Evangeline asked.

"Because the dresses would be passed down and the dyes would have faded over time," Sofia guessed.

Evangeline shook her head. "White was the color of joy in ancient Greece. And then it was the color associated with Hymen, the Roman goddess of fertility and marriage."

"Is that so," Sofia said distractedly, as she bunched the right sleeve around a blue ribbon.

Evangeline looked at the remaining mess of silken ribbons, blue for purity and green for her youth, which lay in the light dust atop a carefully made bed.

Youth had deserted the Melansons' house years before, when Sofia and Jacques sent their five children to stay with relations on Ile Saint Jean. Evangeline was only ten when they left, and remembered little of them besides one of the girls cutting her hair. The parents remained behind in Grand Pre, minding their store as their children raised families in the north. Evangeline realized guiltily that Sofia had not had the pleasure of altering her daughters' dresses for their weddings, and she turned to her friend.

The movement surprised Sofia, and she pricked Evangeline in the side with a needle.

"It's supposed to be good luck for a bride's dress to be torn by her seamstress," the older woman said with a smile.

Evangeline smiled back as she took the girdle off the bed and tied it around her waist. It was bound with the same blue ribbons Sofia knotted at her sleeves. Her mother might have made those knots, Evangeline reflected, and she left them tied as they were.

Evangeline reached next for the delicately embroidered pockets, and heard a crackling as she tied them at her waist. She withdrew a letter from the righthand pocket. Her name was on the outside of the envelope. A letter from her mother, fifteen years dead.

There were three other letters penned by her mother that Benedict had given her when she turned twelve, when she was old enough not to be confused that her mother wouldn't be following after. She had them memorized, and now looked more at the penmanship than the words.

"I thought I had gotten them all already," Evangeline said out loud, but without explanation as she sat heavily on the bed next to the ribbons.

"It's from your mother?" Sofia guessed.

Evangeline nodded wordlessly.

Sofia looked around the quiet bedroom as though she had forgotten something, and then moved to the door. "I'll set out the milk for supper, dear, while you read."

Evangeline had removed the letter from the unsealed envelope before Sofia was out of the room.

Evangeline,

I won't see you wear this dress. Rest assured that my sorrow is relieved by the thought of you swimming in our river, walking the headlands. The apple shoots outside our window must be bearing fruit. I wish only that I could have seen the boy who merits your stepping into my old gown. But, enough.

Perhaps the finest aspect of being born in Acadia is that you are free to choose your husband, and I struggle to conjure a more momentous occasion, an imagining made more difficult with you still writhing in your crib. And do not mistake, though I did not choose your father, his strengths far outstrip his weaknesses. And if his memory (which in our time was fastidious of its details) has not failed him, I imagine he has imparted some of my family's history, while no doubt bending your ear as regards his piratical antecedents. Even so, I hope that you will bear through my telling, for it concerns the dress you are soon to wear, and might even provide you with some inspiration as your new life commences.

This dress was made for Francoise-Marie Jacquelin, when she married your forebear, Charles de La Tour. And though we don't share her blood, as Madame La Tour was childless, she is deserving of our respect (beyond her rich fashion), as she was a brave woman who fought at her husband's side for possession of what would become our Acadia. I should say that she did more than just fight at his side, as she was in command of their garrison when it surrendered to the La Tours' rival, Charles de Menou d'Aulnay, who betrayed the terms of the surrender and executed the defenders. Being of noble blood, Madame La Tour was spared from hanging, but she was poisoned weeks later while still in D'Aulnay's dungeon.

Vengeance found D'Aulnay a few years later, when he drowned mysteriously in the Dauphin. His widow, Jeanne Motin de Reux, was evicted from Port Royal by Emmanuel Le Borgne, a merchant her husband died in the debt of, and, looking for a way to reclaim her lands, she and La

*Tour (who had ceded his claims after his wife's death)
arranged a marriage that must have seemed unlikely, as,
scant years earlier, Jeanne's husband had killed Charles'
wife while their families were at war. Charles must have valued the union, because he allowed dispossessed Jeanne to
wear his widow's dress. They had been married less than a
year when Acadia was occupied by English colonials who,
by virtue of friendships he had made in Boston while fighting D'Aulnay, allowed the newly married couple to remain
in Acadia, where they had five children.*

*The dress then passed to Jeanne's daughter, Marie, who
wore it in another political marriage to a former enemy, Le
Borgne's son, Emmanuel, who was considerably older than
your great-grandmother when they were married in 1674. So
clearly I remember seeing that date scrawled on the cross
atop my grandmother's grave. My grandmother passed the
dress down to her eldest, also named Marie, when mother
arranged her daughter's marriage to Alexandre Gautier. The
marriage was not for political reasons, but for livres, as
Emmanuel had spent his declining years drinking and ignoring his family's condition. Thankfully your father ignored the
bottle instead of me. The Gautiers owned the mills and farms
of Belisle (shrewdly erected at the Dauphin's head of naviga-
tion), and even though my father was the fifth son, he had
lived his life as a wealthy man. He was nearly two decades
older than my mother, who was surpassing beautiful.*

*Despite the circumstantial nature of their marriage,
my mother spoke kindly of my father, though I do not
remember him well, for he was old when I was born in
1696, and died when I was five. It is with such painful
awareness that I inscribe these words, certain in the knowl-*

edge that God will also gather me to His embrace before I have had a proper chance to gather you in mine.

But, rather than mistake the everlasting joy that you have brought into my life, I kiss your cheek, run my fingers through your fine hair, and find the strength to finish my story. It was while growing up in the sawing and heaving at Belisle that I met your father (who knows his family's history better than I, suffice to say that it is a wandering tale). Benedict's precociousness had already won him captaincy of one of our schooners that made frequent trips to the fortress at Louisbourg, a common enough occurrence around Belisle, but an illegal one. Despite our difference in age and background, he asked for my hand when I was only fourteen. My mother refused him, but he remained in my family's employ, and rose in its esteem, until Queen Anne's War finally ended. I remember the last years of the war vividly, as we briefly sheltered distant relations, the Duviviers, who commanded a rabble fighting to wrest Port Royal back from the English. There were hundreds of men encamped around our home for nearly a month, eating our food and drinking all night. It was little surprise to me when they proved unable to take the fort, and returned to Louisbourg in defeat.

The redcoats paid us special attention after that, making frequent inspections of the estate, in which they never seized a person, but always livestock, or a shipload of timber from upriver. The English waited only until the end of the war to take possession of our home, leaving my family to join its kin in France, Quebec, and Louisbourg. As my mother (who was still a young woman thinking of other husbands) prepared for her future in Paris, your father saw his opportunity, and again asked for my hand. Though I was less than excited about the arrangement, as I also wished to see Paris and know something of the world, my mother agreed and Benedict and I moved here to the Minas. My dowry was the lands around you, and together we built the home that your father will raise you in alone.

And I wore the dress, which held the letter you now hold in your grown hands, when I married your father in rustic Saint Charles, here in the Minas. And I hope that you find the same strength in the fine white silk that I did. It is our inheritance, and our reminder, of the world that bludgeons itself, ignorant of the peace your father and I have found here in Grand Pre, where tax collectors, and not soldiers, are the only mark of empire (and may it ever be so).

I have already mentioned the trading by which your father earned his bread, and find no shame in it. More than from any other source, we come from men and women of commerce. Unlike the farmers that have surrounded our family for more than a century, we have concerned ourselves with fur.

Remember then, that Acadia runs deeper in your blood than it does in the farms that even now seem so ancient compared to your cheerful innocence. And though you should never forget that Jeanne's is the blood in your veins, remember also the woman whose dress you wear. She was a particular heroine of mine during the many years when I doubted that I would know the pleasure of your birth. Take her courage as example, and take our story as proof that you will need it.

Your loving mother,
Emmeline

Evangeline considered whether this letter had been written before or after the ones she had already received, which held more tender remarks and comments on her infant growth. The letter with the dress must have preceded the others, Evangeline surmised, in the days after her birth when her mother had planned ahead against a distant wedding that she would not live to see. More yearning emotion cracked through the regal ease of those already read letters, as her mother sickened. The cause had remained mysterious, a wasting illness that seemed rooted in mythical times, when deaths were fated rather than accidental.

The letter certainly offered encouragement and blessing to marry with her heart, though, arriving as she stood already in the wedding dress, the wisdom might have been late received if Benedict had not staunchly echoed the same sentiment throughout her life.

"Marry for love," her father had said recently, "and if you're lucky, you'll be as fortunate as I was, and find a partner who is your better. There isn't a thing in the world that I could do as well as your mother."

"You've always told me that survival is a skill," Evangeline demurred.

Her father had smiled at that. "A meager one it seems. You're pleasant enough, child, but many is the time I've thought that life without her isn't worth keeping."

Fifty-three when she was born, her father had never mentioned finding another woman, or at least, never considered it openly. "I remember her too well," he might say if the subject came up among strangers. "I'm just waiting for my daughter to get old enough so that I can marry one of her friends," was his oft-repeated joke among the men who were regular guests at the Bellefontaine house.

"What friends?" Evangeline might return, if there weren't many visitors.

Her father would be dead before the children she would bear Gabriel were old enough to remember him. It was not so galling with Emmeline. All Evangeline had to know her mother by were her letters, isolated pleasures she would pass along to her children to glean what they could of this corner of their family. But Benedict would be but a shadow flitting across the periphery of her children's memories. When her firstborn daughter changed her family name from Lajeunesse, she would receive this dress and letter from Emmeline just as Evangeline had. And while the La Tours and Gautiers would descend through her offspring, sadly and irrevocably the name of Bellefontaine would be smothered in her.

The letters and the dress were her mother's legacy. She would be Benedict's.

New France 1755

And the streets still reecho the names of the trees of the forest, as if they fain would appease the dryads whose haunts they molested.

BERNARD ARSENEAU WRAPPED THE SHRIVELED HUNKS OF smoked venison in a worn pelt, restoring the meat to skin, and stowed them carefully alongside the snowshoes, wool blankets and short paddles in the belly of the small canoe. He reached for the pelts next, strung through with buckskin in heaps at the side of the bark, and heaved them over the stern onto the pile where they flopped like trout. He negotiated the stocks of the two long muskets until they wedged crosswise atop the assemblage. Possessions secure, he filled his short clay pipe with cut tobacco from the pouch about his neck and lounged smoking against a birch, waiting.

When Augustine finally appeared on the trail from the village, he was distractedly plucking goose and quail feathers out of his unruly graying hair. Three Wyandot crested the hill behind Augustine, and effortlessly outpaced him on their way to a bark hidden in the reeds. As the men glided off, Bernard saw streaks of bear grease and vermilion across their cheeks and foreheads. Augustine joined him and they silently watched the warriors pole south, their shaved skulls glinting bronze in the noon sun.

Bernard tapped the ash from his pipe into his palm and flung it into the lake before taking his bout up front. Augustine shoved them off from the bank, wading into the water and soaking his leggings before clambering in.

"It turned into a bit of a late morning."

"It's not morning at all," Bernard replied as they glided away from the bank where they swapped the dripping poles for the paddles.

"Did you fill the canteens?" Augustine asked.

Bernard leaned back to find one, dunked it in the transparent water and heaved it onto Augustine's lap. The older man sloshed only a bit in his beard as he drank deeply then dunked the bladder again and poured it over his face.

"Another baptism after a night of fire." He held it dripping back into the lake while he gazed back toward the village. "Kindred spirits, those people."

Bernard returned to paddling before responding. "How's that?"

"They've left their ancestral homes behind in search of freedom in the west."

"I wouldn't say many of us got here by choice. Those sauvages were driven out here by the Iroquois, their men were killed in wars with the English, and now these women are forced to marry carrion pickers like you."

"Forced, hell. She loves me. And she doesn't mind that I only stay for a few months at a time. It wouldn't surprise me at all if Mowi had another husband on his way down the river, and good for her." He spat in the water. "Besides, you need her as much as I do. I know you haven't forgotten that my wives have kept us fed these past couple winters, pup. I had to get the second one to balance you out." Augustine started paddling, and chuckled victoriously, "You wouldn't be here at all if your father showed this kind of interest."

They paddled and lapsed into a silence short of anger. Over the last few days yellow leaves had begun to fall and they caught in clumps in the chicots and waved happily in the current.

They sculled north along the lake's western bank for two days before the dark tower of Saint Frederic came into view and late on their second night they made their fire on a gravel island poking up near shore. Four long sloops drifted at anchor in the harbor between them and the granite fortress.

"No festivities tonight then," Augustine complained as they unloaded. "I don't see why you're shy of soldiers anyway. There's little difference between them and us out here." He continued harping while Bernard gathered dry kindling. Their neighbors were burning a large fire against the chill, and the fortress looked like a cauldron ready to spill over on their tiny camp.

"It's late. We're just as well to stay out here."

"Just because a person takes up a life in the wilderness doesn't mean they disdain the idea of the occasional conversation every here and there." Augustine stuck his grizzled thumbs in his belt and prowled the island's perimeter. "This whole rock is no bigger than those ships. I hope this water doesn't come up any higher."

"Sleep on your back," Bernard replied, coaxing the spark he'd kindled. "I was picked up by soldiers once."

"You and your father?"

Bernard nodded. "Not long before he died. We were running ax heads south from Montreal to villages along the Wabash a couple times a year. Trading with Mingo in a mission town not that far east of the Wyandot we just left." Bernard looked back down the lake. "A soldier approached us one night from Vincennes and spoke to my father, and the next day we led two dozen French soldiers up the river to a British post."

"So what, they attacked?" Augustine asked distractedly, staring across the water at the hooded light.

Bernard started in on a bit of venison and waited for his partner to pay attention before continuing, "Against four English, colonials."

"And what of it?"

"We'd been there the week before. They'd been generous, gave us each a Brown Bess," Bernard gestured at his gun slouched atop the canoe, "for a couple ratty pelts and our old muskets. Souvenirs, they said they wanted them to take back to England. They were looking forward to when they'd be shed of the whole country."

They fell quiet, chewing their cold dried meat and speculating on fortune, but shortly footsteps crunched on the nearby mainland. "Who visits His Majesty's fair shores?"

"Frenchmen visiting family," Augustine sang back across the darkness.

"Fine, fine," the voice replied. "We've got some brandy with us. Are you receiving visitors?"

"Come on over." Augustine shrugged at Bernard, who moved wordlessly across the fire to sit near their loaded muskets. The trappers listened silently to the labored progress through the night. Two men emerged dripping from the gloom, water steaming off their bare chests and sodden wool pants as they sat near the fire.

"That's a cold damn lake," Augustine observed.

"It is that," the soldier with the brandy allowed. He upended the bottle and smiled when the cork held, proof of its safe passage. "But a little fire will go a long way."

Satisfied that they hadn't brought weapons, Augustine relaxed into a slouch along the fire. Bernard kept his eyes on their guests as the bottle made its orbit around the flames with the talk.

"You said you were visiting family out here?" The soldier's full black beard hid his mouth, and Bernard told himself he imagined the suspicious tone.

"That's right. My dear wife lives in Missimee."

"That's mighty fine," the same man responded. "If I'm out here any longer I expect I'll get used to a squaw myself." Sitting in front of the fire the half-naked warrior looked like he'd already gone native.

"It's not so hard." The brandy exchanged hands with the laughter, and Augustine started a second round. "Though some men never quite find the taste," he gurgled, looking at Bernard as he drank.

"So what brings all of you around?" Bernard couldn't think of a more casual way to join the conversation.

"We're at war," one explained gleefully. "We're bringing the hammer to the English."

"That's a little hasty," the other cut in, staring at Bernard directly across the fire. "I've learned there are several different ways to disagree, and nothing's been said now that hasn't been said many times before. But my friend's not alone in expecting more boats coming down the river." The bottle was passed to the speaker and he rolled it in his hands, warming it in the fire. "There's been a little trouble further south. We're just reinforcing the garrisons so we can throw our weight around." He shrugged his shoulders after the explanation and drank.

"I hate the damn English," his companion slurred to no one.

"Enough about that," the other man cut in. "As far as we're concerned, when you're in the wilderness, white people are white people and you can't get enough of them."

Augustine emptied the bottle shamelessly before handing it to the sober soldier who took it and settled it among the smooth stones.

"Goddamn right." Augustine belched, and then stood as if to usher them out and the soldiers stood also.

"I hope you gentlemen find another fire when you get back across the water." Augustine stared disapprovingly across the black water.

"Certainly will, gentlemen, and we'll tell them that we've got good Frenchmen for neighbors when we get there." The sober man tipped an imaginary hat and the soldiers waded out into the water, legless torsos hesitant for a moment before they disappeared.

They broke camp in the darkness with Augustine groaning quietly but moving earnestly, and spoke in whispers as they glided past the obelisk and its slumbering garrison, darker than the pitch-black of the predawn sky.

"We've got to keep out of sight for a while, Augustine."

"Easy there, my little doe. You have a finger for every war I've survived out here. We just need to find a village where we can hibernate."

"You heard them, the whole country's already stirred up, and they as much as told us there'll be more fighting before the year's out. We need to get away from the Saint Lawrence."

"To where exactly?" Perhaps because he had the benefit

of twice Bernard's years, Augustine never appreciated being lectured.

"Backcountry, north of the river, I guess."

"Away from people." They paddled in silence for several minutes before Augustine allowed the distance was sufficient for him to raise his voice. "I won't go further than the last village." He softened his tone a bit. "I've always said, if you can't get a sauvage to buy it, there's no sense trying to sell it to me."

"Fine."

The trappers bypassed the tiny stockade of Fort Saint Jean that night, and the slightly larger stone version upriver at Chambly several days later, and reached the main flow of the Saint Lawrence north of Montreal after a solid week of paddling. At Sorel, Bernard found a voyageur headed for Quebec and traded three worn ermine furs for lengths of metal wire. Judging by the splotchy blond beard, the man was as young as he was, but headed indoors for winter.

"These are just over from France," the voyageur gestured to the wires that he'd exchanged without bothering to count. Bernard did, there were two dozen, without their nooses tied. The man gestured to the ermine like the expert he wasn't. "You ever lose one of those little buggers because it ate its way free before you came around?"

"Sure."

"Well, you won't anymore. A lynx couldn't chew through one of these."

The voyageur also offered up two small traps whose iron jaws looked like they might never have tasted beaver. Though tempted, Bernard declined. The tribesmen he and Augustine traded with were jealous of their beaver, and were further offended by the artifice of iron traps on their lakes.

When Bernard returned to their bark, Augustine had loaded them down with so much brandy that it felt like they were towing a body north with them. Downstream of the post, the wide river opened up further and the current slackened, and they crossed to the west bank, and after more than a fortnight's travel from the Wyandot village finally broke from the Saint Lawrence and dug in and paddled against the flow of a tributary north, the furthest north or east they'd been in two mild years spent cruising richer fur lands around the lakes.

The trappers progressed slowly through New France's backcountry, scuffling with their canoe along deserted rivers and lands that had once belonged to the Huron and Algonquin before Iroquois and disease emptied them. The autumn weather stayed mild for two long weeks, as the streams narrowed around them until they grew impassable for stretches, and they were forced to carry their bark and possessions along the gurgling current of the rising land, Bernard driving them onward as Augustine's patience waned. After two days of mostly portaging in search of open water Augustine broke his sullen silence to curse him as they hauled their birch and its swinging pelts on the long march.

"I'm leaving you here in the woods, coward." Augustine looked older than usual, his skin nearly the color of his hair as he panted. Bernard didn't quite feel sorry for him. Neither of them knew exactly when they'd strike the water again, and the temperature was plummeting around them though it was still early afternoon. Over the weeks of travel the leaves had gone from yellow and orange to red and brown, and were now beginning to lay the forest bare.

"You don't even know where we are."

"Damn you if that matters." Augustine dug up a rock and

threw it at Bernard, but missed, and the stone rustled through the dry underbrush behind him.

Bernard ignored him. "We're just about to the Saint Maurice. I wasn't born far from here."

"My old mother might still be alive, but I'm not asking for you to follow me back to Brittany."

"Well, probably time we found a decent camp, that storm's catching up quick." They suffered through another long slough with the bark walls of the canoe scraping against the trees so that Bernard could see patches they'd have to replace before they took back to the water, and they found it, not the Saint Maurice, but a long lake pocked with clumps of beaver-hewn stumps, lying cold and still in the primordial gloom of the evening.

"It'll do." Augustine dropped the canoe and pitched down alongside it.

They made camp with the last light of the cold evening, building with more permanence in mind than usual, constructing neighboring shelters from skins arranged over birch frames, a shape similar to the wigwams they usually slept in, but closed at the top. Both men preferred outdoor fires, and especially after a few weeks' paddle, each valued privacy above warmth.

Bernard awoke to the stench of burning flesh and burst out of his shelter apelike in the sterile predawn, staying low while he looked for his gun. He saw Augustine curled under a blanket with his head pillowed on one of the stones of the fire ring, fur cap inside, half-burned and stinking. Bernard rose, looked his partner over, and after a moment's assessment edged the hat further into the embers with his moccasin. He settled himself with their cache on the other side of the fire and located the new lengths of wire, laid them out on the ground, and then went down to the nearby waterline to find a reed to light his pipe. He tossed the spent brand on the fire and rustled the thin branches. Once the fire blazed anew he sat back and imagined what the thin wires would look like wrapped around the necks of white rabbits.

"Yessir, yessir." Augustine stirred from the ground, non-plussed as he saw that he sat outside of his shelter. "A man could freeze to death out here."

"Your hat's burnt up."

He rubbed his head but didn't respond as he watched Bernard tie the wires into nooses.

"Trying anything larger?" Augustine finally asked.

"Well, I don't expect to find beaver, but I'd set a deadfall if you're willing."

"I might just go hunt up a deer and forget setting any traps at all."

"It's elk up here."

"Stinking venison," Augustine muttered, pawing at the remnants of his cap.

"You could just lay for a bear. One decent bearskin and you won't have to pay so much attention to where you fall asleep."

They set their traps as the storm closed relentlessly, following the same northeast track they had from the lakes. They settled in together after the cold hours afield, massaging their hands before the fire, grumpy from the work and the long portage of the day before.

Following their established custom, Augustine had started his rounds after Bernard returned to camp. Bernard reveled in the crispness of mornings, the soft furs he uncovered damp and glistening, rare as precious stones in a cave. For his part, Augustine would sit up at night, spitting into the fire and following stars across the sky, bottle in his lap, pretending he was a ship's captain at the wheel. Occasionally they might exchange observations over their shared afternoon meal, but usually walked separate but parallel paths through the forest. This evening, however, the gloomy prospect of the heavy clouds motivated a few extra pulls from both men as they sat around their fire, alcohol firing their blood as the temperature plummeted.

"Careful you don't wind up with your head inside the ring this time."

"Kind of you to worry." Augustine drank and breathed out with a whoosh. "No beaver, no people, I hope you're happy." Augustine looked at Bernard as if he'd recently renewed the acquaintance. "I don't think I've ever seen your beard this long. It's certainly uglier every day." Bernard scratched his itchy new growth and silently watched the brandy work down the corners of Augustine's straggly gray whiskers. "How long are we going to freeze our pods off out here?"

"The last few years we've passed through at least a couple villages a season, and we only traded with the Wyandot before we came east, so I figure we need about twice the weight we've got just to last the year."

"You're talking weeks more we'll be out here."

"I'm talking survival, you old drunk. Even if you didn't drink up the money we'd still run out before summer. Then, the only thing'd be the service. Not for me."

"I hate the goddamn cold and this goddamn country." Augustine looked blearily around the campsite. "This wasn't why Henry the Navigator learned to sail. He sailed to find castles and spices and warm beaches crowded with women," he groused across the fire.

"You just ran away from your wife." Bernard didn't mean to rile the old man, but couldn't stop the words.

"One of several," the old man began defensively before hitting his stride. "I'll find another when the time's right." He took a long drink and snickered evilly, "Least I've had more than a father to keep me warm, boy." Bernard remembered that hangovers weren't the only reason they didn't drink together more often.

Bernard awoke the next morning to the hiss of wet snow as it snuffed out the remnants of their fire. A pine bough recoiled and the powder crashed lightly near his shelter. The same hemlocks had kept him up the night before, whispering their protest against the rising wind while he shivered to sleep, hugging his body tight around the angry warmth of brandy in the pit of his stomach.

Though the snow was unlikely to last, the powder would have obscured the castoreum they used as bait. Bernard stiffly untied the lynx pelt that served as doorway, stood outside and stretched, momentarily unwinding his tortured muscles before their daily punishment as he rubbed the frozen pelt methodically, contemplating the dead tail. He slowly opened his mouth and winced as he forced his swollen tongue out into the air, chasing the flakes still intermittently falling as a temporary remedy for his breath. Two dressed rabbits, lightly dusted with snow, dangled cold and dead where he'd carelessly left them swinging on the birch framework over his entrance.

Bernard shook the snow from the light birch snowshoes sitting near the fire, and knelt and clasped the bear's paws over his moccasins. Still bending from the waist, he dragged the heavy string of dirty pelts off his bedroll and draped them over his protesting shoulders for warmth. As upright as he'd be for the next few hours, Bernard watered the cold embers. No matter that the storm had done his work already, it was good luck to piss on a fire at the beginning of a day.

The icy swamp spread out before him, its wetness seeping through his greased moccasins, worth an ermine by themselves two months ago, but the snowshoes underneath kept their traction as he trudged down to the water. The snares and culheag he set yesterday lay north of their riverbank camp, with Augustine's to the south, his plan which had allowed the two men to work side by side for two years without either injuring the other. A lightning-shattered oak stood a dozen paces from him as he reached the water's edge. The boulder of his deadfall was visibly undisturbed at the base of the massive old tree. Bernard quietly cursed to the morning.

He would have a better chance with the snares, though any success was unlikely this morning. The weather would have driven the rabbits, foxes, ermine and minx to ground, though they'd need food again in a day or so.

Hopeful despite the odds, Bernard gave the heavy rock a wide berth to try his luck deeper in the swamp. His snares lay hidden in the high grass along the edge of the slowly flowing water, where he might get anything, though the sleek ermine fur was considered far more elegant and desirable than the lumpy rabbit pelts. His first blaze came into view as he passed the oak sheltering the deadfall, the fresh scar of his knife visible two meters up the trunk of a withered pine.

Before he parted the reeds, Bernard knew his first snare was empty. The cool metal flashed in the sun as he released the tension to spread the scent. Even after snow, the supple wire was easier to untie than buckskin ever would have been. Painful recollections of the piercing teeth of rodents induced a momentary shudder, strong enough to force him to pause and adjust the skins around his shoulders, kneading the fur against his exposed neck. In accordance with tradition, the pelts he wore were pierced through with the same buckskin that captured them, and his stunted spine cracked faintly underneath the dead weight. Daily wear would rub the course outer guard hairs off of the prizes, leaving only the soft fur underneath that would make them worth twice the francs to Europeans traders unwilling to wear out the furs themselves. They had just reached the best trapping of the year, when colder weather coaxed thicker pelts out of the animals they pursued. Bernard looked forward to the shivering season. In his position there was no alternative, no one without a contract could afford to turn down the higher prices paid out for winter kills.

The cold was welcome after an unusually warm fall, but the early snow was a nuisance. Being careful not to put too much weight on the spongy ground, he brushed the white powder away from his snare with the side of his moccasin, exposing the still-green grass. He smeared the fresh rabbit carcass at his belt in a wide circle on the uncovered ground at his feet and stepped out into the standing water of the swamp. His footfalls pushed through the crusted accumulation on the pools, and the ice, still too thin to resist, yielded without a crack.

Bernard slowed as the frigid water lapped over the edge of his sodden moccasins, and yanked the glove off his right hand. He plunged his hand wrist-deep into the icy water, and splashed palmfuls about his mouth. He combed his dark, matted beard, dirty fingernails scratching his chin, splashed his face once more and was prepared for the day, unkempt, but well-scrubbed. A month separated from women, Augustine couldn't be bothered with a triviality like hygiene, but ladies or no, Bernard wouldn't be waking up with lice in his hair and beard like his partner. It wasn't for pleasure of his company but for mutual protection that he had joined up with the older trapper. Only lunatics and

Jesuits ventured into the wild alone. Refreshed, he wiped his hand dry against his coat and glanced once back toward their campsite where Augustine slumbered before he replaced his cap and followed the swamp's edge toward the river, marveling as the sun glinted and reflected off the gathering ice of the open water.

Bernard came to rest again after attending to his seventh empty snare of the morning, squatting on a small hump of earth that protruded from the sucking mud between icy hollows, reflecting on the pleasures of spending the cold months hunting and trapping instead of trading like a merchant in search of bread.

His gaze abstracted with his thoughts in the opaque glare hanging over the swamp, and then focused on three distinct trunks that thrust out of the morning haze. Squinting through the sunlight he could see their leafless limbs arching gracefully above any of their bushy neighbors, topmost branches dancing like whips in the unobstructed wind, so alike in suppleness and length that they might be a single trunk split underground. The dilemma of the terrain made the trees' delicacy all the more aching, as the soft ground would be unable to support even one of the oaks in only a few years. The mound he crouched on undoubtedly owed its existence to a similar story. The trees would collapse, and earth would cling to the exposed roots. Grass would sprout, and then more trees. The longer he stared at the oaks the more majestic they appeared, spiraling away from each other, dooming themselves as they raced for open sunlight.

Bernard turned and waded back through the swamp to the bank concealing his last snare and returned with the wire, conscious of his footing, feeling almost blasphemous as he situated the loop in the swamp grass close enough to the trees that an adventurous climber might reach it. Committed now, Bernard reached up and slowly smeared the freshly skinned rabbit across the smooth bark in front of him. One slow, respectful line of scent each. There was no need to mar these trees with a blaze, a blind man would stop to marvel at their perfection. He returned the flesh to his belt without drawing his knife from its sheath and wiped his hands on the taller weeds shooting up around him, hopeful the residue might lure something hungry in after the storm. Rising up, he turned his back to the sun and returned to camp, the forest sparkling quiet and beautiful before him.

He felt a trace of heat on his way back to camp. Though he hadn't noticed anything else, Bernard backtracked to the little clearing off the trail, and thought he felt the residual warmth again. Bernard sank to his heels, reflecting. Despite drawing closer to French settlement they'd yet to see homesteads, or even sauvages, leaving the wilderness around the lakelands noisy in comparison. This morning in particular, Bernard had seemed the only creature in the forest, and there wasn't any spoor here in the clearing either. Sniffing from his haunches, he did smell a woodfire, moments before he saw a finger of smoke meander into the sky, his cue to return for their afternoon meal. Bernard watched the top of the smoke until it lost distinction in the thin blue sky overhead. He waited, probing the forest's endless stillness for another long minute before he walked back to camp.

He and Augustine were trimming willow branches for plews, in the hopes they would have pelts to stretch, when a tall form emerged from the trees near camp. The stranger waited calmly, leaning lightly on his musket until the trappers became aware of his presence. "Ho. Welcome," the man said, strangely, Bernard thought, as it was he who entered their camp. Strands of wampum ran the length of the thin barrel of his musket down onto the stock, white and purple shells clicking as the newcomer eased to a crouch in front of their fire. It had been a long time since he had seen a white man without a beard and the clean-shaven features were distracting. So were the eyes and narrow-ness of the shoulders, which suggested their guest was too fresh to his manhood to be prowling alone.

"That's quite a gun," was all Bernard could think to say to the greeting.

"Thank you." The stranger nodded and then addressed the space between where the trappers crouched around the remains of their meal. "I'm compelled to inform you that you're not allowed to trap for furs on the boundaries of His Majesty's colony of New France."

"That's a big place. New France," Augustine said, unawed by the weaponry. "We're in it now?"

"You are."

"Then if there were three or four more of you we'd really have something to talk about." Augustine's tone suggested the matter resolved.

"I can offer you full pardons for enlistment." The stranger spread his hands benevolently.

"Enlistment?" Bernard repeated the dread word, right hand around the claspknife in his belt. His gun was below his other hand, but it would take too long to raise the weapon. He listened fruitlessly for the sounds of other men in the woods.

"In His Majesty's army. We'll pay you, feed you and arm you, and when we've laid waste to the English," he said huskily, though his features remained expressionless, "we'll forgive your crimes and you'll be free to pursue your lives as you wish."

"We seem pretty free right now. Free enough that you'll wish your friends had been a little closer."

"I don't have any friends."

"I see," but the rest of Augustine's retort was swallowed in the crunching of the decorated rifle under Bernard's open jaw, knocking him prone with the back of his skull in the snow and his feet straight out in the fire. He scrabbled backwards and kicked the fire, sending up a cough of soot and smoke, and retreated down the slick incline to the water on the backs of his elbows blinking and waving the sheathed camp knife.

He heard a gunshot, and belatedly checked his own chest, then shifted his improving vision upstream where Augustine grunted in surprise, and then pitched face forward in the snow. As fast as he fell he tried to rise, but only managed to flip onto his back where he flailed in the mud. The bullet smoke's unpleasant tang cut through the familiar odor of the campfire.

Bernard pitched his sheath toward the water and rose into a low crouch. The slender assailant stood poised in front of their smoking fire, several paces up the gentle slope. He held a feathered tomahawk and a long knife braced for a charge. "I will kill you if you don't lay that blade down."

The weapons looked ludicrous in the young well-kempt hands, but the conviction in the clean voice gave it overwhelming authority. Bernard pitched his blade up the rise toward their attacker's feet and walked toward Augustine, turning his back on the child official.

"He blew up my leg." Augustine repeated the panicked phrase over and over as Bernard assessed the damage. The bullet had passed through and there was a spatter of blood flaring out over the snow toward the water. The pool underneath the mess of his thigh had already melted the fresh snow and as Bernard watched, Augustine reached for his leg several times but didn't touch it. The trench of the wound was flaked with slivers of bone and leaked irregularly. His friend hissed in anger and gestured for Bernard to intervene as the shooter drew near.

"Heat water," the man ordered.

Bernard did, crouched at the fire watching as the assailant rummaged through their personals for weapons. He ripped the door off Augustine's shelter and punctured each of the corners of the old pelt with knives ferreted from around the fire, and crossed their guns over the stretched beaver before kicking in both shelters. Bernard felt the water and found it barely warm. It hadn't taken long to disassemble a way of life.

By the time it was hot, the man had sliced one of Augustine's shirt sleeves into lengths and had cut the legging away from the wounded limb. The older man's eyes were closed, fending off the nightmare, but they opened when Bernard poured half the water over the wound and set the skin in the snow.

"Brandy?" Augustine said.

Bernard dug through the shambles of Augustine's shelter until he found an unopened bottle, which he poured generously down his friend's throat, holding the gray head up while the stranger finished the field dressing.

"If I'd had to guard you both, you would have been tempted to chance something." The smooth voice and easy philosophy failed to reassure Bernard, or Augustine, whose low insistent wheezings of pain evoked the whimpering of a scared dog. Bernard gave his partner a bit more and capped the bottle without drinking himself.

They stood together and the official focused his attention on Bernard who had to crane his head to meet the six-foot stare. His height and freshly laundered homespun clothes made it seem that the intruder was standing somewhere far away. Bernard felt sure that he heard the metallic twang of a snare releasing in the woods behind him. A rainbow shimmered across the damp cobwebs that ran along the tops of the ferns, but lost in calculation, the newcomer paid the spectacle no attention. "You will have to transport this man in the canoe. We'll arrive in Quebec before dark tomorrow." Far from sounding out of place in the woods, the practiced voice made a chapel of the forest's bare limbs.

Marked with impassive scrutiny, Bernard upended their rough bark, dumping blankets, extra rations, and a bottle of brandy Augustine had squirreled away and carried the canoe over to his shuddering partner. The leg was a mess of cotton cloth, buckskin twine well away from the wound holding the padding in place. Bernard did not have enough experience with gun wounds to know if he would keep the leg.

"Kill him," Augustine hissed from the ground. "Kill him."

"Easy," Bernard said as he squatted and got an arm under Augustine's shoulders, their audience impassive in the face of the comments. Bernard stepped on the edge of the bark and hefted his friend, torso first, into the canoe. Slick with blood, Augustine slid to the narrow scoop of the canoe's bottom where he lay motionless.

A hunter who leaves prey swinging in his snares is bound to swing himself. Bernard remembered his father's cranky superstition and wondered if the snare was Augustine's. He hoped at least that they weren't leaving a doomed prize in the grove, kicking its legs until other predators claimed it.

The man ate a strip of their jerky and offered one to Bernard but the trapper declined. Bernard carried the canoe with Augustine's wounded leg riding in the air next to his ear and as he walked he imagined that he could hear the blood pumping out of the wound in rhythm with his step, though the dressing looked sound when he checked it as he rested his shoulder after twenty minutes of dragging the disintegrating bark.

Bernard had dragged the canoe for half an hour at the same fierce pace, when he stepped in a hole camouflaged by mud and snow. He might not have broken through the ground if not for the extra weight. As his leg gave way, the butt end of the prow slid across his back, and he fought to keep his balance. The small boat perched precariously for an instant, as the rough hull scraped hard against his cheek. He dropped to his right knee on the frozen ground, struggling, but the boat spun off, dumping its cargo before landing on the wounded man's back, curving over it like a turtle shell. The old trapper's wounded leg was first to strike the frozen ground.

Augustine's wail, a high-pitched, hopeless sound, strangely incensed Bernard. He growled back, furious that they'd been taken so easily, frustrated even in the attempt to drag his wounded friend out of the forest in the canoe, and the growl, originally designed to quiet the wounded, became a roar. He stopped suddenly, remembering their captor who stood watching the display, serene despite his protestations. The thought struck Bernard that he might be fouling the last few moments of peace he had left to his life, and it might not be untoward to show the forest some gallantry as he dragged Augustine away, crashing through the underbrush back toward the civilization he and his father had left behind with the farm they worked in his childhood.

Their captor trailed the makeshift conveyance and as they traveled, whenever Bernard chanced a quick look over his shoulder, the stranger's movements over the uneven terrain were so graceful and confident that they seemed to restore some of the tranquility to the ground destroyed in the passage of the burdened canoe. The fancy rifle was slung across the man's back, over the snowshoes, but it would be either the pistol or the short, light blade in his belt that he would reach for if Bernard proved quarrelsome. Which he wouldn't. Augustine was hurt, and they were both unarmed. Bernard considered refusing to continue, walking to your own grave was humiliation enough without hauling a friend along with you, but he decided again against active resistance. The boy's silence was intimidating, but his manner was conciliatory enough to encourage Bernard to wait for a better chance, it was still a long way to the gallows.

Their attacker stood aside stoically as the heavy fearful breaths and strained exertions of the trappers accumulated in the frosty air. Eventually Bernard succeeded in negotiating his partner's flailing limbs and leaden torso back over the lip of the canoe, Augustine now unresponsive even as his leg thudded down the remaining varangues. After his partner was situated, Bernard paused to catch his breath, leaning against the prow with an ear on the quiet hissing through the forest ahead. The deeper pitch of the Saint Maurice proper. The short trek had rendered their canoe unusable without significant patching, but their captor didn't seem preoccupied with the question of what they would do upon reaching the water. If they were headed for Quebec, and there wasn't anywhere else to go, there would be a master canoe waiting, too unwieldy for the numerous tiny tributaries he and Augustine traveled, but sturdier for regular use on the Saint Lawrence's wider stretches.

As Bernard righted the slick end of the sledge on his shoulder, the smooth voice descended over him for the first time since leaving camp. "The difficult part of your journey is nearing its end." Ten minutes later they saw the water.

Four sailors, greasy as rats, impatiently waited in a bateau with six oarlocks and four long plank seats, capable of carrying the seven of them and seven more if put upon. The extra weight lent crucial stability on the larger rivers and the plentiful coastal

bays along the Atlantic coast, but would have been an impossibility on the narrow trails he and Augustine walked. Unwilling
to beach the heavy boat, the sailors had anchored three long
strides out into the frigid water.

"Close enough?" one called to the bank.

The young official ignored the question and turned to Bernard.
"Go ahead," he directed.

Bernard waded out until he was knee-deep in the Saint
Maurice, moving carefully over the moss-covered river rocks,
hesitating to submerge his balls in the freezing water. Augustine
had been quiet for the last downhill push to the river, his energy
depleted by fear and blood loss, and he remained sedate as the
official pushed the prow of the canoe out to Bernard. The trapper found a rock with an edge where he could lock his foot
against the current, and pulled his boat and unresponsive partner deeper into the river. The young official surprised Bernard by
joining him in the water, and together they rolled Augustine on
the lip of the shorter canoe, and then pushed him up into the
arms of the sailors.

As a sailor braced Augustine's leg for the ride to Quebec,
Bernard glanced at the young man standing in the river across
the canoe. The gunman's delicate right hand was on the haft of
his knife in his belt, blue eyes staring steadily down into the trapper's, off-hand gripping the edge of the small canoe for balance
in the stream. The man's readiness and quiet firmness were
unnerving and Bernard decided his best chance at escape still lay
ahead.

Bernard broke off the stare and waded back to shore, dragging his battered canoe back up onto the bank in the hopes that
a future passerby might appreciate the courtesy. As he watched
his abandoned birchbark, Bernard wished only that he could

trade places with it, that he were taken no more into account than his insentient craft, disappearing forever as the current carried them downriver, left behind with his tools, his weapons, and his life trapping in the dark and beautiful forest.

"There aren't many ways for a one-legged man to get by in Canada," the steersman pointed out grimly to Bernard as they neared Quebec the next day.

"I've seen men keep their legs before who looked like they might not." The words of experience might have sounded ridiculous, but none of the other men laughed at Bernard's captor. Neither captor nor prisoner had been given a paddle, and they sat together, facing the steersman in the stern.

Bernard's captor reached over with a piece of buckskin and swiftly bound the trapper's wrists.

"I might not have fired back in the swamp," the man said, his tone one of sympathy more than apology. "This is only to encourage you not to consider escaping. I reacted in haste once, but rest assured, no one would go to this trouble for a hanging."

The stone walls of Quebec had emerged on the Saint Lawrence's jagged cliffs, its turrets mere crenellations atop the massive stone ridge. The city waited still leagues upstream on what Bernard, unswayed by his captor's reassurance, hoped wasn't his final boat ride. He recalled stories his father had told of his boyhood in Paris. The city had been his father's home from birth through his imprisonment in the dungeon of the Bastille at age sixteen. Pere Arseneau had claimed that the famous escarpments scraped the heavens, but his son was doubtful they could be higher than the sprawling ramparts of the city looming above him, their grandeur enhanced by the height of the plateau they guarded. Quebec was said to be the most heavily fortified city in

New France, and that claim alone had kept the trapper from setting foot in it.

Three Rivers, the town where he and Augustine usually bartered their furs, was more palatable, with its collection of longhouses and wigwams huddled in the shadow of a small picketed stockade behind the town. The fort was large enough to accommodate the collection of traders, fishermen and their families in case of Iroquois raids, but indefensible against English cannon. Both English troops and colonial militia each had razed the town in recent years, forcing its settlers and soldiers to abandon their homes in favor of the protection of Quebec's walls, returning months later to resurrect their temporary homes. The squalid huts and fields seemed more dilapidated and less productive every year, and Bernard imagined that one day nothing at all would greet them at the riverbank when they arrived in the spring, flush with fur.

Two days' paddle north of that trading post, closing in on the colony's capital, the muted orange sun illuminated a handful of graceful spires rising above the high plain. As the oarsmen fought upriver against the Saint Lawrence, Bernard watched the low but sturdy stone buildings of Basseville emerge from the early evening gloom, and by the time they discovered an empty pier, he could distinguish dozens of structures huddled between the protection of the cliff and the promise of the harbor. Bernard frowned as their large craft scraped against a piling. The sailors cursed at each other as they struggled to bring the bateau to rest against a pier, the river's current challenging even at the extremes of the harbor.

The night before, the oarsmen had called Augustine's attacker "Young Man," invoking a chilling epithet with which Bernard was familiar only through the wheezy tales of old men.

Never numerous, the order of Young Men was a dying breed, a vestige of the colony's earliest days. Fierce warriors, and preternaturally swift and sure as trackers, they served as scouts and messengers in peacetime and as officers during wars with the colonials or the Iroquois. Legend had it that New France's governors had been unable to find recruits for a colonial military among the traders and fishermen who early on settled in New France. Frustrated, they turned to Paris for recruits. Each time a ship sailed to France for supplies, it would return with a pair of orphans. The young boys would serve as attendants until they were old enough to train in the forest under the tutelage of the Huron and Algonquin, the tribes Samuel Champlain had won as allies for his fledgling colony immediately after establishing the new capital city beneath Quebec's protective cliffs. After Champlain's death, the Young Men continued to enlist young orphans off Paris's streets to replenish their numbers. The men had no families, no property or wealth of their own, but lived true to the tenets of their founder, serving only the interests of the French crown in the New World. For as long as Bernard had lived, they'd been an unseen threat for the coureurs de bois who traded illegally in the backcountry, overwhelming legality by sheer dint of numbers.

Priests had replaced the Young Men on the frontier, to the extent that Bernard had never actually seen a member of the singular order before. One had, however, taken his father, Pierre, out to the homestead south of the capital, when the former convict first arrived in then sparsely settled Quebec with orders to farm the stony ground. The polite deference the oarsmen showed the Young Man assured Bernard that he had been right to choose submission instead of resistance. The trapper knew that these men, renowned for their complete devotion to royal interests, had authority to punish any citizen of New France according to their own determinations. He had not been under the impression that the Young Man's duties included dragging trappers out of the wild to string them up in Quebec. It would have been far easier to ambush Bernard and Augustine in a few weeks, when they would have returned to trade at Three Rivers.

Bernard disembarked behind his captor, his damp, salt-crusted wool leggings swinging uncomfortably against his legs as he reunited with land. He paused to nod his thanks to the oarsmen who had kept them afloat through choppy water upriver. Two of the men passed Augustine to Bernard, who cradled his wounded partner to the pier, taking care that the tender leg didn't again strike ground first.

Soldiers approached down the pier, and the Young Man's voice rang out with assurance, "Take that wounded man to the seminary hospital. I'll keep the other one with me for the moment."

The words gave Bernard hope. Quebec's doctors had enough to handle treating disease and the accidents of daily life on the Saint Lawrence. Presumably they would not treat a man only to have him hanged for his crimes.

Following orders, Bernard left Augustine, conscious but still unable to walk, with the three young soldiers at the pier. A clasped hand and a word of luck sufficed after more than two years of tramping through the cold woods together, sharing their small triumphs and arguments.

"Stay close," his captor ordered, as they entered the crowd of sailors, fishermen, traders, prostitutes, and soldiers occupied with their daily business on the river.

Keeping pace with the long strides of the official as they walked through the working-class slum toward the ridge that shadowed the square buildings and harbor below forced Bernard into an awkward half-running step that strained waning resources he usually considered boundless. From the pier they walked west, up the steep Côte de la Montagne, past several rows of low stone buildings neatly arranged on narrow streets. Many were patched with new stone, reminders of past bombardments that grew less frequent by the street.

Captor and captive passed through a large square dominated by an ancient church. Merchants swarmed them like flies, hawking jewelry and weapons from Europe, and the tall Young Man moved in front of him to part the crowd. One vendor extended knives for their perusal, the blades resting on a large scrap of leather outstretched between his hands. The Young Man struck him in the face. Bernard didn't see the punch, but simply watched the man flop backward onto the stone, steel clanging on the pavement on either side of him. Urchins, beggars and other merchants swarmed the fallen man as they left the square.

The Young Man's moccasins had been dyed red and were distinctive among the leather boots of the citizenry. Bernard kept his eyes on the footwear as they wound through the hubbub. They shoved their way through a last ring of onlookers and followed the cobblestones uphill, the din receding as the street steepened.

Bernard scanned the ridge as they ascended the only path between Basseville and Hauteville, carved deep in the hillside. Quebec was a more pleasant thing for him from above than within, and he thought about the fishermen returning to their wives and children, loaded with salmon. He could imagine enjoying the company and the small warm house on the water, though usually Bernard found it preferable not to conjure alternate lives to the one he'd known, roaming the wilderness in the company of men since the age of eight.

He turned his sights back to the path before him, craning to take in two clusters of spire-topped towers that appeared, undisputed commanders of the high ground, hundreds of meters above the docks below. At the crest of the cliff they encountered a guarded switchback meant to discourage the comings and goings of those who properly belonged lower and closer to the water. Four soldiers stood at attention under a yawning opening that was serving as a gate. Although the men gripped their flintlocks fiercely, their presence was more for show than threat. The gate wasn't the only incomplete part of the defenses, as the wall contained many more gaps than could be intended for postera, allowing passage along much of its length. As the pair climbed higher, Bernard could see craftsmen engaged at several points along the fortifications, their harried work probably motivated by the same rumors of British mobilization that had driven them north.

As the Young Man and the soldiers conversed, Bernard caught his breath and allowed himself to imagine what it would feel like to walk freely out of the city walls. Even if he could, it would be a tortuous walk in fading light to his canoe on the Saint Maurice. The sun perched briefly on the western fortifications before sliding out of sight, drawing the curtain on his dreams of peaceful escape. Bernard had seen these walls and towers several times passing along the Lawrence's eastern bank, but it was the imposing cliffs rising from the river that had captivated him. Inside the new walls, however, the terrain he'd once known lost its significance, the expressionless manmade barriers sealing him off from the comforting security of the forest as completely as if it had never existed.

Stone walls spiraled off to their left, neat, orderly rows of new construction encircling the older defenses where the stones were of all sizes and haphazardly mixed, all arrayed to protect a squat fortress. Past the guards, the trail finally leveled off. Cannonballs were piled neatly near their artillery lining the ridge. The two walked away from the rim of the plateau, toward the collection of towers housing the city's seminary, on a wide empty street running between large stone homes.

The homes gave way to large cultivated gardens, their manicured beauty a stark contrast to the wilds Bernard roamed. They bypassed a pristine church, its stone newly laid and glowing in the shadows that stretched before the two titanic buildings of the seminary. Bernard's captor steered them around the side of the main hall, whose bell tower still reflected the sun setting over the Plains of Abraham. He heaved open a heavy door around the side of the massive grand seminary, and they headed down a creaky wooden staircase, the taller man forced to crouch as they descended. The stairwell led them to a tunnel-like hallway in the building's basement. Torches illuminated thick, white-painted limestone walls. Enterprising craftsmen had carved tiny recessed windows near the hallway's ceiling, guarded from animal intrusion by pronged cat gutters. Bernard's captor silently ushered him through a low doorway marked with two crossed keys. They entered a small chapel, built underground in case of a cannonade.

Once in the dimness of the shrine, the Young Man whispered, "The pew with the others."

Bernard obeyed, despising himself for the ease with which he submitted. He joined five other men, also trappers by their shape and smell, a couple more bruised than he, but mostly hale. Bernard's hope was reaffirmed. Surely they wouldn't be gathered together in a church only to be hanged.

The trappers faced an old priest, hatless by necessity in the low space. The priest's face was pitted with pockmarks, like an animated countenance of the worn stone surrounding them. A bodyguard, his bearing and armament a match for the man who shot Augustine, stood alertly behind the gaunt Jesuit. Without turning his head, Bernard strained to distinguish the breathing of the Young Man behind him from the nervous huffing of his fellow prisoners.

The priest spoke, raising his arm in blessing as he dictated their fate, the sleeve of his robes falling back to reveal his thin limb. "Word has come to us from Boston that the English mean to forcibly remove our cousins, the French Neutrals, from their lands." The Jesuit stared over the heads of the trappers as he spoke, intoning the words as if in benediction. "Already, ships sail from Boston. You will leave tomorrow, and God willing, reach the harbor of Antigonish the following day." He took a long, rasping breath as he waved toward the two Young Men, then continued, "These men will give you your instructions when you disembark, but you should know that the Lord, in his wisdom, sees fit that each man who complies shall receive full pardon for the crime of illegal trapping in New France. Those who wish to warn the Acadians of their cruel fate may go with God. Those who do not wish to do so may remain here in Quebec at the pleasure of his majesty, Louis XV."

Gaspereau River 1755

Like rivers that water the woodlands,
darkened by shadows of earth,
but reflecting an image of Heaven.

GABRIEL WAS STARING EXPECTANTLY THROUGH THE OPEN doorway, peering around Benedict, who turned to her as well, though less desperately, as Evangeline joined them on the porch.

"Gabriel here intends for my grandchildren to grow up choking on soot," Benedict groused from his rocker, gesturing irritably at her fiancé, who sat on the steps, motionless save for the long black hair swatting over his face. Like a horse's tail, Benedict had described it months before, when he saw it bound in the topknot Gabriel wore at the forge.

Evangeline settled the handful of blackberries she carried on Benedict's lap and rubbed the leftover juice into her fingers.

"We're all disappointed they won't grow up to be smugglers, papa," she replied.

"Nothing wrong with living by your wits," her father said more quietly.

"Nothing at all," Evangeline said agreeably, and kissed her father's wrinkled cheek and hurried down the three porch steps, flitting past Gabriel, who stood in her wake.

"You'll have a happy marriage, Gabriel, if you keep toeing the line like that," her father teased the boy from his rocker, but Gabriel ventured only a hesitant wave in reply before following to where she waited for him amid the bare-stemmed roses, their fallen yellow petals still distinguishable from the other autumn detritus.

"He doesn't need any advice from you as to how to treat a lady," she sang back to her father as they walked from her house arm in arm, headed away from town. They strolled past the Melansons' empty porch, and their trail cut into a small wood, bypassing the storeowners' mushrooming gardens of root crops. Stepping out of the late afternoon sun she was more conscious of the heat trapped between them, and the quiet.

"Is everything all right, Gabriel?"

He nodded without looking at her. "My father's coming by later."

"And the forge runs cold." She'd meant it as a joke, but Gabriel didn't laugh. They hadn't had enough work for months. "Don't worry, everything's going to be ready in a week."

"He's worried about the English."

Evangeline smiled and eased under his arm. "You wouldn't let a couple soldiers stop you from marrying me?" She put her hand on his back and felt his breath catch.

A sow moved out of the woods, snorting when it became aware of them on the path. "Never," Gabriel said, relieved. "But it looks like I've got competition."

"You mean I do," Evangeline replied with a smile. "Come on," she said, and led him by the hand back into the unfiltered sunlight of the Labiche homestead where the mother of the house left her porch to pass the time with them. Mrs. Labiche stood in their path, squinting at their approach while she adjusted the ropes of blond hair coiled behind her head.

"Evening, Madame."

"Evening, dear. How's your father?"

"Feeling well, but I'll make sure to tell him you asked. One of your pigs is up the road if you're looking."

"Thank you, dear," Mrs. Labiche said absently, her scrutiny focused entirely on Gabriel. "You all have quite a lot to get together."

"Well under way, Madame," he responded with studied politeness as Evangeline squeezed his side appreciatively.

"Yes, well, good you're going ahead with it." She wiped clear little beads of perspiration off her forehead with her thick forearm and pitched her voice to carry back to the house watching behind her. "My children are getting to be your age, and they're worried how they'll be married at all with the priests gone."

"Mysterious ways, Madame," Evangeline replied.

"Well, we all hear Father Felician's around somewhere now, but what about next year, or in five years? I only know the English made sure to steal our guns before they came to steal our faith."

"Well, they won't get mine," Evangeline said boldly.

"Good girl, that's right." Her eyebrows rose again. "Still we seem worse off every year. I worry so much about you children."

"I assure you that we're going to be fine, Madame." Evangeline squeezed Gabriel's hand to let him know it wouldn't be much longer. "We'll take care of each other."

The matriarch remained unsatisfied. "Plenty of folks seem like they'd rather move along than feed a bunch of English soldiers."

"Yes, I'm sure times are rough all over."

"And we don't have enough to go around as is."

"I just praise the Lord for this autumn's bounty."

"Yes, praise Him." The woman hesitated. "Have a nice night, dear."

"I'm sure we will, and I hope you do the same, Madame."

"Yes. Take care, Gabriel."

"Yes, Madame."

They left the trail for the spreading orchard the Bellefontaines shared with their neighbors, Gabriel's height and fluidity accentuating the gnarled chaos of the denuded apple trees. He raised a limb for her and she led the way between the uneven rows, down the pickers' track into the grove. She valued the trees as much for their privacy as for the fruit. Ten measured paces down the narrow path she turned and kissed him. After a moment Evangeline pushed lightly off his chest and drew back. Gabriel's hazel eyes blinked, waiting.

"Let's go," she said, feigning exasperation, and led them again along the narrow trails until they emerged from the bare trees and heard the Gaspereau gurgle below them. West over the Minas, a few lingering sunrays parted a thin mist of orange clouds, splashing fragmented sunbursts across the paling sky. They sat in the dry grass on the ridge looking down the valley, over the farms they'd passed running along the river as it flowed toward Grand Pre. Across the stream, clumps of spartina waved at the foot of the dike separating the wild lands from the claimed. Behind the barrier, a band of salt-crusted grazing lands dotted with cattle gave way to the smaller rings of older dikes protecting fields of wheat, oats and hemp, and finally the interspersed orchards and houses on the promontory opposite, grease wicks already burning despite the one perfect hour of daylight left.

"It's not as pretty as you are," Gabriel offered.

"And I'll still be here in an hour," she replied.

He had spoken only as preamble, she knew absolutely. Below, on their side of the river, a dozen children piled wood on one of the grassy hummocks of the dike wall. They're only a little younger than we are, Evangeline thought, as Gabriel found his voice.

"I'm ready to get married, Evangeline, though I feel like I belong to you already. I have since you chose me."

The shapes below congregated, the last two coming on a run, and she smelled smoke as the bonfire kindled.

"Gabriel, we were meant to be together. I don't feel like I had a choice."

"I see," he said, but she could tell he didn't. She waited a moment before elaborating.

"I mean I didn't decide to be with you any more than I decided to be born." Hoots drifted up to them as a competing flame emerged on the opposite bank. Both groups retreated to the woods and returned with dry handfuls of hemlock needles that they dumped on the fires, sending little rushes of flame heavenward. She remembered that children used to be chastised for such behavior, but tonight parents remained inside, too worried about the English on the horizon to pay attention to their children on the beach.

"Neither of us used to play on the river."

Gabriel furrowed his brow and she smiled, "Don't worry about that now. I'm nervous because there's something I want to show you."

Evangeline stood up, noticing his eyes on her as she brushed off her wool skirt, before offering him a slender hand and raising up her husband-to-be in his baggy handdowns.

Gabriel looked at the sky, not thanking God for the divine sight, but checking the time. They had until dark before they had to return to meet their fathers. One week away, and little was determined save for the preparations she'd made in secret. Neither they nor their fathers could remember an Acadian wedding without mothers and grandmothers among the celebrants. She almost welcomed the uncomfortable fact of Protestant occupation for the day when the soldiers' presence would mask the immediacy of their simple service hidden away here in the woods. Their choice would become everyone's necessity.

She kissed his hand.

"All in time, my love. We won't be too late."

Gabriel's trusting smile in response made her heart ache.

Turning from the view, they climbed down into a long low hollow running parallel to the river below them, the ridge's rim rampart sufficient to preserve the ornament on most of the trees, splashes of red and yellow brilliant against the pale green hemlock needles. Though the orchard had given out, scattered volunteers persisted along the edge of the forest they skirted.

They picked their way down the short steep embankment at the start of an overgrown trailhead, descending with the sun in their eyes, crunching through the season's fallen leaves as she led them to the center of the shallow depression. After only a brief trek, the small forest opened to a clearing with a slender cross prominent in the grass. Tonight, just short of dusk, her creation seemed two-dimensional and looked like it would better suit a grave. But she knew that the wood would glow in the early light, and the extra ribbons from her wedding dress would catch the sun like flames. Despite her preparations, and even with Gabriel by her side, it was difficult to imagine the ceremony, hidden away with their fathers and Felician in front of the simple altar she'd erected, exchanging the vows that would guide the rest of their lives. Gabriel wanted to marry her, would be happy today, tomorrow, had been ready when they first spoke of it the past spring, but it was important to her that they distinguish them-selves from the dozens of couples who stumbled into declaring their love for each other as the weather chased them indoors for precious months of acquaintance after their hasty courtships. Unlike she and Gabriel, who were bonded through common experience and appreciation of the other's pain, dignified by their exclusivity, destined to love.

They stepped quickly against the lowering night, but Evangeline slowed on entering the clearing, her feet reluctant to leave the woods, as her eyes fixed on the tree above and behind the cross. Standing taller than its pruned and windswept ilk on the tableland above, the graceful old tree still carried the apple she'd checked for yesterday, the flesh still firm under its skin, the late blessed product of a warm summer.

"Isn't it beautiful," she whispered. The last gold of day shone only on the points of the branches twisting upward into the sky. They were far from prying eyes, and Evangeline again felt her desire for Gabriel but resisted the impulse to reach for him by moving across the clearing to the tree. She hefted the apple, felt the weakening stem, and then twisted it free with a violent flourish. The humming branch returned to position trail-ing a rush of falling leaves.

One leaf rested in her hair as she drew closer to Gabriel. Obscure in the semi-darkness, she could no longer see his expression.

"Next week," she said.

"I know," he responded.

"When did you first think that we were going get married?"

"I'm not sure, but before I'd known you for long. I knew that I needed to see you, and that you wanted to see me. And I wasn't nervous when we were alone together. That's probably when it first occurred to me." He smiled at her, not quite satisfied, "Of course, I won't know for sure until it's happened."

"I had a dream about you once," she cut in, taking her turn to answer the question she had posed.

Gabriel's voice intruded on her immediately, almost laughing.

"I've dreamt of you plenty, Evangeline."

"I've only dreamt of you once, the night after we heard about your family." She began talking more quickly now to drown out unwanted memories. "You entered my bedroom," her more carefully chosen remark rewarded with a flicker of interest from Gabriel. "But it was upstairs in a loft, more like your house than mine, except with only one bed. And you floated above me, crying without sound. So beautiful." She remembered his dream eyes, reflecting his nightmare of waves repeatedly smashing a tiny ship, the doomed figures on board the toy-sized craft pitching off in all directions, sinking without struggle. The waves rolled in, and receded. The boat followed over the horizon, and with its departure, the sea's roiling ceased.

He smiled thinly as she extended the apple to him.

"I touched your cheek, and quieted your tears. Your eyes cleared, and I saw that you loved me. That's when I knew we'd be married."

Gabriel stared mutely back at her, eyes wide and unblinking, though she remembered that in the dream, his angelic apparition had nodded in answer to her unspoken question.

"That's when I knew we'd be married," she repeated.

Evangeline stopped speaking and pressed the apple into his palm, and put her hand under his, taking advantage of the opportunity to touch him, supporting his hand as though the apple weighed as much as the tree, as Gabriel raised the apple to his chest, her hand underneath his, the tips of her fingers almost touching the rough fabric of his shirt.

"This is all that I have withheld from you," she whispered. She closed his fingers tightly around it.

Desperate to touch him, to kiss him, Evangeline forced herself away from the boy she tempted, stepping back to the protection of the altar. Gabriel's steady gaze never left her.

"I love you, Gabriel. I've only ever loved you."

Gabriel smiled wide and confident following her declaration. "Everything I have and will ever have is yours. My hands, my heart," his grin turned daring. "My tongue." They kissed until Evangeline stepped out of his embrace. Gradually his eyes lost the look of a feeding animal, and returned to his sweet uncertain gaze.

"Our fathers are probably waiting," Evangeline said to prevent him from having to. It was plenty dark, but the moon lit their way as they walked back to her house, arm in arm, accompanied by the sound of the river gushing past below them. The night breeze was heavy with salt from the reclaimed fields, and as they walked back along the ridge in silence, Evangeline remembered their first kiss.

She had lost control during a dance last spring. Not much, just a brief touch of her lips on the corner of his sweaty cheek as they stood close after a reel. The drone of the fiddles vamping between songs had made her feel hidden and safe, obscured from the prying eyes of newly-married Acadian girls, betting trips to the well or cows to be milked on who would be deflowered next. They had nothing else to occupy their time. Evangeline despised their idle gossip. Gabriel had tensed when the corner of her chapped lips brushed his smooth skin, and the involuntary reaction returned her to her senses. The fiddles were joined by voices, and the pounding feet of their neighbors surrounded them. The tilted eyes and full lips that caused her to pursue Gabriel years ago tempted her as much as they had the first time she saw him.

"What do you think about kissing, Gabriel?"

He showed her.

"I don't see why people frown on it so much," he said as they pulled apart. Then, "Oh," as he saw the Melansons sitting on their porch two short steps from the road.

"We'll be fast," she whispered

The old couple sat in birch rockers like her father's with their knees pointed toward the other. Their chimney stoked and smoking, they remained outside sipping tea, waiting for someone to come down the road. Evangeline greeted them.

"What a beautiful sunset we saw from the porch," Sofia said. "And we couldn't have a lovelier complement than the two of you, could we, dear?"

The old man shook his head vehemently, and leaned forward.

"Out late doing the Lord's work, Gabriel?"

Evangeline laughed and answered for him, "It was a lovely night to take the weather. You both were out late yourselves. I hope all's well."

"Bless you for asking child. Nothing out of order. We're still struggling to keep up since our children have gone." A wisp of thyme came in with the wind from the garden.

"And folks seem to have quite a bit less to pay us with."

"Nonsense, Jacques. The problem is that a store is a difficult thing to leave once you've got it. Especially after all the trouble starting it in the first place. Other people can latch the shutters and leave, but," Sofia waved her hand, encompassing them in their rockers, the house, the young couple and the river valley.

"I don't want to move anywhere," Jacques said. "Did you know that there are only three stores left in the whole Minas owned by honest Acadians? People are selling out to the damn English."

"Jacques," Sofia cut him off. "We've been blessed with more than thirty years together. The Lord will protect us from our enemies."

"Time He got started," her husband scoffed.

Gabriel twisted her hand, and Evangeline extracted them. "I'm so sorry to rush off, but we're late getting home."

"Yes, that's fine child. I'll bring the dress by this week so you can try it on."

"Thank you, Sofia," Evangeline said as Gabriel started down the path.

"And blessings on dear Benedict," Sofia called huskily. "He must be so happy the two of you found each other. Only children in Acadia are rarer than winters without snow."

It was full dark when they reached their fathers, hers sitting on the rocker, Basil Lajeunesse standing stiffly on the ground below so that their faces were level as they smoked their pipes and regarded the approaching couple.

Benedict began needling Gabriel as soon as they came into range of his cheerful wheezing. "There will be plenty of late nights after the wedding, though this eagerness gives me hope I might meet my grandchildren."

Basil grunted, and both men tapped out their pipes. Her father's was of whorled red clay, Basil's was molded from the mud of the Minas, the same clay that peeked out of the chinks in the shingles, absorbing the light like the chunk of gray coral her father kept on the mantle.

"Sorry we're late," Evangeline said, but smiling Benedict had pardoned her before she spoke the words. Gabriel looked at Basil as she addressed her next words to the hulking smith. "I showed Gabriel where we're going to be married."

"I told you, Basil. My Evangeline is beyond the influence of mere ships and soldiers." Benedict sounded as proud of her as she was of herself.

"And Father Felician is willing to marry us next Sunday."

"It's not the presence of a preacher that concerns me." Basil's low, gravelly tone contrasted her gaiety.

"There will only be the five of us, Monsieur, in the woods, far from town."

"It's true," Gabriel added, effusive in her defense. "We won't be any safer if we stay at home and forget the whole thing."

Benedict smiled, recognizing, Evangeline thought, the compassion that Gabriel disguised under awkwardness and a quiet nature. Benedict patted the smith on the arm, sadly shaking his head as the man looked to him for support.

"Sounds like they've made their decision. My friend, through no fault of your own, you may have forgotten the peculiar obstinacy of women," he said gently, speaking directly of death as only the old are allowed.

Basil turned his concentration from Benedict and looked at her holding hands with his son. He shook his head. "Next Sunday. I wish you both every happiness in the world."

An agreement reached, she stretched to kiss Gabriel on the corner of his lips, and stood tall against his chest for a moment until he carried her apple into the darkness. In seven days, they'd go home together.

"Seeing the two of you together reminds me that we have some brushing up to do," Benedict said as the Lajeunesse men withdrew.

"What do you mean?"

"I need to stretch these bones out. I used to be quite the dancer, taught you well enough."

"Are you feeling up to it?"

"I wouldn't want to be the cause of embarrassment on your wedding night."

"I wasn't even thinking that we would, with so few of us there."

"All the more reason to make sure we enjoy the celebration."

She kissed her father and changed the subject. "Monsieur Lajeunesse is as charming as ever."

"I would be thankful that the both of you have independent-minded parents who allow you to marry as you wish. He doesn't get much practice talking over there with just the two of them in that sad house."

"There's just the two of us."

"It's true." He clutched the railing with both hands as they stepped down off the porch, her hand cupped protectively at his back.

"You couldn't have convinced me that my daughter would be the only woman at her wedding." She hadn't quite put it in those terms herself.

"You're right that it's going to be different than we imagined." Evangeline half caught her father as he spun toward her.

"I don't want you to hurt yourself. It's been a long time."

"Lord above. You'd deny me the only responsibility I've got left." He separated from her and spread his hands to show off his balance. "I've lived seventy years waiting to see what it feels like to marry off a child. We're dancing if you have to wheel me in a cart."

He clasped her left hand in his right, put his other hand on her hip and dipped her head back. "I'll have to make sure Gabriel learns something of this before I'm any further enfeebled."

They waltzed around the yard, and Evangeline remembered all the nights over the years she'd danced with her father. He would lead, humming in her ear, smelling of pipe smoke. His smooth hands were the only Evangeline had known before she felt Gabriel's, rough from the forge, holding hers gently when they'd danced for the first time, four years ago. The vitality in his young skin had excited her, and it was that heat, more than anything else, she decided afterward, that had displaced her reason and made her kiss him in front of the town. But even after the brief dance, and her long flirtation with Gabriel, she still enjoyed waltzing to her father's melodies, alone in his arms under the stars.

"I was frightened to dance with your mother at our wedding, you know."

"That's difficult to imagine."

"Well, she was a striking woman. The most beautiful thing there's ever been but you." He turned them back toward the house. "She would be so happy to know that you've found a kind man."

Thoughts of her departed mother dampened her mood a little, but Evangeline knew that she had made her father happy over their quiet years together, and had no doubt that she had been a good daughter to Benedict. He had told her so, many nights under the stars, and he would tell her so again next week as they danced together, their first performance after a lifetime of rehearsing.

Grand Pre 1755

There the richest was poor, and the poor lived in abundance.

OVING CONFIDENTLY IN THE DARKNESS, FELICIAN Abadie followed the crisscrossing swine trails until he emerged from the low spruce and paused in the moonlight to take in the palisade. The waxing moon was shrouded in clouds but bright enough to illuminate the freshly hewn logs held together by leather bands and hemp rope. Only one long half of the church roof was visible above the stockade, vaulting into the muted light like a listing ship. Though shoddily done, the construction represented industrious work, but did not answer the question as to who might attack such an outpost after its soldiers had already confiscated all the firearms they could unearth. The English would leave eventually, and the Acadians would still need their muskets to hunt game and to stalk the voles that undermined their dikes, burrowing mercilessly into the mud walls surrounding their palisades and aboiteaux, reintroducing the carefully irrigated fields to the Minas. It had been one of his great metaphors, Felician reflected, comparing the angry throngs of New England Puritans to a plague of voles. For even as the vermin destroyed a dike, they submerged their own homes. Just so the flood of the Lord would rise up against their Protestant besiegers and wash them back downstream to Boston.

Now though, both his home and God's were enclosed within the English barricade. He wasn't overly troubled by the thin plume of smoke rising out of his chimney, signifying Colonel Winslow's occupancy. It was proof of the Protestant commander's delicacy, as Felician would never have lit a fire indoors in early October. What would the Colonel do in January, when the northern wind howled across the Minas? Perhaps by then Winslow would have left them again to their own stewardship. Regardless, it was an amusing choice of dwelling, as Felician had done little in four years to improve the creature comforts of the simple home. Accustomed to even windier winters on Ile Royale, he disdained the quilts most families used both as bedding and insulation during the cold months, relying only on a thin wool blanket and the thatched crown on his one-room cottage.

The dense cloudbank parted above him and, feeling suddenly exposed, Felician broke off his reverie to continue toward the gathering hosted by Rene LeBlanc. They convened on the notary's holdings in belated response to the summer-long intensification of the English occupation, and to hear from a messenger recently arrived from Quebec. The palaver had been the excuse he needed to return from his refuge with the Mi'kmaq, where he skulked while the English rounded up the priests, Jesuits and Recollects alike, to send back to France.

The tall priest briefly rejoined the trails running the high ground behind the houses before he reemerged from the scrub trees, striding vigorously through the open darkness as though he could wrest back the time spent hiding, aware of the thickening saltiness of the air as the ample house came into view. It seethed with activity compared to its slumbering neighbors, grease lamps and pipes flashing in the gloomy panes as the men inside awaited his counsel.

Felician's people were hungry and sick with worry, but at least they wouldn't be bereft of his leadership as long as he set aside his pride and relinquished his home and church to the English. Sacrifice was the order of the day. Sacrifice, and double-dealing, as evidenced by the clandestine meeting at LeBlanc's home, Felician thought. The notary welcomed the prospect of English rule more than many in his congregation, which had earned him more than the priest's enmity, but the man's integrity wouldn't permit him to betray Felician's whereabouts to the Protestant authorities. Instead, LeBlanc profited off his close ties with the English, carrying requests, orders and complaints back and forth between Winslow and his own people. And, to his credit, the clerk had sent word that Grand Pre needed its pastor tonight.

Felician hesitated briefly outside LeBlanc's entrance, not trying for the moment to distinguish individual words from the muddle of anxious conversations, but merely observing his parishioners. The Protestant lion, reined in currently by Colonel Winslow, could bring only trouble to Felician's flock. Under the best of circumstances, occupation meant possession of a few homes, and the seizure of livestock to provide for the hundreds of soldiers who wouldn't be contributing to the fall harvest. The sacrificed pigs and cows were valued more than the grain, which they still had in abundance, as milk and meat were credited with keeping children healthy through the winter. The soldiers, however, would eat meat, and protest would only result in more troops, and a turmoil that could bring only further trouble to his peace-craving congregation. Unlike some among the Black Robes who ignored these obvious concerns and preach a gospel of war, Felician would obey his heavenly mandate, and Grand Pre would have his honest fidelity to rely on even as its prospects darkened.

The grimy light flickering over the somber faces inside the large living area illuminated little more than the moonlight had outside. Felician paused to look around after crossing the threshold and those closest greeted him with respectfully subdued voices. Men were crowded on benches and tables, sitting on the floor and standing in groups along the walls. Unlike the priest, the crowd was mostly bearded, though there were a few younger men present, their brows knotted to show their seriousness. Felician's smile, warm and vague, was fleeting. He knew that not he, but the mewling majority before him would decide whether they would fight or flee. To win them over tonight he would need to rely on persuasive argument instead of heavenly authority. When it came to basic respect for the deity, the sauvages he'd proselytized were far better Christians than the Acadian farmers who retained much of the spiritual independence of their colonial ancestors. While acknowledging the common sense it bred, Felician mistrusted agrarian cultures, as the sedentary lives of the farmers seemed more easily given over to idleness. Generations ago Grand Pre's first settlers had crafted the mud dikes around the valves of the aboiteaux, claiming long tracts from the rivers and the Minas. Now all their descendents seemed to do was repair the barriers once or twice a year and watch the cattle eat. This notion ran counter to the standing argument among many of his brethren that the sauvage hunter-gatherers were the lazy, allowing for their mastery by the pastorally-inclined Europeans.

Felician quickly brushed off his dark mood. He could not

deprive God-fearing Frenchmen their church, in that his duty
was clear, and there was no one more deserving than the man sitting before him.

"Felician." Benedict Bellefontaine weakly held out his arms
and moved to rise from his bench.

"Sit, Benedict, please." Felician took the man's arm, tucked
it under his own, and sat straight-backed beside him. Despite his
crooked spine, Grand Pre's wealthiest merchant retained a
healthy mane of white hair and the habit of cheerful conversation. "Rest easy about Evangeline. It would be my honor to look
after her." The priest had reassured the old man that if Benedict
planted his feet in Heaven's garden before his daughter married,
Felician would serve as her guardian. Several weeks ago, the
request had seemed strange, with Evangeline's marriage to
Gabriel fast approaching, but Benedict had always been a wise
and good-natured ally, and Felician did not hesitate.

Benedict had been ten years older than Emmeline, his forty-
three-year-old wife, when his daughter was born. Their neighbors enviously observed that Benedict's robust fortitude derived
from his decades spent free of parental responsibilities.
Evangeline was their first and only child, unexpected after more
than twenty barren years of marriage. But the joy of the long-
awaited birth quickly dissolved when Emmeline grew sick and
died after a difficult labor, leaving the infant to her father's care.
Benedict stopped traveling and took the further precaution of
securing Felician's predecessor, Father Maufils, as the young
girl's godfather, a responsibility Felician had inherited with Saint
Charles.

Felician was initially uninterested in stewardship over the
quiet girl. He had asked her to stand as usher at the mass on
Sunday only out of respect for her father, a rare man who could

be generous without motive. But after Evangeline had patiently served as greeter for more than two dozen masses, Felician began to appreciate her calm presence. The serene smile his parishioners received upon entering the sanctuary was the village's closest approximation of eternal beauty. She was thirteen then, and by the time Evangeline began threading red from old English uniforms into her skirt, Felician could no longer imagine presiding over the church without her. Following the example of his old instructors in Quebec, he installed two small mirrors on his altar so that he could observe the congregation without turning. Often his eyes would seek her out, nearly of their own accord, always finding her near the entrance on guard for latecomers. Holy words were the only ones appropriate to describe her devotion and bearing. Four years later, she remained a calm beacon for devout worshippers who saw her greeting as no less intrinsic than his formal Latin one.

As Evangeline blossomed into womanhood, her father meanwhile began to feel the breath of his Savior, and he had asked for a renewal of Felician's vow. Brushing aside the mild affront to his integrity, the priest had reaffirmed his stewardship and performed the Viaticum for his friend before going into seclusion. Benedict appeared tonight, allowed by the grace of the Almighty to cast his vote, and the priest knew Benedict's opinions would hold great significance for those gathered. Many of the superstitious men among the group regarded those closest to God's love as the most prescient. Felician regularly relied on the wise merchant's judgments, and was especially thankful that the Lord granted Benedict life for a while yet. He could also depend on the older man to tell him what had transpired while the priest was away for a month in the wild.

"Well, Father, the Mi'kmaq don't seem to have dealt with

you too harshly. It looks like swimming in that lake took years off you." Benedict grimaced. "Unless you've figured out a way to steal them from me."

"I'd give them back, if it were in my power. Tell me, my friend, how credible is this stranger?"

The priest's brevity brought a familiar grin to the round face. "Ah, Father, he's a different sort. From the smell of him, he's gotten here in quite a hurry, and I'd wager your church it's not the first time he's had to step quick. He says those English ships are coming to make war on us. He claims they've finally resolved to take our lands." Benedict's tone became a touch harsher. "As if he's the first to tell us that smoke means fire."

"I see. Building fortifications, seizing weaponry, sailing warships into the harbor. All as routine as the falling leaves. And neither conviction in God's divine wisdom and mercy nor your cheerfulness can explain away the presence of three hundred more soldiers bivouacked just downstream at Fort Edward. But I agree, you people have ridden this storm out before, and that's the course your Lord and Savior proposes again." Felician steepled his fingers, watching men conjecturing around them.

"You forgot to mention that Governor Lawrence expelled all our priests," Benedict observed drily. "It sounds like you've got strong opinions for someone whose advice is to stay the course."

"I don't remember you entertaining any notions of heroism in the past."

"True enough. And I, and the other old cowards, could probably be convinced to acquiesce once more to live with the temporary inconveniences of submission."

"And Lajeunesse?"

"Well, my new relation has stationed himself at the

entrance. He seems to have already made up his mind."

Felician nodded in weary understanding. "A single day contains only so many miracles."

The smith blamed God, and the priest as His earthly proxy, for the tragedy that had destroyed his family four years ago, shortly after Felician had arrived. His stay in the Minas would soon see him to white hair, notwithstanding Benedict's compliments. Remarkable that he would make the two men family in a few days. It did not seem to matter to Basil that Grand Pre's tacticians viewed negotiation as the only realistic option. Virtually alone among the men in the room, the smith did not cower from the prospect of active resistance.

And here they might have had common ground. Felician longed to return to Ile Royale and join his old congregations as they harried redcoats, to leave these quaking parishioners to their own counsel. He didn't deny that the villagers had their troubles, he took issue only in that they already believed. In his heart, despite his posting, Felician was certain that the great gift of his brief life on earth was to bring true faith and purpose to those blamelessly unbaptized denizens of the untamed woods. No other joy of his holy office approached witnessing the light of faith kindle in another's eyes, and nothing in Grand Pre had so moved him. These faithful needed a calm, steady hand to guide them through their complicated negotiations with the English, not a still young priest with a berserker's fervor for missionary work. And yet despite four years' passage, his baptisms remained glassy-eyed newborns instead of those otherwise destined for Hell's fires.

But now five English warships anchored off Grand Pre. The first priority must be ensuring they didn't use their artillery against the town, as the stranger warned. Felician considered the messenger, sitting alone with his massive head slumped forward from the shoulders, an oddity in the noisy gathering who looked no more capable of speech than the chair supporting him. The newcomer had doffed his fur hat, but this only loosed his matted brown hair, a filthy mane that now flowed nearly indistinguishably into his unkempt beard. As Felician's teachers in Quebec had warned, it was easier to turn a Frenchman into a sauvage than the other way around.

Felician squeezed Benedict's wrist and made for the tiny open area at the center of the room. A quick survey counted more than fifty souls, all men, standing and sitting, conversing and attentive.

"We have a decision before us," Felician began conversationally. There would be time to voice his counsel later in the night. Last but not loudest. "As many of you know, I've been," he hesitated in search of the appropriate word, "in retreat with the Mi'kmaq, for the last month. I return to you, as we've been blessed with fresh news with which to form our opinions."

All eyes slowly turned to the stranger, miserable, hunched over nearly so far as to seem to be seeking out some womb within. Felician prompted him again.

"Welcome, friend. We would be most grateful if you would restate for the record, this for the benefit of our town's notary and our host this evening, Monsieur LeBlanc, the message you've been sent to deliver, which has come to us only in parts. Is the cataclysm upon us?"

The stranger stood reluctantly, the man's artlessness adding to his credibility in the priest's eyes. He spoke, his voice so husky at first that he was forced to stop to clear his throat. "I am Bernard Arseneau. I was sent by authorities in Quebec, a Jesuit." He looked at Felician as if to prove he recognized a priest when he saw one. "They'd gotten word from France that your lands are to be seized by your Protestant masters." Certainly not his phrase, Felician thought as the recitation continued. "England and Boston are arming for a war that's coming up and down the border, but you'll know it first here in Acadia. War is coming, but you don't have an army. And no Canadians or French are marching out of Quebec or sailing from Paris. You can only flee."

The trapper crouched defensively, stocky shoulders hunched and dark eyes darting suspiciously, as he returned to his seat. The man clearly hadn't been among the Acadians long if he thought plain information would result in blows.

Instead of blows, there were angry mutterings that gained momentum as the unpracticed voice trailed off in an apology better made by those responsible for abandoning them to English mercy. Felician wondered which of his brethren had dispatched this luckless man to them. Father Maufils, he hoped, thinking of his old charges on the Minas. Felician was thankful at least that the stranger did not harp any longer on the issue of stooping before Massachusetts' unruly Protestants. The pacifistic course he charted was distasteful enough without a criminal wandering in ragged out of the wild to claim the moral high ground. The priest stepped forward calmly to fill the void.

"Rene, what do we know?"

LeBlanc cleared his throat in unconscious imitation of the stranger before recounting what he was willing to share of the English perspective. "The hundreds of men we've seen disembark and mostly make for Fort Edward are under the command of Lieutenant Colonel John Winslow, who gets his orders directly from Governor Lawrence. I have provided him with a list of the names of the village men. I assure you I had much trouble remembering the names of your wives and children," he added quickly in answer to the men's angry protests.

Felician smiled. The meek old gentleman felt compelled to defend his loyalty and honor, and now the spies and worse cowards among them would scurry back to inform Winslow or Lawrence in Halifax that their informant couldn't be trusted. But the unformed smile dissolved into pity for the notary; the man either offended his neighbors or tugged on the tail of the English lion. Mercy for him, Lord, these are difficult times to pretend at diplomacy.

LeBlanc forged ahead. "Each of the ships that carried the soldiers around the cape from Halifax carry several cannon." This regained his audience's attention. "I don't know their intentions, but we've word there's another fleet anchored in Chignecto Bay, keeping an eye on the border. These soldiers must intend us some discomfort on a larger scale than we've seen, perhaps holding us hostage until the termination of the war with Quebec. No matter the circumstance, someone's going to have to feed the buggers this winter, because I assure you that Winslow has decamped."

Felician caught the chin-wagger veering off to disputatious terrain and cut him off, tempting his night's true adversary. "So, the only option the danger leaves us is to abandon our homes. Are all in accord with the stranger or the clerk?"

And, appreciably predictable, Basil Lajeunesse rose to the challenge. "I do not intend to abandon my home." Conscious or not, the smith had remained near the entryway, towering over a rough crowd of border-dwellers whose presence had forced the male citizenry of Grand Pre to pass through their growling curses and musty smoke before deciding their fate. These isolated men relied more on illegal trade than did Grand Pre's longer-tenured families, whose farms needed no subsidies. The men's guns and homemade goods had been confiscated by the English, even before Felician had sought refuge with the Mi'kmaq, leaving them suffering worse than those who formed his usual Sunday congregations.

"There are more men in this village than soldiers in Fort Edward and aboard ship in the harbor combined. We need to take courage." Basil surveyed the crowd for sympathetic faces before unfolding his plan. "There are a few of us whose homes are north of the Habitant. We maintain regular contact with a large group of Acadians who are building up storehouses all the way from the Missaguash, right under the pig's nose, to the Petitcodiac.

"Myself and Gabriel," he continued, and here father indicated son, who was further behind than the patriarch had hoped, judging from the way the smith flailed his arm toward the boy. Shorter than his father, the boy's head still rose above most in the village, though his frame remained thin despite serving as his father's lone aide these past years. Felician remembered laughing the first time he saw the boy sweating in the dusty spectacles of his trade. But Gabriel had labored doggedly at his father's side, until the priest admitted the boy had a certain grace, tempered by grief, and a candle to Evangeline's sun, but grace nevertheless.

Basil continued, "We've hidden weapons away, muskets, balls, powder, knives, bayonets. We know there are plenty others out there who've done similarly." This time Basil glared into the crowd as he paused. Not too proud to intimidate his audience, the priest thought as he stared down the coal-dark eyes in turn.

"Oliver Thibodeau and some of our neighbors have kept grain and vegetables in storehouses north of town in case some of our homes are lost. I know some among you," the smith flushed as he turned accusatory, "will want to scurry back to the English and report me. Others, certainly, would pursue a different course. Discuss as you want, but neither the English master nor his dogs in Boston are taking my home and forge."

The smith took his seat to general applause. Even as he disagreed, it was impossible for Felician to doubt Basil's courage. The man's enemies would vouch for his honor. But the priest quickly dismissed this notion. The man had lost his wife and three sons and had abandoned caution. Before the next speaker finished, the men would have already forgotten this rush of blood and seen Basil's death wish for what it was. Secular reason dictated that a man who did not care to live had less to lose than those hoping to keep their heads.

Unnoticed in the clamor following Basil's address, and despite his earlier reticence, the messenger again took the floor in the center of the room. "I admire his courage. It is the instinct many of you must have." The stranger did them too much credit, Felician thought. "I tell you there are more soldiers than you know. Thousands scatter all across Acadia, spreading out from Halifax. Just yesterday I passed a dozen ships sailing north into Chignecto Bay from Boston, loaded with troops. Where is their enemy?" Bernard paused. "Here. You are their enemy." As he returned to his seat, he mumbled, suddenly apologetic, "I'd try to escape over the bay and follow the Saint-Jean inland until it freezes. It's a hard road, though, in winter."

Bernard sat, leaving the rest of the crowd to venture their opinions and guess at facts. Henri Melanson stood. The scion of one of the earliest homesteaders who left Port Royal a century ago, Melanson and his clan filled six of Felician's pews on Sundays.

"We'll not leave. The soldiers are going to cause problems and eat our food, but they won't stay here. They left after that trouble four years ago, and we've been at peace since." The man faced down the trapper. "You seem to mean well enough, sir, and it'd be a worse man that criticizes you for traveling on our benefit in this season, but I've got more grandchildren than you've had years, and those babies can't cross the Saint-Jean, before or after it freezes." He softened his tone before continuing, "They need warmth and regular food, and they'll get it at home, where their parents got it, and where I got it, when I was them."

Felician nodded and joined in the clapping, Benedict following suit on his right. Henri had united the gathering, but stout and red-faced Oliver Thibodeau rose to steer their course back into dangerous waters.

"Henri's right. Our families are entrenched. And so we'll stay. But while we sculpted our lands, pulled them out of the sea with our hands, they don't fully belong to us." Thibodeau raised a thick finger, "Yet."

"And when will they, Oliver?" Felician queried, joining the farmer at the center of the room.

The house quieted around them as the red-faced man paused heavily. Thibodeau hadn't expected a rebuttal and looked once at Basil before responding, "When we've successfully divested ourselves of the Anglican tyranny."

"Wars," Felician replied disdainfully, "destroy farmlands more surely than floods, my friend." A fatherly push at the large man's back returned the farmer to his seat. The priest looked encouragingly around the room. "Who else?"

Etienne Gravois spoke up. "There are thousands of peasants in Acadia, agreed, but we're not all built like Basil, and, apologies to him and Gabriel for their tragic loss, but most of us with little ones to look after besides. If we had wanted to fight, it would have been better if we'd done it before people started moving north, away from all this trouble."

"It doesn't look like it would do us any good throwing back in with the French now anyhow," said Antoine Cottard. One of Benedict's old rivals, he had raised three daughters within sight of Saint Charles. "I was in Boston last year. The city is crawling with people. Filthy, poor people, but more white souls than I would have thought bound in all the colonies. I thought then, and nothing's changed my mind since, that it's only a matter of time before the grasping English claim every piece of grass in the Americas."

Benedict chimed in from alongside Felician, "Another point to remember. I'm not alone in shipping cows to Fort Edward every year. Who's going to feed the soldiers if they attack us?" A relieved murmuring accompanied Cottard back to his bench.

Felician's parishioners were frightened, and for the same good reasons as they'd had for the past fifty years. They were defenseless, living in the shadow of an oftentimes tolerant but increasingly bellicose monarchy that mistrusted their language and reviled their Catholicism. If this were Felician's first such meeting, he'd have been on his knees afterward, asking forgiveness for thinking of his cowardly flock without sympathy. Instead, he had come to understand that they relied on faith, both in their God and in the neutrality pacts spoken now by two generations of Acadians, and over the years their stubbornly clutched beliefs had earned the priest's grudging respect. Most of them, wrongheaded or not, had allowed the English to divest them of their weapons. They refused to fight English, French, or native. But they could not defend themselves against the hordes of Puritans in Boston salivating at the thought of annexing their peninsula.

Thibodeau exchanged a glance with Basil and rose, looking more confident now than during his retreat moments before.

"Friends, the soldiers aren't going anywhere we don't make them go. But they don't want to be here, and we do, and any way we look at it, this many soldiers encamped on the peninsula means an end, of one kind or another."

"And if so, Oliver," their host's reedy voice warbled out from the crowd, "what do you suggest we do? They've confiscated our boats, our guns. Felician's hiding from the soldiers, or he'd have been shipped to France. Our representatives are held against their will." The withered town notary stepped forward as he continued, "You tell us things are bad. I'll not disagree, but peaceful negotiation is the only option left to us. We've reasoned plenty of governors out of extreme behavior before. Rational argument was the only choice given our grandfathers, and it is the only option left to us."

Amen, the priest thought. And bless the Lord for simple choices.

"More ships are coming," Bernard snarled, his crooked teeth grating as he spoke. "English troops and ships are all over Acadia, more than just a few here in the Minas. And where is the French enemy?" He searched the room for an answer. "There aren't any soldiers coming out of Quebec or Montreal. The English are preparing to invade the valley from Boston, and you're on your own here. There is only time to run."

Basil could not hold himself back. "They're trying to take our homes, our faith, and our pride. Where do you draw the line? What life do you preserve if you run from your home at a whispered rumor of danger?" Turning more conciliatory, he acknowledged the trapper. "I don't mean to discount the service you've done us with this timely warning."

"Hardly," Bernard declined the praise wearily. "I am telling you only what I have been told to and, wishing to be helpful, what I would do myself."

"We don't have to run," Basil implored, nodding to the trapper to show he bore no hard feelings. "We just need to make an ally of the Mi'kmaq. The tribesmen fight the English in the woods every day. And who can help us reach out to the warriors?"

Felician braced and prepared his rebuttal.

"Father Felician Abadie," the smith intoned, slowly as he joined Felician in the center of the room. "Who is just returned to us after spending a month under Mi'kmaq protection in a secluded refuge while the English erected a palisade around his church." Basil's eyes burned like ingots as the priest met them. "No one's built any walls around my house, Felician," he said coldly, before returning to his familiar boom. "But in spite of the fact that he's our only means of communication, he thwarts the idea of an alliance between our people, something which existed for a hundred years before any of us were around to muddle it up." Basil waited, almost as if struck by his own wit, before venturing on. "If the tribesmen intensified their attacks on the English, and we stopped feeding them and besieged the stockade."

The priest interrupted as he stepped toward Basil.

"Even if I were able to convince the Mi'kmaq to spirit us all into hiding, I fail to see how the sauvages could help us keep what's ours. Should we spend the winter running, as they do, from encampment to encampment? How do you think our children would fare under those conditions?" The two stood alone in the room's center, surrounded by men puffing patiently, awaiting the outcome that would decide their course.

"You're telling me they won't help?"

"I'm saying they can't. The British can't chase the Mi'kmaq from the woods so long as they stay mobile, but their people roam over woodlands, mountains, coasts. We Europeans, for the most part, are stationary creatures." Felician added the last with a nod to the stranger. "There is no place for the Mi'kmaq in the new Anglican world. But there might be one for us if we don't throw in with the natives. We have a chance of surviving as we are, simply by maintaining the status quo. They do not have that choice, and so must fight, just as we must keep the peace and bite our tongues, regardless of the concessions we'll be forced to make." Felician waited a long moment before finishing his case, "We have to convince the English there is nowhere else for us to be, the lands are ours, and we belong to the dikelands. I see no other hope."

They had reached the zenith of early morning, lanterns dim, the moon vanished. It was time for judgment.

The priest stood at the center of the dark room and began his summation. "I've heard three proposals tonight." He held an arm to both recalcitrants, strange and familiar. "Run, pack your families and what you can carry and hie across the Saint Jean on whatever craft you can wrangle, as our boats are confiscated alongside our guns." Felician let his eyes meet Bernard's, who returned the gaze coldly, but remained silent in his seat.

Felician turned to Basil. "We could fight. We have the numbers. But we'll be fighting on our lands and in our homes." Felician felt his adversary crumble before him. "Soldiers hired for pay have no stake in this. If we resist, they will burn and pillage and destroy as it suits military expediency. Regardless of the outcome, there won't be any homes to return to. And where will you keep your families while you're campaigning?"

"Your words make no difference to me," Basil hissed to Felician as he shouldered past him and out of the house, banging open the heavy oak door and vanishing into the dark. The draught of night air cooled the tense room, and the priest had the temerity to smile at Gabriel as the boy followed his father.

"Our hope is the third way, the same choice you've always made, the path of peace. Your fathers and grandfathers settled these treaties with the English, established your neutrality in wartime, and tolerance of our faith. And we promised to respect the authority of the English crown, and we have, to a point."

"Paid for the pleasure," Benedict interjected from the door where he watched the boy who would marry his daughter pursue his father through the gloom. Felician wondered what his friend would tell Evangeline.

"And they will respect our dignity. To a point," the priest continued. "This is a good time to keep heads low, friends, and remember, it's not been war or flight that's kept Grand Pre green these past hundred years and more, but peaceful persuasion. Neutrality is as much a part of us as our French heritage and our Catholicism. You've been stubborn as mules, to your credit, and unlike so many others you still farm your lands here in the great meadow. The best in Acadia."

The deep darkness gave way to the first gray light as Felician spoke, though the lip of the southern highlands still delayed the sun's meeting with the Minas.

"Pray to the Lord to deliver us from the heaving monstrosity of the English war machine," he intoned. "Ask him to stand by our side in this time of upheaval, and remember that our God is Lord of Peace, and He smiles as He looks down upon us, quietly toiling here in our fields and shops. Ask His blessing that we might continue to do so till He calls us to serve at His side."

With that, the first rays struck the Minas, glittering across the calm water and brightening the fields and homes sheltering in the lee of the uplands between Port Royal and Grand Pre. As the beams broke through the windows, Felician joined Benedict in the doorway to watch the dawn over the lands they hoped to keep. Distracted, he intoned the rest of his blessing more quietly.

"Thank you for this morning, Lord, and for every peaceful day you keep us safe in our homes. Amen."

Habitant River 1755

Over the joyous feast, sudden darkness descended.

HEN JULES ROSSELIN FOUND GABRIEL AND BASIL outside their forge north of the Habitant, they were staring out at the lichen encrusted rock of Cape Blomidan. The horse's heavy panting intruded on their silence from a distance and Gabriel turned to watch their visitor's progress, though his father took no notice. The clanging work of the forge often allowed customers to reach the shop without their knowledge, but since the soldiers had moved their own smithy into town, there was rarely enough work to fill the hours. The horse clomped through the bindweed, crushing the dried pea husks as it shifted its feet to drink from the trough beside the shop. "Colonel's called a gathering for tomorrow morning," Jules reported, his wide belt jiggling over the saddle as his mount finally came to rest. "Winslow says it's required for all men older than ten years." The derisive snort was a match for his mount's slurping grunts.

"That's us, then."

"Peculiar that Winslow's insisting we bring our snotnoses.

Bad enough he's got news that the rest of us need to hear," their visitor said, as he tugged his reluctant horse away from the trough's scummy water. "He's insisting we arrive by seven tomorrow morning. Tell him this is harvest season, and he'll tell you there's a war in the offing. There still aren't many of this sort that've mastered dealing with regular people."

Basil grunted his thanks, and the man was off, galloping west along the Habitant toward the Thibodeaus, their closest neighbors. Prodigious farmers and breeders, the Thibodeaus were independent-minded Acadians. The large clan took advantage of its remove from the stockade and garrison to horde huge grain surpluses, which Basil and Oliver Thibodeau already planned to use to feed insurgents through the winter. Gabriel turned back to the blood-red cape, the wild vista here raw compared to the tame Bellefontaine lands along the Gaspereau.

"Well, boy, no reason to wait any longer to clean out the forge. I'll see if there's anything worth eating tonight."

Wordlessly following his father's command, Gabriel reentered the forge, which had darkened quickly on the short autumn day. He raked out the coals from under the forge with the alder broom, separating them with the twigs before stamping them out on the dirt. Evangeline's father often remarked that no one had dirtier sabots than a smith's apprentice, but over time Gabriel grew to believe that old Bellefontaine approved of smithing, his mercantilist soul satisfied so long as his daughter didn't marry a farmer, even if she was determined to break his heart with a working man.

Gabriel gripped his tongs and set to work fishing the iron nails out of the water pail where his father had plunged them, dropping them on a shelf above the cooling bucket. He knew that Benedict had a good bit of money in a few ships still sailing out of Boston, and he and Evangeline seemed to be managing despite the fact that the old man hadn't appeared to work in the four years Gabriel had known the family. He and his father were certainly scraping for bread. Regardless, Gabriel was grateful that Benedict was warming up to him. It had been months since Gabriel had heard, "He seems nice, but I certainly wouldn't marry someone I couldn't talk to. Poor lad can't help but bore you, can he?" It was either a sign of the old man's deepening respect or perhaps his advancing age.

Brushing aside thoughts of his future father-in-law, Gabriel raised the thin eight-foot bar up to its resting position. He pumped the bellows at the scattered coals, turning a few of the dark lumps red with a final burst of soot and hot air. His father insisted on carrying these stubborn coals outside to the trough by hand, preferring not to contaminate the bucket of water near the wall of the small shop where they dunked the red-hot metal after it was shaped. There was no cause for a real fire today, but his father despised half-measures. Deeply indoctrinated, Gabriel hadn't bothered to ask if they'd use a full ration of coal this morning, though they needed barely more than an hour's heat to pour the couple dozen half-pennies.

The English soldiers had grown suspicious of their fluctuating prices, and a new smith had been engaged from Halifax so they could avoid patronizing the local craftsmen. Worse yet, the soldiers had siphoned off the food surpluses that usually allowed the local farmers to purchase the services of the Lajeunesse forge. Still Basil refused to react to the indignities, allowing himself only a tight, superior smile, despite his full knowledge that that the seizure of all Acadian vessels, from schooners to canoes, meant the trickle of coin through the villages had dried up. Stubborn about the English, stubborn about the coal.

Gabriel knelt, not taking his eyes off the recalcitrant coals his father would burn but not waste and gripped one in his right hand. His hand searing with pain, he rose, made a quick look around the forge, and walked to the entrance to dunk his hand into the standing water they left for the horses. He opened his hand underwater and set the coal adrift. Neither father nor son had likely changed the water in the trough for three weeks, as neither would consent to lug water short of absolute necessity, holding the volatile substance accountable, along with the angry whimsy of God, for the drowning of his mother and older brothers in the Minas, sinking them with a load of unworked iron on their return trip from Beaubassin.

Keeping the trough water fresh had been Daniel's chore, and it was one of a host of minor duties father and son took turns neglecting. Daniel had been two years older than Gabriel, but now Gabriel was older than his brother had ever been, proved by the reflection in the stagnant water though the face he saw was angular compared to his memory of his brothers'. He turned away from the trough and hefted the shovel from its resting place under the eaves of the tiny forge. His ritual having proved his virility, he would want the use of his hands on his wedding night.

By the time Gabriel finished in the shop the cape was lost in shadow and his father sat on their front stoop, smoking his pipe and staring toward the Thibodeau farm. Basil distractedly gestured him toward a chair positioned across from him, a surprise to Gabriel, as conversations with his father rarely lasted long enough to merit sitting down. He approached slowly, but sat quickly after glimpsing his father's disapproving expression. The chair Basil had set out was the small one he and each of his brothers had used as young children. Gabriel remembered his mother reaching him down small spoonfuls of mush she'd sweetened with molasses, a memory that might have been lost forever if not for his gigantic father perched awkwardly on the stoop. The chair had outlived his three brothers, but his father had some time ago simply sawed the arms off, declaring, "We'll keep it because it's still useful."

As they faced each other, Gabriel wondered if his father had dragged out the small chair for nostalgic reasons or if he'd purposefully chosen it to retain his height advantage. Gabriel knew better than to believe chance ever played a role in his father's decisions. There his father sat, leather apron hunched over his knees, cracked glasses tucked into his apron collar, his shining eyes fixing Gabriel intently even as he rapped his pipe against the retaining wall of the house.

"So, we're to meet with this Colonel tomorrow in the church." It wasn't a question, and Gabriel didn't respond. His father continued, "And you're expected, though you're a boy. Hell, children are expected, of an age that'll make you appear a man." Basil kicked the earth and looked over at his son, silent. He put the pipe down, thought better of it, and reloaded it from his pouch. Basil's restlessness disturbed Gabriel. He resisted pointing out that he was fully seventeen years old, and that he'd be married inside of a week. Still, the silence stiffened and, perhaps aware of his feelings, his father kept his eyes on the tobacco he glommed into the pipe while he changed the subject. "What did you think of that stranger?"

"He's not giving the same advice as Felician," Gabriel responded loyally.

"Nor supporting the course I proposed."

Gabriel fell silent, trying to imagine his father peacefully abandoning the home where his sons had been raised. He thought instead about dying in the house, circled round by implacable redcoats firing volley after volley into the tiny dwelling. He took inspiration from this more likely scenario. "Looks like he'd be handy if the British come calling."

"Yes, it's a shame to disagree with him. Honesty's plainer on him than the scales on Felician. The priest is right, though, that one trapper isn't much favor from Quebec. They've got their own garden to tend." He puffed awhile. "No, we're on our own. Probably have a decent chance if everyone stands up for what's his."

They silently reflected on this possibility.

"I'm not leaving you here."

"I'm not asking you to. Still, a man with a wife might want to think about moving on," his father added.

"Maybe some of them will come around tomorrow."

"It's the ones who've already made up their minds that you want with you, boy. And I fancy you won't catch that trapper or old Felician at this meeting." The big man bestowed a conciliatory smile on his son, his teeth flashing white from within his jet-black beard. "At least I'll get to set foot in that church again without listening to that spindly bastard." Basil hoisted himself to his feet and turned to face his son, "Better to know than not, that's what my father used to tell me." The towering figure turned, his head nearly even with the hammer and anvil Henri had carved on a cedar plank hanging above the open doorway, as he entered their dark home.

They reached the stockade well before seven the next morning, near the head of a line of hundreds of proud and angry Acadian men, and just ahead of rumbling storm clouds high over the bay. Soldiers opened the gate in the stockade to usher them inside the compound, searching each man in turn for weapons, though the English had already confiscated their guns and ammunition during the summer. Only a few knives had been discovered among the crowd before Basil's too was taken and stuck, quivering, into the barricade with the others.

The scowling men of Grand Pre were compressed into a narrow file by an armed crowd of irregulars who cast them disdainful looks as they kept the locals from straying through the compound. The rising sun was still low and mostly obscured behind thin, dark clouds that turned everything inside the compound the color of steel. The ground around Saint Charles didn't look as different as it might after being walled off for months, Gabriel reasoned hopefully, just a little muddier. In the place of the garden Felician had kept there was a low gatehouse with a long common bed visible through an open doorway, and the new smithy just beyond. Their competitors had their fire stoked, the spent smoke joining the haze of dozens of wet campfires belching their own gray tendrils as the militiamen heated coffee and smoked meat confiscated from the farms of the men streaming before them. But in spite of everything, it kept the feel of a temporary encampment, Gabriel thought, housing men that smelled like the livestock they'd stolen. There was a bottleneck somewhere ahead of Gabriel, the tense crowd shoving and cursing at one another, until suddenly a pistol shot cracked over the furor.

Whatever its intent, the shot halted the procession. The soldiers turned from their breakfast fires, and edgy guards leveled long rifles at the line of unarmed men which now stretched from the gate toward the mouth of the church. The thin chain of farmers constricted in fear, though from Gabriel's vantage it seemed that those in front had glimpsed something horrible in the maw of the familiar church. A redcoated officer strode forward with the smoking pistol. He kept the line waiting as he methodically holstered his weapon, removed his black hat by its crown, and then swept it theatrically toward the front of the line. After waiting a moment for their comrades ahead to grudgingly resume the march, Gabriel and Basil filed quietly into the commandeered sanctuary, alongside its other wary former parishioners.

They remained near the entrance, his father restless inside the armor of his blacksmith's apron, intent on his neighbors pouring in, nodding to a few while Gabriel examined the familiar confines that had stood empty for the past weeks. The wan light of the morning was made more opaque as it passed through the eel-skin panes, and almost as though straining through a muddy waterfall, he could barely make out the altar Felician had partially stripped before fleeing. And yet Gabriel was struck by the impression that the building was missing something beyond the golden emblems, and that though compared to the grounds the interior remained almost untouched, it was different beyond the dust. He'd yet to settle on an answer when the procession finally ceased, and was followed hard upon by Colonel Winslow, the stern voice imperial rule since early that summer. Four redcoats carrying bayoneted Brown Besses accompanied the tall Colonel, trailed by a graying man without a uniform who entered with the enthusiasm of a man walking to his hanging. The Colonel made no motion for quiet, but the restless stilled themselves as they could and muted conversations hushed expectantly.

Gabriel could read English slowly after two years of evenings spent studying with Evangeline, but he was nervous and did not understand the Colonel's first words, addressed to his escort. The tall man's crisp French was plenty clear. "This man, Isaac Deschamps, will read my orders aloud so that your situation becomes clear." The timid civilian moved forward to accept the scroll, and Winslow stepped back behind the translator. His face expressionless, framed by its grim curls and black hat, the Colonel vaulted more than a foot above Deschamps, imbuing the reluctant voice with the full force of the crown's authority.

Gentlemen, I have received from His Excellency Governor Lawrence, The King's Commission which I have in my hand and by whose orders you are convened to gather to manifest to you his Majesty's final resolution to the French inhabitants of this his province of Nova Scotia, who for almost half a century have had more indulgence granted them, than any of his subjects in any part of his dominions, what use you have made of them, you yourselves best know. The part of duty I am now upon is what though necessary is very disagreeable to my natural make and temper as I know it must be grievous to you who are of the same species. But it is not my business to animadvert, but to obey such orders as I receive, and therefore without hesitation shall deliver you his Majesty's orders and instructions to wit. That your lands and tenements cattle of all kinds and live stock of all sorts are forfeited to the crown with all your other effects saving your money and household goods and you yourselves to be removed from this, his province.

Thus it is peremptorily his Majesty's orders that the whole French inhabitants of these districts, be removed, and I am through his Majesty's goodness directed to allow you liberty to carry of your money and household goods as many as you can without discommoding the vessels you go in. I shall do everything in my power that all those goods be secured to you and that you are not molested in carry-

ing of them and also that whole families shall go in the same vessel and make this remove which I am sensible must give you a great deal of trouble as easy as his Majesty's service will admit and hope that in whatever part of the world you may fall you may be faithful subjects, a peaceable and happy people. I must also inform you that it is his Majesty's pleasure that you remain in security under the inspection and direction of the troops that I have the honor to command and that until departure you are the King's prisoners.

The hush that had originally descended so that those closer to the altar could hear deepened into a breathless silence as the speech continued uninterrupted. They kept waiting as the words echoed interminably in the hollow church, praying as he was, Gabriel thought, for some form of reprieve to emerge from the unconscionable declaration.

His father broke the silence with an inarticulate roar as he lunged across the room. As Deschamps scurried aside, and the Colonel reached belatedly for the pistol at his belt, a part of Gabriel absently thought to envy the sound, certain he would never muster such a passion. One among the English would feel their pain.

But Basil's berserker rush ended before Gabriel or any other of the stunned Acadians moved in his support, as the redcoat to Winslow's left met the charge, driving the butt into the side of Basil's head, the wooden stock splintering with the sickening crunch of bone.

Gabriel's hand clenched into a fist, his first movement since his father had rushed from his side. Basil's attacker backed to the door with his ruined weapon as the remainder of the escort lowered their muskets, but Winslow stepped forward without reaching for his weapon.

"There are three hundred soldiers outside, British regulars and colonial militia," the Colonel spoke loudly but without haste, making certain he was understood. "Any further attacks against a representative of the crown will be regarded as an act of war, for which both you and your families outside the stockade will be held accountable."

He stopped speaking as Gabriel, his hands lowered, walked forward to kneel next to his father and feel the heartbeat in his wrist. When he raised his father's head off the bloody floor, Basil's eyes fluttered. The Colonel stared down at them for a moment before issuing quiet orders to his guard that Gabriel managed to decipher despite his preoccupations.

"Take both to Captain Murray. Tell him to have someone see to that man, and then introduce them both to our custody." The slightest of shrugs preceded his parting words. "Sometimes the son pays for the father."

Two soldiers hoisted Basil's frame up onto his son's thin shoulders, and Gabriel staggered out of the church stooped so that he could only see the boots of the redcoat who had cracked open his father's head. He struggled behind the two soldiers the short distance to Felician's house, where they lifted Basil from his shoulders and hauled him inside.

Entering, they found a smooth-cheeked officer standing over a map of the Minas unrolled on the priest's kitchen table.

"If this man were hung," Murray ignored Gabriel's angry stare, "then we wouldn't have to worry about it happening again tomorrow. He wants us to find a doctor when the governor would have him strung up from the steeple."

The officer unsheathed his sword and laid the heavy

weapon over the map. "Find a sawbones, then, if that's what he wants," he said, "I can watch these two bleed on the floor."

Murray turned to Gabriel and spoke more slowly, exposing a mouth that looked to be missing half its teeth. "Don't let me know that you're here."

A militiaman came in shortly to relieve the Captain, but it was several more hours before a ship's doctor passed through to check on his father's seeping wounds. Pausing in the doorway to whisper to the guard and finish his pipe, the small man swayed unsteadily into the room, briefly casting an eye toward the patient without a word to Gabriel. The redcoated doctor stooped over the smith, reaching out unsteadily like a child dared to wake a slumbering troll. Gingerly he cut the blood-soaked hair away from the wound, pouring water then liquor onto the deep gash to clean it. Without ceremony, the man tucked a fragment of skull into the breast pocket of the smith's blood-soaked leather apron before expertly sewing the wound closed with metal wire. He spoke to Gabriel in effortless French as he worked.

"Not many of us get the chance to keep part of our own scalp as a souvenir." The doctor cackled and took a sip of the liquor. "I don't believe that your father's going to be the first to die here." Realizing how his words could be misconstrued, he coughed loudly to cover his indiscretion. "What I mean is that I don't think your pa's going to die. I just saw someone I was told didn't have any family in the village. He stole a canoe from the harbor and was pushing for sea when they shot him." The man paused to search for a clean piece of cloth in his bag, found a likely scrap, and tied it tightly against the wound. The doctor panted slightly from his exertions, brandy rising from his breath and sweat like discarded medicine. "They had to paddle out after him and tow the boat back. The man's still breathing over in the chapel, but he's sure to be dead by morning." He offered the bottle to Gabriel, "Have a drink, son. It'll help you sleep."

Gabriel was sure the man he described was the trapper, who must have taken his own counsel and run, just as his father had fought. Hard ends for the independent thinkers.

The doctor's creaky voice began again. "You'll all be free to take your personals along with you. That's what your women are doing right now, packing." He took a last drink, then shrugged apologetically. "The colonies," he toasted, before corking the bottle and departing. Gabriel was left alone again with his unconscious father, free to let his imagination conjure the worst from the doctor's words.

The meeting in the church might have been his life's defining moment, Gabriel reflected, and he hadn't acted. No one had, except for his father. Perhaps they would have had a chance if they'd fought, and certainly some families would have managed to escape if they'd run. His father wouldn't have run, no matter what others did, and Gabriel knew Evangeline wouldn't have left Benedict who could neither run nor fight.

Images of Evangeline materialized before his eyes. He saw her gliding around her home's modest interior, while Benedict observed from his rocker, occasionally gesturing for a particular curio to be packed. Bellefontaines would not be rushed. Father and daughter were perhaps most alike in their self-assurance. Armed men at the door, Benedict would think to ask for his Virginia tobacco, which he was never without, though he knew Evangeline could not stand the smell of it, and complained whenever it lingered under the eaves of their house.

Evangeline's mother's comb, inlaid with silver, was a present to her father from a fellow merchant in Boston. The large silver coin stamped with the Sun King's leering face that Benedict carried with him whenever he traveled. Emmeline Bellafontaine's wedding gown carefully packed in their cedar trunk. Evangeline had told him how heavy the delicate-looking dress was. He might at least have seen her in the dress if they were to have ill luck for their wedding.

Evangeline would move to the bookshelf, making sure her father saw her reach first for their well-worn Jonathan Swift, even before wrapping her Bible in a scarf and laying them in the trunk with the dress for protection. Most of the books, prized possessions of both father and daughter, would be too cumbersome for the uncertain travel before them. Gabriel would miss the books as well. He loved the scent of the old leather covers, redolent of evenings outside in the damp, apple-infused air of the Gaspereau, the smell merging with the musk tones of Evangeline's home. He had hoped it would be what their home would smell like.

Gabriel and Basil kept no books, which was for the better now, because there would be no one to pack them. Whoever entered their empty house would find beds disheveled, cupboards bare. He slept in the loft's four beds indiscriminately, and all were unmade. His father had built the beds as each son outgrew his crib in turn, but Basil had not set foot upstairs since the drownings, and so Gabriel slept there alone, with memories of his brothers invading his nights and filling his dreams with their speculative personalities.

Although the two of them cooked simply and required only small fires for heat, their chimney pumped thick gray smoke regardless of the season, and the smell of wood smoke hung heavy in the house. Downstairs sooty hangings covered the interior. They never troubled to remove the winter insulation from the walls. His mother had always celebrated the arrival of spring by ripping down the furs and fabrics, but since, the untouched draperies had hung stained and reeking, darkening the cabin so that father and son increasingly moved about in solitude, a consumptive dust filling in the air between them.

While Evangeline and her father were saying goodbye to their home by the river, he and his father had already seen their house for the last time. Gabriel felt sure that though some might return to Grand Pre, he and Basil were not destined to be among them. Both would be happy not to look out over the unforgiving face of Cape Blomidan again.

With his father ensconced in Felician's bed, Gabriel settled under a thin blanket on the floor. The night was restless, and he woke once to change the bandages his father tore loose as he tossed about in his painful sleep. In the dark of the night his father had reached over to him, sobbing Henri's name, but the smith woke the next morning with his wits gathered more closely. By the next evening, Basil began cursing his captors, and it was generally agreed that he would live. They were removed to the hut guarding the southern gate of the stockade where they had entered, chained to the back wall of the hasty structure. They were casually guarded by whichever soldiers were sleeping between shifts. Other soldiers sat by the gate, drinking and harassing villagers who attempted to visit the Acadian men Gabriel learned were still imprisoned in the church. The redcoat who'd struck his father visited them their first night in the guardhouse.

"I'm happy to see you're alive. Acadian skulls are thicker than English muskets." The man's French was almost as good as Winslow's, his words slow but clear. The man was thick and breathed heavily through a lumpy nose. He lowered a pot of stew onto the dirt floor between father and son, and extended a loaf of bread uncertainly toward Basil. Garlic in the stew's aromatic steam washed over the cell like a memory of the fields outside.

Basil took the offering wordlessly.

"All the malcontents are being sent south within the month, and you'll be going with them," the man said. He waited a moment. "Do you know anyone there?"

Basil stared coldly at the soldier, who turned away without meeting the gaze for long, as though this was the outcome he had expected. Only when the redcoat's hand touched the door handle did his father speak, his voice cracking after two days of disuse, "What about spoons?"

On the seventh day of their captivity, Gabriel and Basil joined the mass of prisoners from the church in the early morning cold of the stockade. They waited for nearly an hour with two militiamen before following at a short remove behind the ragged prisoners, Winslow careful before committing his more incendiary prisoners.

Outside, the men of Grand Pre found themselves surrounded by nearly two hundred soldiers in formation. Despite the precautions, Gabriel heard shouting from the front of the line, and the procession had ground to a quick halt before he'd left Felician's threshold. He waited to hear gunfire, but after only a few uneasy minutes the Acadians resumed trudging out of the stockade in their hundreds.

Gabriel and Basil fell into step with four men newly brought into custody, two of whom were wounded. Father and son trailed the others, immediately behind a man whose head was wrapped with clumsy bandages. Gabriel thought that he leaned heavily on the man next to him, but then realized that it was the other man's limp that accounted for their halting progress. Basil's feet dragged heavily as well once they started downhill, following the line of willows that ran halfway to the landing at the Gaspereau's mouth.

Past the trees the trail was constricted by lines of oxcarts and small wagons, and villagers crying out in panic as they recognized their neighbors among the grim parade. The line ran nearly the entire mile remaining before the lapping water where the ships bobbed in the low tide. As the prisoners passed into the encampment, redcoats shoved them along as the din intensified. Soon the men were calling back, ignoring their captors and stopping in places along the crowd. Despite the chaos, Gabriel and his father were attended closely by redcoats who prodded them downhill. They kept watch for Evangeline, but neither saw her as they were hurried downhill. It looked to Gabriel as if the causeway was lined mostly by mothers who kept their children behind them, staring with nervous wonder at the tattered men streaming down the hill, so dirty and ragged from their week imprisoned in the church that it appeared as if the hillside were rolling down to the harbor with them, the land subject as they were to imperial whimsy.

Even as they neared the harbor, Gabriel remained hopeful that he hadn't missed Evangeline, though he occasionally called out above the clacking sabots and similarly desperate cries. Reunited families began moving downhill together, but now near the head of the column, Gabriel, Basil and the other four malcontents were hustled toward the harbor in advance of the other men beginning to cluster along the shoreline. It was then that Gabriel finally saw Evangeline, standing out several paces in the incoming tide, scrutinizing the oncoming men with a heron's intensity.

She started toward shore when she saw him, and they called for each other in the same moment. To Gabriel she looked like a mermaid become a woman at the shore, her brown hair bound and swinging behind her head as she loped gracefully past Benedict, who waited at the edge of the cold water. Her father gave him a low wave, flat palm facing the earth in a gesture of farewell.

"Gabriel," Evangeline screamed. People turned at the sound of her voice.

Gabriel's ears thrummed. Soldiers were everywhere in the chaos, and one had smacked him sharply in the head. He shook off the soldier long enough to meet her eyes, five meters distant. "They're taking us to Carolina. I don't know anything else. I love you."

"I'll find you," she shouted back, as he was dragged away, and roughly manhandled into a canoe at the water's edge.

"I love you," Gabriel shouted helplessly again as they were propelled across the water. The landing, usually so sedate, was swamped with wives and daughters from every settlement in the long valley. It would not be possible to fit all of them in the ships as well. Who would keep them safe from the rapacious colonials?

Onboard it took two soldiers to prop Basil upright and propel him down the hatch into the bowels of the ship, his linen-wrapped head rising well above both soldiers like a grizzled bear's. For one last moment, Gabriel scanned the beach for a last glimpse of Evangeline across the tidal water. The soldiers reached for him next and he struggled vainly away from the hold as the men roughly shoved him backward down the steps into the darkness.

Grand Pre 1755

✦

Seize them, and whirl them aloft, and sprinkle them
far o'er the ocean.

E VANGELINE'S FATHER CLUTCHED HER HAND AND GENTLY
drew her away from the beach where she stood looking
at the deserted deck of the *Success*.

"Do you know that I don't recognize one of those ships?
There was a day when I could name half the boats in the
Atlantic." Benedict's watery eyes sharpened on her. "What kind
of cruel man names a prison boat, success, I don't know."

As they returned to their belongings, Benedict released her
hand and leaned heavily on their cart.

The village and her father had been wrong, Evangeline
thought. This time had been different, and now Gabriel was
gone. She'd heard many desperate scenarios these past weeks,
but no one had predicted this bleak a turn of events. The
English were forcing them out of Acadia, and there was to be
no return. She wondered how much her identity had been
determined by this land. She would continue to refer to herself

as an Acadian, regardless of where they landed. Her children, though, might not.

Benedict caught his breath and noticed her consternation. "We will find him, Evangeline."

"Have you been to Carolina, Father?"

Benedict shook his head wearily. "Georgia, but it's close by. There's every chance that we'll be taken to Boston, where I might still know a few people who could help us."

"I don't want to ask these people for anything."

"But I've been waiting seventy years in the hopes that I'd become a beggar." Her father's expression was more sympathetic than his tone. "Take heart. You're my girl, you can do anything. And you will find him." He coughed and surveyed the scene around them, watching families industriously unloading their carts and building fires. "Why would they want to do this? I have no answers."

"The English? They are leeches trying to suck the world dry."

"My dear, I've found that as individuals, they're much the same as we are."

"We are not taking anything from them," Evangeline repeated firmly, amazed that her father's equanimity remained as unwavering as ever.

"Come, Evangeline, we're lagging behind." Benedict indicated the long path vanishing beneath a patchwork of makeshift shelters.

Evangeline watched two boys she didn't recognize tie a square of sailcloth to tool handles they'd anchored in the ground, fixing the other ends to the handles of their upended cart. A good idea, and certainly an improvement on whatever she and Benedict were about to engineer tonight. Evangeline turned back to their pushcart, docked next to the Labiche clan, who remained their neighbors even in exile. Her father sat on the ground beyond, staring into the stream that ran the length of the path from the church to the harbor. She unfolded a blanket from their cart and wrapped the wool cover snugly around his shoulders.

"Father, just sit there. I'll find a book for you."

"Don't bother, the light will be gone soon. My legs are sick of holding the rest of me up, and apparently remembered they had a choice in the matter." Benedict cupped his head in his hands. Just moments ago, she had been ready with recriminations for his having them remain in Grand Pre, but now she only worried for her father.

"This has been more walking than you've had anytime recently," Evangeline remarked softly. It was difficult for her to think of her father as infirm. He had certainly been graceful enough waltzing with her a few short days ago.

"Walking," he snorted. "I'm ripe for travel."

"Sit for awhile, and I'll unpack."

Madeleine Labiche was standing at their cart when Evangeline returned from the water, and the older woman embraced her.

"How awful this is." Madame Labiche might have considered the possibility that one day soldiers would forcibly remove them from their homes. She had certainly always been forthcoming with warnings that Evangeline was glad to dismiss. "Why don't you bring your father over to our fire, dear?"

"We wouldn't want to make more work for you."

"Nonsense, there's just the two of you, and the fire's already started. Bring your things, and I'll get your father." The stout blonde woman heaved Benedict to his feet, wrapped an arm around his waist, and led him the ten steps to their crude shelter. Evangeline followed their plodding pace with the two-wheeled cart.

"They took Jean aboard this afternoon," Madame Labiche said. She had been talking to Benedict but now turned her attention to Evangeline, who settled alongside her father. The new-comers stared across the fire at the Labiche children ranged around the camp.

"He wasn't guarded by soldiers like I saw with Gabriel," Madame Labiche continued. "Jean told us we'd be joining them out on the boats."

Evangeline turned to gaze out at the boats anchored out in the dusk. Accustomed to an unobstructed view, the ships' foreignness made them appear enormous in the shadows.

"Where are Julian and Jana?" Benedict asked.

"I sent them off to hide."

"Wise mother," Benedict said, batting ineffectually at a fly. "I wish I'd had the same foresight." He started coughing again.

"I have a bit of brandy for that cough, Monsieur."

The fire brightened as one of the children dragged in a branch with dead leaves still dangling in clumps, and her father nodded in the fresh light.

"I'd be much obliged, Madame." The woman found the liquor after a quick rummage through her possessions. The Labiche's cart was a match for their own, though it provided efficiently for seven rather than two.

"Here's the bottle, but I'm afraid I didn't pack anything to drink out of."

"It won't be the first time I've been reduced to such straits," Benedict said, and with a jerking motion he reached up to clasp the bottle. He coughed violently after a swallow, and Evangeline snatched the bottle from him, returning it to their friend.

"Not the fault of the liquor," he rasped when he was able.

"Jean's kept this bottle for years," the woman said apologetically.

Benedict smiled.

"Ages better than some people do, I'm afraid." The wind picked up, rustling the cord grass crowning the dikes, and Evangeline stared across the Minas, trying to make out Gabriel's ship. The children scuttled about her, piling up wood and vying with their new neighbors for the closest tinder. It was growing cold to ford the stream, so they left the fallen fuel in the birch woods across the water for future days.

On all sides, families stretched quilts and sailcloths as overhangs, tying them off to shovel handles repurposed as corner posts. A mother with a gaggle of children captured Evangeline's attention as she fashioned a frame of long birch branches, interlocking at the top, which looked to be wide enough for all of them. Nearby, a family chocked the wheels of their oxcart and was already bedded down beneath it.

Unaware of the industry surrounding them, Benedict dozed with his chin on his chest, and Evangeline draped her blanket over the one already warming his shoulders. She walked to the stream, startling a raccoon drinking on the far side of the little flow. The creature retreated up the closest tree, watching her intently until it was several meters up, and then continued climbing slowly and confidently out of sight. The raccoon would no doubt still be here in the spring, drinking from the stream and enjoying its view of the Gaspereau, but she and her father would not.

"Evangeline," Madame Labiche called. Evangeline rushed

back to her father's side at the fire. "He's cold," she continued anxiously as her children heaped more wood onto the fire. The two women eased Benedict closer to the expanding flames. Her father moved groggily in and out of sleep even as they edged him toward the warmth. The heat was oppressive to Evangeline, but despite the sweat that rose to his skin, Benedict felt cool under her fingers.

He found her eye as she arranged herself alongside him to rub his back through the blankets.

"I'm not sure there's any colonizing in my future."

"Hush now," she said, and he obeyed without comment. His lack of rejoinder was worrying, as acquiescence was uncommon in their family. Beads of sweat formed on Benedict's forehead, and soon he was coughing weakly again. On their mother's instruction, the Labiche children began dismantling the two carts, adding the reclaimed wood to the heap that already burned brighter than the neighboring fires.

Evangeline fetched her father's water skin. The worn leather was filled with what might be their last taste of the Gaspereau. Holding his square head in the crook of her elbow, Evangeline poured Benedict small sips and watched him swallow laboriously.

Eventually the children went to sleep, huddled together under blankets on a pile of cord grass, and their mother took over feeding the fire. In the glow Evangeline saw color returning to her father's once ruddy cheeks, but her hope faded as the tone of the wrinkled flesh deepened to purple, vivid even in the inconsistent firelight.

"No good," Benedict muttered.

"What, pere?"

"I'm no good to you anymore. If you weren't the girl I

raised, I might be worried about you."

"No." It was unimaginable to her that he would die here, outside, on the first night of their exile.

"Yes, I'm afraid." He started to cough, but could not gain enough air.

"We just have to get through the night."

"You have a lot longer than that to worry about." She started to argue, but he shook his head as vigorously as he could, supported by her arm.

"I don't."

Evangeline began to cry, and her father shook his head more gently now.

"You'll have more than luck, child, if I have anything to say about it. Remember everything that you need to and do what you can to forget the rest. Think about the varied life ahead as a blessing, because it comes for you regardless." She kissed him on the lips, hoping to breathe her life into him. Benedict smiled gamely. "It won't get any better than that. Never has."

Evangeline rocked her father gently. He looked reassuringly at her. The effort is what's important, his eyes strove to convince her, no matter the outcome.

"You'll find Gabriel, Evangeline. Know that I pray for both of you, that the two of you find happiness together as your mother and I did." He tightened his grip on her hand, and they sat that way as the fire burned down and her father's shivers ceased.

The next morning, Evangeline and Jacques Melanson pulled her cart, heavy with Benedict's body, through the stockade entrance, sweating a little from the climb. Sofia Melanson followed behind the procession, keeping the blanket tucked over

Benedict's body so only his stocking feet were visible to torment his daughter during the ascent.

"What do you want?" a redcoat soldier hailed them in graceless French. "Acadians are to remain in the encampment until departure," the man began before the sight of Benedict's lifeless body brought him up short.

"I've come to bury my father," Evangeline replied in English. The words felt emotionless in the foreign tongue. The soldier nodded and waved over a companion as the Melansons closed ranks behind her.

"She says she wants to bury her father," the first soldier relayed to the second man, who wore his coat unbuttoned, his stained undershirt overlarge and flapping in the breeze.

"The Colonel is going to want to know about this," he replied. "You found them. You tell him." He turned back to Evangeline.

"I'm sure you know where the cemetery is better than I do. I'll find you a shovel," he said in French.

In a few moments, Evangeline and the Melansons entered the cemetery grounds. Jacques insisted on digging the grave himself, next to Evangeline's mother in the Bellefontaine plot. Sofia meanwhile went to the well and returned with a bucket of water. The two women were wiping Benedict's face and neck clean with the smudged linen of their sleeves when Colonel Winslow, tall and heavy, emerged from the church, his soldiers following behind him like children vying for their father's attention. The officer looked around the small cemetery and strode purposefully to their plot. As he drew up formally before them, his officious bearing and stance caused Jacques to stop digging. Hunched over in the trench, the elderly Acadian gentleman appeared knee-high to the commander. Other movement and conversation in the compound ceased, as all eyes were trained on the commander.

"I've been informed that a man died," he said, staring straight ahead, his formal French matching his posture. Evangeline stood protectively over the cart that still held her father, unwilling yet to surrender him to the ground. The man fixed her with a glare. "Are my men responsible for your father's death?"

"There's little doubt he'd still be alive if we weren't forced out of our home," Evangeline said.

The man seemed unfazed by her answer, and asked more softly, "Perhaps it was a more complicated question than I intended. How did your father die?"

"He sickened and died in the weather last night. He was unwell."

The Colonel bowed his head respectfully. "I'm terribly sorry for your loss, Mademoiselle. Though I am thankful," his voice returned to an angry boom, "that English soldiers aren't accountable for this tragedy." Winslow turned back to the soldiers, his voice like a whip.

"The coffin," he ordered. He was compassionate again as he addressed the three Acadians. "We found one in the church. My men will bring it out to you." The Colonel extended a hand to Jacques and helped him out of the shallow indentation.

"If it wouldn't be too insulting, perhaps you'd allow me to find someone to finish that grave for you. I truly hope not to have to dig another."

Jacques looked to Evangeline, who stood helplessly by the cart. The Colonel removed his hat smoothly, and tucked it under his right arm. "Are these people your family?"

"No, sir."

The officer took her hand proprietarily as he led her away from the gravesite, tucking her arm under his as he led her toward the church, in a deliberate display of cordiality for his soldiers milling inside the compound.

"Do you have any other family in the encampment?"

"No, sir. My father and I have lived alone since my mother died in my childhood. His father was from Ile Royale, and my mother's relatives live in Beaubassin. We have no family in the Minas. My father left me to the care of Felician Abadie, our priest, who's locked on one of your ships." She had an empty pain in her head from crying through the night, but she faced the officer stoically, relating the facts as unemotionally as she could manage, even as behind them Protestant soldiers dug her father's grave.

"I see."

The Colonel sounded displeased and she stopped talking. The church was mostly empty as they entered. Four soldiers were bickering as they negotiated the coffin through the church's small side entrance, but they fell immediately silent on the Colonel's approach. Beyond them, Evangeline saw the Labiche twins, Julian and Jana, huddled at the church's entrance as though afraid of what awaited them in the open. Maybe they were smarter than she'd guessed, Evangeline thought. They were the oldest in their generation of Labiches, about a year younger than she was, and born already when their parents bought land from Benedict that he might have passed on to other children if he and Emmeline had been luckier.

Evangeline left Winslow's side to embrace familiar faces she never thought she would miss. The twins whispered their condolences.

"Your mother told us she sent the two of you off yesterday," Evangeline said softly.

"They caught us looking through our house for food," Jana hissed angrily. "Neither of us wanted to run away. There wasn't anywhere to go."

"So we came back," Julian finished.

Winslow needed only to shift his feet to command their attention. "I've sent to the ships for the priest. Until we find an appropriate guardian, I entrust the three of you to his care."

Felician arrived that afternoon to officiate Benedict's burial, and the Melansons, Jana, and Julian joined Evangeline in laying her father to rest. They planted a shoot of French willow at the head of the coffin, the outline of which Evangeline felt she could still see through the veil of disturbed earth.

"Your father was a great inspiration," Felician told her afterwards. "His wit and compassion were the equal of any man I've ever known. Though I try to love without prejudice, there was no one I valued more." He looked her in the eye for a moment. "And I won't forget my promise to him, nor ever neglect my duty to you, as though I were he." Felician held her for a moment and then followed a redcoat back to Saint Charles.

"It's still Acadia underground," Jacques remarked to Evangeline, "and any bit of Acadia is better than where I'm likely to end up. Your father rests next to his wife, right where he knew he was going. He's better off than most of us, so long as you keep heart and a hold of his memory."

In the church that evening, Evangeline mentioned the Colonel's help in securing the priest's release, but she learned others felt differently about his kindness.

"Winslow," Felician scoffed at the mention of the man. "The coward marched me out under cover of darkness that night after they boarded everyone. He didn't want to offend anyone's sensibilities needlessly while he unburdened them of their homes." Felician took a deep breath. "But here we are, and we must find solace in our faith in the face of temporal injustice. These are people who need to hear that their Lord loves and succors them still."

Returning from the cemetery they found that Winslow had culled the sickest and the oldest Acadian refugees, leading nearly two dozen people out of the chill damp around the harbor.

"He thinks that if he keeps them alive long enough they won't be on his conscience." The priest's anger blazed anew as he watched scores of elderly file unsteadily into Saint Charles. He calmed himself again as he looked into her eyes. "The Lord is giving us an opportunity here, child, a way for us to keep our hands busy and our minds occupied in the face of the unspeakable." Evangeline followed him down the rows of elderly and sick, asking after their origins and praying with them for deliverance from their oppressors.

Food from the English mess followed the new arrivals in the door. "You'll eat as often as anyone else," the soldier claimed.

"They'd rather starve themselves and keep us under guard then spend a few hours harvesting a year's worth of food rotting on the vine," she said to Felician.

"I pray it means they don't intend to keep us prisoner much longer," he responded.

Felician, Evangeline, Jana, and Julian slept in pews near the altar after long days watching the soldiers through the dirty windows and tending to the older inmates. The wind howled their first couple nights in the church, cold enough that they occasionally saw light snow gusting through on the breeze, though none accumulated. Despite the better protection afforded by the church's solid roof and walls, Felician was forced to perform last rites for two more victims in the days that followed. Neither had worshiped at Saint Charles. Like most of the elderly in the church, they were from the communities near Fort Edward.

A bloodstained stranger lay in a corner of the church, after the ship's doctor had left him for dead earlier in the day.

"I'll have someone dig a hole," Evangeline had heard the doctor say as he left.

"Who is he?" she asked Felician.

The priest shook his head sadly. "He was our aid from Quebec." But Felician's prayers appeared to work where English medicine had not, and the man still lived. He hadn't moved from the corner, however, and seemed not to understand where he was when Evangeline sat with him, cradling his head so he could sip some water, as she had for her father on the beach.

Some nights later, the soldiers who delivered their food curtly informed them that there had been an escape from the ships in the harbor. The villagers excitedly gathered to speculate over the identities of the men now free to run for their lives in the woods.

"Gabriel wouldn't leave his father," Evangeline said simply when the Melansons tried to convince her that she might have reason to hope.

"We've already left ours," Julian said.

The twins remained in limbo in the church. As runaways, they were not allowed to rejoin their family, and were shunted temporarily onto Felician after being warned against future disturbances they weren't bold enough to consider.

Though only sixteen, Julian already carried the odd heaviness of a peasant in autumn, heavy skin layered in soft folds atop the muscles underneath. Between the puffiness of his expression and the near-blond fineness of his hair Julian looked several years younger than his twin. Jana had developed fully years earlier, and was shorter than her brother to the point that even Evangeline had heard others say that her height was in her chest. At sixteen, her movements were vested with a weary sadness, sentiments Evangeline thought must have been increased by the Labiches' lands on the highlands above the Gaspereau. Like her father and the Melansons, most of their neighbors possessed some means beyond farming, while the Labiches toiled simply alongside. In one of their rare conversations over the years, Jana had mentioned hopes of joining an aunt in Port Royal when she was old enough.

And yet, Julian and Jana were considered capable to care for themselves. Being a year older than the Labiche siblings, Evangeline felt troubled. If it had been determined that she needed a guardian, why didn't they?

Few of the older Acadians seemed to sleep at all. Those who were able to walk paced the aisles at all hours, stopping regularly at the small fire kept smoldering in the chimney near the side entrance, where the less ambulatory kept their own vigil. The children, as she and the twins were called, were encouraged to keep their distance so that the adults could speak openly about their despair. Evangeline didn't bristle at being grouped indiscriminately with the Labiches, as she might once have. She did feel like a child, surrounded by the elderly in the church.

Five days after Benedict's death, and six since Gabriel was rowed out to the *Success*, the compound emptied except for a handful of soldiers at the gate, watching as their fellows rounded up the families still encamped along the path. Evangeline followed Felician and the twins outside the church, where they climbed a ladder to the roof, and from their makeshift perch they bore witness to the dismantling of their village.

They watched hundreds of soldiers march downhill from the stockade in their blue and red coats, pouring through the encampment like a single organism, collecting people as they churned through the crowds. The maneuver seemed to be proceeding more smoothly than at the beginning of the week. As easily as with any other domesticated animal, Evangeline thought furiously. So many people docilely submitting.

The temporary shelters had multiplied in the week Evangeline had remained in the church. Now the closest were only a stone's throw from the stockade, and they stretched all the way down the path to the harbor. Sturdy birch frames had replaced the hasty shelters she remembered. Using extra clothing and quilts for insulation, the Acadians had created a colorful patchwork of second homes to abandon.

Barking dogs drew her attention to the fact that the dispossessed were mostly empty-handed. They had left their pets behind, as well as their livestock, hobbled in the narrow corridor between the stream and their structures.

"Why didn't they put everyone on the boats the first day?" Julian asked. Evangeline had wondered this herself.

"There are too many people out there to survive very long on just a few ships," Felician replied. "There were too many even before they started loading these families."

"Where are they taking them?" Jana asked.

"Gabriel shouted to me that he was being taken to Carolina. I don't know where that is." Her skin crawled at the admission. It wasn't far to the ground, but the height was seclusion enough from the turbulence below to feel traitorous.

The main body of soldiers pushed over the bridge halfway down the hill, where the path crossed the stream and descended more steeply. The vanguard kept its formation to the water's edge, where the soldiers moved along the shore, overturning and dragging canoes to the edge that lapped out quickly with the tide. The newly visible mud made it appear as though the warships had drawn closer to shore. Evangeline watched as hundreds of people emerged from their wigwams and sailcloth-roofed shacks. Julian and Jana silently fixed on the spot where their mother, brothers, and sisters were leaving behind their cart and any belongings they'd salvaged from their farmhouse. Evangeline could not distinguish the Labiche clan from the crowd of unfortunates.

"I'm sorry," she said to Jana on the roof beside her. Brother and sister remained transfixed by the suffering unfolding below. The hobbled animals stood in place, calm compared to the dogs that were more prevalent than Evangeline ever remembered. Above the bridge, Evangeline watched as a mother and four children were dragged away from a chest they'd dragged with them from their wigwam. The upper tier of hovels above the bridge emptied quickly, with abandoned chests left in place of their owners.

Her chest was below where she'd abandoned it with its precious cargo. Benedict's books, Spanish coins he'd saved from Havana, her mother's comb, letters between her parents from her father's travels. Her mother's dress. All dust beneath the boots of their invaders.

Her attention shifted to the throng crossing the water. The canoes, burdened with ten and twelve bodies each, struggled out to the English ships, as the shouting grew more distant. The deepening silence below contrasted sharply with the grim violence on the beach as the stockade's soldiers forced the people of Grand Pre to the flotilla.

"I swam out that far before," Jana said, pointing to the ships.

Evangeline nodded, though she never had. Neither she nor Gabriel had ever done much swimming.

"Those holds were already choked with people," Felician crossed himself. "I hate to think that we're better off up here."

"When do you think they're leaving?" Evangeline asked her guardian as they climbed back down the ladder.

"Soon. They can't keep that many people on those boats for long. Even an English officer must recoil from watching a thousand people starve in front of him."

"Then I need to try to see Gabriel tomorrow."

"Winslow won't let me out of the stockade, even to escort you to the water. We've asked."

"No one can stop me if I go by myself."

He looked at her sharply, late in realizing her intentions. "You can't go down there without me. Remember what you just saw, girl."

"I have to see him before they take him away from me. Maybe he knows something more about where they're sailing." Her tone sounded more pleading than she felt.

"It's too dangerous." Felician looked startled.

"No more dangerous than missing my last chance to see Gabriel."

"Evangeline," he began.

"You can't protect me from that, Father." Evangeline waved her arm petulantly toward the harbor. "If I'm lucky they'll just put me on board with Gabriel." She softened her tone. "Forgive me, but I've been looking after myself for a while."

Evangeline smiled at her scowling guardian. "You can watch me from the roof."

Evangeline saw smoke rising west of town the next morning as she prepared to leave the stockade. The compound was quiet that morning. Many of the soldiers had not returned the night before, and she guessed now that they had slept in the looted houses they'd yet to burn. Inside the church, she hadn't been able to differentiate the smell of the smoldering homes from the incessant campfires along their prison's outer wall, but in the open the vaulting acrid columns of smoke took on their own character. She imagined the sweat on benches, the must on the linens, the grease on railings where generations had rested their hands, all burning before her. Evangeline momentarily took heart that the smoke was too close to town to be her home on the Gaspereau. Though that day would come as well, she could be spared until after she had said goodbye to Gabriel. Carolina was an ocean away. She tried not to think about how long they would be apart if Gabriel sailed off without her. She felt like she'd been struck dumb for their brief exchange in the harbor, and he deserved to know how she felt about him, that she would think of him for the rest of her life, no matter how it would be spent.

Many of the makeshift shelters were already collapsing after standing untended only a single day. She saw clothing, toys, and utensils the villagers had left behind in their haste. Dogs prowled the leftovers but shied away from her, already understanding that it was safer to avoid people.

Evangeline had felt relatively safe the past week, deceptively isolated from the desperation outside the stockade.

The soldiers rotating through guard duty inside the church had treated her with cordiality as they brought in rations of hardtack and water, in deference to their commander's orders. But it was clear to her now that she had passed beyond such protection. Before she reached the bridge, Evangeline glimpsed three men, armed but not wearing uniforms, sitting close by the derelict path. They were cooking hunks of a pig they'd wastefully butchered outside one of the deserted shacks. One of the animal's hoofs, attached nearly to the shank, lay before her on the trail. The soldiers had spitted the fatty meat on bayonets, which they suspended above a wooden trunk they'd fired for fuel. The smoke smelled like burning hair, and she realized that the chest must still be full of clothes and everything else the family had thought to carry with them.

By the time Evangeline crossed the plank bridge halfway to the harbor, storm clouds hung between her and the stockade, another unpleasant portent on a day that needed none. She stuck to the middle of the track in the darkening afternoon, away from the ruined dwellings and pillaging soldiers. Before she left that morning, she had mixed a little of the molasses the Colonel had given them with some ground cornmeal to make Indian pudding. She carried the pudding with one of her father's shirts and a couple pairs of leggings that she had left in the cart to cushion Benedict's body. An appropriate dowry for an imprisoned groom, she thought sourly, and it would have to do because it was all she had. She had never wanted to return to the encampment for her belongings, in case she wasn't allowed back in the church, and now everything that she had saved was gone.

Evangeline walked downhill as quickly as she could, swinging the basket to help pull her through the deep trenches gouged by the hundreds who'd carried, dragged and wheeled their belongings through the mud. Black flies tormented her neck, face and hands as the path flattened in its final stretch over the tidal lands claimed from the Minas.

At the bottom she saw dozens of soldiers competing with gulls and sandpipers as they picked through the upended carts, stuffed chests, and pieces of broken shelters, this last remnant of her village's prosperity rising in rings from the water in unconscious imitation of their dikes. Much of what was carried out of their homes lay scattered in heaps, distracting the treasure-seekers who took no notice of her.

As the trail became impassable, Evangeline surprised two angry gulls picking at the empty eye sockets of a cow's head, the birds flapping their wings and crowing madly but not budging from their prize. Just as the men were drawn to loot, the birds and flies mindlessly swarmed the slaughtered animals of Grand Pre.

Out on the mudflats sat a low, crude watchtower, nothing more than an upturned wagon atop a pile of wood. Another heap of wood to be burned after satisfying the marauders' temporary needs. Past the watchtower and receding shoreline, the low clouds rendered Cape Blomidan so misty and vague that Evangeline couldn't tell for sure where the usually distinctive red rock ended and French Bay began, though she'd admired the view in all seasons over many years. The large canoes that had been used to reach the ships on previous days were upturned, but with no other way to reach Gabriel's prison Evangeline headed across the beach to the colonial militia. She thought again about where the laden ships might be going. She had never even been to Boston, and tried to recall her father's descriptions of the crowded port. It was difficult to imagine houses nearly as far as you could see in all directions. Dozens of large vessels passed through Boston's harbor every day, unloading landless immigrants along with whatever goods survived the crossing. Glass and guns mostly, Benedict had said. As a girl listening to her father's stories, she had looked forward to her first trip to the English colonies.

Evangeline was not eager to engage the militiamen. These dirty ragmen were here to burn Grand Pre and pick its bones, with no care for the kindness an officer might have shown her in the stockade.

One of the men hailed her in English as she started across the mud.

"No visitors. Ships are off limits." A few long strides carried him across the mudflat to her. She'd watched the four soldiers gesturing at the heaps of waste and spitting tobacco as she approached, their dirty blue military coats a shade darker than the heavy afternoon sky. There were no other Acadians in sight, and only a scattering of other soldiers. Grim awareness dawned on her that there was nothing she had to persuade these men to let her see Gabriel, nothing even to prevent them from dumping her in the Minas.

The man unsheathed his knife, and she backed away from the dangerous gleam, ready to run, but he kept the blade at his side as he approached. He gestured deliberately at her basket with the knife and then pointed at the ground with his index finger. Evangeline mutely lowered her burden to the dirt.

He bent down, still without a word, and jabbed his knife twice into the clothing. Satisfied, he squatted back on his haunches and scanned the path she'd just walked.

"You walked down here, alone, expecting to be let aboard ship." The soldier spoke slowly. "But you didn't realize how alone you are." He saw the fear flash across her eyes, and recognition lit his own. "You can understand me," he murmured, quieter than before, though Evangeline still refused to acknowledge her accuser.

He looked appraisingly at Evangeline's breasts, staring at her as if he believed her muteness also blinded her to his lustful gaze. He rose deliberately and walked slowly around her. She tensed as he passed behind her, again ready to run, but he circled back and met her wary stare again before he continued speaking, making sure he had her full attention.

"There was an escape yesterday. The cowards dressed like women and snuck out pretending to be their mothers and daughters." His leer became a cackle as his young face pinched up close to hers. "No real men here, but you probably know that better than me."

Evangeline snatched up her basket and spun on her heel, returning to the bleak path that led back through the empty refugee camp crouching in the marshy lowlands. One mistake among many, she thought of her effort. Holding her breath as she skirted dead animals amid the remnants of the shelters, she picked her way through the heaps of abandoned possessions, listening to make sure she wasn't followed. As she looked up toward the village, the smoky air seemed to rush down toward Grand Pre, funneling into thicker columns and consuming portions of the town like tornados touching down, as clapboard frames and plain wooden furniture vaporized into grim mist. Evangeline stopped before an open chest. Tiny rocking horses, tops, and carved dolls spilled from the lidless coffer, trinkets that could have been hers. She settled her basket, plucked a small wooden crucifix from the box and turned it over in her hand. Evangeline had been convinced that God had withdrawn His protection from this land since the day she buried her father. Even so, she pocketed the crucifix, deciding she'd give it to Gabriel if she could persuade the Colonel to let her visit the *Success* once she got back to the stockade.

Loud laughter interrupted her reverie, the source close but hidden. She heard nothing else, and wondered what in the carnage might have prompted such a reaction. Evangeline strained for a last glimpse of the ships through the mist and conceded at last that she and Gabriel might already have seen each other for the last time in Acadia.

The soggy air finally turned to a steady fall of rain. Appropriate, Evangeline thought, as the remains of the collapsed hovels looked like an enormous shipwreck washed in from the Minas.

At least the new rain chased the salt and smoke from the air, Evangeline thought as she slogged along. Her shoes were splashing as the soft ground gave over to puddles at the base of the hill, the long path to the stockade dissolving above her. Her basket grew heavier on her arm, and she saw it was waterlogged.

Fifty meters inland of high tide, it felt as though she had traversed a mountain. Her single night out in the wet shelters was spent somewhere nearby, though the landscape was unrecognizable. She remembered anew the sinking moment when her hopes for her father died.

The bottom of her wool skirt was covered with the cold gray mud of the salt flats, tiny mussels clinging to the wet tresses. The heavy wool trailed behind in the rainwater as she hiked uphill, splashing the backs of her stockings. She followed the path carved by the dispossessed multitudes whose footprints now rapidly filled with water, rendering the course a slippery ravine as it steepened.

Unable to continue, Evangeline waded toward an overturned oxcart alongside the path, and hoisted her basket up onto the sturdy wooden frame where they sat, soaked through but free of the mud.

Picturing returning to the church with the pudding she'd prepared for Gabriel worsened her depression, but she forced her mind to her more immediate concerns. She had barely begun to climb the hill, but was surrounded by the remains of shelters, these fractured pieces still promising some relief from the weather. It was only six oozing steps from the wagon to a length of sailcloth, and she ripped it loose from its birch frame. The wet sheet was heavy, and brought her to her knees, but Evangeline regained her footing in the downpour and returned to the wagon. The mud squelched into her shoes as she gave the big sailcloth an ineffectual shake. She wrapped herself in the cleaner side and clambered up onto the wagon to sit beside her basket, which she draped in the folds.

The rain smacked down on the sheet covering Evangeline, a match for her tears as she stared out into the torrent. The swollen current began dislodging more objects from the path's outskirts, bonnets and sabots floating past, chests banging more noisily downstream.

A weak thump at the base of the upturned wagon brought Evangeline out from under the sheet to find a dog with its skull caved in. It was stuck against the corner of the wagon jutting prow-like into the flood, the back of the carcass thumping limply against the wooden side. She perched on the edge of the wagon and stared down at the small brown hound. She extended her legs, hands fiercely gripping the slippery corner for the support necessary to bring her outstretched foot into range of the pitiful animal. Evangeline kicked the dog's rump and screamed as her foot sunk into the limp flesh without dislodging it. She grunted loudly, exorcised the disgust from her shoulders, kicked the animal harder, forcing it out into the current. The stench had already subsided by the time she returned to cover, wrapping herself in the sail, furiously rubbing her wet cold skin, lost in the sodden layers of linen and wool.

She huddled on the wagon watching loose pieces of temporary shelters wash down to break on the dam of Acadian possessions sloughed off in the final crunch of bodies as the families of Grand Pre boarded the cramped ships. Several distinct lightning strokes pierced the gloom and struck the higher ground closer to the church, each accompanied by a magnificent crack of thunder. The lightning was gone after the quick display, and only by staring north after it could Evangeline glimpse occasional flashes moving into the distance over the mountains to the Mi'kmaq lands at the heart of Acadia. The thunder likewise withdrew to growl from a distance, a caged observer to the destruction.

The sky brightened, though the new stream continued to displace chests and unidentifiable flotsam down the steep trail well after the rain slackened and almost apologetically faded to intermittent drops. Evangeline shook the sail loose. At this point a drizzle wouldn't bother her or the basket. The ground was slippery but firm around the wagon and Evangeline slid down the wooden side, keeping her feet as she hiked away from the rampaging flood. Further along, she started to see more debris that hadn't washed down the hill and after prowling for several minutes came across a large unopened chest.

Evangeline untied her linen bonnet and draped the muddy cloth along the curve of a wigwam that had remained as solid and untouched as the chest alongside it. Bending from her back, as her father always warned her not to do, she managed to open the sturdy spruce lid on her first heave, the hinges swinging without protest to clang to the side. Brushing aside the men's clothes stowed on top, she uncovered a clean if slightly damp brown coat, in a style that matched her own, but much larger. She dropped her old coat at her feet and stepped into the overlarge one, freeing her feet from the sucking mud. The generous fabric of the new coat felt warm and comfortable against her neck and she ran her hands through her muddy, tangled hair and rested a moment, content for the moment to have survived the storm intact.

As she stood, she felt someone's eyes on her. Turning, Evangeline saw the soldier who had denied her access to Gabriel's ship. He was standing near the bottom of the hill, partially obscured by the shelters, but pointedly staring up at her. His blue uniform was soaked. She was close enough to see where he had pushed his sleeves off his bony wrists and forearms. He stood hatless and did not carry his musket. He was breathing heavily, and when Evangeline looked at his face, she saw him staring back, not with the imperious mien from before the storm, but with an uncertain, guilty look. Evangeline turned uphill and ran, her long, dark hair whipping behind her in wet knots. Starting as if from a dream, the man below ran after her.

Evangeline didn't panic as she ran, calmer confronting this immediate danger than she had been during the storm. She was

fast and could keep pace with most men her age over long dis-
tances. She stayed away from the parallel streams and angled out
of the encampments, hoping to outdistance her pursuer on the
firmer ground uphill. After a long minute's sprint, she hesitated
long enough to peek over her shoulder. Her shallow breath was
just now visible in the crisp air following the rain. The soldier
was no closer than when the chase began, running through the
wreckage with his eyes fixed on her.

The afternoon storm had finished what the looting began,
scattering the abandoned belongings, posts and sails. The debris
slowed her progress, as she was forced to plant every step with
great care so as not to be tripped up in the morass of splintered
wood and torn fabric. At last she was in the clear, west of the
tents running back to the church on a parallel course to the
flooded and empty hovels.

Evangeline's breaths were coming in deep gasps as she
crossed ever firmer ground above the marshy fields. She sprint-
ed, less concerned now with losing her footing as she followed a
ridge running parallel to the shore which would take her back to
the bridge. After fording the path, she reached the stream, only
to find the bridge washed out. Frightened, she spun around,
looking for the soldier, and for the first time she felt anger well
up inside her, directed irrationally at Gabriel for his inability to
protect her.

Evangeline plunged back across the path near the Dubois
farm. Knowing the land was a benefit, but of little advantage
without knowing the soldier's whereabouts. The mud of the
salt flats was mostly past, and with fewer ruined dwellings in
evidence, she followed along the edge of the path to cover
ground quickly. The shelters thinned to a single row beyond
the bridge, and there was little evidence of foot traffic on this

part of the path. Here the deluge had done little more than rush over the grass, lending a freshness to the air. Soon it would be time to put herself in God's hands, and leave the intermittent concealment to cross the water. There appeared to be several places she might ford the stream where the slope leveled off, and once across, she could improvise a route back to the church. French willows emerged from the next series of ridges in her path, their silhouettes like stubble bristling in the sun's rays. A little farther above the harbor and she'd be able to see the steeple poking out from the new palisade. Although she saw no sign of the soldier, she didn't allow herself to imagine that he'd peacefully returned to his post.

Evangeline stomped her sabots to loosen her legs and took off as fast as she could, sweating despite the cold. Her father hated to run, and had credited his glib tongue to an early disdain for both running and fighting. Gabriel was faster than she, skinny but strong from the forge, and yet she had outraced him from the Gaspereau to her father's house once the past summer, with Gabriel running as hard as he could. Bolstered by the happy memories, she still could not keep from panting as she continued, slowing a little as she looked for a place to cross, unable to believe how tired she was. The thought of what would happen to her if she were caught spurred her on, however, and she dashed across the stream at the next point where it appeared shallow, hitting the water nearly at full speed, her right foot then left landing solidly in the rocky streambed.

Back among the more intact shelters farther from the water, her exhausted mind flickered over the memory of how she first learned of Gabriel's fate. She had left her father to look for Gabriel in town the night word filtered back to Grand Pre's anxious women and children about the edict delivered in the church. A crowd of women gathered around the mouth of the stockade as though despite the news their husbands and brothers and sons were about to be released. Gossipers told her that Gabriel's father had attacked Winslow and they were both being held under guard in the church. At that point she was worried they'd both be hanged, so in that regard at least, confinement on the *Success* was preferable. She had run to town without stopping that night, a distance similar to that from the harbor to the church.

Now that she was on the right side of the stream, the church couldn't be more than ten minutes distant. Less than that. Inside of ten minutes she and Felician would be demanding to see Winslow. She gulped at the air, its clean scent lending her legs another surge of life. She kept her eyes on her feet as she dashed around potholes and refuse in the trail, concentrating on not turning an ankle.

She passed a wigwam, caved-in and unremarkable save for the panting soldier who emerged from behind it. His blue elbow struck her eye like a flash of lightning, the bone meeting her eye socket directly, knocking her from her feet. Her face rested heavily on the pungent grass, which, incredibly, seemed barely wet. Evangeline pushed onto her elbows and hurriedly drew up to her feet, unavoidably lurching downhill as she fought for balance. She tottered, unable to open her eyes wider than slits due to the overwhelming pain driving into the side of her head, her ear at the pain's center, where the throbs started and stopped. The soldier was three steps away, nothing between them. He seemed to be rambling, his words difficult to make out through the ringing in her ears.

"I'm sorry. That was quite a chase. Barely kept up with

you." He approached her, hands outstretched, palms out, as if seeking understanding. "Don't worry, shhh."

Evangeline had begun to back away from him downhill, the way they had both just come. He caught her quickly, the hush barely off his lips, and gripping her fiercely by the shoulders, flung her to the ground. Her run became a tumble, as she flipped twice, head over heels, before skidding to a halt. Her coat had caught on a rock and ripped free, leaving only a sleeve behind, but slowing her so that she lay with her left arm twisted beneath her, inhaling quickly and quietly as pain lanced across her body.

Evangeline raised her hand to touch her right eye, massaging lightly around the brow. At least she landed face up this time. She needed to try to run again, but her head wouldn't clear.

"Neither one of us looks our best, I'll believe that." The soldier laughed nervously as he advanced, trying to assess how much damage he'd done before he came closer, whispering conspiratorially. "Shhh. Bet your head smarts, doesn't it? I didn't want to come here and do this. I'm Simon. We weren't asked if we wanted to come here. They didn't even tell us what we'd be doing, fighting native bastards, guarding women and children and men without spunk." He spoke between labored breaths, one hand braced on his knee. "It's not your fault your men are cowards who wouldn't fight to protect their families. I won't hit you anymore. Pretty girls shouldn't be hit."

The words flowed in a sing-song Evangeline might have used a skittish animal, meaningless sounds spoken to try to calm her. She was thankful his nasal voice kept to English. She blinked her eyes, half-successfully clearing the right one. She shook as he came down the hill toward her, still whispering, trying to convince her to stop resisting.

His heavy breathing above her slowed a bit and deepened, his body steadying itself for what his mind had already concocted. Her legs writhed in the long grass, but she was still dazed from the fall and couldn't will herself to stand up.

The soldier seized her, his bony fingers clamping down on the muscles of her calves, his clammy sleeves dripping rainwater. He lifted her legs slightly off the ground and began dragging her. Evangeline dug her hands in as they went, uprooting clumps of the slippery grass, the earth breaking loose in clumps of salty soil. Held by her legs, she was stuck on her side, unable to see where he was taking her, her eye still blinded from the initial attack. She cried out as loudly and desperately as she was able with the wincing pain in her skull.

They splashed through storm puddles of standing water, cold in the evening air. Her calves, stiff from the grueling run, screamed under the soldier's grip as her fingers groped futilely. Muddy masses of her wet hair fell across her face with each pull of her attacker's arms. All at once, the sky was replaced by the dank, musty smell of dirty canvas. The coward had brought her inside a tent, she thought, and slammed her fist angrily against the earth floor.

No doubt discomfited by the open hillside littered with evidence of crimes already committed, he'd dragged her inside one of the hastily erected shelters that had guarded a family as they waited to say goodbye to a husband or father. The desperate sadness of parting hung in the air despite the rain, a last testament to the inhabitants of Grand Pre, packed like cattle on the foreign ships. Evangeline felt a pang of loss even as she sensed the man's furious lust, and her sadness became a white-hot anger that fueled a more determined resistance.

The soldier's wet jacket hit the ground on her right like

an unlucky goose, flapping once and lying still. Her legs and hips felt dislodged, shaken, but intact, and Evangeline rolled onto her back so that she could again see out of her uninjured eye. No sense playing dead, she thought, and looked her attacker full in the face, plainly surprising him. There was something in these small victories. He was fumbling with the fourth button of his breeches, rushing to finish what he'd begun. Simon, how she despised knowing his name, was tall, forced to hunch over in the tiny shelter, and more slight even than Gabriel under the wet wool shirt that clung to his scrawny chest. He'd freed himself only enough to poke partially through the opening of his sodden blue pants. It shrank into the folds of his fly once he became aware of her attention, as afraid of her as she was of him.

Her respite was short-lived, however, as Simon quickly ripped through the button, and stood naked before her except for a dripping shirt so dirty its color was indistinguishable from his flesh. Another small victory that she was still fully clothed save for the bonnet left downhill. Accustomed to bathing outdoors, his nudity was not unfamiliar, but seemed grotesque inside the tent.

"This isn't the first time I've been with a woman," he boasted loudly, and grabbed his penis as if to demonstrate his claim. "But this will be the first time I've tried a Catholic whore." He paused, purposeful and suddenly rakishly sure of himself. "It might be more than a year before I get back to Boston," he murmured. It could be forever, Evangeline thought. He stepped forward suddenly standing to her blind side, so that she was forced to turn her head toward him.

His hand clamped over her mouth as he dropped to the ground beside her. She gasped. It was happening to her now. His

closeness was terrifying, the enormity of his menace, his undi-
rected gaze freezing her. The soldier remained calm as he stifled
her scream in his muddy palm. He seemed much more certain,
kneeling next to her now, one hand swallowing her mouth, his
other holding his knife near her good eye.

"You see this, don't you, girl? Be still now," he commanded before chuckling. "You'll be surprised how fast this is
over with."

Simon's hands disappeared from her mouth and hip as he
straddled her, his bare legs pinning her squirming ones in place.
She screamed, terrified, and he backhanded her with his left
hand, bloodying her lip.

"Quiet, bitch," he hissed. He plunged his knife into the
thick wool of her dress and sawed quickly through the fabric,
tearing open the front as she dragged her fingernails across his
face. He punched her this time, and she was helpless as his fist
crashed into her bad eye. The pain dazed her, and she stopped
resisting for a moment. He jabbed his knife in the ground next
to her and dug his fingers into her stomach hard, rolling her over
after his grip was secure.

She got her wind back as she felt both his wet hands on her
bare legs, tugging the stocking down off the left. Evangeline
rolled to her right as hard as she could, away from the grasping
fingers, her legs colliding with the knife handle stuck in the grass
a moment before. The impact knocked the weapon loose, and it
landed alongside her. She grabbed the blade and brought it
straight up into his descending hand, stabbing right through the
palm. Simon howled in pain as she let go of the knife.

Evangeline got to her feet shakily as Simon reached with his
uninjured hand for the knife. She kicked him just as his hand
closed over the handle, her sabot striking him hard across the

nose with a satisfying crack. His hand moved from the knife to his broken nose as he fell back onto the grass where Evangeline had been prone just moments before. As quickly, things might change again, she thought. She rocked her leg back and kicked him again, connecting solidly with his left temple.

Blood now ran unchecked from the naked man's nose, but otherwise there was no movement from him as Evangeline gathered up her ripped dress and staggered from the tent.

A wet smack replaced the fresh crack of the whip after five lashes. After ten strokes, blood began to trickle down the man's legs, and he stopped crying out as the leather bit into his naked back. Evangeline's attacker had been dragged, naked and unconscious, from the tent to the whipping post planted between the soldiers' tents and the church. Though his comrades were not able to revive Simon until after dark, Colonel Winslow insisted on bringing out torches so that all could see the spectacle of his punishment. The lines of sullen, grimy soldiers, sick of their wet camp inside the stockade, were bordered on all sides by small columns of redcoats, their uniforms glowing demonically in the firelight. Facing the English and their vassals was a crowd of nearly a hundred Acadians, the huddled refugees interned in Saint Charles Church that composed the last remnant of Acadia in Grand Pre.

The bedraggled villagers had turned out from the church following a soldier's invitation, "The Colonel's going to put a new shirt on the man that came after your girl."

Evangeline came only after the Colonel personally asked her to attend the sentencing, and she'd agreed, though her left eye was completely swollen shut and she swooned if she stood up for too long a time. Simon's wrists were bound to the top of post, which kept him on his feet as the sentence was carried out. Alone among the witnesses, Winslow had provided her with a chair, and Felician stood behind her, holding her gently by the shoulder as they watched the torture, his hand clenching with each strike.

"Fifty lashes for this man," the Colonel had shouted into the night after firing his pistol into the air, the loudest words she'd yet heard from the loud man. He returned the weapon to its holster. "And fifty for any other man who approaches any woman in this village."

After twenty-five lashes, another soldier took the place of the first striker. Evangeline thought she'd become inured to the sickening sound, but when the wet smacking started again, she vomited on the ground between her legs, and Felician carried her back to the church.

Grand Pre 1755

Hanging between two skies, a cloud with edges of silver,
floated the boat, with its dripping oars on the motionless water.

TWELVE FRESH GRAVES KEPT BENEDICT COMPANY IN THE cemetery behind Saint Charles. The ceremonies had been grim, and arrived so quickly after her father's that they blended seamlessly into a continuous grieving. Evangeline washed the bodies and smoothed the faces of the gray-haired matrons and voiceless old storytellers in preparation for the burials, each time remembering the feeling of wiping her father's face outside the church. Meanwhile, the hardier men among them pried charred planks from the floors and walls of the abandoned homes to build the coffins.

"The English burned the village, but they have graciously allowed us to bury what they missed," Jacques observed bleakly as they loaded another body into his rude casket. Grime seemed the main difference between the living and the dead, Evangeline thought, watching his palsied old hands shake. Now that the ships had sailed, Grand Pre had been reduced to the tired and sick, leaving the old storekeeper as one of the stoutest among them. Of the church's healthy occupants, only Felician, Jana, Julian and Evangeline were younger than grandparents.

Each time one of their number was interred, Cecile Bourgeois, a widow who'd lived within forty paces of the church all her life, shrilly proclaimed, "The last body laid to rest in Acadia." Then the dwindling church dwellers would straggle back to their quarters as Felician and Julian filled the grave with dirt. Julian, in particular, took ownership over the grim chore, and dug many of them himself.

The Labiche twins seemed to have taken the departure of their family in stride. They kept their thoughts to themselves even shoveling alongside Evangeline in the cold ground. And it seemed that Julian and Jana alone among the refugees slept soundly in the disintegrating church. The four pews set aside for younger backs remained intact near the denuded altar, but the rest had been broken down for coffins and firewood. Jacques and Julian had salvaged four fire plates from abandoned chimneys, and they'd laid them in a square just inside the entrance at the side of the drafty hall. A large fire burned there at all times, in addition to a small fire in the hearth just inside the small narthex. Soldiers had dumped heaps of animal feed, brittle after being left too long in the ground, at the door. Those who were able stuffed the chaff inside of blankets to prop themselves off of the cold floor. Evangeline made beds for those too weak to help themselves, but most of those who might have required such assistance were already dead.

She and Jana had gathered turnips and cabbages from nearby fields, and they stewed them with salt pork, eating winter soup daily until the greasy residue discolored the ceiling of the church.

"I never used to mind it," Evangeline gagged to Julian as she scraped the overcooked flesh off the sides of the cauldron back into the condensed broth, holding her breath to keep from retching. The meal simmered incessantly above the fire, and every morning the residue was caked onto the interior of the iron pot.

"I'll do it for you," he said.

"No, I'll finish. We could use some more water though," she said. Though he didn't relish the duty, Julian almost always brought water from the well, as Felician attempted to limit the girls' exposure to the militiamen outside the church.

There had been no trouble since the flogging. Whether out of fear of other reprisals or newfound sensitivity, most of the soldiers had vacated the compound after the deportation. They especially stayed away from the graves that mushroomed toward the militia camp, and now bedded down in Acadian houses they had yet to burn.

The refugees buried Cecile Bourgeois in silence with one week left until Christmas. Felician performed the service immediately following the day's Advent mass, and kept the ceremony briefer than usual.

"Too eerie, even for the priest," Bernard mused when Evangeline checked on him later that evening. Despite the heavy losses sustained by the Acadians in the church, here was their messenger, clinging to life.

"Stop that, girl," he'd wheeze at her as she prayed over him on one of his better days, when the worst of his wounds had closed up enough for him to sit up for a few hours. He'd been struck twice by musket fire. One musket ball had not punctured the skin, and left only an ugly black bruise spreading from his right shoulder down his back. The other shot had passed though his right side, tearing holes in front and back, but though several of his ribs were broken, none appeared to have been shattered by the musket ball. His wounds left him with little mobility in his right arm, but for the most part Evangeline could only speculate about his condition. The trapper remained tight-lipped about his injuries, only bitterly thanking any who assisted him, as he remained largely unable to use his arms.

Kept busy in the church, Evangeline did not leave the compound for weeks at a time. She stayed close by Felician, no longer joining the harvesting expeditions in the untended fields, until one day the soldiers began noisily removing their weapons and gear from the stockade. Finally, they were informed that the Colonel was off to war. A considerable uneasiness accompanied the news that he was leaving.

"Remember, not only can it get worse, it probably will." Jacques' pessimistic slant made the rounds amongst the church's chin-waggers. Though not previously tempted, as most were not, to look over her burned home, Evangeline used the impending departure as motivation to revisit the hovels while still under the Colonel's token protection. Within the week, Winslow and most of the soldiers would board the last ship in the harbor, and it was difficult to say whether it would be better to join them, sailing to God knew where, or to remain among the dead and dying in the church.

It was a clear beautiful day in early December, and no one had died the night before, so Felician was available to accompany her. On her request, though, her guardian remained on the ridgeline, watching her pick her way through the icy debris as her hair danced out from under her hood, obscuring her vision.

The ordered paths amid the hovels had fallen victim to the frigid whistling winds carrying ice and hail that battered the sacked encampment. The time and snow obscured last year's deportation, though bones, picked clean and widely scattered, informed her that something was the richer for all of it.

The tent wasn't distinguishable from any of the others, and Felician must have been searching for a while before he found her, sitting inside with her fists clenched, staring at ground that looked the same as the ground everywhere else, trampled and abandoned. She didn't know how long she'd been sitting, and he didn't ask her. They walked numbly uphill toward the church, following the last bit of the track that she didn't remember running, and paused to speak only when they'd gained the rise. Felician did not touch her, but she could feel him close to her elbow.

Evangeline spoke first, "I'll be happy when it's finally our turn to leave."

"I can't even imagine, child."

"It's strange not to see anyone on the rivers, isn't it? One of the sights I'll miss most, probably, is watching everyone snowshoe by with carts and sledges." She smiled a little. "Snow has a wonderful ability to reinvent things." It felt clean outside, away from sick people and overcooked soup.

"How do you feel now?" Felician asked.

"That I'm ready for the rest of my life to start."

The next morning she watched Winslow depart, his soldiers marching out of the stockade's mouth without a murmur, off to serious war at last. The village felt different, tenser even before they'd finished boarding. Voices in the church remained hushed throughout the day as the soldiers went about their business outside, aware of the dangers threatened when the powerful felt less secure. Captain Osgood inherited command of the remaining garrison of fifty soldiers, mostly New Englanders, marooned with their feeble captives.

Deferentially, the soldiers made themselves scarce, wandering along the coast, peering expectantly out to sea, back toward their New England homes, waiting, praying for the Minas to deliver more boats so that the tangible representation of their guilt, this needless suffering and loss of life, would be removed at least from sight, if not from mind.

Christmas was weeks past when two sails came around the cape. The water might as well be frozen for how slow they progressed, Evangeline thought, watching from the church roof as they inched closer. She felt a little flutter of hope and let it breathe. That they were here to remove the refugees from their dead homes was knowledge enough. The confines of the dilapidated church had long felt unbearable. And no matter where they went, she'd be nearer to finding Gabriel.

The next morning, Osgood marshaled the remnant of his soldiers who shouldered their weapons and accompanied the surviving Acadians to the coast. The twins helped the infirm outside the church while Evangeline changed Bernard's dressings and Felician prowled his church.

"Last off the ship," Felician said, and smiled for her. She was surprised to realize he too was happy to be leaving. There was no reason he could have to stay, but she had not thought before to ascribe feelings of preference or desire to her guardian.

The trapper's dingy shirt made a sucking sound as Evangeline lifted the sweat-soaked fabric, gently gathering up the ends. She slowly uncovered his hairy stomach, chest, and finally the wound itself. The sticky poultice Felician applied yesterday was the color of Minas mud, the salve's main ingredient. During the night, Bernard's exertions had reopened the wound, and dried blood had seeped through the cracks in the daub.

When she finished, Felician helped her situate their patient's dense weight on a pushcart, each heaving on two ends of an old quilt they'd repatriated from the piles of damaged goods still looming between them and the harbor, its usefulness eroding daily in the damp winter. The trapper looked uncomfortable, but didn't protest, and she tucked the quilt in around him, remembering doing the same for her father's body the morning after he died.

Last and least of the three pilgrimages from Saint Charles to the harbor, she and Felician lugged Bernard at the rear of the creaky, tortuously slow tramping of hoary feet. By the time Evangeline left the stockade, the nearby houses were already in flames. The soldiers had probably just turned over their breakfast cookfires, swallowing the last buildings in Grand Pre in loud crackling. Hungry dogs followed the procession, nipping at the heels of soldiers and Acadians alike, howling when they were kicked, more frightened of further abandonment than physical cruelty. Evangeline could not believe how skinny the animals had become already, as though the land had already been deserted for years. Like the twins, the dogs kept returning, looking for food.

Julian helped her drag Bernard up the gangplank and aboard ship, going down in the hold first before she pushed the sled and her patient down to him. Shadows coated the interior and they found him a place against the wall, the trapper silent but conscious, eyes flashing wetly in the darkness, squeezing hard on her arm though he didn't seem aware of it.

"I'll check on you after everyone's loaded, just try to lie still," she said. The man banged his head back against the floor in response, defiant within his limitations. Evangeline smiled and laid her hand on his forehead to find that it was more feverish than when she'd checked in the church, and then felt a different hand rest on her back, close in the perpetual dusk below deck. Julian reached for her hand, and she let him help her to her feet. He moved toward her, and she ducked out of the way, turning the attempted kiss into an embrace. It was dark enough in the ship's bowels that he might pretend it was his intention all along. She held him for a moment, and pulled back shaking her head gently as the boy limply disengaged.

She patted his hand, though, before she left to climb back onto deck, and saw hope flare anew in his eyes, a beatific but dangerous sentiment to cherish in the gloom.

When she returned to the deck, the *Dauntless* was following the setting sun toward French Bay. Columns of smoke rose into the red sky from the village on the hill. The reasoning behind razing the village remained unclear to her, despite the rampant speculation from old gossips she overheard during the cold months she should have spent in Gabriel's arms.

"It's even more insulting to be kicked off your land by people that don't want it for themselves," Jacques said, voicing part of her reflection. "I've never heard of it." Sofia put her hand on her husband's shoulder.

"There's no reason for those soldiers to stay once we're gone," Evangeline said. "It looks like the whole world is on fire." It seemed unlikely that anyone would ever be compelled to claim the tumbled chimneys and haunted fields.

"The English are owls to our mice," Felician said bitterly. "They did this because they could."

They're more like vultures, and we're the carrion, Evangeline thought, but kept quiet.

"It's beautiful," Jana said, and started sobbing on her brother's shoulder.

"The fires?" Evangeline was compelled to ask despite the girl's tears.

"No, Grand Pre. I've never seen it from the water."

The Acadians comforted each other throughout the boat, but Evangeline felt the same numbness as when she'd prepared the strangers for their rest in the church. The destruction of her village paled beside the loss of her father, especially after two months of praying, only to leave it for good. And even her father's death draped in its larger naturalness paled beside the uncertainty surrounding Gabriel. His was the only death that might touch her now.

As they passed through the gut out into the bay they joined three other ships sailing south from Chignecto. Night fell before their ship churned into the Atlantic, but the ocean winds tossing them into one another in the hold made it clear when they'd passed beyond the bay. If it wouldn't have made her sound like Jana, Evangeline might have mentioned that she'd never traveled so far from home. Lightning struck the foremast late that first night. Evangeline hadn't heard any thunder over the waves smacking the sloop about the sides and ringing through their confinement, and had assumed the roughness of the travel was customary.

"I had not hoped that the Lord would be so quick to punish the heretics," Felician observed grimly.

They held hands below deck in the pitching waves while their captors tried to save the ship. Unaccustomed to the heavy swells, several passengers became sick in the close quarters, including Bernard, and Evangeline retched trying to clean up his vomit. One wave made it completely over the gunwales before crashing, swallowing a mast cleanly with its trappings. They listed for several hours while the pilot waited for light, and eventually headed northeast. They drew closer to Acadia's ragged Atlantic coast, the percussive booming of waves on cliffs so unlike the ebb of the Minas. They passed Cape Sable and cruised through a perfectly still night, the overloaded vessel hanging in the water like a gigantic jellyfish. They were forced ashore the next afternoon, and the dozens of prisoners watched as the ship lurched north toward Halifax. Ten soldiers and two barrels of water remained with them on the stony beach.

"Well, they wanted us gone, but not very far," Evangeline said to Felician, who frowned at the ship.

He gave a rough little laugh. "When what you wish for is worse than what you have, then especially, may we receive our Lord's blessing."

After the boat was gone, they climbed away from the beach, following the soldiers up a trail until they reached a pine wood more reminiscent of home. Evangeline and Jana scoured under the snow at the edge of a frozen lake until they had handfuls of brittle boneset leaves. They returned to a triangle of large fires, wetter branches and people stretched out to dry inside the perimeter. Jana brewed tea while Evangeline followed Felician on his rounds amongst their patients. Three soldiers returned with a deer, and prisoners and captors huddled together for the night.

Evangeline woke early, disoriented until a breeze off the ocean reminded her of where she was. A soldier sat awake in the darkness, tending one of the fires. Whose purpose was served by all of this suffering? It was not for his benefit that they had been taken from Grand Pre, Evangeline thought. Moving quietly, she left the camp without being detected.

Walking away from the water, she sightlessly picked her way up a ridge, using tufts of grass to pull herself along. As the slope leveled above the camp, her groping hand brushed against something sharp, and she recoiled, fearing for a moment that she was snakebit. It was too early in the season, she reassured herself, nudging the ground with her sabot. She dislodged a spear, the shaft broken a hand's width below the blade. She would do well to remember that things could always get worse, Evangeline thought, sucking the cut on her palm. The sounds of morning stirring reached her from below, and she moved further through the blackness so that she wouldn't be visible after sunup.

Evangeline sat alone, watching the first curve of the disc of the sun rise over the sea, as the entire panorama of water flashed silver in a brief oceanic homage to the coming of the new day.

The water faded to blue, and the sun took on color as it climbed. She saw a ship on the edge of the horizon, easily distinguishable from the *Dauntless* even at this distance. Seven masts porcupined the vessel. Squinting harder, she realized there weren't any sails up, rather the ship rested at anchor. Which was impossible that far out to sea. Evangeline found a strip of bark, brushed the loose dirt off the top, and used the cool, damp wood to shield her eyes. The sun rose higher, but the glare on the horizon persisted, as though a second sun, brighter than the first, prepared for its ascent. And now it seemed that the ocean's earlier hue was concentrated into a heavenly white-silver fire that radiated out over the water from the ship. And in that far-off light, so distinct from the yellow glinting on the tall masts, it seemed that men, solemn and beautiful in their armor, walked with dread purpose across the surface of the water.

Wafts of deep musk, like the incense Felician kept but rarely burned in Saint Charles, drifted in over the ocean, briefly replacing the damp earth smell of her oak visor. Then the sun rose a little more and she couldn't see anything but water, though it seemed that in this vision, unlike a dream, her participation wasn't necessary. The men in their glittering scales of armor required no audience, and would continue unabated.

Evangeline kept watching until late in the afternoon, when the refitted *Dauntless* sailed back to anchor at the beach. The next morning the Acadians became cargo again.

They discharged in Baltimore after a week in quarantine, greeted like old friends by the crew who helped the elderly arrange themselves in the rowboats. Evangeline sat with them, apart from Felician and the twins, watching the low wooden houses lurch closer with the stroke.

"Here you are, girl," one sailor said to her once they were ashore, pushing a shilling into her hand. He only came up to her chin, and it made her feel like she was taking money from a child. "Good luck to you."

The sailors moved en masse toward the closest structure on the docks, a long one-story wooden building so loud that it could only be one of the taverns her father had mentioned as being prevalent in foreign ports, but that were entirely absent in the Minas. The Acadians slumped on the dock, or atop barrels, staring with disbelief at the town whose buildings were clustered far closer together than Grand Pre's. There was a line of homes on a hill west of the harbor, and what looked like a couple dozen more dwellings north of their wharf. Two men crossed paths with the crew of the *Dauntless* and headed toward the new arrivals.

Felician joined them outside the crowd of refugees. Evangeline kept watch on the town, but the sailors had disappeared and the street remained empty. Uncertainly, she joined the priest, thinking to help with her English, but he was already engaged in French with a man who had the exaggerated thinness of the recently ill. The heavier man at his side glowered at the translator suspiciously and he unrolled a parchment.

"We've got a newspaper here in Maryland." The French speaker gestured at the paper. "And they seem to have taken your side." He paused to blow his nose loudly into a handkerchief, and the other man shook his head and withdrew.

"My name's Lucas, ma'am," speaking to her, "and Mr. Gwinn's our sheriff."

"Oh, excuse me," Lucas interrupted himself. "We've brought water." He pointed to barrels of fresh water waiting on the pier, then to a few baskets of bread alongside. "And food."

"We appreciate the generosity," Felician said. "But these people are going to need milk and meat."

"Good thinking. We'll get meat, and some butter too. Do you have anyone you could send with us to carry it back?"

The man looked at Evangeline, but the priest called on the twins, who followed Gwinn back to the town in mute procession. Evangeline stood with her guardian, watching as Jana and Julian vanished into the same tavern that swallowed the ship's crew.

"Where do we go?" Felician's question sounded more ridiculous than it was, with the crew gone, only Lucas stood with the dozens of newcomers. She imagined a fearful populace keeping watch from the safety of the homes.

"I know that you're not the ones that asked for the trip, but these people here are surprised to see you." Lucas looked behind him, and then at the ground. "But there's this article from the Gazette. Maybe its author has an idea for you."

They looked at him blankly.

"It's the newspaper down in Annapolis. Henry Brandt writes for it. He lives in one of those new houses on the water, and says we need a paper of our own." The man shook his head in disbelief. "He's a compassionate man by local standards. I'll take you around tomorrow to meet him, and I'd rely on him. Meantime, we'd better get you people away from shore, get a fire going and leave the future in the future."

Lucas led the way away from the docks, pushing a one-wheeled cart. They headed east along the water, and directly came to a decrepit wall on which construction looked to have been long abandoned.

Lucas had little trouble guessing her thoughts. "You probably wouldn't believe we finished that wall, brand new, five years ago. It lasted for one winter before people started dismantling it for firewood. You know how people can be. Once someone looked out for themselves above the rest of the community, we all did."

"There's barely anything left at all," Evangeline said. They could have stepped naturally over the barrier along most of its length.

"It's been a cold past couple winters, I'm sorry to tell you," Lucas replied, looking uncomfortable. "Not helping matters, we had a freshet last year that took out several bridges, and we've just about finished it off finding pieces to fix them."

He and Felician set to work ripping pieces of the wood loose, and Evangeline wheeled the first cartload back to the wharf. She slowed on nearing her people, and leaned against the handle of the cart to watch a man with a fishing pole wander over and, in English, ask one of their codgers how long they were staying. He repeated the question louder twice before returning to his course up the beach. She dumped the load and wheeled her way back to Felician and Lucas.

"Where are we going to sleep?" Evangeline asked her

guardian when she returned. Felician looked at her tiredly, the dark rings around his eyes a match for hers. He considered the disheveled Acadians by the water, before looking helplessly at the harbor, toward the ship that had almost suffocated them over the past week. Yet it was the only familiar landmark in the foreign port.

"Not there, in any case," she said reassuringly, but Felician's neck stayed hunched between his shoulder blades as he considered the *Dauntless*.

Before sunset, dirty children arrived in small clusters, jabbering at them in rapid English she had trouble understanding. Eventually, from a seat on a piling, she informed a small crowd of youths that they were Acadians, good Catholic people, and that they had been taken by force from the homes, and that they had nowhere to sleep and no food. One of the young boys started crying. "Bring your mothers," Evangeline told Baltimore's children.

That night, the refugees gathered and prayed for deliverance, huddled under their worn blankets. They'd moved a short distance from the chilly water, but remained leery of entering the unknown town to seek out warmer accommodations.

Employing the soldiers' tactic from their night on the beach, they built three fires and huddled in the warmth between. Julian and Jana returned with jerky and butter, and they settled in the lee of the rise west of the harbor, wheeling the trapper over in the cart they'd used to haul fuel. He remained silent and cold to her touch.

Lucas brought the newspaperman to see them the next morning, and they followed him up the street leading from the dock. They passed the tavern and half a dozen homes that didn't look like they would last two winters on the Minas and soon stopped before a rambling structure no sturdier than its neighbors, but much larger, with a grand front porch that was missing several floorboards.

"This one?" She couldn't believe it. "This is one of the largest buildings we've passed."

Brandt nodded proudly. "Damn near the only two-storied building in Baltimore, unless you count the steeple on Saint Paul's."

"And no one wants it?" Felician inquired, sharing her wonder.

"I think there might've been some talk as to what to do with it, but in the meantime, it's certainly the biggest empty space around here where you people can get out of the weather."

"Who used to live here?" She couldn't picture the family, and was embarrassed to realize that there weren't any two-story houses in Grand Pre, that she'd never even seen one until she was forced into the larger world.

The newspaperman inhaled deeply. "This was Edward Fottrell's house. He came over from Ireland, with an inheritance he used to have this built. He only lived in it a couple years before he disappeared." He didn't leave them time to wonder. "Dead, went back home, moved on further west, shaved his moustache and married a squaw, I don't have any idea." He smiled at Evangeline and smoothed the thick black growth on his lip proudly. "And there's no use in asking somebody else in this town something I don't know. I've tried it several times."

"Bless you for your assistance, sir," Felician said.

"Well, Father, it's my pleasure. I meant what I wrote in that article, and here I am proving it. Doing my duty as a proud Catholic, though it costs me twice as much on tax day." Another smile for her before adding, "And I got to practice my French on a young beauty in the bargain." Twice her age and half her height didn't stop the man's hopes.

"Thank you so much for everything you've already done, Mr. Brandt," she began. "And forgive me for asking, but do you know how I could get in touch with other refugees?"

"You mean the boats that stopped in Annapolis?"

She shook her head. "The man I'm supposed to marry was deported to Carolina."

"I'm sorry, dear." His expression was grim. "That's the first I've heard that they're taking Acadians that far south. But I'll keep my ears open."

"Thank you, sir."

"Don't let hope carry you away, this war has more than just our corner of the world in chaos."

Felician led the procession around the curve of the harbor, up Calvert Street, his black robe a warning against the deathly wrack of the forty lost souls tramping behind. Evangeline followed last with Julian pulling the half-dead trapper with them in the wooden cart. Finally they reached their lodging at the north of the town, raised on an elevation she appreciated more for towing the trapper's weight on this second visit.

A gray-bearded man in a long black coat was there, talking quietly with Felician, but he had gone by the time she'd stowed her pallid patient in a corner of the vast drafty house. Inside, the emptiness made it seem even larger.

"That was Charles Smith," the priest said as she approached. "A generous friend of Brandt's. He brought us these blankets that he rounded up from his friends, and he said he's sending over food." Almost one cover for each of them, heavy wool blankets without holes. Felician clapped his hands happily. "Between these and the walls we'll almost be too warm tonight."

The house had a separate kitchen on the first floor, but no other partitions. From the first, Evangeline and Felician spread their blankets upstairs with the twins, willing to suffer the draftier conditions in exchange for privacy denied those unwilling to climb the stairs.

Charles Smith returned the next day with his wife Abigail, bringing iron pots, wooden cutlery, and oats. That night Sofia presided over their first independent meal since winter soup at the church. The resulting porridge wasn't delicious, but Evangeline was happy that she hadn't been asked to cook it.

Instead of cooking, she borrowed a hammer and nails from the Philpots, a young couple with four children already, who were building a home next door on Calvert Street, while Felician investigated Baltimore's church. When he returned, she and the twins had lined the worst of the gaps on the first floor with old coats and the thinnest of the blankets.

He nodded at their work. "Excellent. We'll get more blankets and do the same to upstairs, and then everyone should have room to sleep."

"What did you think about the church?"

"Nothing compared to Quebec, but not too shabby for a Protestant frontier town. They've got an organ." He looked around. "I'll make an altar downstairs, as Mr. Smith said that Catholics here who have room keep them in their own houses. And for now at least, room is the only thing we don't lack."

Evangeline walked along Charles Street, west past Saint Paul's and the brick buildings gathered near the water. There weren't many of the structures, but their presence made the town feel larger than Grand Pre or Port Royal, even though there didn't seem to be more people here than in its Acadian counterparts.

She was happy to not have company, as she despised asking for handouts with spectators, a concern she weighed against her safety. She didn't care for begging money in any case, but felt that she was best suited for it, and accepted the duty so long as her humility went unobserved. And though they went barefoot in their new home, the forays presented her with opportunity to wear her old sabots whenever she went *collecting*, the term she'd come to prefer.

She knocked on the first door past the church grounds on Baltimore Street, and was greeted by a large man in a vest, clearly just home from work though she didn't recognize him from previous expeditions. Exposure to Baltimore's pale-skinned population was a pleasant reminder of her healthier complexion.

"Good evening sir."

"And to you, young lady. What brings you around?" His tone sounded like she wasn't the first alms seeker to his door.

"I help Father Felician run the hospital over on Calvert Street," Evangeline trailed off expectantly.

"Yes, you people have already asked for and taken everything I can spare."

"Well, sir, as I mentioned, I make the rounds for the hospital. It's my job, and no one else would have come by on our behalf."

"There have been plenty of strangers asking for money lately."

"Well, sir, let me be clear. We have cooks, and plenty of clothes and linens, as we keep losing patients. I am asking for money, but not for myself. Change your mind and we can all rest easy, knowing that you've helped keep these poor people alive."

He shook his head with a smile that wasn't for her benefit. "Hold on a moment."

The man left the door open, dug something out of his coat slung over a large table in the main room, and on his return took a short stovepipe hat off the antlered rack by the door and stepped outside.

"A pretty girl like you shouldn't have to beg for money." As he said it, she was almost off the porch, ready for this response at every door, but then he upended the top hat and extended it to her.

"But if you do," he dropped a piece of eight dully into the felt, "It's only appropriate that you come to the door with a hat in your hand."

Evangeline took the offering and recited her refrain, "May the Lord bless your charity." Appropriate for any circumstance, she felt, worthy gift or none at all, and she left the condescending man to his evening.

Several houses along the construction turned wooden, and the homes and people were newer to town. These families had retreated from western settlements endangered by their proximity to the French forts just across the mountains. The roughcut homes of these former frontiersmen promised no great wealth, but she avoided the houses more because circumstances encouraged these settlers to identify the Acadians with their distress. Evangeline tucked the coin and her bonnet in the pocket of her cottonelle, pulled on the top hat, and turned for home.

The Acadians spent the spring refashioning their new home. They filled the worst remaining chinks with their traveling rags after bartering for or being given sturdier replacements by their new neighbors. Better prepared for cold weather, they turned their attention to beds, piling chaff for pallets along the walls of the large downstairs room high enough so that old knees would be able to stand unaided. Blankets were hung to screen the sleepers from a visitor's initial impression. Felician stood in the foyer on Sundays, with the front door in place of the altar at Saint Charles, and the blankets tied off so that he could be seen. Her old duty as greeter rendered unnecessary, Evangeline watched the service from the stairs.

Only Felician, Evangeline, Jana and Julian slept on the upper story, the stairs a luxury come too late to be of service to the older Acadians confined below. The four of them slept together in the expressionless room until the heat inspired her and Jana to fashion another partition so they could strip to their underclothes to sleep. More used to privacy than Julian, Felician hung a blanket for himself as well, and Julian slept in the open alone.

"Four of us up here, and four dozen of them below," Evangeline observed to Jana one night. She had heard the other girl stirring, but Jana made no response. "At least we've moved the cooking outside."

"Until the winter, anyway," Jana said.

Though ordinarily a sound sleeper, she awoke one night to find herself alone. She didn't call out, but crept into the main room, where Jana had curled up in bed with her brother. They slept, holding each other familiarly, and Evangeline wished desperately for the press of a body against her own. She returned to bed and sat, hugging herself, long into the night.

"Are you afraid you'll get sick?" Julian asked. She was carrying chamberpots out from the sickroom for him to dump in the street.

His hand brushed hers as he took one from her. It felt deliberate, but she couldn't tell when she met his eyes. It would certainly be an odd moment to pursue his interest.

"I've never been sick," she said. "Most of these people are just old."

He nodded as though he hadn't considered their age and left with the pot.

"I'm fine, girl," Bernard said as she approached his bed. "I can take my own pot outside when I've filled it."

"You're welcome to take them all if you'd like."

He laughed. "I was only raised to look after myself."

She could have said the same, but her curiosity was piqued by his response. "And where was that?"

"I was born on a farm near Quebec."

"Did you spend much time in the city?"

He shook his head. "My father and I ran away when I was young."

"You ran away from your own farm?"

"It wasn't ours exactly. I don't remember much from there. My father said he wasn't cut out to be a farmer."

"That sounds like my father. What about your mother?"

"She died the winter before we left."

"I'm sorry," she said. There was plenty of death in the world for the living to bond over. "My father raised me also. My mother died just after I was born."

He nodded his condolences. "Nothing to do but miss them, I suppose." There was something newly vulnerable in his voice.

"How old are you, Bernard?"

He grinned. "Probably younger than I look. A gunshot will add a few years, my partner used to say."

"So how old?"

He looked up at the ceiling, and then back to her. "Twenty."

She laughed, but he seemed serious.

"Two years older than I am." Between his posture, beard, and gruffness, she would have thought he was closer to twice her age.

He guessed her mind. "Some of those years went on an awful long time."

Though their guests that summer, Brandt and Smith chief among them, mentioned only the unseasonable cold of recent years, the Acadians complained mostly of the unrelenting mugginess, a torpid heat they'd never felt before that left them praying for winter. Instead, as August rolled toward September, rain wracked the town for weeks, and drips upstairs became leaks, until there were as many catch basins as patients.

Near the close of the month, Brandt stopped by for the first time in more than a week and sat on the porch with Felician. Evangeline carried out tea from the kitchen and sat on the steps alongside Brandt. She welcomed his visits as they otherwise existed in ignorance of the world outside the walls of their refuge.

"Who fixes roofs around here?" Felician asked.

"Who doesn't, Father? This isn't the only one in town that's leaking." Brandt waved his hands to ward off the whining words. "I'll bring some pitch over this week and we'll have a go at it. Not wanting to climb around up there is probably why this house has sat untended for years. That's not why I stopped by, though." Brandt's tone was pointedly ominous.

"What brings you around then, son?" The weariness in Felician's voice was tragic, but he sat up straighter after seeing her look, and fixed Brandt with his stare.

"I hear more of your people are on the way."

"From where?"

"No idea, Father. But presumably your country had more in it than a few old invalids."

"Well, point them this way, and they can help me with the roof."

"I will. I've been watching the harbor for wooden shoes for days, though I'm sure we'll all know when they get here. You know yourself that new additions don't go unnoticed in our community."

"People have been generous with us," Evangeline interjected.

"That's good. I hoped, and even expected, that you all would find a warm enough reception from the people about town, and I'm happy you got it. Most of us believe it's our Christian duty to extend some care and support to those in need, and even the stingiest admit it's disgraceful to think about kicking those old folks out of their homes. I'm grateful that most people in Baltimore are sensible enough to realize that's not what an invasion looks like inside. You all have gotten the short end. Meantime, though, the war's not going well."

"If I'm not missing it, that's a long way around to your point, Monsieur. But as far as the war goes, much depends on your perspective, doesn't it?"

"No, Father. The way things are, if things go poorly for us, things go poorly for you, and if that sounds threatening it probably should. Here it is, plain as I can make it. Forty people on death's door are one thing. Boatloads of families on top of that are another. And we've got our own flooding back into town every day, chased back here from out west, scared of the Indians, and scared of the French."

"It sounds like we have quite a bit in common then, people displaced against their wishes by circumstances out of their control."

"I guess that's why I'm not a priest," Brandt said. He pulled his hat snug against the drizzle, tipped it to her, and departed.

Felician sensed her thought as they sat on the porch, obvious as the rain. "I wouldn't expect that Gabriel would be on any of those boats. Brandt tells us they're coming from Acadia."

"We can pray."

"I'll pray with you child, but I'm afraid you may have a longer wait ahead of you."

Evangeline looked at the few small houses visible down Calvert Street. "Where are they going to put all these people?"

"Well, many of them probably won't go further than Annapolis, and they'll probably take some across the bay, but it sounds like the rest are going to walk right up here."

Brandt was right, as inside of a week three sloops anchored in the harbor below Calvert Street, one discharging Acadian families, the other two English soldiers who looked out of place in the wooden town. The redcoats bivouacked for a night and moved west. Julian and Jana led the Acadians up Calvert Street. Evangeline and Felician moved the children into the first floor of the church, and their parents slept outside in the damp with the mosquitoes. Charles Smith came by the following morning, and took the newcomers to property he'd convinced the town to let them use. The adults set to work on rude shelters, packing mud bricks in gangs, working as they had for generations raising dikes against the Minas, though in exile the women worked alongside the men. Four mud longhouses soon stood on Charles Street, and the families that were able moved into the hovels. Two dozen of the oldest arrivals and five children orphaned remained with them in the house.

"The whole village is intact again," Evangeline said to Julian one evening as they watched the Melansons tear cabbage for the stew. The new arrivals had animated Grand Pre's weary leftovers, and it did them all good to be around families again.

"You make do with what you have sometimes," she began, and then realized the connotation her words might carry with Julian. She wished, for the first time in years, that she might live out her days as a man where her accidental flirtations wouldn't be taken as seriously. "Have you ever thought about what it would be like to be a girl, Julian?" she asked him instead.

"I feel like I know a little bit, because of Jana." He stopped, unsure if he'd answered. "At least I wouldn't be digging graves, I guess," he finished, frowning.

Evangeline frowned with him. She could only be blamed so much for Julian's discomfort. She deepened his attraction by doing nothing.

"I'm going to see about that girl's fever," Evangeline said stiffly, reminding him they all had responsibilities they hadn't asked for. "Maybe you'll have one less hole to dig."

She stomped upstairs, happy for an excuse to storm off, but aware she'd have to apologize later. She was sick of Julian and already sick of Baltimore. The English were losing each battle they fought, Felician assured her, but after every loss, boats of new soldiers arrived to march west.

Over her oatmeal Sofia reported that two of the boys were running fevers. "I don't want to trouble Felician needlessly. It's warmer here than we're used to."

Evangeline left the spoon sticking up out of the bowl. "Yes, it would be snowing back home by now. Let me see about them, Sofia, you were right not to bother Felician."

The boys were shrunken, and lay feverish and naked on the floor where she had put the trapper when they first arrived months ago. They were slick with sweat when she touched them.

"I fed them broth, dear," Sofia said from behind her. "They wouldn't touch any bread."

"They're breathing slowly to be sweating like this."

"Good girl. You know what to do."

Evangeline didn't, but she wiped the perspiration with rags, and prayed. She watched as pools of water formed in the elbows, in the crook of their emaciated necks, and went to get Felician.

The next day the boys stopped sweating, exuded now an arid heat, and they stank despite the water and lye she scrubbed over them. Quiet from the beginning, neither spoke at all that day, even when Evangeline discovered blood behind the whites of their eyes and asked them if they hurt. They weren't bloodshot, rather it seemed the irises floated in blood.

That evening, one of the new arrivals, Francis Bauer, helped Felician deliver four more patients, a boy and a girl on a sledge, and an older man and a woman about her age.

"We've got a problem." Felician beckoned her out onto the porch where the man waited for Felician's questions. Both were covered with mud from the streets.

"You brought a lot of sick people with you," her guardian began.

"They didn't come with me any farther than Charles Street. I've got my own children I can't go near now after dragging these people up here."

Felician nodded. "No one else since you've been here?"

He shook his head, thick angry motions reminiscent of Gabriel's father.

"So you don't have any idea what they might have?"

"Could be the water we've been drinking. There was plenty of diarrhea on the way down here."

"I don't think that's what we're facing here."

"No, I agree with you there. Listen, I appreciate that you're taking these people into your care, and I can bring over anyone else that gets it. Otherwise, I suppose I'll set up out here on the porch and I'll help you how I'm able, though usually my wife would doctor my children."

"Can you bring her?"

"There may still be a time when somebody has to doctor them."

The following morning, Evangeline started her rounds with the young woman, who had been the previous night's most responsive patient. "Is anything different today?"

"They are," came the listless response, accompanied by a slow point to the two boys, curled up and kneading their stomachs with their fists.

"They're not as hot as they were yesterday, but their stomachs are cramping. They're fighting through it, and so will you." Evangeline didn't mention the purple tongues that she helped Felician lance late last night as the other patients shuddered in a semblance of sleep.

A few of those already in their care began complaining of being overheated, rare for the elderly in mid-November, and that evening the little boys' skin turned gold as she and Felician doused them with water, fighting off flies that swarmed about the sickly bodies. Felician prayed over them as the boys spat bile to match his robes, and the fifth day of their care ended.

They didn't wake up the next morning. When Evangeline found them, their skin had faded to the worn bronze of an old statue, and their stomachs were bloated, the distension even more obvious after the months of malnourishment marked by the tiny hands, wrists and arms.

"You're stronger," Felician said to the other sick children, nearly ten now in various stages of degradation.

"You are older. You will survive. You've all been sick before," he told the other patients.

Henry Brandt walked through the new sickroom downstairs, more slowly than she expected, and waited until they were back on the porch.

"Stranger's disease," he commented as he sat down on the porch step, "when they turn that yellow. It's been through here before, but still the sheriff's going to have to quarantine all of you."

"Do you," Felician began.

"Know anything useful? Not a damn thing, except that you can survive it. I'm so sorry about those two boys. There's no reason to mention to Gwinn that I stopped by."

It didn't snow for two more weeks and the lower sleeping quarters became cramped with the sick and dying from the shacks, though the downstairs remained roomier than the ship's hold. Finally a freeze brought an end to the stream of patients, God's icy breath extinguishing the plague. Julian and Francis Bauer dug graves in the mud and they piled in the newcomers they would never know and six of the elderly who'd wintered with them in Grand Pre. The day before the snow finally fell, the trapper turned yellow.

Felician prayed for Bernard as Evangeline rinsed him and apologized for not paying closer attention that she might have recognized sick from wounded.

"Oh, I've been hot since we got here, girl. I was trying to convince myself I didn't have the damn thing. And your ministrations didn't seem to be changing much for those people anyway, if you'll forgive rudeness in a man whose life you've already saved." He waved a jaundiced hand, "Enough now, Felician. This is a hell of a way to figure out who's right about all of that."

He threw up the black bile, but his eyes never turned to blood, and though he remained jaundiced through the new year and his breathing stayed slow and weak, eventually the trapper recovered. He joined seven survivors.

Baltimore Town rescinded the quarantine on March 14th, 1757, one day after Evangeline's nineteenth birthday.

South Carolina 1756

Loud from its rocky caverns, the deep-voiced neighboring ocean speaks, and in accents disconsolate answers the wail of the forest.

G ABRIEL WATCHED A THIN TRICKLE OF BLOOD ESCAPE FROM the dirty linen wrap around his father's scalp and ooze slower than tears down into Basil's bristly sideburn.

"Papa, your head," Gabriel said, pointing at his own, and Basil probed a finger under his bandages. They huddled in the dank splintery darkness of a hold along the low curve of the schooner's bow with four other men who merited unusual confinement. Viktor sat patiently in the gloom of their first day together and waited to continue his tale.

"Unlike you in Grand Pre, we've been living with Fort Edward in our midst for years now, so a few more soldiers would have been tough to spot." He paused. "If they hadn't been colonial militia. So, something was in the air, and when they sent out the call for us to gather at the fort to discuss the return of our guns, we here wondered if there wasn't more to it." He paused a moment to let their shared wisdom sink in.

"But they came after us quick enough after they settled everyone down over at the fort."

"Where were you?" Gabriel asked.

"Hiding out in my farmhouse," Viktor answered. "I wasn't going to that gathering, and let other folks know they were welcome to wait it out with me." He chuckled, "Probably safe to say that I spread the word further than I might of. My farm was more than a league from that fort, and the militiamen were there by evening."

"We were still talking about what we should do, when we saw the torches," Philippe cut in. He was a younger man about Gabriel's age, wild-looking with hasty bandages around a head wound.

"They didn't need them for light yet," Viktor continued, "and it is a frightening prospect to have those blue bastards advancing on your homestead. But we had loaded muskets, and we made it to the windows to open up on them as they threw the torches. I know that I hit one."

Alain coughed at the door.

"We hit a couple of them," Viktor amended, holding up his mangled left hand for emphasis. "But they shot back, probably near twenty of them. Even through my house, both the boys were hit in the first volley, and we gave in pretty quick. That thatch catches quick in October."

"So what happened to your hand?" Gabriel asked Viktor.

"Oh, this is old. You probably can't tell in this damned darkness, but my hairs are growing over the stumps. My mother chopped off those last two fingers when we were splitting wood, probably thirty years ago, now."

Alexander Soulard, Philippe Boiselle, Viktor Doucet and Alain Toussaint hailed from the Pisquid settlements, a people

Gabriel knew only from their occasional business. As their ship made its heavy way south, the six of them pursued their acquaintance over Alexander's right leg, which jutted out into the scant communal space, under a barrage of accidental movement. He'd been shot through the thigh in the fusillade, but the bullet missed the bone. The ship's doctor patched him up along with Philippe. A ricochet had torn off most of his left ear.

"Although none of us charged Winslow in front of his men." Alain's remark was followed by hearty assent from the others who all acknowledged that they wished they had the bravery. Gabriel wondered if praise had been the speaker's intention.

"Speak for yourself," Philippe countered. "I would've gone right after them if I hadn't been busy looking for my ear."

Alain and Basil, their representatives to their captors, flanked the low hatch. Gabriel sat next to his father, then Alexander, Philippe, and Viktor back around to Alain, the wounded ear and leg arranged next to each other, so neither was tempted to lean toward the largest space permitted between any two of them. He and Gabriel were in the worst position, Viktor claimed, as the other four had corners to lean against, while they were forced to sleep leaning against someone else.

Alain had served as a notary to the former governor. "I retired when Lawrence took office in an attempt to avoid spending my final years in handwringing," he said helplessly. "Though I imagine a cell in Halifax would have to be some improvement over this."

Alexander's father had replaced him, representing the several Acadian hamlets around Fort Edward, and had been detained in Halifax for the past two months. Philippe was the sixteenth child of a family near Viktor's north of the Pisquid who'd been passed between his older siblings after his parents died. He disobeyed the summons, he said, "Only out of ordinary distaste for English dickering."

The six men were confined to their hold for the entire journey down the coast, listening enviously to the noisy daily exercise of their fellow prisoners, parading down the corridors and up on deck. But neither the large ship's unfamiliar lilting nor the barely potable water reduced any among their number to the vomiting that neighbors claimed was rampant in other parts of the ship.

"I wonder how long until they let us off," Alain said.

"I hope it's soon, because I'm sure they didn't have people in mind when they carved this space out down here," Viktor replied with an eye on Gabriel and his father folded under the low ceiling. The lingering odor of coal, which seemed to intensify rather than diminish over the days at sea, validated his claim.

They took turns standing and stretching as they could in the center of the low room during the day when a dim light seeped through the walls and doorway and they could make out each others' faces, rather than during the interminable opaqueness of the winter nights. Philippe and Gabriel helped Alexander to his feet, and supported him while he put some weight on his functional leg so that he might have some motion left when they were eventually let off the ship. The dark was punctuated with surprise whenever one of them awoke to the press of sweaty strangers in the dark, jolted from thoughts of their capture, their terrorized communities, and the prospect of a life in prison. There were torments aplenty to haunt the half-sleeping hours in the cold blackness, nightmares that Gabriel shared with the others, but staved off with dreams of Evangeline. The dark here was only a shade darker than the night they'd spent spear-fishing on the Gaspereau.

"No different than if we were underwater," Alexander's hoarse voice had commented on their first night, any sound startling close in the lightless hold.

"We are underwater." Basil's fatalism had tended towards despondency since their capture. Guilty, and with matters beyond his control, he abruptly ended attempts at conversation at night, welcoming his demons privately. Respecting his father's pain, Gabriel did not mention that Basil's outburst cost him the chance to get on deck to see Evangeline like the less threatening deportees.

All of them were equally ignorant as to what had happened to those that were left behind, and they found common ground in their seclusion. The three older men also shared their widower status, which gave them less interest in discussing the past, and how they might reclaim it.

After five days of blindly churning through the ocean, Gabriel found the lack of movement discouraging as the *Success* moored in the foreign harbor.

"Is that how long it takes to get to Carolina?" Basil didn't answer his question, as he never gave an unsure answer, and Gabriel spent the darkening hours in fitful sleep alongside his silent father, tall men with cramped knees hunched in their sweat stained rags against the damp wooden hull, listening to the wind howl as sick men retched foul water all around them in the schooner's bowels.

After one day at anchor in the new harbor, the departing crew passed a last time down the narrow passageway to inform their prisoners that all were now confined to their holds, and that the entire vessel was under quarantine until the sickness passed.

"Small need for a messenger there," Alain said. None of the

six of them evinced the wasting sicknesses plaguing their neighbors, and to minimize exposure, only Alain, from his post at the
hatch, interacted with the slaves who doled out hardtack and
chamberpots reborn as water carriers, his honor as the oldest.
They sat quietly and shriveled with hunger and cold like grapes
dangling impatiently on the vine as the weaker clusters dropped
off around them.

Twice over the next week the wind howled so as to blot out
even their own voices, and they vomited throughout the hours of
the ship's pitching and rocking. Only the cessation of these
fiercer storms brought any lasting quiet to the *Success*, silencing
all but the most desperate, who continued calling out eerily, like
the only survivors of a battle none of them had fought.
Eventually, gulls calling overhead in newly cleared skies drowned
out the exhausted sick. The second storm was worse than the
first, and the next morning, Gabriel awoke as if from a dream to
the reek of the hold. He retched, but had nothing left to purge.
Even his father finally slept, extended beyond the limits of his
strength, with his massive frame leaning against Gabriel, past
caring about the filth and discomfort.

The day after the second tempest they were remembered,
and the slaves returned, marching through the prison ship with
tall baskets of steaming rice that they ate with their dirty
hands.

The next day when the door opened, no rice came, but a
soldier gave them news that they were being moved. The emaciated men slowly unfolded themselves from the constraints of
their tiny prison, and were led down the deck to canoes waiting
to take them to shore. From the beach, Gabriel looked up into
the gray sky, his senses recoiling from the vast world. Their cir-
culation restored, Gabriel and Philippe helped Alexander to the

ocean, the water as cold as glacial runoff, the beach's only obvious concession to winter.

"Let's see that leg," Philippe insisted. The flesh was pinched at the edges of the thick black scabs. It didn't look like he had enough skin to go around.

"You're lucky you can hide that under your trousers," Philippe said as he rinsed Alexander's clothes in the surf. Gabriel held Alexander's elbow, and after a cursory look, kept his eyes off the wound.

Gabriel's wet clothes were full of heavy salt, giving the rags the scratchy feel of new wool. He was happy to be a little cleaner as he took in the unfamiliar specter of other people, forms for the disembodied voices that had kept them company over the past weeks. Besides the *Success*, three other ships were disgorging passengers south along the beach. None of the other boats was familiar from the Minas, their passengers seized from Acadian communities other than Grand Pre. He had no idea how long they'd been treading water alongside these other ships and hundreds of people.

A river marked the northern boundary of the beach and scrub behind, a narrow strip of firm ground that was several hundred meters at its widest. The land gave way quickly to a vast bog, and gradually, the marshland narrowed their habitable island as it stretched south, though the beach continued for several leagues, occasionally split by creeks trickling in from the marsh, before it ended in another flow. Across that stream sat a small fort with a single tower, only six meters tall, but twice the height of any natural growth on the island. There wasn't a fort guarding the wider channel to their north, just a few soldiers observing the hundreds of Acadians from a lonely harbor empty of other activity as they arrived. The land was steeper on the far side of the river, and the trees quickly grew into a forest. Smoke from a city's numerous chimneys left a smudge over the scraggly trees just up the river, obscuring the refugees' westerly gazes and turning them east, to scour the endless sea. Their crimes forgotten, or even unknown to their new captors, the six men were treated with the same neglect as the other prisoners, loosed without reference to their separate status onboard the *Success*.

The site the older men chose was at the northern end of the beach, sheltered by the dune rising up along the bank of the river, and backing up against a little copse of the gnarled trees.

"You look better." Basil nodded his approval at Gabriel's appearance. "I could stand a bath myself." His father bled from shallow lacerations on both arms, the result of clearing the tufted grasses and cactus from the edge of their camp. After the older men took their turns rinsing off, they pillaged the nearby beach and riverbank for driftwood until they had heaping piles, enough to sustain several nights of blazing fires. Alain passed around rough pieces of bark he'd stripped off the stunted oaks, and they dug beds in the cold sand, keeping the loose stuff close to the trenches, to cover themselves up at the end of the night.

"I'd almost forgotten what fresh air smelled like," Gabriel said as he sunk his oak bark shovel into the pile of cold sand. "I'm tired just looking at all this comfort."

"That's the attitude, Gabriel," Viktor said, patting his recessed paunch. "Another week or two of captivity and I might be thin enough to start looking for another wife."

Around them, the *Success'* passengers divided into bands and occupied themselves scavenging for materials to build shelters and light fires while tending to the sick. As the sky darkened on their first night in Carolina, Etienne Gravois walked into the ring of their firelight.

"Basil, Gabriel, I'm so glad to have found you. I've just found my mother up the beach with my brother's family. Is it all right to bring everyone over?" His clan waited in the dark, more than a dozen shadows. His father and Alain exchanged a look, and his father stood up.

"None of us have been sick, Etienne."

"We haven't either, Basil."

Basil hadn't reused the filthy wrapping covering his wound, but, in spite of the crusted blood, looked whole and menacing for the first time since entering the church.

"You're going to need to make your own fire."

"This is absurd. My family's freezing. It's December."

Basil dug around the logs at the edge of the fire and drew one out, its tip as red as from the forge.

"It's best if we keep to ourselves, and then this sickness won't spread further than it has to." Basil motioned with the brand. "Walk down the beach aways and dig up some grass."

Etienne opened his mouth but said nothing, standing stunned for a moment before regaining his composure and leading his family away. Gabriel gathered up an armload of wood and followed his father down the beach where he dumped the gift and returned to their fire without a word. Neighbors from home were quickly become strangers, Gabriel thought.

The next day redcoats led a delegation from the city, several men wrapped in gray winter coats that brushed the sand as one stepped forward to speak loudly in French.

"You have arrived in Charleston, South Carolina. I'm sorry to have to inform you, but the sight of the ships was the first news we had of your coming. And, though it won't increase our safety, I'm compelled to inform you that the English in the colony's capital hardly outnumber you here on the beach. You are prisoners here, and you will not leave this island." He waited for his words to sink in. They'd arrived in the captivity before it even existed, Gabriel thought as the man continued. "I have more despairing news that I will not withhold, though it also might work to our detriment. There is no reason for you to entertain the prospect of returning to your homes, even after the war's conclusion, as there is nothing to return to." Gabriel heard several men around him ask neighbors what war the man was referring to.

"We did not ask for you to come here." The delegate wasn't mincing his words, but these last were finally met with shouting, and two muskets were fired into the air. "Despite the circumstances, you can rest assured that the food will improve as we in Charleston become more equipped to feed the guests that Our Lord has thrown upon our mercy."

After the visit, rice became their daily staple, floated downstream from Charleston on rafts or paddled in canoes, and toted in huge baskets to the beach from the river by slaves, unaccompanied by the few soldiers who remained with the small crafts at the river. It was often still pleasantly warm, but plain even compared to his father's cooking.

Gabriel and Philippe spent their time finding the longest pieces of wood they could, mostly drift as the scrub oaks were twisted beyond usefulness. In time, Alain assembled a wall with the lengths, a windbreak curving to the northeast, parallel to the low dune, with the ends of the sticks deep in the sand, and braced in the spreading branches of one of the trees. Alexander and Alain peeled off the bark from the support branch and its trunk, and wrapped the strips around their frame. Gabriel and Philippe brought handfuls of mud from the marsh and filled in the gaps in the barrier, and soon their bed trenches were well protected. The wall shielded them against the worst of the wind, and they stacked their wood inside, next to a fire that looked bright compared with those they saw farther south over dozens of less finished camps along the beach.

"That's fine for now, but we've still got to get off this island," Alain said that night as they admired their work.

The Acadians eased the food crisis by dying in droves over the first blustery weeks of winter, falling victim to disease, or exposure, or swallowed by the ocean. Most of the refugees recognized the freezing salt water as their best protection against the unfamiliar sicknesses birthed in the swamp that trapped them on the beach, and regardless of temperature, the six of them got in the water each day. So Gabriel was forced from his fear of the churning water, though even on calm days he remained aware of the relentless tug of the waves threatening to draw him out to be remade in the inhospitable wider world. His lasting fear was not from the power of the waves, though they had claimed several lives among the inexperienced swimmers who thought to use the ocean to escape. As Gabriel swayed to sleep with the sea each night, what he remembered was one man, striding out into the surf, and indistinguishable from the other bathing refugees until they became aware of his head, bobbing above the water not north or south along the coast, but out, far enough that it looked like there might be a chance he'd find the strength to cross the limitless horizon.

Eventually, Alexander healed enough to trudge around on the beach behind Gabriel and Philippe, exercising his leg while they gathered wood or fished a river unable to provide for the hundreds of Acadians. The three of them canvassed the northern edge of the island, claiming everything that drifted down the river, leaving the beach to other scavengers.

After a particularly bitter night, they came upon six boys walking up the bank. Gabriel recognized Baptiste Gravois and his younger brother. No greetings were exchanged, but the younger Gravois called out as they approached.

"We're gathering this."

"This is our wood," Philippe responded. The riverbank was lined with drift from the night before.

"You're always out here."

"Yes, we are."

The spokesmen squared off in advance of their parties. Alexander and Gabriel moved up alongside their companion.

The younger boy made a show of looking around before he turned back swinging at Philippe, who expected the deliberate punch, and took it on the left shoulder as he slammed the smaller boy in the chest, and followed him down to the ground.

Gabriel faced off against Baptiste, maybe drawn up against each other out of familiarity. The smaller boy raised his fists, scared, and Gabriel caught the front of his shirt with his left hand and cracked him in the eye with his knuckles. Baptiste sprawled out on the sand, but didn't seem to be hurt too badly as he covered his head with his arms.

"Stay down, and keep away from us," Gabriel said fiercely before moving off to help Alexander battle against two boys who fled as he approached.

"What happened?" Basil asked. Philippe had taken a few punches and blood from his nose was obvious on his shirt, though otherwise they had acquitted themselves well and returned carrying the wood in high spirits.

"We were in a fight," Philippe said, speaking first as he had before.

"With who?"

The other men continued to let Basil handle the interrogation.

Now, sensing real danger, Philippe looked to Gabriel, and he answered his father.

"With Baptiste Gravois, and some of those boys who were over here the other night." There was no reason to mention the little brother.

"Why?"

Gabriel waited a long time, but no one else spoke.

"Over wood."

"Was anyone hurt?"

"No one was hurt badly. I don't think any of them looked worse than Philippe."

His father shook his head angrily, and closed his maul of a fist.

"You think that's the answer? Fighting with all these people here?"

Gabriel shook his head as humbly as he was able.

"Apologize." Basil looked at the others for the first time. "All of you. And take them wood you brought back."

A barrier, unchallenged since Basil refused the Gravois that first night, had already existed between their fire and those down the beach, a divide that deepened after the fight. The weeks passed, and the ocean, already titanic in its winter majesty, seemed to swell further with the spring, huge frothy waves that crashed on the beach with a young man's vitality, but for all their violence, rode no closer to the fragile camps. The frosts came regularly at night for more than a month, turning the pale sand whiter, like a new crust of sugar carried in from the islands. Only once did they see flurries that dissolved into the ocean without sticking to anything but their lengthening hair.

"I hope that Evangeline and Benedict are better off than we are," Gabriel said to his father as they watched the snow.

Basil grunted, "It would have to be a pretty miserable place to make this one look welcoming."

Soldiers who guarded the food allocation had told Gabriel that the other ships from the Minas sailed for Massachusetts, Maryland, and Pennsylvania, but they heard nothing from them over the winter.

"How am I going to find her?" Gabriel asked his father. Basil stared out into the ocean while the light snow blew cleanly over their faces.

His father looked over at him bleakly. "You need to make sure that you keep yourself alive that long. Once we're out of here, we can worry about finding Evangeline."

They weren't the only ones chafing in their captivity. Several days after the confrontation over the wood, word passed up the beach that a large group had set off across the swamp the previous night. No one was exactly sure how many, or what their intention was when they made it through.

"And that," Alain said, "is the rub. Not crossing the swamp, but where we go afterwards. We don't seem to be guarded, but surely they'd take offense if we accidentally came too close to the city."

Gabriel and Philippe walked the beach the next day, but disagreed on their guesses of how many hundreds were still left after the winter. As the days grew longer, word of more attempted escapes came to them sporadically, even in their isolation, but the outcomes remained mysterious, as there was no communication, or even knowledge of whether those fleeing were alive or dead. Neither guards nor slaves ever made mention that some of the Acadians were missing.

"They probably just think they've died of some malady and we stuck them in the swamp with the others," Basil said. "No one's been out to count us."

Seemingly since arrival, they had watched from their camp as neighbors hauled their dead to the swamp, feeding the disease with the festering bodies it had already claimed. But they did notice that by late spring, the daily ration the slaves carried out had shrunk, and after walking the beach again Gabriel guessed their number had been halved between sickness, flight, and occasional drownings. What had truly cured his fear of water, Gabriel reasoned, was the lurking swamp, clearly more a harbinger of death than even the powerful chill of the waves. It was clear to all of them that the swamp would have them unless they forced a more violent end at the hands of the soldiers who might wait for the escapees past the pestilential margin.

One spring morning they awoke to find the Gravois and their camp departed without a word for one of the vacated sites further down the beach, and they were isolated in their captivity again. Before they could even locate their old neighbors, the fire ring was claimed by a group of Mi'kmaq, who migrated from further down the beach.

"I'd heard the sauvages were part of the last escape attempt." Viktor said that night as they watched the newcomers settle in, speaking of the most recent exodus from their prison.

"There was an escape recently?" Alexander asked.

"That's the word from down the beach."

"Where do you think they go?" Alexander asked.

"Maybe the redcoats shoot them?" Basil said.

"Stop scaring the boys," Alain said. "That emissary said there were hardly more English than there were of us."

"Well, our numbers have thinned since we arrived," Basil said.

"Even so, all of those people can't be soldiers," Alexander said.

"Smart lad. So if they're not being shot, what exactly is happening to them?" Viktor asked.

"Maybe they're just rounded up and put in a real jail in town. The English found new prisons for all of us before we left home," Basil settled on another negative possibility.

"Which means we should wait for some kind of distraction before we try our escape," Alain said.

"Like what?" Gabriel asked.

"Well, things change slow enough around here. We'll know it when it comes," Alain concluded hopefully.

"So what should we do about the Mi'kmaq in the meantime?" Gabriel asked.

"Stay away from them so they don't infect us," Basil said.

"What makes you think they're contagious?" Viktor asked.

"What makes you think they aren't?"

The rain began with huge slow drops, individual beads of warmth devoured on impact by the gray, churning ocean as the fourth ship and last bedraggled member of the incoming convoy emerged from the heavy mists hanging over the harbor's mouth. It quickly intensified, loudly pelting the prison's sugarcane fence as they were hurried away from the swelling waves back to the flimsy captivity. Across the river, their refugee countrymen disembarked as the short deluge slackened, leaving them to mill about on the beach like gulls waiting for a feasting tide.

"Goddamnit," came the high angry whine of a South

Carolina man on guard, one of the few words Gabriel always recognized. It seemed directed at him, though it could have been any of the twenty of them standing in the breakers, staring across at their kin. The guard turned away.

The newly arrived Acadians piled off the boats, dragging and pulling each other, but otherwise empty-handed. Gabriel remembered staring across the water that first time, a sinking realization in the quiet white beach. Of course, they and their crude huts must loom large in the imagination of this second wave of deportees, proof they weren't going back. After a moment of watching the frail newcomers, Gabriel figured most knew before they arrived that they were unlikely to see home again.

Gabriel saw neither Evangeline nor her father among them.

"That bunch isn't from Pisquid, or your village either, I'm sure," Alexander said what Gabriel already worried over as they sat squinting at the opposite shore. The newcomers still wore the wool pants the earlier exiles had long since transitioned to stuffing in the walls of their shanties.

"It doesn't matter where they're from, this is exactly what we've been waiting for," Basil said.

"They'll be confused tonight," Alain said. "This is the best chance we've had yet."

"Or are likely to get," Basil said. "Let's find out who else is sick of this place."

The large group of men staring at the arrivals through the tangled cane and thorn abandoned their study after he finished speaking and peeled away from the perimeter to spread the word through the compound. Gabriel caught his father's elbow.

"I need to make sure that Evangeline isn't over there," he said quietly.

"We're leaving in a few hours, Gabriel," his father said. He looked at his son. "How do you intend to get across?"

"Swim, I guess."

"Why don't you carry a piece of that wall down to the river. With a little cover we might be able to cross unnoticed."

"You'll come with me?" Gabriel asked.

"You're not going over there alone," his father answered.

They waited until near dark, and pushed their float out into the river, kicking quietly for the opposite shore, loud with the barking of the colonials as they sorted through the newcomers. They had to swim hard in the middle of the river as the current pushed them toward the sea, but crossed easily, and waded out, dripping, but otherwise unremarkable among the Acadians crowding the little harbor they had overlooked for the past half year. It was refreshing to be out of their proscribed confinement, even if only to visit another prison, Gabriel thought, looking hopefully around in the sultry summer dusk.

"Let's go," Basil said. "We've got two hours, maybe, before we need to get back."

They were longer than that, moving up the beach, asking after Evangeline and Benedict, but everyone they asked hailed from the settlements around Beaubassin, though many of them had gotten further north even than that before being apprehended. After walking their length, they stood considering the silhouettes of the new schooners, as though the ships might still be holding the two they sought.

"We should go, Gabriel," Basil said. They retraced their route, back along the harbor to the river, but their float was gone.

"It's probably in a fire by now," Gabriel guessed while his father eyed the river.

"Stay just upriver of me as we go across," Basil said in response.

"We shouldn't look for something else?" Gabriel asked.

Basil shook his head, "It's getting late, son. We had better make sure we don't get left behind."

Despite the exhaustion, Gabriel couldn't sleep when they returned to their camp, and could tell from the occasional rustlings that his father was as awake as he. The rain had cleared the lingering humidity, but the night remained far warmer than his loft would have been this early in the summer, or almost ever out on the peninsula with the bay blowing. The bright stars helped him forget his home's smoky bedding back in Grand Pre. They were slightly twisted in this southern sky but more familiar by far than the moon, tonight just a fingernail's sliver, low and yellow as it sank into the ocean. His father sat up, checked their canteens, and found them already full of tepid river water.

An hour later, he and his father squatted with their companions. Dawn whispered over the velvet waves, and the darkness of the beach hummed with the unseen preparations, as those who would flee began to lose patience waiting for the sun's arrival. Someone would break, would fly too early, but that was the elegance of the plan. Wait until someone doesn't do what they're supposed to, then follow their lead. Numbers, dim light and the sleepy confusion of their foe were their timid allies. The six of them wouldn't be the first to break, but they weren't going to be the last out either. Basil led them and Viktor and Alain brought up the rear. Between the men, Gabriel and Philippe flanked Alexander in case his leg gave out in the swamp.

The sound of movement rolled over them in the pre-dawn blackness, and unbidden, they joined the herd. Gabriel helped Alexander through the sugarcane perimeter and then walked slowly behind his father, waiting as Alain and Viktor cleared the barrier. They picked up their pace, still stepping carefully over the sandy soil, and finally, as they became comfortable in the dark, trotted across the sands with the irresistible feeling of the stampede all around, Gabriel keeping his left foot in his father's right footfalls.

Angry shouts turned them haphazard for a moment, but they started quickly when they felt no hands, and saw no nearby torches. Basil slowed their column again moments later, surprising Gabriel though he heard splashing all around him as they reached the swamp, alive with grasshoppers in flight, muck sucking their feet out from under them like grasping hands.

Gabriel had looked over the marsh several times a day during their months of captivity. Usually, it seemed a pathetically slim barricade between their captive isolation and freedom. Its thinness disguised its true purpose, strangling them with diseases born in its filthy pools. So you waded through a swamp, the sensibly cautious among them asked, then where did you go. Outside of smoke from the city, the scrublands offered few clues as to their surroundings.

The water was at his boots, then hip deep, as they waded over roots, stumps and thick marsh grasses which Gabriel mistook for snakes several times. Then he tripped over a stump and went down, crying out in surprise, then fright, as he recognized the round stump as the skull of a corpse. He stayed on his knees in the muck helplessly for a moment before his father yanked him to his feet, and they slogged on, racing the outlines of other escaping men as reflected light gripped the coastline in glorious anticipation of the day.

The exposure as the light broadened into full day gave them second life, and they kept moving through the afternoon, their column breaking into a ragged pack, exhorting each other as they jogged, taking strength from the nearness of so many other runners, all moving slowly, blindly west through the balmy summer morning.

Gabriel ran, bumping his father occasionally and being jostled from behind, but within an hour they outdistanced much of the headless mass of men they raced. Visible in the daylight they saw they were paced by five of the Mi'kmaq as they turned north away from the bulk of the exodus which steered south along the coast.

The three older Acadians, decision makers still in exile, discussed their limited options in front of the boys.

"If we head south and get ahead of the pack we might be able to get our hands on a boat." Viktor puffed, still hoping there might be a return to his fields.

"Most people are headed south," Alain ventured neither support nor discouragement. "We'd be with a larger group."

As Basil pointed out to the others, there were certain to be more settlements further south along the coast, and the risks were probably greater there than in a straight break for the interior.

"Lost is the best you can hope for when you're running away," Basil philosophized.

Despite hearing infrequent gunshots in the distance, they slowed in the afternoon sun, and finally contented themselves with walking until they found a damp gully, where they collapsed, seeking any refuge with Charleston's smoke seeming right before them. The stream was a disappointing trickle in the gash on the lush landscape, even in spring a low flow. The heavy grass they'd been trampling for the past few hours grew over the bank's edge, jutting out like the mustache over a pronounced lip. Gabriel ducked his head under it, out of the sun, grunting fiercely as he propped himself on his elbows to drink from the canteen, one of two that had sloshed with every step of the morning, his thirst eventually distracting him completely from fears of pursuit.

"It's not that hot a damn day," Basil barked as he joined Gabriel in the shade. His chest heaved as he slurped on one of his canteens.

"How's the leg, Alexander?" Gabriel asked.

"Fine," he answered.

"Let's wait until dark," Alain said with an eye on the sun. "In a couple hours we can move undetected."

"And then what?" Viktor asked.

"We can follow this creekbed west and hope it leads us to actual water," Alain suggested.

"Good enough for the present," Basil said.

Exhausted from his search for Evangeline the night before, Gabriel slept deeply until his father's firm hand woke him in the darkness.

They ran in file through the night, listening for sounds of pursuit during brief pauses to allow Alexander and Viktor to catch up. As the sun rose, they found a grove of pines and collapsed into the needles.

Gabriel woke in a sweat. He sat up without sense of where he was or how long he'd been sleeping. The afternoon sun was bright above them. Water, he thought, feeling the back of his tongue swollen and plastered on his throat. He stood, groaning out loud as his thighs once again were forced to bear the tiresome burden of his body, and found a half-full canteen.

His father rolled over in alarm at the noise, and then gave

him an angry stare. The other men grumbled themselves awake while Alexander slumbered undisturbed. Seeing him, Gabriel was tempted to try for another hour of sleep. They were all accounted for after the dark, disorienting marathon.

"When did it get so hot?" Philippe croaked. "My ear's sweating."

Gabriel laughed with the crowd and started rubbing on his thighs, digging in as hard as he could with the heels of his palms.

"We need to find some water," his father said, right to business.

"There's Charleston," Alain said, pointing to the smoke in the eastern sky where Gabriel had grown accustomed to finding only ocean. "We've put the city past us, at least."

"So where do we go now?" Gabriel asked.

"We're going to have to find some food somehow," Viktor said.

"We can manage with just water for one more day," Basil responded. "Chew on some bark if you get too hungry."

"We should try to get farther from Charleston before we chance a farm," Alain agreed. "People around here might be accustomed to escapees."

They ran again that night, and foraged for groundnuts the next morning, uprooting the flowering vines, and chewing the tubers as they walked slowly that day.

A thin column of smoke rising peacefully into the light blue sky greeted them the next morning when they awoke.

"They'll have some food," Philippe said.

"Maybe they'll give us some," Viktor said.

"Or turn us in," Basil responded.

"He's right," Alain said. "There's a war going on out here, and we're the enemy."

"We can't eat roots forever," Philippe complained. "They probably have an orchard."

They considered the smoke for several minutes.

"Fruit is hardly better than foraging in the woods," Alain said. "We need to get in that house."

"Let's go see what it looks like," Basil said.

From the woods a pasture stretched up to a large clapboard home, with roughcut windows facing all sides. Tree limbs hung visibly heavy with peaches on the slopes near the dwelling. The ground smelled fertile, and several cows ranged about the house.

"This is not going to be easy," Basil cautioned.

"We can't attack those people," Viktor said.

"We're not going to starve out here," Basil answered.

"What do you suggest?" Viktor asked.

"We wait until nightfall, and then surprise them," Basil said.

"No," Alain cut in. "It will be hard for us to see what we need to take, and easy for us to get separated afterward."

"So we're just to barge in?" Alexander asked. "How many people do you think are in there?"

No one answered him. After a few minutes a boy emerged from the house, and walked down to the stream at the edge of the cleared ground. The Acadians watched him fill the buckets. The boy returned slowly, the water buckets sloshing heavily at his sides.

"We should follow him in," Basil whispered.

"I can't do this," Viktor said.

"We don't have any choice," Basil returned coldly.

"Stay out here and gather peaches," Alain suggested. "The rest of us will go."

"What do we do when we get inside?" Gabriel asked his father.

Basil looked at him for a moment. "I'll go in first with Alain."

"But when we get inside?" Gabriel asked again.

"If we get our hands on that boy, they'll give us food to make us go away." Alain said.

"This is insane," Viktor interrupted. "We don't have any weapons."

"No, but that's something else we'll need," Basil answered. "Alexander, find a musket. Philippe, get everything you can carry from the kitchen. We'll keep the family at bay."

A girl in a white apron emerged from the house and scattered feed for the chickens that gathered noisily at her feet.

"There's our hostage," Alain said. "We need to go now."

The girl turned from them, clucking at the chickens, and the men burst from the woods, not ten meters distant. Gabriel covered the ground fastest and seized the girl's arm as she ran to the house, jerking her off her feet as she screamed. The others passed him and barged through the front door as he crouched beside her.

"We're not going to hurt you," Gabriel said. "We just need food."

He heard shouting inside. "Come on," he said.

Gabriel pulled the whimpering girl to her feet by wrists that felt as thin as his thumbs, and followed the men into the farmhouse.

The family was eating dinner. His father fought with a man over the table, where an old woman still held a trencher of stew. Philippe and Alexander menaced another woman and two boys who huddled in the corner. There was a door behind the table, and another opening deeper into the house.

"We need food and clothing. We don't want any trouble." Alain was shouting as Gabriel entered.

"Susan," the woman cried on seeing the girl in Gabriel's arms.

"Hold on," Basil said to the man struggling in his grasp. "He's got your daughter."

"Go on, boys," Alain said.

"We need food, Madame," Philippe said to the woman. "Give us what we want, and we'll be gone." He pushed her through the open door into the kitchen.

Alexander took a musket down from the fireplace.

"Give that to Alain," Basil said. "And go see what you can find."

Alexander obeyed and followed into the kitchen. Gabriel backed away from the others with the girl, pinning her to his chest while she struggled in his arms. He heard a noise behind him, and turned to see a boy enter the house carrying a musket as long as he was tall.

"Alain," Gabriel shouted, clinging to the girl.

Alain turned at his cry and saw the boy.

"Don't shoot," Alain said, as the boy fired.

The musket ball struck Alain in the stomach, erupting out his back to thud into the wall behind. He collapsed into a sitting position on the floor.

"Alain," Gabriel screamed again. Philippe and Alexander ran back into the room, loaded down with plunder.

Basil threw the man he restrained to the floor, and took the musket out of Alain's hands.

"You two get moving," Basil commanded. "Gabriel, drop that girl, and help Alain."

Acting as he was bidden, Gabriel lifted the older man to his feet as carefully as he could, and dragged him backwards from the house, trailing his friends. Viktor came on a run from around the house, bare-chested with his shirt tied into a sack and full of fruit.

After what seemed minutes, his father emerged as well, pointing the musket back through the open door. Basil took up Alain's legs, while Gabriel hefted under his arms, and they staggered down the hill into the woods.

They covered little ground in the hours following the raid, limited to the stumbling pace Basil set, carrying Alain on his back. They called a halt before sunset, and Basil and Viktor tried patching the musket hole with hurried poultices of moss and mud.

"I told you we shouldn't have done this," Viktor said to Basil as they worked.

"It may as well have been my idea," Alain said weakly. "Leave me alone, neither of you knows what you're doing."

He sat just outside their fireless circle at the foot of a tall-trunked maple, while they looked over their dearly bought spoils.

They had the musket and a cavalry officer's blade Alexander had discovered to go along with Philippe's sack of cornmeal and potatoes, and the unripe peaches. They ate handfuls of the cornmeal dampened with river water and bedded down for the night. Viktor took the early watch, and the night closed noisily around them, as Gabriel tried not to imagine soldiers happening across them while they slept.

When they woke the next morning, they found Alain, dead, holding the sword in one hand, his head slumped to one side as though examining the pommel of the weapon.

"It was right next to me when I went to sleep," Alexander said. "I didn't hear anything."

"I fell asleep," Viktor confessed. No one spoke for a moment.

"He couldn't have gone any further," Basil said.

They used sticks and rocks, rather than the knives, to dig the grave, but still the peaty earth gave way easily before their simple tools, and the hole was dug in an hour.

They walked slowly that afternoon, the boys respectfully trailing out of earshot of the men as they talked.

"I've never seen anyone die from a gunshot before," Philippe mused.

"You still haven't," Gabriel pointed out.

"I've never dug a grave," Alexander said.

"I dug one for my sister Jacqueline's husband last summer," Philippe said. "He fell off his roof, not that far, but his head hit a rock and he died."

They walked onward, the two of them looking at him expectantly.

"When I was thirteen, my mother and three brothers drowned in the Minas," Gabriel said quickly. "We never found their bodies. We had a service, but my father and I didn't dig graves."

"Do you have any other brothers or sisters?" Alexander asked.

"No."

"Jesus," Philippe breathed.

They walked for a while, following a stream running through a limestone trench that was already deeper than where they'd buried Alain.

"We haven't seen a fire since the farm," Philippe broke the

silence. "How far do you think we're going to keep walking?" he asked.

"Until we find the French colonies west of here," Alexander said after a moment's consideration.

"We're sure they're out here?" Philippe asked.

Alexander nodded. "You remember that man back on the beach mentioned a war. We've got to find whoever's fighting the English, and then we can go back home."

"I don't see us going back to Acadia," Gabriel interjected.

"Where will you go?" Alexander asked.

Gabriel shrugged. "We haven't talked about it." He knew no alternatives. "There's a girl I've got to find before I start calling anywhere home again."

Huddled in the rags of their clothing, they didn't make a fire for more than a week. The forest stretched south behind them, with no change on the horizon save the same steady rise they'd climbed since burying Alain in the hills below them. Soon the men stopped hearing angry squawking from squirrels and chipmunks displaced with their passage, and finally they were alone in the woods, though they saw traces of camps everywhere. As the weather cooled, they reused fire rings most nights, warily, but without incident.

"Why do you think this was abandoned?" Gabriel asked, as they passed over ground which had recently housed a village, fire rings and partial frames of shelters plain among the already canvassed ground.

"The war," Viktor said. "Anyone who is able is running from these mountains, because the armies are going to meet each other on one side or the other, and maybe both. We're just on a different border between the empires." He stopped to look back through the woods. "Losing a home remains, by a narrow margin, better than losing one's life." He spat in disgust.

"But why leave?" Alexander asked. "We haven't seen any soldiers."

"The woods have grown quiet these last weeks, haven't they?" Basil asked, and continued without waiting for affirmation. "There's been fighting near here recently."

They walked through colder days and freezing nights, which brought an end to the gnats and mosquitoes that had dogged them closer to the coast. Most days the boys took the musket ahead to hunt, and they rarely had meat to complement what they could graze. As the nights grew colder they smeared the deer fat on their faces and hands for protection, and eventually insulated their clothing as well.

"Old men always say that bear grease is the warmest," Viktor complained as he smeared it on after warming it in the fire.

"You are an old man," Philippe said, hesitating and watching Gabriel and Alexander.

"Well, that's why I'm saying it, for your benefit," Viktor replied. "This deer wouldn't keep my toes warm if they were in the fire."

"Be thankful that we've got it," Basil said of Gabriel's kill. "I haven't heard much out there lately."

They continued north as the trees finished dropping their leaves, the mountains shrinking in the distance beyond like men growing older. Finally they came to a pass where the foothills only rose to larger versions of themselves, and they followed deer trails across the high valley away from the looming peaks to the south.

One day, in the cloudless distance to the east, Gabriel saw

the smudge of fire. They had been running for months without ever losing sight of English fires, he thought.

The following day a storm blew the smoke against the peaks and they could taste the ash on the breeze, though they could no longer see the army.

"They're gaining on us," Philippe said, and rattled Alexander's sword. "We're lucky you've got this."

They headed downhill through fallen snow, waking before light and walking until after dark as the days got shorter and colder. Finally they saw more smoke on the western horizon, familiar enough that Gabriel worried they'd circled around, or the sun had somehow misled them. Soon after seeing the sign, they heard shouting, French shouting, and realized that this smoke of war meant an end to their wandering.

The empty fort trembled as they were led to the quartermaster's office. The room was a dank hovel crouched below the western wall where they found the fat officer removing his gray wig, which he left off his desk as the men filed in. The scalp dominated Gabriel's attention, the man's voice ethereal in crowded shadows.

"You men will have to remain here until the imminent hostilities are concluded," Pritchard, the French soldier, told them. "There is every possibility we will require the services of militiamen before the campaigning season closes. Otherwise, I've a need for laborers." The man interrupted himself with a long, wet cough. "Either way, you'll be fed, and for another day or two I can promise a roof over your heads, so that's something anyway." He passed a pouch of tobacco to Viktor, adding, "For starters, though, men that've run bare-assed from Carolina probably haven't been holding much smoke. Welcome to the service of His Most August Majesty, King Louis."

The fat man housed them in a low guardhouse just inside the east gate.

"You can sleep where you like tonight," Pritchard told them. "We'll see if the men these beds belong to return."

Gabriel dreamt of Evangeline that night, tipping her over into a canoe, falling naked on top of her, her hair on his arm, her hand reaching down, closing over him, before he realized it was his own under a scratchy wool blanket. Gabriel sat upright in the darkness. His father snored next to him, his face thankfully turned away. He couldn't see if anyone else on the long bunk was awake.

Gabriel went outside to calm down. He hadn't been in a bed since the night before Winslow's man struck his father down in the church, and he hadn't been near a woman in the weeks since they raided the farm.

That day, they joined the wounded regulars on the eastern wall as shadows of people crested the ridge to their east, the track toward the approaching English army, screeching as they came.

"The Delaware," filtered down the line of warriors, but Gabriel waited until his father let his musket rest on the parapet before following suit.

"You might not get to upgrade those firearms after all gentlemen," Pritchard said, glassing the incomers. "There seem to be more headed this way than went out in this morning."

"You sound disappointed," Basil commented, not trying hard to hide his disdain for the quartermaster.

"Mouths to feed, sir, and I'm the one that finds something to put in them."

Another smaller column emerged behind, the French van-guard. It still looked to Gabriel like they might attack the fort. It certainly looked like they'd be able to splinter the palisade they stood atop. The stacked logs looked like they might be able to stop a bullet.

"Would these stop a cannonball?" Gabriel asked.

Basil frowned.

"These walls?" the quartermaster interjected in his father's place. "No chance," he said with a snickering certainty before speaking louder for the benefit of the thirty or so men watching their army return from the field. "When the English reach those cliffs with their cannon, this place is dead." And returned to his lisping speaking voice, addressing the newcomers, "Get your hands on some food if you get a chance, and figure out which boat you're getting on."

"You've just won a victory, and you're still running away?" his father said incredulously.

"Monsieur, this is a simple matter. They can shoot at us, and we can't shoot at them. Look at those ridges. Our intelligence says the English and their colonials number in the thousands, with dozens of artillery pieces." He bit off his rant, and quietly said to Basil, "My intelligence says we're burning the fort tomorrow night."

Gabriel exchanged a glance with his father, and saw he wasn't going to ask any more questions. "So, where are you going?"

"South, boy, to find some French territory the English aren't quite ready to piss on." He looked around at the refugees on the parapet. "Does it make any difference, so long as I'm willing to bring you along?"

They returned to the guardhouse that night, which they now shared with a dozen unfamiliar men. Happy with the news they wouldn't have to defend the fort against the British, their new bunkmates didn't raise an objection over the unusually cramped quarters, and five of them ceded their bunks to sleep on the floor in front of the fire.

His father remained wary despite their overt friendliness, and sat upright in the corner of the bed, watching the long row of sleeping men. Gabriel slept, but he dreamt of blades, knives and bayonets, flashing and stabbing at him through the windy, empty darkness. He awoke with a start to find his father still awake, still staring down the long bed. Basil put his hand on his shoulder. Gabriel didn't fall back asleep, and feeling his restlessness, Basil removed his hand, and they kept vigil over the sleeping soldiers together.

The next morning they helped the French garrison carry ammunition from the fort to the canoes and barges that bobbed on the river, awaiting cargo and men to row them south. Once they had packed nearly two dozen of the small vessels full of provisions, Gabriel, Alexander and Philippe swam out into the river with some soldiers, one per boat, and they tied the flotilla together, passing heavy hemp rope through oar locks or cracks in the rafts. The water was refreshing, but all three of them were covered in mud by the time they finished slogging back across the beach to their clothes. Unlike most of the soldiers they got back into their rags while still wet before following the men they labored beside upriver to a rock beach.

The swimmers sat alone while other hands busied themselves in the fort, drying off in the midday sun and contemplating the unwieldy vessel they'd created in the channel. They sat in a loose circle and the man on Gabriel's right produced a pipe with blue beads and teeth dangling in short strands beneath the bowl.

"My mother told me God and His Majesty would save this land," he said as he tamped fresh tobacco down into the bowl, "but I see no evidence for it."

Gabriel forced himself not to look around for Basil on the empty riverbank before he puffed on the tobacco in the bowl. He didn't cough as he exhaled, and handed the pipe over to Alexander who inhaled dramatically and passed it along to Philippe, who blew a thin practiced-looking stream of smoke. Gabriel didn't know if his friends had smoked before. There hadn't been any tobacco over the months of wandering.

While they were securing the goods in the river, the Delaware and Wyandot had gathered brush together for the fire and now they heaped their tinder around the base of the fort, occasionally calling to one another. Basil saw the three of them headed up from the river and waved them over to where he, Viktor and the quartermaster lurked twenty paces from the fort's southern exposure. French soldiers in uniform dragged resisting prisoners out from the fort. Enough wood-smoke hung over the dismantling camp that Gabriel hoped the pipe smoke would be indistinguishable on his breath, but when he approached he saw his father had other concerns. French soldiers dragged their prisoners out of the fort, roughly lining them up along the wall. Their actions were in marked contrast to two Delaware, who went down the line, tenderly painting the English faces with ash. The twenty-two men stood, crying, praying, or silent, the blackface incongruous with the blue uniforms.

"We've got nowhere for prisoners now." Pritchard weakly defended the indefensible.

Another Delaware came forward with a spear, and started prodding one of the condemned. The man stood on the end of the line closer to the Acadians, shouting, "Cowards," at the French troops that encircled them.

"Cowards. Cowards. Cowards." He shouted each time the sauvage stuck him with the spear, louder and louder. After several strikes against the man's torso the Delaware backed off, stepped violently on the tip of his weapon, and broke off the stone point. He held up the edge for the man to see, close without threatening, and then put the spearhead in the soldier's coat pocket and left the now silent Englishman alone.

His father reclaimed Gabriel's attention, arguing with Pritchard.

"Then why did they bring them back here after the battle?" Basil had been addressing the official, but turned to him. "Military justice. Never has been, never will be such a thing. I'm not watching this."

"Then go wait by the water," Pritchard said simply. "Once the shooting stops, come on back and you can finish loading up."

The Acadians headed a little way down the river and stood in a group in the path until they heard the shots, three clusters of them. Gabriel wondered how many had been killed in each round.

His father shook his head and started up to the fort. "I'm going to get someone to take us out of here."

"I'll come with you," Gabriel said to his father's back as he followed Basil back to the fort. Torches were being lit ahead, in large numbers, too early to be needed for light. The bodies were still slumped in front of the wall as they approached, but a few had already been dragged around toward the gate facing east, where the English army would approach if the fort's defenders weren't already burning it to the ground.

A row of stakes had been driven into the ground before the

fort, and Gabriel watched one of the sauvages use a sword like a saw to behead the executed. The man worked methodically, severing heads as the executed men were dragged over to him. Others took the trophies and, howling, impaled them on the stakes. One missed his mark, cutting his hand instead on the stake, and flung the head away like it had bit him. It rolled awkwardly, and came to a rest with its face in the dirt, as though ashamed without its body.

"This is disgusting."

The tall officer who spoke seemed younger and cleaner than the other men, watching in horror only a few steps from Gabriel and his father. He started toward the bloody Delaware who crouched over the heads, changed his mind and stopped. The man looked around frantically as the Delaware were joined by the soldiers who had remained near the fort, and were now stripped to the chest from the heat of the fire, drunk, and moving toward the corpses. He drew his pistol and fired it in the air, but the shot was widely ignored.

"I'm leaving here tonight and I'll take anyone with me who wants to come," the officer called out loudly.

"Let's go," Basil said.

He turned to follow the officer, but Gabriel didn't immediately obey, captivated by the dark blood trailing down the lances, making new necks of the stakes.

"Gabriel." The edge of panic in his father's voice was unfamiliar, and he listened this time.

"What's happening?" Alexander asked when they reached the bank.

Gabriel just shook his head, unwilling to describe what he had seen. He waded out to a canoe where Basil was already positioned in the stern.

The Acadians paddled away with Pritchard and his goods, trailing the convoy as it carefully maneuvered through the night on the wide river that appeared darker for the lurid intensity of the pyre they passed.

Baltimore 1758

*Each succeeding year stole something from her beauty,
leaving behind it, broader and deeper, the gloom and the shadow.*

S PRING CAME TO BALTIMORE, AND EVANGELINE AND Jana sat on the front porch, tying fans out of turkey tails sent to town by Acadians who had been bound out to nearby farms. After the first winter on Charles Street, Governor Sharpe decreed that any unmarried Acadians older than fifteen had to secure employment. They worked for most of the year, but were allowed to return to the cities for the cold months when travel or escape would have been difficult. The system also meant that the plantation owners didn't have to feed the Acadians when they weren't working. Felician had prevailed on the sheriff that he needed help at the hospital, but his entreaties were received less sympathetically as the war raged on. Bernard and Julian would be gone for months next year, as there was additional need for tobacco pickers after the militia marshaled out. Even the tobacco farms kept poultry, however, and the Acadians gathered the feathers and periodically sold the fans at the Calvert Street dock. When measured against selling the fans to leering sailors and wealthy women who would use them for a few moments and pitch them in the harbor, Evangeline preferred just being given money in charity.

Bernard emerged from the house and lit his pipe. Felician followed him out clutching a recent issue of the Gazette.

"Governor Sharpe issued a law that prohibits Acadians from leaving town without a passport." Felician looked at Bernard as he spoke.

"That sounds like something a person would have no reason to want," Bernard said.

"It's insulting," Felician said. "Brandt told me they've been readying this since Fort Oswego fell. At least we'll know the French are winning the war when we don't have meat."

"And if you want to leave town?" Bernard asked.

"You have to get the passports from Gwinn. And he's not going to hand one over so you can head off trapping."

"Then there's no reason to ask," Bernard said. "But there's also no reason not to have meat on the table."

"Do you think this is worth the risk?" Evangeline asked Bernard.

"It doesn't matter. We are not going to disobey the law," Felician said.

"It won't be you that's breaking it, Felician. And this law applies to Acadians, which I'm not."

"That's not how they view you," Felician shot back. "You'll bring the militia down on us. I don't remember you having much luck evading the English in Grand Pre."

"No, I didn't, Felician, you're right. Don't concern yourself. You'll just have to turn me in if you're uncomfortable," Bernard replied. The men looked to Evangeline, but she gave no further hint of her thoughts.

That evening, Jana discovered a bloody newspaper left on the front porch and brought it upstairs so they could examine it together. The first page described the slaughter of a garrison after its surrender at Fort William Henry. Inside, Brandt had written of a family forced to abandon their saw mill outside Frederick for fear of French attack.

"That's not human blood," Bernard said.

"How do you know?" Evangeline asked.

"I'm just guessing."

The Acadians avoided Baltimore's citizenry as much as possible in the days following, but eventually Evangeline cautiously resumed her collecting. Not begging, but rather collecting for the hospital, she said, as she went to the Smiths, the Lows, the Woods, the Gays, the Carys, who owned the inn by the dock. The Fottrell House had been a remarkable piece of charity, but much of the friendliness in town had deteriorated since.

A servant greeted Evangeline at the door and withdrew to alert the master, leaving her alone in the foyer of the Smiths' brick home.

"Hello, Evangeline," Charles Smith called from inside. "I'll be with you in a moment." She stayed in the hallway by the door, glad for a chance to look into the rich man's mirror.

She wouldn't be parted from the top hat which she wore now tucked down over her hair, and was pleased to see how she was holding up underneath it. Her cheekbones were a little sharper, but the angularity only gave her a seriousness she might have lacked with softer features. Her skin tone hadn't faded in exile. It was still the color of a fallow field needing just a little rain, as

her father used to describe it. "My little squaw," he would sometimes call her as a girl. Nearly all the Acadians appeared dark-
complexioned and exotic next to the Marylanders, who carried
their pastiness like a shield. She tilted the brim lower over her
eyes, frowned, and reset it a little higher. Squinting at the reflection caused faint crows' feet, and she smiled, imagining the wrinkled old walnut she would look like as an old woman next to
Gabriel. She had always wanted to be older than she was, though
the reasons had changed.

Besides the hat, she was wrapped in an oiled cape, covering her black dress and stockings. All her clothes were black.
She'd adopted her guardian's raiment, and now thought it suited her as well as him she thought, the color of mourning appropriate for the time and the newly unwelcoming city. Despite the
drab ensemble, their few remaining patrons, Charles Smith
included, preferred that she made the rounds collecting, and it
gave her a reminder to look after her appearance more than she
might. A couple years of lean eating and hard living had stream-
lined her already small face, and the mature, frightening beauty
of a woman had replaced her girlish attractiveness. She felt the
difference, knew it as men stopped talking to her in passing on
the street, though they still stared. She would have been upset if
they had.

"I should give you that mirror," Smith said, also admiring
her reflection. "You've got more reason to use it than I ever
will." Evangeline couldn't help but notice that he didn't move to
take it off the wall.

She turned and smiled at him. "Please don't ask me to insult
our most sympathetic supporter, Monsieur."

"Well, you know we're happy to help. Someone's got to
take what we have." The Smiths were childless, and though his

wife looked like she still might be in her forties, Evangeline hadn't mentioned the unexpected happiness of her birth in her mother's advanced age. She didn't want to deprive them of possible hope, but she felt hers was an exceptional case, one that while not without precedent, didn't allow for similar accounts.

He gave her a change purse and Evangeline pocketed it with the same motion, keeping the exchange as unobtrusive as possible. The Smiths' unflagging generosity was overwhelming. Someday, she would again be the one extending the full hand.

"Thank you sir. Blessings on you and your wife." She started toward the door, but looked back at the man. "I wish that we didn't have to keep coming back to you, but you should know your money kept people alive last winter."

"Hush, girl. You and the Father are the ones doing the work." They moved to the door and he let her out. "I just hope it doesn't rain on you today."

As Evangeline sat in the kitchen with Sofia after dinner, they were interrupted by a crash on the thin wooden wall of the hospital, followed quickly by another. Tempers had been flaring in Baltimore since the massacre at Fort William Henry, and hecklers from the Rogers' tavern had tormented them several times since the weather had warmed, singing drunkenly in the windows. It sounded like a larger gathering tonight.

"God damn the French. God save King George." The drunks unified their intoxicated chanting.

"God will damn you," Felician called back from the porch, loud, clear, and sober.

Evangeline left Sofia in the kitchen and found Julian staring uncertainly at the door.

"Are you coming, Julian?" she asked.

"Father Felician told me to stay inside." Julian saw that he had missed a chance to prove his bravery. There was more shouting from outside, and they went out onto the porch together.

Felician stood on the stairs, clenching a musket, but not aiming it at the small crowd standing in the street. Outside of more bottles, the five men weren't armed. Bernard stood in the porch's shadows, even quieter now that he was healed. He'd been waiting for this, she thought, for some violence in which to prove himself. No, in which he could repay his debt.

"I thought there were only old women in there," one of the men acknowledged her presence. Another started up the steps.

Felician backed away and raised the musket.

"There's just one shot in that gun," one of the men said. "Go on and get her."

"Easy for you to say," the man in the lead responded as he stopped on the first step.

A bottle flew out of the crowd, invisible in the darkness until it struck Felician. He staggered backward and the crowd advanced. Bernard met them, charging down the steps and knocking the first man from his feet before plowing into a second. The others surged over them.

"No," Evangeline called, too late to stop him.

"One of you is about to die," Felician screamed and aimed the musket.

The men paused, and Bernard emerged from the melee, dragging a man back toward the porch by the hair, his knife at the drunk's throat.

"Maybe two," the trapper said.

"Stop this," Evangeline implored, and stepped forward,

placing herself between the musket and their besiegers. "We wish you no harm. We don't have anything to do with the war. The only way we get news is when one of you comes by drunk to curse it at us. We didn't even know who the redcoats were until they burned our homes."

"You attacked us," one of the men said. He pointed at the trapper. "We're taking him to Gwinn."

"No, you are not," Bernard said.

"No one's going anywhere but home," Evangeline said. "And when you do, remember that it's been three years since we've seen ours. Let him go," she said to the trapper.

He looked up at her for a moment, and then shoved the man toward his fellows.

"There's suffering enough to go around," Evangeline said.

The men in the street stared up at the porch, contemplating their odds.

"Leave us alone," she screamed at them, loud enough to carry past the men into the dark houses of their neighbors who permitted this abuse. "We don't have anything you can take. Go home," Evangeline finished. The drunks' hostility drained into the street and they withdrew.

Bernard and Julian kept watch at the door. Evangeline followed Felician upstairs where he removed his liquor-soaked robe and put on a linen shirt before pacing angrily.

"They're just angry that they're losing the war," Evangeline said to calm him.

Felician nodded sharply.

"They know that they'll never be able to take Quebec." Felician gathered himself for a moment before continuing. "The city is built on cliffs rising straight up from the Saint Lawrence, a river nearly as wide as Maryland's bay. Even compared to the

old cities of Europe, the fortress is impregnable. And the seminary," she'd heard much on this subject already, "is without
compare. Its spires are the most beautiful object man has fashioned in the New World. And even the church's walls are thick
enough to stop a cannonball." He remembered the object of his
anger. "By contrast, this has and always will be a worthless frontier town."

Despite the priest's rage, she appreciated his image of the
holy fortified capital, majestic above the river. After losing their
homes, it was good for all of them to hear of something that the
English couldn't conquer.

Felician's anger had abated by the time he finished mass the
following morning, and he was cheerful as he sat on the porch,
preaching still though his audience had dwindled to only her and
the twins.

"Remember the Exodus. The Lord said to his people, I will
not go up among you, or I would consume you on the way, for
you are a stiff-necked people. But as I told Benedict in Grand Pre,
rest his soul, implacable stubbornness is the great virtue of your
people. And we can say with conviction that the Lord does not
condemn his people for stubbornness. Rather, it is a quality he
sounds in his greatest champions. Human tenacity acting in con-
cert with faith is what sustained the Israelites in Egypt, and it is
what sustains us now."

He looked at her, and spoke as though the twins didn't
stand among them. "Remember also, from the Exodus and the
promised conquest of Canaan. God said that he would send an
angel before the people."

Felician went to relate the previous night's events to Gwinn,
and after he had gone, Bernard and Julian left to check on the

traps. Evangeline and Jana distributed cornmeal mush and tea among the elderly residents. If people took sick again as they had that first winter, they would return the house's downstairs to hospital quarters, but otherwise, they only accepted people into their care when they had a bed to put them in, and no one had died in months. The mud houses had expanded, and most families now maintained their own shacks along the stretch now called French Town.

She and Jana heated water and took it upstairs to bathe. Ever since Evangeline was a girl, soaking her hair in warm water had been one of her favorite sensations. She sat on the floor as Jana brushed out her tangles.

"It's about to go curly on me."

"I don't ever remember it this long," she said.

"I forget that we grew up as neighbors."

"I don't."

Jana fed her hair into the water in the silence after her comment, and Evangeline took a turn brushing out Jana's hair, lighter brown and finer than her own.

She remembered how she'd looked in the mirror, and considered Jana's breasts. Evangeline might have wanted them for herself if they didn't look so heavy and ripe. But the girl was pretty.

"Has anyone caught your eye lately, Jana?" Evangeline asked.

"No, I suppose not." It didn't seem like the girl wanted to talk about it, and Evangeline tried changing the subject.

"It felt good to shout at those drunks last night, like I purged something. It's strange that I couldn't have said those things if I were a man. Or at least, my angry words wouldn't have ended the hostilities." Evangeline shrugged. "It's important to remember the power that we have as women, when the world so frequently tries to remind us of our fragility."

"Like the soldier in Grand Pre?" Jana asked.

Evangeline nodded. She was able to think of the blue-coated man without overwhelming fear or revulsion by now, though she still couldn't stand to think of his name.

"Speaking of an understanding of your power as a woman," Jana began, "you must have an idea as to how my brother feels about you."

"I think that I do."

"I've noticed you've gone out of your way not to be alone with him."

"I have, but not because I don't trust him to act like a gentleman."

"You don't want to encourage him, but you don't want to tell him no."

Evangeline waited for a moment.

"No, I won't tell him no. But it's not going to happen." Evangeline turned in the tub, looked into the sad brown eyes, the same as her brother's. "I don't see love as a choice, Jana."

"I'm not sure Julian does either."

That's not the point, Evangeline thought, as the girl's argument took on a higher pitch.

"The two of you could have a life together, where there's so little opportunity for the rest of us. There's a chance for some real happiness with a boy who's loved you as long as he knew you existed."

"That's sweet, and I wish happiness for Julian, but I wish to wait on it myself. The catastrophe doesn't exist that would blot out my feelings for Gabriel. I'm not sure when or how I'm going to see him again, but thinking about that meeting, that's what gives me strength. Gabriel's a part of my life, the part I'm most conscious of, even without him being here. I think about how what I'm doing here might impress him. I think about him every night before I fall asleep, and I know that he's thinking about me. I love him, and I'm going to find him, and we're going to have our life again. And I'm going to be the same woman he knew. Things might happen to either of us that we can't control, but what is in my power to do to stay true to him, I will." Gabriel with another woman felt ludicrous, impossible, stranger even than imagining herself with another man. She remembered that he preferred to do what he was told.

"What if one of the things that happens to you is that you never leave this town? This war could last ten more years."

"Ten or one hundred, my heart's gone with Gabriel. When we can finally leave, if we still haven't gotten any word of him, I'll follow my heart to find him. My instincts will lead me to him. And I know it's going to work, because I'm going to keep searching until it's true."

"That sounds a little far-fetched."

What did this farmer's daughter know of far-fetched, Evangeline thought. Wasn't being stripped of your homes in a war that devoured your youth far-fetched? Evangeline sighed and got dressed.

"It's all I have."

The girls fell silent, considering the impassible terrain between them, and Jana left the room before Evangeline thought of anything else to say.

She was still sitting in the bedroom, lost in thought, when Felician came back from the docks. "Nothing new today," he said, and then noticed her introspection. "What's wrong?"

"I've been talking to Jana about her brother," Evangeline ventured what she considered her simplest problem.

"And Jana wonders why you still wait for Gabriel?" he guessed.

Evangeline nodded. "Jana says he's been in love with me for his entire life." She didn't know why she sounded miserable about it.

"And what do you say?"

"That there aren't two of anything, or anyone. I told her that my heart has gone with Gabriel, and I can only follow." She looked at him, near tears. "What do you think, Father?"

"I think that affection cannot be wasted. Even if your love can't reach Gabriel, still, that affection lives on in you. That which the fountain sends forth returns again to the fountain. Draw on your well of patience, and do not put aside your labor. In sorrow and silent affection you are strong, and patient endurance will purify you, and Gabriel as well. What you suffer will strengthen and purify the union that awaits you, and render it all the more worthy of Heaven."

"I wish that's what I had told her."

"Have faith in your convictions, and everything will be as it should."

"So, I have become like Hannah," Evangeline said.

"How do you mean?"

"Praying desperately to the Lord."

"For Gabriel, not a child," the priest replied.

She raised her eyebrows sharply. "I understand that. But what she was asking for, she knew she wouldn't get to keep, either. Gabriel and I will never be young together. But rather than giving my child as a servant to the Lord, I give myself. And to serve Him, I serve you, with my youth. If I can get to Gabriel before either of us is entirely gray, there's hope for us. Until then, I'm yours."

Bernard called them awake upstairs one night, holding a candle while Evangeline and Jana joined the men in their quarters. Bernard rolled his blanket up before facing them.

"I was wrong about the traps, Felician, though I wouldn't say you were right."

"What happened?" Felician asked.

"I found a boy caught in one this morning."

"What? Is he dead?" Felician asked quickly.

"No, but I mangled his arm. I never used these damn jaw traps in Canada."

"Why did you try them now?" Evangeline asked.

"Because that's what they use around here. And because there's more meat on a deer than on a possum. I never used to bother with elk or deer at all, but you won't catch one in a snare."

"Where is the boy now?" Evangeline asked.

"I carried him and the cursed trap to the smith so that he could cut it off. It looked like wolves had gotten after him."

"Have you spoken to his parents?"

"They'll probably claim I was on their land. I didn't seek them out."

"Very kind," Felician said.

"I left the boy my money pouch," Bernard said quietly. He checked to make sure his knife hung at his belt. "I'm leaving."

The priest scoffed. "Will Gwinn hunt for you?"

"If Gwinn's all that comes after me I can hide uphill. Town sheriffs aren't my worry."

"I wish you weren't going off like this," Julian said.

"I only wish it hadn't taken that boy to make obvious what should have been plain from the start." Bernard slung his roll on his back and looked across the faces of the small crowd. He nodded. "Take care of yourselves, and keep an eye out for me if you're ever on a river." He disappeared down the stairs and into the dark night.

Fresh from Sunday's mass, Evangeline headed down awakening Calvert Street, through the door of the Cary's Inn on the water, followed by Jana and then Julian, their reluctant bodyguard. The only movement in the bar was a hefty man she didn't recognize, his apron and consciousness all that separated him from a man who slept undisturbed with his face on the table, right hand gripped tight around a mug. The barkeep left the slumbering drunk's table untouched and swung toward them, an earring glistening in a sweaty ear as he sized them up.

"You're a bit ahead of the after church crowd. This morning we've just been catering to last night's patrons."

"We don't want anything to drink." Her tone conveyed her lack of amusement.

He looked at her. "No, I guess you don't. Well, if you girls are looking for protection from the scurvy-looking fellow that followed you in, I'm your man." He belched, found a half-full mug on the bar and gulped it down.

As crass as the barman was, Evangeline briefly wondered what sort of reception she might have gotten across the street at Rogers'.

"We're hoping you could show us any recent lists that've come into town."

The man nodded, put down the empty mug, and belched again. "Where are you interested in?"

"Carolina, sir." Politeness cost her nothing.

"Carolina, hell. They're either dead already or they wish they were. Girl, Baltimore is Canaan itself compared to that place. Consider yourself lucky to be up the street with a roof over your head."

She didn't react angrily, but calmly asked, "Do you have one?"

He looked through a sheaf of papers nailed behind the bar and ripped one loose. "Here you are, Madame. It's only a few weeks old, but it sounds like they've had trouble counting them down there."

There were no Lajeunesses on the smudged scroll. There were a couple Labiches, but Jana shook her head when Evangeline pointed out the name. "Not our family."

Julian stood above them, glaring protectively as new customers began to shoulder their way inside. Evangeline took the parchment back to the bar where the bartender was filling the unwashed mugs from a keg, excess beer spilling down his wrist and dripping onto the floor in intervals when he lined the full mugs on the bar for his drinkers.

"No luck, girl?"

She looked at him, and he shrugged. "Take it to heart that whoever you're looking for is better off not having his name on that paper." He jerked his chin toward his task. "Hang it back on the peg for me, would you."

She did, turning away for only a moment before she felt his wet hand climbing up the back of her leg. She spun, striking out and hitting the mug he raised as a shield against her attack, splashing its contents over the nearest of the Sunday drinkers.

"My mistake." The man withdrew as far as he was able in the narrow space. "You can't blame me for trying."

She stood, angry and irresolute for a moment, then seized the wet handle of a full mug and splashed it over the man, who only started laughing.

"My mistake, girl, as I said." He raised his hands in surrender. "If I had more sense than I do, I wouldn't be slopping up dregs."

Julian made his way up to the bar, his expression betraying his desire to intervene and his lack of knowledge of what he might do.

The barman tugged at his wet shirt and said, "Let's call it even."

Fuming, she brushed past the lout and into the handful of gawkers. As she reached the door, the barman called after her.

"It might be better for everyone if you let the priest do the checking in from now on. He's not nearly as tempting for us sinners."

The derisive laughter followed them out onto Calvert Street, and defeated, they walked back to the hospital without a word among them.

New Orleans 1760

⌘

Soundless above them, the banners of moss
just stirred to the music.

GABRIEL AND PHILIPPE WORKED A TWO-MAN SAW THROUGH the trunk of a cypress, toiling alongside other teams of men similarly engaged in clearing the spongy ground, widening and straightening the trails leading north from the buildings and plantations of New Orleans to the harbor on Lake Pontchartrain. Once the trees were down, the usable trunks were cut to length and hitched to horse teams that dragged them back to the city for the palisade. The cypresses' wide bases made them imperfect for wall-building, yielding fewer posts than it seemed the felling deserved. But it was enough that they hadn't lacked for work since arriving in the city two years ago, carrying with them threats of English attack on the colonial capital. And despite their efforts alongside the other itinerant craftsmen of Louisiana, the palisade and moat around it were still unfinished, leaving months before they'd have to wonder again how to would pass the days.

"It's fine with me. There aren't enough of us around here," Basil's excited boom carried clearly over the noise of the dozens of men laboring in loose gangs between them.

Gabriel straightened up, grinning to see Basil with an armload of branches carelessly thrown over a shoulder, free left hand patting the back of a stranger. The sailcloth sack on the man's back meant he'd gotten off a boat, and the fiddle meant he didn't work. It was not like his father to welcome vagrants, Gabriel thought, before the skinny stranger clutched a hand over his father's forearm and Gabriel realized the man was blind.

"Gabriel," Basil bellowed. "Finish up, and let's get back."

Gabriel passed Alexander the saw, and nodded to Philippe at the other end. "You boys don't mind. We've got company."

He reached his father and shook hands with the stranger, guiding the man's wrist with his left hand. "Gabriel, sir, Basil's son. Pleased to meet you."

"Good grip, son," the man replied, his wrinkled face pinched in a smile under a floppy black hat. "It's a pleasure to meet any stalwart from home. I'm Michael Dagonet, most recently of Saint Domingue, though I was born and raised within sight of the fort at Annapolis. At least that's what they told me," he laughed to himself.

It was nearly a mile back to their lodgings, and longer each day they cleared the ground toward the immense lake. They'd been in the flimsy house for over a year since inheriting it from a German family moving to join relatives up the Mississippi. They still had several Germans for neighbors, people with whom they had little contact, and a few poor white creoles, but most of their neighbors were former slaves.

"Visitor," Gabriel barked as he held their mosquito netting, discarded linens patched with their old clothes, so Michael could enter. Acrid smoke drifted lazily in through the back door.

The trick to living in a house full of men, in a city full of men, was to drink when possible, and a jug was the plank table's lone adornment. Viktor or Philippe were usually responsible for procuring cheap rum or wine made from pineapples or strawberries to supplement the weak cypress beer they brewed in the partial shade afforded by the house.

"Luckily, we don't have much cluttering up the place," Gabriel said. He rested one hand on the sack the man had carried from the worksite.

"I'll put that on your bed, and I'd be happy to lead you to it whenever you'd like."

Michael smiled appreciatively at Gabriel's understanding. "You're a rare gentleman, Master Lajeunesse. Having little has made me embarrassingly possessive of those few treasures I've managed to hang onto through my traveling years."

Gabriel put the bag on his usual mattress, stuffed with gray moss harvested from the cypress, alongside his father's, which was identical down to the smell. There were three pallets in each room, and on the rare occasions when someone asked for the use of their extra, or on the more regular occasions when Gabriel stayed up drinking with Alexander and Philippe, he slept in the smaller bedroom with his friends, where he had carved *Success* above the door and given the bedroom a name. Each of them had some money squirreled away under their pallet, except Gabriel, who kept his Spanish coins with his father's.

Viktor came in the back door, straining with a heavy pot he set on the table to steam. There were no indoor kitchens in New Orleans, even the largest houses downtown had a separate area for cooking. The earlier residents had put a roof over a clay four paces from the back door, and the house hadn't burned down yet.

"Fish stew," Viktor said happily. Whatever was inside, it was burned, and Gabriel wished there was less of it. "I'd have bought bread if I'd known were entertaining a traveler from home."

"Oh, I left home long ago. I haven't been back for several wars."

"Well, it looks like you missed your chance if you hoped to find Acadians there when you arrived," Basil said. He poured a little liquor in four mugs and passed them around the table.

"I hate to hear it," Michael said after he drank. "Though that's the rumor that brought me up from the islands." He extended his mug and Basil refilled it.

"What can you tell me?" Michael asked.

"There's not much to tell," Basil said. "The English took our homes without a fight."

Alexander and Philippe entered the house where Gabriel half-listened to the older men.

"You're a damn boiler," Alexander accused Viktor as he ladled out the plates.

"What you boys don't understand is it's unseemly for a man my age to be cooking dinner at all." He spat his evening refrain as he tossed the stew onto plates.

"Yes, it's a passable experience only if someone can't hold it down." Alexander was combative after the extra work.

"Well, you won't be getting soft and fat on my cooking, and you can thank me at your leisure."

Viktor bowed his bald head in apology to their guest. He smiled when he realized the gesture wouldn't be appreciated and talked loudly to make up for the mistake, as though not only the man's eyes were impaired.

"As I said, I'd have fancied things up a bit if I'd known we were having a brother Acadian to supper, but family forgives all, as my mother told me."

"Well, I've nothing to criticize. You'd be a rich man in the islands, cooking like this."

Gabriel assumed Michael was merely being polite. Gossip had people eating out of golden bowls in Havana, and presumably the food they put in them was better than the slop Viktor concocted daily. Regardless, the chef appreciated the compliment.

"Another night cooking for a bunch of strange men," he commiserated to the blind man. "At least one's decent about it."

Viktor was invaluable to their group, a man who'd ceded his worldly ambitions after he'd found himself unable to defend his home. For Viktor, like Basil, this had been the ultimate insult, a blow to his masculinity so deep that it shook his personality loose from its moorings. But more naturally than his father, Gabriel thought, he'd embraced his role as a vagabond, confronting his bitterness with humor.

"I'm going to sample a bit of rum on the porch then." Philippe stood first.

"Boy, I've told you before, it's only rum till it passes down a good Acadian gullet, at which point, it becomes brandy." Viktor shouted to emphasize his point.

Basil shook his head. "Acadia stopped somewhere back where it wasn't so hot. What they've got is Louisiana rum, and they paid for it with pistolleros." He stepped out the back door.

"It's a sadder world than I imagined, my friend," Viktor said as he led Michael outside by the elbow to join Basil for their evening ritual of blowing smoke over the weedstrewn garden behind the house.

The younger men claimed the front porch where they stared

lustily toward town. "Partnered in the business of staying alive," Philippe had described their trio as they headed south down the Ohio and the Mississippi, fleeing the fort.

Alexander retrieved the liquor, stumped back with his left hand pressing the scabbard against his leg, the right swinging a bottle they'd secreted in the dugout in front of the house.

"Ripe," he snorted before passing the bottle to Philippe, who drank more effortlessly. The rum attacked the back of Gabriel's throat in turn. Like being choked on flowers, he thought as he gagged.

"Gabriel, I heard your father call Evangeline your bride-to-be, yesterday, when you were giving your letter to that crew," Alexander said.

"So you weren't actually married? You've been a free man this whole time?" Philippe jeered.

"We were pledged to each other. I don't feel that the actual day is what matters. We're still going to get married, as soon as I see her again," Gabriel said defensively.

"How long did you know her back home?" Alexander punctuated the question with a slurp of rum.

"More than three years."

"And you never?" Philippe asked without hesitation.

Gabriel looked around. Unsure of exactly how to say no, he convinced his audience without words.

"Never." Philippe shook his head. "Once, back home, I slept with a girl from Grand Pre the second time I saw her."

"Bull," Alexander said, usually willing to protect Gabriel from the worst of Philippe's harassment. "Unless you're trying to tell me that was only the second time you'd seen your sister."

"She wasn't my sister."

"She looked a lot like you, from one farm over."

244

"She was visiting from Beaubassin."

"Your people never got up that way?"

Gabriel laughed as the bottle went around and Philippe fell silent momentarily before returning the conversation to its original source, albeit less aggressively.

"So, Gabriel, what are you going to do with your bride when you're reunited?"

"I don't know. I was going to be, maybe am going to be a blacksmith. Otherwise, I guess I'm equally adept at everything."

"That's the attitude," Philippe encouraged. "Stay positive."

"I haven't seen her in longer than I've known her. Almost five years," Gabriel realized for the first time.

"How long do you think you'll wait?" Alexander asked.

"I'll wait forever."

"Had you even heard of New Orleans before we got here?" Alexander asked, but didn't pause for him to answer. "We're stuck at the end of the world. A decent girl would only wind up here by accident."

"Evangeline doesn't do things by accident."

His friends exchanged a glance. Alexander drank.

"Well, you're out of luck, then, because that's the only way I see an Acadian woman ever setting foot in New Orleans. Women come after places are civilized, and the English are certain to chase us away again before that happens."

"Then I'll find her after the war." Gabriel took a confident drink, remembering that he had a prospect, at least. More than these two.

"Who knows, maybe she's in town somewhere, looking for you," Philippe speculated.

"We would have already heard. You're not going to believe it when you see her. I'm not going to believe it when I see her again." Gabriel laughed, brash. "I didn't know how lucky I was."

"Don't worry, we'll introduce ourselves."

Alexander steered the conversation away from Philippe's teasing. "I'm not certain I'll see a beautiful woman again for the rest of my life. Even when a gypsy shows up, it's a blind old beggar." He took a long, angry drink, backwashing into the bottle as he pulled it from his lips. "I don't know what my father did to deserve to have his line peter out here in the swamp."

They chopped down trees for two more days, working laboriously through fatter trunks as the trail crossed a marsh. They had stayed away from the trench of the Saint John as best they could while hewing their course to the lake, and as the line between river and land blurred further, felled only the trees needed for the trail. The spurned cypress appeared squat and ugly from a distance, but magisterial from under the waving gray moss, casting saggy judgments on the foresters as they hurried about their labor. The largest one Gabriel saw rose above a waterless depression, its bulbous torso surrounded on all sides by knees that had dried out years before when the water fled. He often thought of Evangeline when he saw that solitary tree standing in the little bowl of the dry swamp. Like the tree, or the fruit on the apple behind the altar they never used, she would still be standing when everything else, himself included, had crumbled into ruin.

Mosquitoes harassed them each day as they returned from work. His friends usually judged the bugs a greater evil than further exertion at the end of the exhausting days, and ran home as fast as they could. Gabriel walked with his father, watching enviously as his friends disappeared up the trail. He silenced a mosquito in his ear.

"Do you want to go ahead?" his father asked.

"No, I'm fine."

They tramped along in silence for a minute as the woods opened to the cleared lowlands surrounding the city, the evening's swarms further darkening the sky.

"Seven men," Basil said suddenly.

"What?"

"That's what it would take to get me running. If only six men charged me, I'd stand and fight. Seven, though," he sighed.

Gabriel smiled at his old man, pleased as always when his father's sternness vanished. It had happened more frequently as the months tumbled past in their new home. "We just had to get Basil warm," Philippe joked once over dinner after his father told them about wrestling pigs in Port Royal. "Four years with the man, and he's opened right up."

Gabriel squinted at his father. "What would you do if they were armed?"

"That wouldn't change anything." His father scowled. "Six men," and clapped his hands violently together, crushing whatever flew in front of him.

A young woman with blond pigtails watched them pass from her lawn where she hung wet clothes out to dry in the sodden air. Gabriel smiled and nodded without stopping, and they were past the first woman he'd seen that day. Their shack came into view soon after. The German girl was practically their neighbor. He decided not to tell Alexander and Philippe, as they would be on daily parades in front of her door until someone started shooting. In New Orleans, one learned the importance of defending what was yours.

The past spring, with the palisade already halfway finished, a visiting engineer had offhandedly described the city defenses as trifling before sailing home to France. Days later, the first team of laborers was conscripted to work on a moat at the foot of the insignificant palisade, and now the boys observed their Sabbaths digging the ditch in front of the uneven posts they had sunk in the mud earlier in the week, the labor force buoyed by a huge influx of slaves, spending their off-day working for pistolleros. Theirs was a lot an Acadian could appreciate, compulsory service for five days, one day to grow food, one day to earn money. Even so, the slaves seemed proud of their recognized right to move around more or less at will, which made Gabriel wonder what the slaves' lives were like in the other colonies. The Creoles that owned them were dandified to the point of disdaining moat digging altogether.

"Though they're not quite so heartless that they won't pay others to keep their families safe from the English," his father remarked whenever the subject of the wall came up.

He and Viktor were also spared the servile digging due to their age, and spent their Sundays on the hill behind the palisade, installing banquettes and barbettes for the troops and weapons Gabriel saw no evidence to expect.

Alexander surveyed their line disgustedly, and spat. "Men at home, and men at work."

Gabriel spat in response, sweet wine never failed to sour next morning's breath. They started digging again, slopping the ooze in which they stood onto the bank of the three-foot wide ditch.

"This isn't as glamorous as building the wall by far," Philippe laughed. They shoveled.

Gabriel found a chunk of cypress and flung it at the wall. The fresh-cut twenty-foot barricade was still less impressive than the works about Fort Duquesne that had been deemed indefensible, but it was towering enough to provide shade for its creators who gratefully labored in its shadow after the sun crossed the river.

"Boys, this has got to be the easiest place to build a moat I've ever seen." Philippe was bent at the waist, hacking from mixed exhaustion and hilarity as water seeped up under his shovel. "Unless we just wanted to dig in the Mississippi."

Gabriel shoveled alongside his friends in companionable silence, too exhausted after the week for much talk. They slopped through the leavings that the artisans and workers had discarded during the construction, everything buried deep in soggy loam after only a few months.

Just past midday, Captain Bedard, the officer who'd led the protestors and squeamish from the fires of Duquesne, walked down from the incomplete fort to watch them work.

He and his gray uniform were clean, and he looked closer to their age than he was. He surveyed the plains beyond, scouting imaginary adversaries, waiting until his presence gained their attention. "If you boys wanted to join the militia, I could get you out of this pit on the weekends." The crisp voice was friendly. He sounded like a man eager to help those less fortunate.

"How are you involved, sir?" Alexander said, snapping to attention in the moat.

"I've been assigned to train new arrivals to defend our fair city in the event of attack by the vociferous English." The priggish words sounded almost like Benedict's, the condescending mockery of an older, smarter man. "Which means I'll give you guns, and feed you like kings two days a week."

"I'm ready now," Philippe said. They all were. The Captain had known them for his men.

"The first hitch only lasts a season, and then I'll decide if I can make you into real soldiers. You can start next Saturday at dawn, and leave the ditch to the less fortunate." He kicked a loose chunk of mud back in the moat. "We muster in the plaza between Saint Louis' and the water. You don't get uniforms."

"So we're going to defend the city?" Gabriel asked.

"Oh, Gabriel, you speak. Yes, you'd be called to defend the city if the English attack. But it's a busy time to be a soldier, so I may find more for you than that."

The Captain left, and Gabriel stuck his shovel in the mud.

"Stopping already?" Alexander asked.

"Talk to me when you finish the tree you started last week, runt." Gabriel followed the scratch in the earth line that defined the shape the moat would take over the coming weeks, worrying over how to tell his father what he wanted to do.

The finished palisade gave way as it met the hump of the town's levees near the river. They were larger than the dikes they'd built in Acadia, but without any conceivable drainage, stale brown water gathered at the base of the inland slope though the dikes hadn't flooded over in the year since they'd arrived in town. Standing in front of the stagnant pool, black women passed gourd cups of river water among the workers. Gabriel fell in line behind Jeremiah, a neighbor his age, but with a wife pregnant for the third time.

"Are you going to the square tonight?" Gabriel asked, by way of greeting.

"Yes, indeed. You listen?" Jeremiah's voice had stunning resonance for a man even skinnier than Gabriel.

"Every week." Gabriel searched for an appropriate compliment. "An old fiddler moved in with us who says that's what he hoped he might hear after he died. He spent all last week trying to capture it, and won't play any old songs unless we ask."

Jeremiah smiled, the black skin around his lips cracked and peeling from the sun. No one was coming to spare this man from digging. Gabriel looked back down the trench.

"Do you think this ditch is going to help anything?"

"Well, the English are going to hate wading through the mud to root us out, at least."

It was nice to have found another optimist. "I just hope we don't have to abandon this one, too." The man looked at him quizzically. "My friends and I came here with soldiers who abandoned Fort Duquesne without a fight."

Jeremiah nodded. "Our defenses on the Gambia didn't do us much good either."

"I've never heard of that river. Where is it?"

"It's back in Africa." The man pointed down the Mississippi. "Straight down this here, out to the sea, sail till you forgot what land looks like. Then you find Africa." He laughed once loudly. "But, I've never been."

They looked out across the Mississippi, as wide here as the Minas at its mouth, but more different than he and Jeremiah, a more impassable wall isolating the city from its plantations and the great gaping swamp.

"We should just cross the river," Gabriel said. "We'd be safe in the swamp."

"From the English maybe."

"Who else is there?"

"You might have to worry about the runaways."

"Oh. They live in the swamp?" Though Gabriel knew the Chitimachi had once lived along the slow rivers west of the city, the swamp seemed as untouched as the bottom of the ocean.

Jeremiah spat and nodded. "They've got villages out there

older than New Orleans, folks that escaped from the first plantations around here who never came back to see what they were missing."

Monday was their lone personal day, and so the Acadians often drank heaviest on Sunday, but no matter their state or the weather's, they all gathered together in front of their house to listen to the singing and drumming of their neighbors.

Gabriel piled a piece of stewed whitefish atop his Sunday bread and headed outside last, in the order he had arrived. No women and no favorites in Viktor's kitchen.

He joined Alexander and Philippe atop the upturned back of the unused pirogue they'd inherited with the shack. Michael and his father sat on their two chairs, situated on either side of Viktor, who manned the wide wooden stoop that the boys shared on the weeknights. The hunk of fish that Gabriel bit into was overcooked but already cold. He meant to harass Viktor, but the sun caught his attention as it slipped below the horizon, and the blue sky became a deep yellow, and just as the new color completed its conquest, the drums began, infrequent and curious thumps that would slowly grow, suddenly cease, and build again.

The blind man gasped only a little at the strawberry wine. "Made here in Louisiana," Viktor said as he took the bottle.

"Amen," the fiddler responded.

The wine circled back to Gabriel's outstretched hand, and he took a respectable gulp that he held it in his mouth, swallowing only after his cheeks began to pucker.

He imagined black faces staring at each other over low fires, bright enough only to illuminate the white of the old men's beards. They would be as filthy from the day's work as he was, sweaty and encrusted with the blood of crushed mosquitoes. But there was something timeless about the gathering in the square that made Gabriel more aware of Louisiana's isolation. Here, they sat at the edge of every world. No one really knew what the boundless swamps, rivers and plains surrounding them contained. The Acadians in particular had no knowledge of what lay beyond the Mississippi, though the breathy voices that they listened to from the front yard each Sunday seemed to hint at the swamp's pulsing heart, exhilarating but exhausting, a passionate rhythmic world. The sound, rising up in one voice, deep as the Mississippi, threatened to sweep him away with the violence of a flood.

The powerful chanting overshadowed the day's menial labor, the voices roaring in a chorus that overflowed the ditch, a sensation that faded as the voices stilled, while the accompanying drums receded to a quiet but ominous thumping, conserving their strength.

The swamp was the linchpin of their new home, Gabriel realized. To explore and understand it would be to come to grips with his new identity. It wasn't he that had changed, it was the world under his feet that had become a different thing, shifted, shed its skin to reveal the murky tropic surrounding him.

The yellow sky watered, as though adjusting to his drunkenness, and then faded swiftly to a wan gray that shed light enough only to prove its opaqueness. The color of the absence of light, Gabriel thought, as the voices rose again. Stars poked out of the sky in time with the drumbeats.

The keening finale whirled and quieted, fading out singly so that he only became aware of the absence when a few female voices still hummed to the night. And these voices finally, simply quieted, replaced by the laughter of people walking toward them, and exhausted sighs of goodnight as the performers returned home. Then only the cicadas were singing, rasping so loudly that Gabriel wondered how he'd ever heard anything above them at all.

Only after they were gone did he realize that some of the goodnights and partings that he'd heard were his friends wishing him well as they staggered to bed. He perched atop the pirogue, his balance still perfect, always a source of pride, and looked at his father through the dark, trying to think of something to say about the music.

"Well, damn," Basil said.

"What's wrong?"

"That we're stuck here in this swamp, with you going off to fight for people that sat on their hands while our homes were taken away." Basil waved his arm angrily, the motion making him visible. "You're wrong about this Captain. You saw what those cowards did before we left that fort. You saw that, but you're going to join up with them anyway," he continued, raising his voice, "and leave your home, which you should be defending, as my responsibility." Basil laughed coldly. "Shooting someone that comes to your door. That I can understand. Not tramping around interfering with other people." He pointed his finger accusingly at his son. "Official business is what got us removed from our homes."

Gabriel found his angle. "What home?"

"The one I'll be painstakingly crafting with my own hands so that you can raise a family in it once you've returned to your senses. If you're not killed or maimed." Never one to overlook a detail, his father included the possibility that he'd live but suffer a disabling wound. "Maybe when you get back you'll remember that it's only in our homes that we're worth anything to ourselves or anyone else." His father stopped and cleared his throat after Gabriel's huff. "Or maybe there's a little amendment needed for some of the old ways."

"So where do you think we should settle down?" Not in this city, he knew that much.

"West. There are a couple trading posts along the Atchafalaya, but I hear the better land is along the Teche. We might have a few years before the English find us."

"Like Acadia before our people came out there."

"That's my boy."

"I'll need to find a squaw." The time spent in camps of men had shown how easy it was to discomfort his father, who didn't respond. Gabriel tried again. "So, what are you going to do with your hermitage?"

"I'm going to build a place where your family can live. The rest is your business." His father's simplicity was staggering in its complete dependence on Gabriel.

"I won't leave for weeks, if at all. And it will get me out of the trench. You're already building the wall full-time."

"Only because they need at least two capable hands for every dozen doing the construction up there."

"Regardless," Gabriel said. "Next spring we go to work."

"Then that's all I can ask for."

"And you've got a fiddle player now."

"Yes, to remind me of home." His father remained a difficult man to cheer.

Gabriel drank and thought for a moment. "Of the sparks of your forge, brighter than the stars above New Orleans."

Basil stood up, leaving him to follow.

"Goodnight, son," he said from the doorway.

Louisiana 1763

⁓

Slowly, slowly, slowly, the days succeeded each other.

GABRIEL ARRIVED AT THE DECATUR STREET TAVERN EARLY, but checked for his friends nevertheless. Four men drank at the bar, eyeing him narrowly from above their beards, and Gabriel took a bench at one of the empty tables behind them. He was pleased to arrive first and start on the weak beer before his friends joined him. He jumped up from the dregs of his second mug when they came in, Alexander stumping in with his sword clasped to his leg, Philippe with clean white bandages over his ear, a sharp contrast to his new black three-cornered hat. It seemed like more than three months since Gabriel had last seen them. Even without uniforms his friends parted the growing crowd of drinkers as though blaring bugles.

Their clean-cut appearance was a stark contrast to his own. Gabriel's hair was as long and unruly as when they left South Carolina, and in his sweat-stained cotton shirt and wool pants he looked only better fed than the boy who had arrived in the city years before.

"What happened to your head?" Gabriel asked Philippe as they sat down, prompting knowing laughs.

Alexander answered for him. "He's improved the telling of our failed defense of Acadia."

"The story's changed a little over time, I grant you. Anyway, nobody wants to ask about an old wound, but several of the ladies I've met have been quite curious about bandages." Philippe slapped Gabriel on the back. "In fact, I was planning on getting creative tonight."

"Where are the drinks?" Alexander asked, looking at the empty mug in front of Gabriel.

"You have to go up to the bar and get them."

Philippe looked at Alexander, who sighed before extracting a purse he laid on the table.

"Thank you, Captain," Philippe saluted after helping himself to a few coins and departed.

"That looks heavy."

"I've had a bit of good fortune lately."

"I heard we were losing the war."

"Actually, we've already lost."

"What do you mean?"

"It's over." Alexander said as Philippe returned and set the mugs down loudly, sloshing foam over the table and onto Gabriel's pant leg.

"You haven't even fought yet. This is Fort Duquesne all over." Gabriel didn't know why he felt betrayed. He'd left the militia after one season's useless patrols east around the lake. He regretted that he'd been forced to return the boots when he left the service.

"I see what the problem is," Philippe began loudly, the tone alone raising a smile on Gabriel's lips. "You're bitter we weren't killed so you could finally have your pick of New Orleans' five single ladies. Afraid not, my friend, we return alive and well, and in Alexander's case anyway, damn near hitched."

Gabriel pointed at the purse. "She must have some money."

Alexander drank nonchalantly. "That's just an officer's payday."

"Oh yeah?"

"It turns out the Captain's daughter fancies our friend's peculiar stride." Philippe couldn't even drink his beer he was so desperate to spread the news. "He was made a company commander after a couple of kisses. Just think what he's going to get when he gives that man a grandson." Philippe shook his head.

"I can't believe the war's over," Gabriel said. They looked at him sharply as the comment brought attention from a few of their neighbors, and they didn't have to ask him to change the subject. "So what are you two going to do?"

"Well. Anna's on her way over here to meet you, so assuming that goes well and she doesn't change her mind "

"You mean her father doesn't," Philippe interrupted, laughing.

"I'm going to marry her sometime next year."

"Unbelievable. Congratulations." Gabriel raised his mug in salute.

Philippe seemed to have heard only the first part. "That's what I've been saying. You're lucky if you see a squaw a week out on the damn coast, but here Alexander will be going home to one night after night. All the damn luck." Philippe dipped back into the tooled leather change-purse and went for another round.

"So." Gabriel didn't know what to ask, he'd assumed he'd be the first of them married.

"She's beautiful, Gabriel. And smart. You'll see when you meet her."

"What are you going to do for work?"

"You remember what Bedard said when he hired us out of that ditch. There's as much work for a military man in peacetime as in war. Chasing Indians up the Mississippi, making sure the English keep the treaty we'll be forced to sign."

"Escorting the Bedard family about town," Philippe said as he returned. "Kissing ass."

"This softbelly's backing out on me though," Alexander told him.

Philippe faced Gabriel. "I'm sick of listening to officers, and was thinking maybe your father would like a turn bossing me around."

"You want to trap with us?"

"Well, I haven't found my own rich girl yet, and I don't see the point of sitting around here drinking and waiting to get my throat cut by some wharf rat."

"Here she comes," Alexander said and they turned to the door. A girl wearing a blue dress that hooped out around her hips and a wide white hat stood in the door.

All three of them stood on her approach, rickety chairs clattering. Philippe removed his hat with a grin for Gabriel. The girl came over and kissed Alexander's cheek.

Gabriel held out his hand. "Gabriel Lajeunesse. Pleased to meet you." He had nothing else to say. They shook by the fingertips.

"Anna Bedard." The pretty girl sniffed the air around him

and turned up her nose, but didn't lose her smile. "You look like a farmer."

"Well, I do some farming."

"Nonsense," Alexander said, "Gabriel's a notorious hunter and trapper, out there in the wilderness, with nothing but his gun and his pirogue to interfere with life's simpler pleasures. He lets his father dirty his hands in the soil."

"That's right," Philippe broke in, "and they hitch Michael to the plow."

His friends howled. After they finished their beers, Anna looked at Alexander.

"Well, it's good to put a body with the name. You can imagine I've heard a great deal about you." She doffed her hat to Gabriel, as a man would, and then to Philippe in turn, "Always a pleasure, Master Boiselle."

"So where are you two headed tonight?" Philippe was brazen enough to ask a question Gabriel had wondered about himself.

"Oh, this city's full of things to do compared with plenty of the places my father's been stationed," the girl said lightly.

"It's nicer than a coal room on the *Success*." Gabriel's comment met with the requisite murmurs of agreement from his friends.

The men shook hands around and the couple was off across Decatur toward the riverfront.

"Women make everything different," Gabriel said, as they watched Anna lead Alexander by the hand toward the water.

"Yes, they do." His friend watched closely for another minute. "She doesn't have any sisters. I asked."

Gabriel didn't respond and they breathed in the river in silence.

"How long are you going to wait for her?" Philippe asked.

"Evangeline," Gabriel sighed her name to the night.

Philippe laughed. "A while yet, I guess."

"I think sometimes that it would be easier for me to wait for Evangeline if I knew what I was waiting for, you know?"

"I think that I do."

It was better all the time that he was joining them on the Teche, Gabriel thought. He and his father could use a little cheer.

"I don't know where these thoughts come from," Gabriel said, searching the sky as though looking for the particular star.

"Not divine inspiration, my friend, but just a bit lower."

The two friends returned to the four glasses and drank for a while reflecting on their less than ideal state as single men in a world with alternatives. Soon enough, though, Gabriel found himself gushing over his frontier life.

"You'll be on your own again, Philippe. Making decisions for yourself like you should be. The camaraderie of the trail, without the hardship."

Philippe emptied his mug and set it carefully in front of him on the wobbly table, peering grumpily over it at Gabriel. "You don't see that many girls out west, do you?"

"You don't see that many around here either, remember?"

Philippe did not answer, and after a moment went to pay for two more beers.

"So, I'll come back for you in two weeks," Gabriel said when he returned.

"Yes, fine, we'll try the summer out there, walk a day in your celibate shoes. Get barked at by your angry father. Basil still comes along, right?"

"He wouldn't miss it."

"Well, if there's some plan in the doings of my life, I sure don't see it."

Sweltering heat woke Gabriel. He had sweat through his clothes, and his face was slick with it. It was hard to imagine how he'd slept at all. His head throbbed as he sat up, the jungle cure for humid nights exacting its morning revenge. His jaw worked grudgingly open and closed and he spat dry white foam on the floor, but his tongue was still plastered to his throat, and he tried again. Light streamed over Philippe, who was asleep peacefully on the little room's only bed. He was lucky he'd wound up on the floor, otherwise he might be even later meeting his father.

He crossed Decatur to the riverfront and strolled up the street toward the public wharves, still spitting the night's residue over the pilings toward the river.

Their pirogue was already packed. Basil helped Michael aboard after he saw Gabriel and waited for him to take his place upfront.

"Ready, Gabriel?"

Gabriel swallowed bile and nodded seriously to his father.

"I'd be happy to paddle," Michael offered, long bony fingers extended as proof of his intent.

"We have our system." Basil answered, loud enough to be heard in the city. "This might, however, be a good time for a little music."

"Indeed, you both know that northern boatmen measure their distance in songs," the fiddler made one of his favorite observations as he raised his instrument to his shoulder, whistled a few notes and set to.

The fiddle's shrill bowing was painful in Gabriel's head as he and his father pushed their burdened pirogue away from the dock, and they headed upriver with the fiddler performing from his seat between them on their canvas-wrapped provisions. Gabriel breathed a little freer once they started paddling. As his head cleared, he was nearly able to convince himself that they paddled the Gaspereau, bringing a minstrel to Evangeline and Benedict's fire.

But despite years on its shore, the Mississippi merited no comparison to Acadia's waters for Gabriel. There, the music danced and skipped off the surface of the streams, and rang back in your ears. Here, the muddy water sucked everything in, fastening the music with a sorrowful weight, suitable only for the contemplation of unrecoverable and inarguably better times. His home was in the north, until Evangeline joined him here and they made a new life with the fat cypress, the moss, the teeming cloudbanks of midges, the alligators. It wasn't quite what they'd envisioned in her orchard.

"I'll never leave Grand Pre," she had told him.

"You're not even curious. The whole world? I'd like to go to Havana," he'd said, inspired by her father's tales from the extravagant city.

"Gabriel, if you can't be happy at home, you can't be happy anywhere."

"I'm happy here. Completely happy."

"Then why leave?"

He smiled sadly remembering her obstinacy. She'd need it undiminished now.

Michael began bowing *The Blessed Valley*. Gabriel hadn't heard that song since he was exiled, but recalled the song's final line. *Better to have loved and lost than never to have loved at all.*

This referred equally to the girl who was the subject of the song, and Acadia, but Evangeline would be both for him. The meaning behind the ground that he walked, the reason something was home and something else was not. Though they'd yet to share one, he felt sure of this.

That was the lesson of old Acadia, faithfulness tried and rewarded. So he toiled through the war years, patiently waiting for his wife to fall into his arms. Now eight years waiting. It occurred to him again that he refused to consider the possibility that she had died. That he might wait all his life for someone that wasn't coming.

A raft of Germans floated past them, headed downstream toward New Orleans, a mother and father with four skinny children, blond creatures with long arms and legs hanging off their flat boat as the young parents clucked at them in their strange tongue. Their boat was covered with deer hides, jugs, and painted baskets.

The men, Basil and the German, exchanged greetings, his father's conveying gruffness, but respect for the man's cargo, the other's simply preoccupied.

You're a child yourself until you have children of your own, Gabriel recalled the saying from home. That buck in the other pirogue might have been his age. When they were alone on the water again, Michael returned to his music.

The palmetto roof of his unfinished house flapped open in welcome as they slowed to a halt on the mud and the three men pitched forward in unison.

"Home at last." Gabriel clapped Michael on the shoulder and helped him out of the boat as his father stepped free, the shallow water splashing knee-deep as he dragged their craft until it lay snug between cypress knees at the water's edge. The bark on each side was scrubbed smooth from the practiced maneuver.

His father's home was a blockhouse without the lookout, a squat rectangle of interlocking cypress logs. Basil had completed the defenses by chinking out firing holes for muskets in each corner. They slept in a loft despite the oppressive heat to escape the soggy ground for a few hours at night. His friends had dubbed the paranoid structure Fort Lajeunesse.

"What happens if they attack while we're cooking?" Viktor had asked his father after they completed the fort.

"Your worry," his father had replied.

More recently, Viktor had moved a mile upriver, to a modest home modeled off their old shack outside New Orleans, preferring to spend his waning years in hermitage. "It has grown to be a depressing thing to wake up and see you every day," Viktor had told his father.

Gabriel's unused home lay past the cookstove, across a seasonal finger of the Teche. They'd built it quickly, raised on the stumps that survived their earlier building. They'd followed local custom and mixed the hanging moss with river mud for his walls, but inside everything waited on Evangeline. He hadn't put up shelves, hadn't filled in the frame of a wall dividing the interior into two rooms, and as of yet there were no tables or chairs. He stepped through the wall, taking advantage of the convenience while he still could, and moved to the only piece of furniture, a bed. He lit two stubby candles that lay against the back wall to augment the light coming in through the open door, and sat cross-legged at the side of the bed. *Acadia 1755*, the year of their separation, greeted him, scrawled deep into the wood. He had hewn the bed from a solid cypress trunk, claimed before the pecci fungus hollowed the heartwood, as it had done to several of the surrounding trees they'd cleared for the homes. Its huge stump now served as a table outside the kitchen, on the high, dry ground that had allowed the truer growth.

"Where do you want to build?" his father had asked as they'd surveyed the property from the bank two years ago.

"I'm not sure, but I want the wood from this tree." Before they chopped it down, the cypress' branches had extended twenty meters to dangle its moss over the swamp.

"Well, I've been sweating since Acadia. Just make sure you leave me a little shade."

With the bed fashioned, Gabriel found himself still unwilling to move to the rest of the house. Instead he had attached a shelf to the footboard, and more recently had begun carving rough figurines out of long leaf pine. Gabriel began with Evangeline, but was dissatisfied with his early results, and he found more success shaping the soft wood into a bushy tree that would serve as the apple tree under which they would have been married. Gabriel tried again to carve her after his skill progressed, and now she stood alongside the tree, one hand reaching toward up toward it, the other arm crossed over her chest. His best moments were spent imagining her admiring his work for the first time.

Gabriel had selected a nicely sworled piece to represent himself, but was uncomfortable carving it, and so the block stood unfinished on the other side of the apple tree. He was well under way on a figure of his father now, carved from a large piece of pine, with one arm raised above his head clenching a hammer.

He shaved pieces of the base, shaping the anvil and differentiating it from the leg so that it looked less like his father grew out of the anvil, and instead stood beside it. Outside, Michael's warbly voice rose to accompany his fiddle, a local ballad Gabriel had come to recognize.

Prepare me oh Lord, to sail me on that ship, that ship that's sailing by. The days seem like years to me. I once had a sister, but now I have none. Prepare me, oh Lord, for that ship that's sailing by.

Gabriel put his work down and walked around the bed to look at his fiddle, propped in the corner, still new under the gray dust. He turned back to the bed, where he'd etched *Louisiana* into the opposite plank, the date of their reunion yet to be determined, he thought, looking back at the instrument, though he was still hopeful about the one and the seven.

The next morning, he sat in a pirogue in the mud along the edge of the Teche, intent on a gray squirrel, its back legs balanced on a root within his arm's reach. It ran its tiny black eyes over him a couple times, but didn't seem to recognize him as unnatural or separate from the environment they shared. The squirrel readjusted the large green acorn in its mouth with the fingers of its front paws, then got down on all fours with a fluff of its tail and bounced away, taking the treasure home to its winter store. His father shot the deer just after the squirrel vanished from sight, though presumably he hadn't also been watching it.

The dead deer rested in the pirogue between them as they returned home. Basil had shot the animal at the base of its long neck as it strained upward. It still surprised Gabriel how much foliage the deer actually ate. As smiths, the only animals they had needed to concern themselves with were flustered horses. His father sighted as it gnawed its way up a tupelo branch and waited until the animal's neck was outstretched before firing. It dropped in the clearing with the hole through it, mid-chew, right where the leaves would have passed with its next swallow. Gabriel was happy to take the seat in the bow on their hunting trips. Alive, deer resembled a moose. Dead, the reproachful brown eyes reminded him of an abused dog's.

Basil slung the gutted carcass onto the bank for his son as he stepped into the brown water to secure the pirogue in their pier of living cypress. Michael sat outside the house on his chair. He didn't call a greeting as he heard them, but quit murmuring to himself and started creaking away on the fiddle he lifted from his feet, nothing Gabriel recognized. The fiddler claimed African spirituals were better suited to the climate and liberally sprinkled his Acadian repertoire with songs he'd picked up in the city.

"It's better we have a little music to go along with this," Gabriel commented to his father once they had it spiked onto the side wall of their kitchen. The Crucifixion was how Basil referred to the process on cheerful days. This was a more ordinary day. Basil only nodded and slit the deer open, starting above the back white-stockinged feet, running his sharp, old blade up the chicken-thin legs.

"Go on, son," Basil said.

Gabriel took the toothed saw to the deer just below the knee, removing the back legs while his father hacked off the tail. After he sawed off the front legs as well, Gabriel left the tool with the hooves and went to fetch the beer. The fiddler waited on his father's porch, instrument quiet but at the ready.

"Quitting, Gabriel?" Michael asked when he heard him pouring the mugs. "Don't go easy on yourself, boy. In music or work, it does no one any good." He stared blankly off the porch over the Teche. "We measure ourselves against the eternal standard set by all other men, Gabriel, those who have already lived, and those yet to peep awake." The fiddler swung around and fixed him with eyes as watery as the river. "God will judge you in your time, but there will be plenty of people to impress along the way."

"Alright, Michael," he said. "I'll practice."

But the fiddler wasn't listening. Having picked up his instrument, he began talking to himself with a self-interest Gabriel envied.

"This reminds me of a song I learned in the city." Michael started bowing, working slowly up and back the G and D strings, took the bow away and called in his wavering voice out over the river, *I didn't know I was going to have to pray so hard. No Lord, I never knew I'd have to pray so hard.* He sang with emphasis on know and hard.

Michael kept playing as Gabriel crossed the yard with the mugs of beer. He sat them on the stump outside the kitchen and helped Basil stretch the hide off the meat, both of them sticking their hands inside the membrane, ripping loose the unwilling skin loose. He held it taut while his father cut the skin free. Basil nailed the legs to the wall, where the pelt flapped alongside two older ones. Gabriel trailed after and scrubbed the blood and bits of meat off the inside of the pelt and left it to dry. His father returned from the house where he'd taken the venison, accompanied by Michael, who wailed, *Which way has my redeemer gone. Which way, Lord, which way has my redeemer gone.*

They drank their warm beer and regarded the neck and head of the deer, propped up so that it appeared as though the rest of its body was buried underground. The brown eyes seemed not quite lifeless enough.

"I've got a couple things to take care of next door."

From the porch came the wavering voice, *He took my money to New Orleans. He took my money to New Orleans.*

His father nodded, and Gabriel set his mug down and marched across the swampy ground, kicked his boots off against the frame of his house, and walked into the empty shell, the fiddler's strains filtering in through the bousillage as naturally as the dust. *Lord, I don't want to die in the storm. No, Lord, I don't want to die in the storm.*

Baltimore 1766

Many, despairing, heart-broken, asked of the earth but a grave.

THREE SLOOPS ANCHORED OFF THE NEW PIER AT CALVERT Street, and Felician trod down to the dock to watch as his congregation prepared to depart. Autumn's browning was in little evidence across the treeless city. The crisp weather had drastically improved the odor of the filthy streets lined with troughs and sewage, and even took the edge off the harbor's rankness of dead fish. Robicheaux from Beaubassin, Melansons from Grand Pre, Dugas and Ponces from Port Royal. The Acadians were advisably seizing their first opportunity to quit the town they'd been forced to occupy for the duration of the war, and now several years of peace, which brought no immediate change to Baltimore's Acadians. Governor Sharpe's ban on traveling west out of sight of the city was shortly to be lifted, though the victorious English had yet to determine whether or not they were to be considered citizens of the empire, or, if they were free to make their own way, where they would be allowed to settle. So far, the English seemed only to hope that they would dissolve into the mist like the French resistance, Felician thought bitterly. Something akin to hearing he'd been born of different parents, or that Louis converted to Protestantism, was the force of hearing of the fall of impregnable Quebec. And yet that sting had faded, lost in the bilious rage of Anglican bureaucracy.

And finally the English had sent trim sloops, freshly constructed for the war, to carry the Acadians away from Baltimore. No matter that the boats sailed for Saint Domingue, a sugar colony with as many similarities to Acadia as Winslow had to Evangeline. Those departing felt the need to start afresh greater than those like she, who still sought the lost. Some had boarded ships to return north, but, arriving in Acadia, they'd been confronted by Scotsmen who plowed their fields and lived in earthen hovels erected over the fresh ruins. Those disappointed souls had spread the sad news along the coast, and few now considered that Acadia could be home again.

Felician spied Bernard on one of the ship's decks, and thought for a moment that he witnessed the trapper's return to the city, before remembering that Bernard had been living for weeks in one of the vacant huts after his unceremonious return. Moving along the pier, Felician hailed another familiar face busy with the unloading.

"Monsieur Bauer, I didn't think you were taking ship."

The burly man settled the cask he'd been carrying on the ground, and leaned on it as he spoke to Felician.

"No, Father, I'm done putting my family on boats. These still need to be unloaded, though, before anyone gets on. No extra weight."

They'd heard recently of a transport overburdened with four hundred exiles from Ile Royale, Felican's old post, which sank on its way to England, drowning hundreds.

"Good for you. I wouldn't say the sugar islands hold any personal appeal."

Bauer grimaced. "It seems like Maryland ought to be hot enough for anyone. Plenty of others seem to like it well enough."

There was no denying the city was flush with immigrants, Felician thought. The Acadians were the only ones who seemed to have an interest in leaving. "You've heard that Acadia's already resettled."

"No sense beating that horse, they can have it. We were bothered there for more than a hundred years." Bauer shrugged, unwilling to dwell on his fate.

"I admire your equanimity, Francis," Felician said. "It's probably why you're an excellent father."

"Most people will recognize what they're forced to," Bauer responded. "I'm going to see who else is leaving."

"Fair enough," the priest said. "I believe I'll determine the opposite."

Felician meandered up Calvert, his usually rapid stride slow as he looked over his shoulder at the Acadians waiting with their meager belongings for the unloading to finish.

He was passed by a rowdy crew, bragging as they spilled into Payne's tavern, adding to the cacophony within, where three ships' worth of men tried to get drunk before they were forced back to sea. Like those it followed into Baltimore's harbor, the small fleet had carried immigrants, arriving nearly as cramped as the Acadians had at the war's beginning, with many in as desperate a state of need. Their hospital had found a second life giving families new to the colonies a meal or two and a place to stay for the night. Otherwise, the city was trying to forget the hundreds of Acadians it festered over during the war.

And now, after ten years' close confinement, they would give up this temporary home that none of them had asked for. The only experience he had to compare it to was the siege he'd been present for at Louisbourg, though there they had been fighting back, rather than impatiently waiting for those more powerful to determine who was strongest before all could continue with their lives. Felician recollected the nearly two months trapped with the sweating, powder-encrusted and wavering garrison, carrying a musket at night and rebuilding the walls with the noncombatants and soldiers rotated off guard, more of those last available in the siege's final days as their defenses contracted. From the outset, most in Louisbourg considered their situation hopeless, and the ranks of those unwilling to mount counterattacks outside the walls grew as the weeks dragged on, and the militiamen crept closer. The Massachusetts men had seemingly brought every cannon in the colonies, and they used them, firing into the city from their advancing batteries until finally the warships that had blockaded the harbor sailed into the city and forced the French surrender.

And so Louisbourg was surrendered, and he spent a winter in Paris before a ship returned him to New France, and the Mi'kmaq of Ile Royale, though he avoided the repatriated fort. No one was going to come reclaim Acadia for the Acadians, Felician felt, nor now Ile Royale. Many times since their arrival he had argued that the French were certain to outlast the English. But the grand stone seminary and fortresses of Quebec and the rows of towers and cannon of Louisbourg rested in English hands. The Anglicans did not lack guns or people, and the French had an answer for neither, Felician thought.

Rather than sulk down streets lined with the rough

dwellings of the victors, he turned for Saint Paul's, a retreat he sought more frequently despite its creed. James, the pastor who kept the church, was a kind man who'd arranged for a letter Felician wrote to be sent to France several years before. Several days ago James sent word that he had received a reply, but Felician had not yet claimed it for fear of learning of his reassignment.

Although bleak communications should be familiar by now, he thought with as a scowl upon reaching the bricked enclosure that distinguished Saint Paul's from its city. James knelt inside the low walls opened onto a path, sweating through his linen shirt as he removed loose bricks from the way. He stood to greet Felician.

"You've come for your letter," he said after they shook.

"If you don't mind, James."

Felician settled himself on a pew in the center of the soaring brick nave, relishing the rare tranquility of any empty shrine, until James brought him the envelope, holding the broken seal out for inspection.

"Only under mandate, Felician." The younger man looked at him sadly. "I'm sorry."

"I knew you'd have to open it, James."

"I'll leave you in peace," James said humbly, and returned to his work outside.

Only for a moment did he wonder about James' discomfort before leaning forward over the letter and squinting until he could make out Father Maufils' script.

Felician,

It is a blessing to know that you yet labor among the living, and I pray that this letter finds you ministering to your chosen in health. Your wish to somehow remain in the colonies (after this luckless war finally ends) may be easier to grant than you imagine. For it is no longer to Quebec or Paris that you need look for direction, as France, in his ignorance and rage, has turned from our Jesuit Order. We lost His Majesty's favor with Pere La Vallette's ships off Martinique in the war's first days, even as you chose to cleave to your congregation and accept exile in the English colonies. The loss of the sugar money left the Order destitute, and even so, the others with a stake in Martinique dragged us before the courts as accountable for their losses.

The colleges were closed last year, the year of the peace, 1763. Earlier this year the Order was formally banished, from any lands His Majesty still lays claim to, and we were informed that we would have to renounce our vows to remain in the protection of France. It was an exceedingly rare choice, and we were scattered, many to holy Rome, though doubtless not to remain. I am past the age where I wish to travel only to travel again, and write to you with three days left until Christmas, which I will celebrate this year in Spain.

I am deeply grieved that I cannot provide better succor for you, nor better guidance than to trust in Him, and to follow His vision as best you can. For as unwelcome as the Anglican has made you in that land, such is the reception you should expect in any of the courts of the kings on this earth. I pray for Benedict's soul in Heaven, and am relieved to hear of the care you have taken of Evangeline in his stead. You have my admiration for the selfless fortitude you've demonstrated in bearing this burden longer than you had any reason to expect. But, in this madness, every life saved is a miracle.

Short of another, I do not expect to see you again in this life, though I will certainly write if His Most Christian Majesty shows us leniency. It is better, however, to entrust what hope we have in other vessels, none more upright than yours, my friend. Go with God,
Pere Maufils

Rather than the feelings of loss and resentful anger directed toward the ungrateful monarchy his predecessors had fostered for centuries, what the priest felt, overwhelmingly, was relief. Duty wouldn't take him from Evangeline's side, so long as he chose to remain, and so long as she would have him there. Guiltily, he considered that with all the turmoil around him, both here in the colonies and for his brethren in France, he might have more concern for those beyond himself. But he was happy to see much of his congregation sail away, for their sakes, and for his. And he remained so in the face of the loss of the Order that had nurtured him for the length of his conscious life. He, who previously had no thought or wish for anything but his labor, was relieved to see his mourning charges depart. He walked home in distraction, thinking about what he would say to Evangeline when he arrived.

Felician didn't walk up the steps of his church-in-exile, but down the narrow lane alongside, to the cemetery. Not quite as large as the one behind Saint Charles, it lay hemmed in by new houses which obscured the still dramatic ascension of incoming ships up the Patapsco. Ten years, and thirty white oak crosses. Of fewer than two hundred Acadian souls brought to Baltimore in the early years of deportations. His steps carried him to two graves strewn with aster. Sofia Melanson, at rest beside her husband, her grave easily distinguishable without the light grass that covered most of its neighbors.

He and Evangeline had spent enough time in Baltimore. They could leave, or they would rest here with those they had put in the ground. It didn't seem like enough, not for his Creator, not for himself, and certainly not for the beautiful woman walking out of their house toward him.

"It makes us seem pretty fragile," Evangeline said when she joined him.

Evangeline looked vulnerable indeed standing before the cemetery, like she'd be comforted if he put his arms around her, and so he hugged her close, greeting her with the physical contact he felt they both needed. "You put flowers on Sofia's grave," Felician said.

"Not as often as I should."

"I've been thinking there's more of this world for you to see. Your father would never forgive me if I let you spend the rest of your life in Baltimore."

"Well, I certainly wouldn't paint traveling in the glowing terms my father used, but just being allowed to move about relieves a certain weight."

"Free to seek inspiration in the continent's hidden corners?"

She smiled wistfully. "Watching those ships readying to sail, it reminds me of home."

"That's enough time spent staring at graves today," he told her. They left the crosses for the cavernous house, but he caught her elbow just outside.

"I told you I sent a letter to France, asking what was required of me with the end of the war." He withdrew the letter from his threadbare robe. "I received Father Maufils' reply."

Evangeline drew in her breath. "When I saw you standing outside" she said, but then stopped talking and looked down resignedly, turned almost to a young girl again before him.

"It's not what you think, dear, nor what I expected. Or could have. The Jesuits have been banished from France."

"What does that mean for you?" she asked quickly.

"It means that it's time I sought my own relationship with the Lord."

"You're not going back to France?"

"No. I wasn't going to leave you, Evangeline."

"And now you won't have to," she said with a smile.

He tilted her chin up. "I was not going to leave you."

Jana came down the steps from inside, walking fast and cradling a load of dirty rags.

"Hello, child," Felician said, imperceptibly distancing himself from Evangeline.

"Hello, Father," Jana returned.

They went inside without another word to the girl as Felician wondered if, like Evangeline, Jana had watched through the window before going outside.

Evangeline woke him that night, bent over his pallet, sobbing and shaking both of his shoulders.

"Father." He could barely understand the words through her tears. "I dreamt of Gabriel. Trapped alone, in a ship at the bottom of the ocean. And then, I realized that I was in the ship with him, and that I couldn't breathe. That's what woke me," she cried helplessly.

"Oh, darling." He held her tightly, trying to ignore the fact that they were alone in the room, in his bed. "Just a dream," he whispered in her ear. "You're fine, you're safe."

"I only see him die in my dreams," her sobs continued slower. "What if he is dead? What if Gabriel drowned? What will I do?" She moaned.

"I'll take care of you, sweetheart. We're not going back to sea."

"But what about Gabriel?"

"This is probably because of the shipwreck we heard about." He ran his fingers through her hair and realized he'd never really done so before.

"We haven't heard anything from him." He knew it wasn't the first time she'd worried over that fact.

"I know."

Disease and worse neglect than they'd suffered in Baltimore hadn't left many survivors in South Carolina, and it had been difficult to keep her spirits up as no mention of him surfaced from Charleston or any of the neighboring ports.

"I meant what I said," he said seriously, to try to wrest her attention from her sadness. "We need to leave. There isn't enough for you here, and it's past time I provided you with something better."

"What do you want to do?" Evangeline asking for advice wasn't much more common than her tears.

This was a matter he'd given much thought. "You're a born healer, Evangeline. God has given you a gift, and it's time we put it to better use. We'll head west. There will be plenty of people who have suffered greatly in the war, who need us."

She looked at him without the immediate rejection he'd feared. "When?"

"As soon as this spring, after the weather breaks, we'll leave this town and make a new life." He held her in his arms, rubbing her back. "If Gabriel's alive, it's likely he's gone west himself. It's easy to get lost on the frontier." And so might it be for them, Felician thought.

She nodded, and rested her head on his shoulder.

"Your life waits for you still. And I will make sure that you find it." He stopped murmuring, but kept stroking her hair as she fell asleep in his arms, as she had when they shared a pallet in Saint Charles, after the militiaman attacked her.

Felician eventually slept as well. When he awoke she was not beside him. He lay on the pallet for a moment, inhaling her smell, remembering what her breath felt like on his face. He felt reborn. The Lord had seen fit to grant him a partner for his work, and that partner was the woman he loved. He knew that he loved her, but what form that love would take, the Lord still kept hidden from him. In this instance, Felician felt that too much consideration might be destructive. To examine the intricacies of the issue might illumine those smaller pieces, but would create new problems when the parts were returned to the whole. Only God might probe those larger mysteries without shattering them. Faith meant believing their Lord would bestow meaning onto their wandering.

He thanked Him for the blessing that they were together at all.

Evangeline wasn't downstairs in the kitchen. Fottrell's two-story building had survived yellow fever, a second wave of Acadian immigration, and the resulting backlash from Baltimore's frightened English population, better than the neglect that preceded their occupancy. It stood stoic as its onetime residents had moved to the mud huts on Charles, and now sailed for islands even old Benedict hadn't seen.

Felician headed for Charles Street, to see who among French Town's residents hadn't taken ship. It was a warm day, but he strode briskly, not succumbing to summer's torpidity. Though he thought himself hale, he felt especially young this morning. The only indication of time's passage was three silver streaks cutting front to back in his otherwise coal-dark hair. The only person to whom the years had been kinder was Evangeline, another sign of God's grace in the girl. His charge was old enough now to be mother to half a dozen children if she and Gabriel had been left unmolested in Grand Pre, and he wondered briefly how differently she might look. Felician pitied Gabriel for the life that might have been his with Evangeline, but he rarely felt sorry for her while in her presence.

Otherwise, the years of hunger had sapped the vitality of many of them. Especially with the elderly in his and Evangeline's care, casualties were enormous. Since they were dispersed, births had been exceedingly rare. The trapper had remarked too truthfully after that first year's sickness that the Acadians buried their race in the mud huts.

Felician changed his mind once he reached the dwellings the trapper had spoken of, and now sheltered in himself. He had the winter to count the remaining Acadians. Instead, he walked quickly down the street to the docks, drawn to an inordinate number of gulls that filled the void of the departed ships with their cawing. Pity on these weary souls, Lord, light their way home.

A man he didn't know approached him once he reached the water, wretched with scurvy, seasalt encrusted on his clothes and splotchy beard.

"Father Felician? You probably don't recognize me. Alderic LeBlanc. Rene's son."

"Alderic, forgive me, it's been years. Is your father?"

"He died years ago, Father. Thank you for asking."

"I'll remember him in my prayers. Where were you taken?"

"Philadelphia. With my parents and most of my sisters. But I've been crewing up and down the Atlantic since before the war ended, looking for the rest of my family. Along the way, I stumbled into a piece of news for you."

"Yes, son?"

"I spoke to Jean Dugas, from Grand Pre. He took a turn as a hand on a ship that passed through New Orleans, and he spoke to Basil Lajeunesse, down in Louisiana, Father."

Felician started at the name. "Praise the Lord's abundant mercy."

"Indeed, Father," LeBlanc said.

"Did he mention if Gabriel, his son, were with him?" he asked without hesitation, like ripping off a scab.

"Yes, alive and well, though he wasn't with his father at the time."

"Less than one year ago?" Felician asked, and LeBlanc nodded.

Peace changed everything, with communication foremost among the differences. They'd gone years without word of what lay over the horizon, notwithstanding Bernard's limited ramblings. The man couldn't help but to break the law. But now, correspondence pieced the world back together.

"No word." Felician hesitated.

"Yes, Father?"

"On how they're making out. If they have a family."

"They're trappers, Father. And they're successful enough that they had pelts to trade. That's all I heard."

"Thank you, son. This is unlooked for news, indeed. Blessings on your travel."

Felician walked away from the man absently.

Evangeline would be ecstatic. Her confidence rewarded after the years of pining. Gabriel was alive in the world, waiting for her. And woe be unto the lad if he'd forgotten her, Felician thought, after the line of suitors she'd ignored for a decade. It surpassed coincidence, to finally hear of him only after they were ready to consign Gabriel and his memory to the past.

He forced himself to walk slowly up Calvert Street, from the dock to the church, frowning at the rabble that had washed up on Baltimore's shores over the seven years of wartime. The war's limbless veterans hunched together outside the tavern entrances, begging handouts from the profiteers entering one of the establishments that had grown like spores alongside the two already crouched near the docks.

"You are welcome at the Fottrell House, if you would care for something other than liquor," Felician said to the men as he passed.

The end of the war had brought these new refugees to replace the Acadian variety it first dumped on Baltimore. There were disaffected peoples anywhere he cared to look, with those closest to him already begun another journey without enthusiasm. Though at least the Acadians chose from amongst bad options this time, Felician thought. It was a kind of progress. And that was the extent of the progress permitted him in His master plan. Which apparently wouldn't involve proselytizing the souls of the borderlands between the empires, in favor of him delivering up Evangeline to Gabriel.

He and Evangeline would have left for the west that spring. Returning soldiers assured him that plentitudes of pagans' souls persisted over the Appalachians. They might have founded a mission town, along some stream west of the dividing mountains, to save those who would be in need. The war had made westward travel more possible, despite the bear attacks and sauvage raids frontier settlers continued to warn of. He might have suggested English landowners, urban living, and disease bred in the swamps of the coastal cities, but Felician was not asked what his problems were. Even by Evangeline.

He needed to get the vitriol out of his system so that he would be himself, so that he would be the most reasonable advisor he could, when he did find her, because she had a decision to make. No, she didn't. Her path was chosen for her, and his was to follow her and protect and guide her, and that was all. She had need of him as he was promised to her, and she had Gabriel waiting for her. She had been his responsibility before she was his love, and that responsibility remained, to deliver Evangeline to Gabriel Lajeunesse, who had sailed to Charleston but was no longer there. The sum total of ten years of separation preyed on Evangeline, her cross to bear as she nearly said herself those years ago, comparing herself to Hannah. He didn't delude himself. The weight of her commitment and conviction drew him to her as surely as it drew her to his office.

He went up the steps and bypassed the porch where the old women greeted him as he passed, needing to find her and put his hopes to rest before he returned to his proper duties as minister.

Francoise still cooked for them, the last of four women who'd originally served in the kitchen. Porridge, porridge and gruel was how Felician remembered it, but as their household grew smaller, there was more meat in the diet.

The priest ducked in the kitchen, waved at Francoise, but left quickly when he didn't find Evangeline within. He heard the woman follow him out, but he didn't look back, and the cook didn't call out as he marched upstairs. She was rinsing his other shirt in a basin on the floor, softly humming a song that he couldn't make it out from the door.

"Evangeline," he beckoned from the doorway, "I've just heard some news." How innocent he sounded.

She joined him unhesitatingly, the two of them sitting in his room. He loved being alone with her, behind the curtain. There was nothing romantic in the notion that she grew more attractive by the day, simply an observation of a natural phenomenon. Every girl was pretty as a child, but only the truly beautiful caught more eyes as they aged.

She noticed his study. "What's wrong, Father?"

"Nothing, child. We've had blessed news." You, you've had wondrous news.

"Yes?"

"Gabriel's alive. He and his father are in Louisiana. A man I spoke to saw Monsieur Lajeunesse. He said they were trappers." He spoke slowly, not wanting either to shock her or be forced to repeat himself.

"Gabriel." She said his name like it was a food she'd always wanted to taste. She looked away and then was in his arms, sobbing, her wet cheek against his chin. Her long legs pressed against the length of his. She'd always been too beautiful for a daughter, he thought as she cried, a happy, heaving awareness of the years she missed and those she might still have. He hadn't yet heard the prayer that could be answered to everyone's satisfaction. She was dry-eyed in an instant, and drew herself out of his tight embrace.

"Did the man know anything else?"

"Nothing."

He could most likely have kept the news from her for the two months before their departure. Once they left, traveled west beyond the larger settlements, it was unlikely that they'd hear much from other people, or that others would hear of them. It would be enough for the two of them to subsist in their life together, as they had in the early, busy years of the hospital. She would have been his, a promise made permissible because of its conditional nature.

I am not your father, you are no longer a girl, these were the new recognized facts of their relationship, much else was yet to be determined. She was betrothed to Gabriel, and they needed to wait for the war to end so they could leave. He had waited, patiently, without expectation, until he became convinced that God had need of them elsewhere, and to fulfill His holy will they needed to return to proselytizing the unbaptized. And she'd been a willing convert, after a longer stretch of time than what he'd previously considered a restrictive posting in Grand Pre, bless the Lord for His strict lessons. Divine mandate suited them both better than waiting for their last patients to die, there was more that they were needed for. They were not called simply to wither away in this English port town.

And once they were away, they might make their lives together. But that wouldn't be the line of their destinies, though they didn't look to branch yet, either.

"Oh, Felician. After the dream. I'd never come so close to giving up hope."

He remembered the dream then, and saw hope for them both.

"There's another way to get to Louisiana. The colony lies at the terminus of the Mississippi. We could travel to the river, and then follow it south, to Gabriel."

"What do you mean another way? We can find a ship going to Louisiana, can't we?"

He waited for a moment before responding. "Only last night you dreamt of shipwreck and the sea rising to swallow the clouds."

"We'd just heard of the ship that sank on the way to England. You said so yourself. I could have been reacting to that."

"I'm sure that you were," he said gently. "So, we heard of a shipwreck, and the next night you dream of calamity at sea. Then we finally, after years, we receive word of Gabriel."

"People have just sailed south." She saw it now as a missed opportunity.

"To Saint Domingue. We wouldn't have known that Gabriel was in Louisiana."

"You don't want to hire a boat?"

"They infrequently sail so far south. But, there might be a better choice." She looked at him, still awash with the news, amazed that Gabriel's existence could be so removed from his actual presence.

"What choice?"

"We said we would never trust ourselves to the English again, and we don't have to. Louisiana is where the Mississippi meets the gulf. We intended to leave Baltimore in the spring, and we will."

"We're not going to leave until spring? How will we get to the Mississippi?"

"Bernard can help us get there. He's trapped the Mississippi's headwaters."

"If he wants to help. I thought you didn't care for Bernard."

"Well, at least the man has enough sense to avoid idleness."

"That's kind of you, Felician," she said approvingly.

He shrugged away the praise. He wouldn't trust Bernard

alone with her, the man's interest was as clear and painful as a simple adult fumbling with a child's toys. "It's clear the man wants to leave Baltimore as badly as anyone."

Evangeline nodded. "So, we'll walk to Gabriel."

"Your trial may seem unceasing, Evangeline, but it is not as bottomless as your faith." He inhaled thickly, "For God speaks in one way, and in two, though people do not always perceive it. In a dream, in a vision of the night, when deep sleep falls on mortals, while they slumber on their beds, then he opens their ears, and terrifies them with warnings, that he may turn them aside from their deeds, and keep them from pride."

"The dream is warning me not to sail, or we'll perish in the ocean?"

"Easy child. Your people are experienced in travel's perils, and dreams are confusing things. Which is not to say that you're wrong. Perhaps we have been warned."

They sat quietly reflecting together, until Evangeline stirred. "Will you stay in Louisiana when we get there?" Evangeline asked.

"Well," he started slowly, as though only now realizing. "I can't go back to Quebec, and the Jesuits are banished from France and out of favor with the Holy Father in Rome, so I suppose I will serve God as his individual instrument as best as I am able." He paused and smiled at her. "Once I've seen you safely to Louisiana."

"It's across the country," she wriggled her slender fingers uncomfortably. "I can't imagine that you, or anyone else would be willing to come."

"It's certainly proper to thank Him for His mercy, dear, but don't hold yourself accountable. Each of us wants to leave, we just lacked the destination." Felician kissed her forehead where

her hair met her skin, feeling more like the man who'd scaled
peaks on Ile Royale.

Winter in Baltimore had left Francis Bauer's clothes fitting
him awkwardly, Felician thought when the man came to the
church looking for him. Sometimes the largest among them
looked the skinniest.

"Father Felician, I heard you could help me get a fair price
on some horses." The voice was respectful and quiet standing in
the hospital annex.

"What are you looking for?"

"I need two work horses, big, healthy and younger than
not."

"I see. Where is the farm you're planning to start?"

"Well, Father, we've been told that we're free to go as we
please."

"Yes, that's the official word. Part of the peace."

"There's cheap land west of Hagerstown. With some animals we could be settled by the end of the year."

"I see," Felician said vaguely. "The four of you only
Francis?"

"Only my family, yes." Bauer stood up straighter as he
spoke.

"You've spoken to Evangeline regarding," Felician hesitated briefly, "our plan."

"She mentioned you were considering heading to
Louisiana." Bauer knotted his brows, angry over being forced
into gossip, Felician guessed.

"Did she mention that we might all head out together?"

"She told me that I should see you about getting some horses."

"Well. If you're establishing a homestead in the great

unpeopled west, and we're headed along the same path, what about safety in numbers as far as we care to venture together?"

"What if we're taking you out of your way?"

"I'm sure it's best for all of us to have a little company through one winter to get our bearings, before we push south."

"Well," The man stopped for a moment, looking around the offer. "Can you help me with the horses?"

Felician left for the new Gazette office after speaking with Bauer, his first trip there since it had opened with the new year. Brandt had settled his business on Charles, not far from the emptying mud huts already eroding at the heart of the burgeoning town. The newspaperman's chimney sent up one of the few plumes of smoke on the lonely street. Brandt occupied his solitary perch at the center of three paper-strewn desks, press equipment sequestered behind a new interior wall. The newspaperman pushed a chair to the priest.

"You heard that they're raising funds for more ships this summer?" Brandt asked.

"We've been hearing."

"The money's right, Father. They're vouching for it down in the capitol. The Governor is more fed up with you Acadians than we are even." He ran his hand atop the few slick strands of hair he had left and pushed them across his head in the other direction. "What are you going to do? There are hundreds of Acadians up and down the colonies."

"There have been all along."

"True enough. And it's hard to blame clamoring for homes after ten years without."

"Though you say otherwise."

"I'm a company man, Father. But, like I was saying, the Crown's flooded the colonies with money since the war ended, and there's enough of it now that we can see about doing the least service for a disenfranchised people."

"You mean that you've become rich enough that you can afford to pay to dispense with discomforting reminders of the recent struggle."

"Take it how you will, Father. Sharpe is hiring boats enough for anybody that's left that wants to sail down to Louisiana, where it sounds like they'd actually welcome your presence."

"The last people to try sailing out of here are still on disease-ridden islands down in the Caribbean."

"Yes, travel's uncertain, Father. You know that. But you've heard the rumors, and I'm telling you they're true, that the next ships through here are taking Acadians to Louisiana."

"Well, if you're telling me, there's no sense asking anyone else." Felician stood up before adding, "I'm still tempted to be a bit suspicious around English boats. Take care of yourself, Henry."

Later that day, Felician stood on the dock on Calvert Street and watched the trapper's tar-streaked hands twist apart the hemp rope. Neither had sought out the other since Bernard's return.

"Would you want to come with us?"

"I'll be of more use on the trail than here."

"So you'll help us?"

"I consider myself to be in your debt, Felician. And though shortly returned, I've no reason to stay." Bernard shrugged.

"So how would you take wagons west?"

"Whose wagons, Felician? What are we taking?"

"The Bauers are starting a farm."

"So we'll be following their wagon train." Bernard tailed off, and Felician imagined the realities of animal dung and axle repair competing with Bernard's yearning to be purposefully free of Baltimore.

"You mentioned that you traveled by boat before you came to us in Grand Pre."

Bernard nodded at Felician's memory. "They're cleaner than animals. Plenty of men I knew, my father among them, ran a long way to avoid spending time around pigs and cows."

"Well, as I said, the Bauers have heard there's land available and that the Governor is welcoming honest settlers of any creed along Braddock's road."

"That's convenient, because that road is the only way we'll get very far in the woods with a wagon and a bunch of cows."

"So you got out that way on your travels?"

Bernard frowned and shook his head.

"Horses for the wagon, and goats for milk. That's all they have."

Bernard looked at the frayed rope in his hands. "They seem like helpful people."

"They are good people. And if we travel with them, we can keep plenty of food around while we get accustomed to the trail. And we can help the Bauers get safely settled. Besides, Evangeline and the twins haven't traveled like this before, so going slowly seems the prudent course."

"No, they haven't. I don't imagine we'd have to worry too much about her, though."

Felician nodded. Evangeline would be fine in any situation he could envision. "I think a larger group is safer all around. The war's just over. There's bound to be someone still in that borderland we've got to cross." Convinced they were of a mind, Felician patted the trapper on the back, "Once we leave the wagons behind, though, we'll have to find a river. I don't intend to walk the whole way to Louisiana."

Maryland 1767

⚬

Sometimes they saw, or thought they saw,
the smoke of his campfire.

ERNARD HAD RETURNED THE PREVIOUS SUMMER, CURIOUS
to see what had become of the boy. He told Bernard
that he had already kissed three girls, and that two of
them had only done it because he was missing his arm. The boy
said his parents told him that girls would stop being nice to him
when they found out he couldn't do as much work on a farm.
The boy's parents held him accountable, not Bernard. The boy
didn't care what they thought, he was going to hire on a ship in
a year or two.

You only needed one arm to turn a wheel in most weather,
Bernard had agreed. He left the family the bale of skins he carried, and he left the boy a hatchet.

He'd arrived at the Fottrell House after dark, but despite
the hour, they had opened a bottle of brandy, and he had walked
to the dock with Julian, Jana and Evangeline, and they stared at
the ships in the moonlight, and he told them that Augustine had
died in Quebec.

Bernard spent the autumn picking tobacco on a plantation east across the bay. Julian arranged for the work, he had been bonded out to the farm with dozens of other Acadian men, and since the war, had worked for a wage. The sprawling fields stretched along the Manokin River, and they slept nearby, in cabins open-faced to the water that would shelter livestock over the winter. Julian told him that the plantation had been a preferable arrangement during the war, with few overseers who knew the men were returning to families across in Baltimore. And there was always plenty to smoke.

That winter, they returned with the other men, and he joined Julian and Francis in picking oakum at the docks. On the rare occasions they were paid in coin, Bernard sent his with Julian up to the hospital. He had a rifle, a knife, and a year's worth of tobacco, and he didn't yet want to confuse the issue with additional possessions. Usually they exchanged the oakum for small casks of beer, which they could lug north to the sprawling lumber mills out of town whose workers appreciated the service, and offered four pelts instead of the three the brew was worth in town. If the weather didn't allow for the trip, they would drink Bernard's cask in the hovel he had chosen to see him through the snow.

Julian's guilelessness and Francis' directness endeared both men to Bernard, and his friends' inclusion was reassuring, as he remained wary of Felician. Their relationship had not warmed since he recovered from the fever. Bernard considered himself beholden to the man and disliked him for it. But he did remember the steel of the priest that night on the porch. They had stood together naturally enough when there were larger enemies about. And no matter his personal misgivings, at least the next time he was ambushed there would be more than Augustine running his mouth for reinforcement.

Which was good, because today he followed the man into the wild. They had saved his life, and fed him for a year while he waited for his strength and color to return. But he followed them into the wilderness not to repay what could not be repaid, but for a chance to show the best of himself. It did not exactly matter that their purpose was Evangeline's safe delivery into the waiting hands of a man she'd last seen as a boy.

He and Julian walked at the head of a pair of open wagons, each pulled by two heavy beasts. Evangeline rode with Jana and Felician up front, and the Bauers brought up the rear. Francis had purchased the plowhorses with Felician's assistance, and the animals dragged goods to weigh down ten canoes. Ground corn, rice, sugar, peas, chocolate, cured meat, rum, and two hogsheads of tobacco jounced behind Evangeline and the priest alongside two spare muskets and the Bibles Felician had brought to hand out in the woods. The lead wagon with its weapons and libations was off-limits to the two boys, Frederic and Eugene. The family hauled saws, axes and other tools and sundries for constructing a home at the end of the trail.

The conveyances bore all the possessions seen as necessary for the family to start a farm, and everything he and Felician thought the five of them might require between here and Louisiana, if they augmented the foodstuffs along the way. It didn't look like enough for crossing a largely uncharted territory, but that was the beauty of the unknown.

Bernard turned back to mark their progress, and his eyes drifted to Evangeline who rode with the lead team next to Felician, taller than the priest in her hat. She saw him and waved, smiling. He waved back and then turned to catch up with Julian. The girl was impossibly aware, he'd never managed to watch her without her knowledge, probably the result of a lifetime having her least movements observed.

That night, with Baltimore's smoke still visible to their east, they gathered around a large fire and Felician blessed the inception of their groaning journey.

"Years ago, I compared the Acadians to the Israelites, who endured their captivity through unwavering tenacity and unshakable faith. Now, after ten long years among the pharaohs of Baltimore, we begin to fulfill the triumphant promise of His will." The priest inhaled and continued. "Remember though, what has brought us this far. Let us honor the Lord by persevering over the trials of our upcoming journey. Trust in Him to know what we can bear, and in His mercy, to shield us from what we cannot. Allow Him to guide us past the obstacles of this life until He welcomes us in the next."

"Amen," Bernard watched the others intone with the priest.

Bernard wondered who else in the company saw beauty around them but felt nothing for the words. Francis, perhaps, who tended the fire and smoked impatiently during the sermon. His family, though, joined Evangeline and the twins, either content to listen, or held in line by the priest's authority.

Those first years in Baltimore, mass had been the finest part of Bernard's day, and he considered that his bitterness might stem from the loss of those peaceful moments. Sitting with his feet propped on the railing, smoking and imagining the ritualistic muttering of his companions inside, he could almost laugh at the path that had landed him on that porch, watching detachedly as the strange town filled in around them.

"The physical world is to Heaven as infancy is to conscious life," he remembered Felician telling him once. Bernard reflected on that often while sitting on the stoop, happy as a baby puffing his smoke heavenward with no more awareness than an infant's cries. How many times had he watched sunset alone while they worked at their foolish mysteries inside?

But his humor didn't last in the intimacy of the trail. The peaceful solitude he'd known was displaced by a purposeless sensation brought on by the others' prayers, an unquiet he was unable to dispel by carrying on with the chores of the camp in the meantime. The priest's lofty words made him feel a fool.

And this was just the well-trammeled beginning, the easement provided by established routes through the woods and scattered farms. Soon would come the limbo of the forest, where though they could be sure that others had preceded them they could still become lost. And, finally, the true wilderness, where all might be unmade.

They fell into something of a rhythm, walking to the pace of the plodding horse teams, animals for whom the journey was only the beginning of their sentence. He was happy when Baltimore and its hamlets receded into the woods behind them. After two days the wide beaten track was the only sign of the civilization they'd left behind.

At night, while they shared a fire, the family maintained their separate identity, and seemed to have the greater purpose. Despite the knowledge that they were pushing on for Louisiana, the Bauers' unknown destination seemed less nebulous, with children already in tow, their future assured. Evangeline hadn't spoken much as they left the city, and he was disappointed, but maybe this didn't feel like a beginning to the girl as much as a continuation of the incremental progress of the preceding years. The first couple nights she had mostly talked about the creeping pace of the horses. But on their third day on the trail, she started out hiking upfront with him and Julian, both of them so unnerved by her presence that they walked the first hour without letup and wound up well ahead of the train.

They halted where the trail eased around a small, boulder-strewn hill. Bernard scrambled up one of the rocks and surveyed the ground they'd covered, guessing how far back in the woods the wagons might be. Evangeline walked over to him, leaving Julian sitting and staring at the way ahead. Bernard climbed down to her, but had nothing to report, and looked around, suddenly uncomfortable. They watched a small squirrel with black spiky fur running along a tree root as it snaked between the large stones, examining and rejecting acorns that seemed fine to Bernard. He guessed it wouldn't be so picky in a few months.

"You don't have to go very far for the animals to be entirely different," she said to him staring after the squirrel.

"That was a strange-looking squirrel," Bernard agreed, studying her profile for a moment. Under the stovepipe hat her stiff jaw and clenched cheek almost looked like a mask. Evangeline turned and met his eyes briefly, and then looked back after the squirrel, leaving him disappointed, though she hadn't frowned noticeably to see him staring. Her expression hadn't changed at all, like there was nothing that he might have been doing except looking at her.

"Have you ever seen a bear?" she asked.

"Lots of them." He frowned as the wagons become visible through the trees. "I never had the same trouble with them that I have with people."

She laughed, though he hadn't meant it as a joke. "We had one, the nicest rug in the house. My father brought it back from Boston before I was born. That bear might have come out of these woods." She looked around as though expecting her words to make it true.

"Here they come," Julian said, and they fell back in with the caravan.

Each day was more beautiful than the last, Bernard thought the next morning as Evangeline joined him again at the head of the procession while Julian kept his sister company behind. Thick soles on his moccasins, a nearly new fur cap, no heavy pelts, and the unusual company of a beautiful woman on the trail. Evangeline was quiet again that morning as they started walking, but the birdsong and sunshine encouraged him to try his unpracticed hand at starting a conversation, though it took him a moment to settle on a topic.

"I don't like riding in wagons either," Bernard said.

"We're going so slowly." Her pain was his.

He looked at her, aware as always that he'd happily do anything that she asked other than deliver her into the arms of another man. "I can't imagine you married."

That made her laugh a little. "Yes, you can. You know I get enough of that from Julian."

Bernard smiled and nodded though he hadn't known. He only knew that Julian wanted her, but it made him happy that she confided in him.

"It's hard to believe we're walking to Louisiana," he said, suddenly seeing the expedition as daring rather than drudgery.

"A boat would have been a lot faster," Evangeline said.

"I thought this was your idea."

"It was."

"Those sugar islands sound like Hell on earth."

"And people drown."

He nodded, and they walked quietly for a while, he hoped speculating on the disasters they'd escaped. The deciduous forest that had carried over from Baltimore was giving out to sloping hills, a beautiful country, but too open for beaver, and rockier than the wagon wheels would prefer.

A week from Baltimore the rutted trail met Braddock's Road. The new track was broad, and had seen heavy use enough that the grass was gone along much of its length, and trampled in every clearing spacious enough to camp in. When they crested a hill, they could see another caravan following them west. They passed no one that day or the next, and covered the packed earth swiftly until it started raining.

Bernard woke to another morning with their disparate company. Two slow weeks on the military road had given them renewed appreciation for the full days of clear skies they'd had leaving Baltimore. It was threatening again when he woke with the light, poor luck after a downpour the day before kept the wagons motionless for hours. As he feared, he felt drops before he'd even stirred the embers.

Back under the shelter of the wagon, the rain plunked loudly on the canvas tarpaulin covering the foodstuffs and dripped off the sides. After a few minutes it slackened, reaching them only in pats and drips through the oak canopy overhead. The noises were quickly drowned out by appreciative birds returning to the morning sky. Bernard left the shelter with their song, ignored the lingering drops and started scooping the wet ash of last night's fire into a hole he kicked outside the dirt ring. Francis came out directly from under his wagon, his boys on his heels, embarrassed not to have been first. Julian stayed put, sitting next to Evangeline with their knees not quite touching. Afforded a reason to be in close quarters with her, he wasn't budging.

It hadn't been Bernard's intention to disturb the camp, but he was waking up early after only a few weeks on the trail, his back knotted worse than after months of carrying pelts through cold forests. He felt twisted around the wound in his back, as though the bullet hole was his body's new origin, the center of the painful life he'd regained.

Bernard left the Bauer children to hunt for dry tinder and walked into the woods. Not far from camp he found a mature oak with a thick limb running parallel to the forest floor. He climbed the ivy-entwined trunk, reached out and hung from the limb, breaking off thick chips of bark as he found his grip. He gasped out loud in relief as his vertebrae adjusted, then blew out more calmly for as long as he was able, smelling the moss under his feet. With a pattering in the leaves above him, the rain began anew.

"Goddamnit," he said halfheartedly, as he was joined under the branch by beetles and black ants displaced by the rain. The shower halted, even faster than its predecessors that morning, and the insects dispersed as quickly as they appeared. The ivy glistened in the early light, appearing as waves dancing up the big trunk, cresting in the leaves that bent back toward him. With his arms raised, Bernard could smell old sweat, penetrating the veneer of last night's fire.

Leaves scrunched as someone headed his way, and Bernard released his hold, slipped off the branch and landed solidly. He started walking toward the oncomer, his back somewhat improved. In the aftermath of the rain a second dew covered the ivy and fallen leaves, and in that moment, stolen from weather, companions and time, Evangeline came toward him. The brightening sky glared off the wet leaves, and it looked like she walked across the sun. He was happy not to have been caught in the tree.

The rain had flattened the crown of her hair, but otherwise

the dampness only made her beautiful hair fresher, more in keeping with the forest they traveled.

"Are you hurt?"

"No." He was flattered that she paid enough attention to know he was concealing pain. "I was scouting for sign of other travelers."

"Did you see anything?"

"It's just us." Bernard looked around as he spoke, as though making sure. Another rainfall began above them, but failed to penetrate the canopy.

"Then there's nothing to stop us from another day." She came a little closer, and he could smell the smoke from the new fire on her.

"Nothing at all," he said, now staring into her eyes.

"Let's get back to the others." She spoke gently, as if not wanting to upset him, and he followed her under the dripping trees.

After several weeks the rain gave out, and the miles passed easier again as the horses scampered over the dry earth in relief. The road barreled forward through the wilderness like the scar from a cannonball. They climbed a hill one night to make their fire above the reach of the flies, and cooked trout Felician and Francis had caught. Sated, Bernard stood on the rise watching evening swallow the pristine wilderness. So long as he kept the horses in their traces out of sight, he could convince himself they were the first come to that hill above the stream.

"Not a bad place for a farm, eh, Francis," Bernard said, sitting back down with his fish. The crisp skin crackled like a second fire in his hands.

"It's too hot," Francis said tersely, only beginning to eat after making sure his children hadn't swallowed any bones.

"Well, it's easier to take out here under these tress than it was in Baltimore," Marguerite said. "Really, the heat was a godsend, drying up the roads."

She turned to him. "Do you like the fish, Bernard?"

Francis was a lucky man, was what he thought. "Very much," he said. "We rarely ate it in Canada."

"Even on the river?" Marguerite asked.

Bernard nodded. "The best voyageurs only eat moose tongue. The rest of us made do with bear or possum. But we only ate game." It seemed a strange custom now that he considered it. "Though there were plenty of fish to be had."

Frost came early to the foothills, and after they saw it, Francis and Marguerite began scouting the terrain for a homestead for their family. They finally called a halt after a week of slow travel over rocky ground past the sturdy cabins that identified themselves as Hagerstown. They slept under their wagons on ground that the parents would soon work with their sons. A spring gathered speed as it ran south from the foothills to plunge into the Potomac.

Halfway to the river, Bernard and Francis dug notched posts into the hillside and braced a log in the forks while the others gathered oak branches. They built the roof on the second day, filled the worst gaps with bark. It would be a more than passable livestock pen, Bernard thought, and it should keep them from freezing over the winter. They built a large fire outside the shelter's open face, and Bernard stayed up late that night with the two older men, drinking a little rum while they contemplated their sleeping companions.

"Rocky soil," Felician commented, fidgeting under himself and digging one out as proof.

"Good for walls," Francis returned.

"I don't think we've seen a Frenchman since we left Baltimore."

"No, this doesn't seem the place to look."

"So you'd have your grandchildren raised speaking German."

"So long as I get them, they can speak any way they like."

Francis offered the bottle, but the priest shook his head.

"For luck?" Francis asked.

Felician drank. "There's only hurt in there," he said as he passed the liquor back to Francis. His black robe melted into the night beyond the fire's reach.

"I can't argue with him on that," Francis said as he passed the bottle instead into Bernard's outstretched hand. "I'm going to have to set up a still."

"He makes me miss a man I never thought I would have."

"You mean your old partner."

"I liked him alright. I can admire anyone that makes their own way. I just never felt sentimental about the relationship. He was a rough old bastard." Bernard drank. "But my best days all seem to end up like this," he pointed at the fire with the bottle. "And he felt pretty similarly, I think."

"Bernard." Francis' tone was sharp. "I understand why they're going south. The girl, the priest, Julian and Jana have their reasons, and I know that you've told me you feel obligated."

"They saved my life, and I can help them out here."

"Neither you nor Felician even knows where the damn Mississippi is."

"The Mississippi's west, Francis. A good bit west."

The man laughed. "So you'll be a boon to them, no question. But that gets at my point, in a way. You've lived plenty of years as your own man, but you've got more life in front of you than you let on. Stay here, marry some girl that comes along and get on with life. There are more folks coming this way every year, and I'd be proud to have you as a neighbor."

"I appreciate it. But I told her I'd get them to Louisiana. It's not much, but that's what I've got."

"I know, son. But it's a difficult thing, envisioning the bunch of you all winding up happy."

Louisiana 1766

∽

*All things forgotten beside, they gave themselves to
the maddening whirl of the giddy dance.*

GABRIEL MET THEM IN THE SAME TAVERN ON DECATUR.
Nothing had changed inside the low building, peace or
war, boatload of arriving Acadians or not, the same
unremarkable men drank and elbowed in the dim greaselight
before loosing themselves onto the muggy night. And Gabriel,
Philippe, Alexander and Anna downed weak cypress beer spiked
with rum, Gabriel drinking faster than his friends. After touching glasses, they stayed quiet until Alexander returned with the
second round.

"Evangeline's not on the boat," said Philippe, as though she
wouldn't be sitting alongside them now if she had been on the
boat. Gabriel had trouble imagining her drinking a beer.

"I'm sorry, Gabriel."

"Thanks, Alex," Gabriel replied. "Thank you," he said to
Anna who rested her hand on his.

He looked to Philippe, but after introducing the subject his
friend had fallen silent.

Gabriel finally started talking again. "Philippe and I spoke to a woman named Perrine that knew her up in Maryland, only a couple years ago." He started hopefully, but trailed off and looked into his empty mug.

"And she's still got you in mind," Philippe said helpfully.

"There was no mention of a man."

"Are you going to go up there?" Alexander asked him.

He shook his head. "She already left town." Gabriel paused, hoping he didn't sound foolish. "But it sounds like she was heading for Louisiana. The woman said that she was looking for a man."

"She's coming to find you?" Anna asked.

"At least she was," Gabriel said.

That was the sum of his information, related just hours ago on the old city docks, as he and Philippe questioned the disembarking families.

"Now I have to keep hoping that she knows where to come claim me. Unless I want to walk into the woods in the hopes I see her." Gabriel sighed. A little hard information just made his suffering seem more commonplace, and left him feeling more distant from her. The vanished promise of his life with her in Acadia would forever cast a pall over the the paltry remainder.

"So, these people are from Maryland?" Alexander said, feigning interest to distract him.

"Some of them. Some are still sweating with fever from the islands."

"Well my father didn't complain about it," Anna said. "Plantations as big as this city." She looked around the table. "Each of you would have a stable of girls down there."

"I wouldn't take it," Alexander denied flatly.

Anna smiled at his response. "He sounded happy enough."

Alexander huffed and took their mugs back to the bar to be refilled, while Anna turned her attention to her husband's friends.

"I think this upheaval has spoiled an entire generation of Acadian men."

"Not me," Philippe said. "I'm headed to those docks tomorrow to see who needs an escort out west."

"I don't doubt it at all, Philippe. I've heard that you're both in luck, though. These people are all headed out to the frontier with the two of you."

"My father will be thrilled," Gabriel said.

Philippe laughed, and slipped the bottle of rum he'd smuggled in up to the table. "I can't believe I survived two days with the man."

"I'd love to meet him."

"Well, you may have to come to us," Gabriel said, "because I don't remember the last time my father stepped foot in New Orleans. In my father's mind, little good can come from leaving home. He probably still thinks we'd be forging iron in Acadia if we hadn't gone to church that day."

"How long does it take to reach the Teche?" Anna asked, apparently more serious than he'd thought at first.

Gabriel frowned at the question. "It's not the sort of thing you want to commit only one length of time to. We got back this time in three days, but you'd have a hard time dragging Alexander that fast." He timed the statement with his friend's reemergence with the drinks.

"The limp looks good," Philippe said and he splashed rum into the mugs.

"Thank you." Alexander grinned and turned to Anna. "Nibble on my ear there, darling."

"How's the Captain treating you?" Gabriel asked.

"Awful since he left for Mobile to negotiate with the English." Alexander laughed to take the sting out of his words. "Now I'm accompanying those prigs upriver to make sure that the tribes don't attack them."

"And he misses having his old friend out on campaign," Anna said to Philippe.

"He couldn't help me with this," Alexander demurred, digging out a letter containing his orders from her father. He unfolded the paper on the table and squinted at the document.

Alexander, I will assume this missive finds you and my daughter enjoying the fullest bloom of health and contentment. Mobile's charm is matched only by the compassion of its English commander, whose considerate behavior I can only hope to be able to repay in kind one day.

"That means it's not going well," Anna said.

Alexander nodded and resumed.

He has claimed, however, that several English ships traveling north up the Mississippi have been waylaid by sauvages that he is certain were our staunch allies, the Choctaw. The commander insists that we are responsible for correcting this confusion on the part of our friends, though I did try to persuade him that we'd lost the war, and with it much of our former influence in the region. To ensure our compliance, he is requesting that I remain here, which unfortunately leaves me little choice but to dispatch you up the great river to remind the Choctaw that English vessels are to be allowed full liberty of the Mississippi's waters. Take with you the knowledge that my affection for you is greater than could possibly be the case if you were actually, Alexander stopped midsentence.

"Scion." Gabriel read the word. "Like son."

Scion, Alexander continued, *of my noble loins, and forgive me for depriving you again of your lovely bride for the sake of these trivialities. Best of luck in this endeavor, your grateful Captain and father.*

Alexander shook his head and looked at Anna. "I guess I'm leaving you alone, love."

"I suppose so," she said and looked at Gabriel. "How did you learn to read so well?"

He hesitated before sharing this memory. "Evangeline taught me."

"She must be quite a girl," Anna said.

"She was teaching me English."

"I can't read English," Anna said regretfully, as though she just realized it was a possibility.

"It's absolutely critical out there with the deer." Philippe laughed at his own joke. "I'm just lucky I had Gabriel to translate."

As summer turned to winter, the newly arrived Acadians settled west of the city along the Teche and the Atchafalaya. They diked the turgid water to protect their fields in as close an approximation of their Acadian farms as they could engineer in the swamp. Philippe moved downriver to join the exiles.

Gabriel sat on his father's porch with Michael, listening to him fiddle while his father hammered together a shelf inside.

"I haven't heard you playing lately, Gabriel," the blind man nagged after he finished his song.

"No, I haven't felt like it much."

"You haven't had much to say to anyone either. I've told you, boy, there's no better cure for loneliness than singing about it." And the fiddler did so, solemnly singing, *I once had*

a mother, but now I have none. She's gone to her home on high.
Prepare me, oh lord, for to sail on that ship. When the ship
comes sailing by.

He put his instrument down.

"The small amount that songs lift the spirit is an important amount. The Lord has done me a great service in giving me extra motivation to play the fiddle," Michael gestured to his empty eyes. "A noble craft where the product of my hands is as evident to me as it is to the rest of you."

He took the instrument up again. "I've not known the pleasure of a wife, either, you know. But there are plenty that might consider us fortunate to have escaped a woman's tyranny."

He bowed his strings, fingers deftly racing as he sang, *Well I married my old wife and there ended my life. You never seen a woman blow so cold.*

Michael offered the instrument to the younger man, but Gabriel gently pushed it back toward him.

"Music doesn't have any answers when it comes to Evangeline. And the older I get, the more years that lie between us, the less I feel like singing about anything at all."

He left the man on the porch, and returned to his empty house to stare at the bed he hadn't yet slept in while the fiddler droned on.

Gabriel loaded the traps in his pirogue and left early the next morning with Philippe, paddling north, happy to be away. He rarely ate with the older men, and could barely remember the last time he'd exchanged more than a passing word with his father.

"What about keeping a little closer to home this time?" Philippe asked.

True to his word, his friend had courted a new neighbor

devotedly enough to get her pregnant, and married the girl before she was half a year in her new home.

"There's no reason to exhaust ourselves. There're still enough deer that we could shoot them from your porch."

"Fine with me," Gabriel responded. He would have preferred to spend a few days camped out away from home, but instead said, "Pass that brandy back here."

Philippe grunted in surprise. "Pretty early start on the day."

Gabriel took an angry drink from the bottle, and settled it between his feet without a word.

"We may have to make it our regular practice," his friend said after a moment. Gabriel was unsure if he'd ever heard Philippe sound sheepish, and he was pretty sure he wasn't referring to drinking in the morning.

"Shorter trips, you mean."

"I'm not sure. Rosa isn't really crazy about all of this. Her parents have four hectares right alongside mine, enough room so that they've started farming corn."

"You want to be a farmer?"

"I don't know about that."

"You hate to work, and anytime you go down the river you can see for yourself that as many crops are failing as are taking."

"Well, it's in my blood. Besides, what I'm going to hate is being gone for days at a time once she's done being pregnant. All that sweat starts to pay off."

"Jesus," Gabriel said, realizing he would be out there alone.

"Yes, well, I'm reforming. Not reformed, though, and Rosa has girlfriends over for dinner half the nights of the week, tempting me from my virtue."

"How long do you have to wait?"

"You mean until she has the baby? Two months." He spat

in the water. "Damned if she wasn't pregnant before I even got started enjoying myself. Alexander must know something I don't."

They shared a look as they drifted atop the dun water, and Philippe changed the subject. "You know, Rosa's got a friend with blond hair and big, beautiful breasts. Why don't you come over one night and get her off my imagination? I'd consider it a favor."

"Maybe."

"Or what, Gabriel. These are Acadians, no different than the woman that you've been waiting half your life for, except they've been here for half a year now while you've been watching your father and Michael shrivel up in that cabin."

"People saw Evangeline in Baltimore. Unmarried."

"A lot can happen between here and there. Listen, Gabriel, I'm almost thirty now."

"So am I." Gabriel interrupted, quiet but firm. "Speaking of my old man, he'll need more than stories to tan."

They dug in, and pushed sullenly a bit further upriver. In this swamp, there was little difference paddling out or returning home, on this water, he never really felt like he was moving at all.

News that the birth went smoothly restored some energy to the Lajeunesse household, as they prepared to host a celebration for the new parents, though it still struck Gabriel that no two people were more unsuited for throwing a party than he and Basil. His bitterness didn't stop the day from arriving, but he insisted on handling the cooking, keeping himself busy outside while Basil and Viktor smoked and listened to Michael's fiddle until the couples arrived.

Short, red-headed Rosa beamed over Philippe as they stood

on the porch greeting Basil and Viktor, who took turns pounding him on the back. Gabriel waved from the cookfire, but stayed with the stew. His friend shouted a greeting inside to Alexander and Anna, and he joined Gabriel, leaving his wife on the porch with the men.

"How goes the cauldron, Gabriel?"

"Hello, Philippe." It was a gorgeous evening, the usual swarms of mosquitoes shrunk to solitary irritants. "Congratulations."

"Thank you, thank you." Philippe sniffed appreciatively. "Viktor will be ashamed when he smells this." He took the ladle from Gabriel. "Go and be polite for a bit, I'll keep an eye on this."

Inside Fort Lajeunesse, they crowded around their only table to celebrate with a feast of venison steaks, fish and rice stew, real brandy, and beer they'd carefully brewed in the shade of the roofline behind the house.

"Clara Boiselle," Viktor said as he shook his head. "At least she has a decent mother."

Philippe smiled, and addressed Alexander. "I'll bet these rude old men didn't even know they were Spanish citizens. What do you elderly gents think of Governor Ulloa."

"You were right to think I don't pay much attention to talk of politics," Basil said.

"And none of us pay much attention to your talk, Philippe." Viktor laughed.

Gabriel headed outside directly after he ate to smother the fire. His friends had become men, while he remained mired in unnatural childhood, cordoned off with life's veterans out in the swamp.

They were out of water in the kitchen, and he took the pail down to the Teche, and when he returned, Anna was sitting on the stump that he'd felled for his bed, watching him drag his feet back up toward his duty.

"You look like you're having a good time," she said.

"You know me," Gabriel replied.

"There's nothing worse than when other people's happiness makes you miserable."

"Thanks for understanding."

"I was referring to myself."

"Oh."

"It's entirely more difficult to say how much you're missing as far as marriage is concerned."

"I've always hoped I was missing quite a bit."

"Don't torture yourself." She put her hand on his arm. "Put that water up here and I'll help you scrub the plates."

Gabriel did, and they stood outside in the darkness and the leftover heat of the cooking fire, wiping the wet wood clean and listening as the Teche lapped up the bank toward them.

Maryland 1768

Loud in the midst of the music, heard she the sound of the sea.

VANGELINE SAT ON A STUMP IN A FIELD OF THEM, WATCHING the Bauer children swordfight at the edge of the cleared ground. Beyond the boys and the three-walled shelter where they had spent last November, the forest was beginning to leaf out. From her vantage, Evangeline could see holes in the thatched roof they'd hastily bundled the previous fall, but it had served to keep the rain out until they had raised a cabin.

That first month had been further discomforted by the necessity of warming bousillage in the firepit dug in the shelter's open side. While the women heated the material for the walls, the men began to clear land where Francis would lay a crop the next year.

They were so efficient in completing the Bauers' home that Evangeline believed the snow settling in thickly around them was all that kept them from constructing the rest of the village. The potential for settlement drove home the truth that she was the only one with a reason to push on to Louisiana. Why drag this unaffiliated assemblage across the wilderness? There were certain to be other Acadians than Gabriel in Louisiana. But if that was all her companions sought, they could remain here, or with seemingly more reason, return to settle among whoever hadn't been carried from the north by the English. But the five of them would push on together, and maybe Jana and Julian would settle alongside her in Louisiana to restore the world its balance.

Evangeline certainly didn't begrudge the stop. She had been happy to pitch in, and the cabin's sturdy roof had been a boon in winter. The snow had fallen thicker than she'd ever seen, yet the clean wintry expanses of this western land were reminiscent of home. Nothing brought people together like building a house, a lesson regularly reinforced back in Acadia, and just as true here in the foothills of the English colonies. The shared work had generated a goodwill that hadn't been evident slogging up the road. Even Felician and Bernard, who evinced no desire to possess homes of their own, walked proudly through the empty cabin, talking of the boys growing up secure. No matter what else resulted from the leagues of wandering, there would be this happiness for a deserving family.

Thinking about the miles ahead, she again wished that she smoked a pipe. She had envied Bernard's excuse to leave the close house that winter, quietly puffing around staring after his smoke. What she didn't want was the little hole he'd bored between the bottoms and tops on the right side of his mouth where his little yellow teeth clamped around the wood stem of his pipe. Evangeline pictured herself, stooped and with fine gray hairs poking from her cheeks and chin, puffing her smoke as she chased her still young children through the humidity of her imagined Louisiana riverbank.

Marguerite and Jana walked up from the shelter and chose

stumps, and the three of them watched Francis trek across his boggy ground to round up his sons.

"If I never smell that mud again it will be too soon," Jana complained.

Marguerite shrugged in response. "It's a thankless chore, but it won't hurt to have our walls thicker for when we don't have so many bodies warming the cabin. I'd prefer you all weren't leaving."

Frederic ran back toward the woods away from his father.

Marguerite started to rise, but Jana stopped her.

"I'll get him," she said to them. "Don't worry, Francis," she called as she chased the boy down.

"They hate to bathe at this age," Marguerite said as Jana caught the recalcitrant and led him to his father, waiting in the cabin door where he prevented Eugene from running after his brother.

"You've got a good man, Marguerite," Evangeline said.

"I'm sorry to be the one to tell you this, Evangeline, but there are no good men, just the ones that behave if someone tells them how to act as they ought to." The woman inclined her head toward the cabin. "There's one in there waiting who looks like he'd listen to you better than you have any right to expect."

Surprised by the woman's directness, Evangeline glanced at Jana walking with Frederic. The other women must talk about her and Julian when she wasn't around, Evangeline thought.

"I've never understood why people are so repelled by the favorable regard of others," Marguerite continued. "One other person that wants the best for you should be enough to satisfy an entire life."

"I don't think loyalty comes first," Evangeline responded. "You're true to someone because you love them. You can't grow love in reaction to charitable behavior."

Marguerite waited a moment before speaking. "I met Francis five days before we were married. I had been married already, but my husband died our first winter. My parents waited until the next summer to make the arrangements with Francis. Our marriage has taught me that if you act one way, quite likely you will start to feel that way as well. Showing disproportionate regard and generosity to another can grow into love. If you don't figure that out sooner, you'll learn if you have children."

They left the Bauers in early March, and forged ahead on the road, five on foot and one pack horse led by Felician in the rear. Spring's cheerful growth seemed to mock their efforts as they began another year of travel without the certain reward of new life. It would be better, she thought, if their journey was instead against natural time, if they traveled from the old leafless thornbushes of Maryland to new spring in Louisiana.

But the birds chased insects with youthful abandon rather than autumn's desperation, the water flowed strong and healthy downhill to the Potomac, and they started through the brilliant sunlight to Gabriel. Besides, there was no certainty that a year would see them to Louisiana, as Bernard reminded her the night after they left.

"I don't know how long it will take," he said in exasperation. It was an overly common topic, Evangeline acknowledged sympathetically. The cabin had been an unusual experience for the trapper who had spent as many years as the rest cloistered in the hospital back in Baltimore. She begged his patience, and asked again what he did know.

"I've never been, and I can't even say for sure that I'll know it when we get there. We might be a year wandering just to find the river if this road doesn't last." Evangeline reassured herself with the knowledge that Bernard consoled himself with worst-case scenarios.

She welcomed his dourness as a shield against the grim repetition of tiresome days before them, as well as against the equally tiresome parade of Julian's passive flirtations, or the random intensity of Felician's attention.

It started drizzling early in the afternoon, which discouraged the little talking that would have been done between saving breaths. Walking ahead and apart from Felician, Evangeline ducked her head against the moisture, and kept her eyes sharp on the slick grass, as she imagined Bernard might at the front of the line.

Evangeline doubted that there had ever been a time when Bernard was a woman's favorite. Not through fault of the man so much as peculiarity, she thought. It was the lack of love, not a physical wanting, that she considered crucial to Bernard's perpetual gloominess. She felt that sex must change a person like a gunshot wound, a physical knowledge and awareness denied to the inexperienced, as wars were truly known only to those who fought them.

To be one's love was another matter, and here she felt more expert. The idea of love, the idea of Gabriel, was sustenance in itself. Here, she relied on the memory of her father, who kept his happiness alive those long years alone after her mother died. More than just wearing a smile for her sake, he took solace in the certain knowledge of his former joy, and the awareness that some would never be so fortunate. That your soul might one day find a union with another's should be enough for any hopeful person, Evangeline thought, and the knowledge had merit even without the tangible presence of the other. How those who didn't understand this, and to her it seemed the world's entire remainder, steered themselves through their lives remained a mystery.

Though she still lacked the forgiveness of a mother, Evangeline thought, as she watched Julian step on a fuzzy bramble to clear the way before her.

"I'd better get accustomed to stepping over worse than that," Evangeline said as she passed without taking her eyes off the ground. The trail would afford more chances for intimacy than the Bauers' two-roomed cabin, and she hated to think she'd have to start fending off his soft passes already.

The light rain didn't fade completely for several hours, and Bernard brought them to a halt at the next hill they reached, where they spread out to make an early camp under the partial dryness of the pine boughs. Complaints were plentiful that night, despite the shortness of the day, backs and legs that had happily forgotten the ceaseless rigor of hiking, strenuous even compared to the varied lifting and hauling of home-building.

"I'd forgotten that even your arms get sore from walking," Jana told her brother as Evangeline settled in alongside them for the night.

To avoid the commentary, the next morning Evangeline started out alongside Bernard at the front of the procession, thinking to set a faster pace then they'd managed the first day in the mist as their muscles grew accustomed to the journey.

It didn't feel like a particularly fresh start, Evangeline thought, though the sun was hot on the rising land about them.

"Can we get that far today?" she asked Bernard, pointing out to where the road wound out of sight, climbing a pass.

He nodded, and gave a little smile probably meant as reassuring. "Sure."

The grin wasn't contagious.

"It's going to take us weeks just to get to the river," she said, and Bernard nodded, verifying the distance by saving his breath for it, she thought. If only speaking the words could make it true, Evangeline thought, but they still had to walk there. And the only speculation she could engender along the way was in contemplation of another weary day, rendered both more difficult and meaningless by the unrelenting sequence unraveling successively after. Her father would have disowned her if she couldn't make better conversation.

He nodded again, "And then we need boats."

They walked in silence for several minutes before Bernard changed the subject. "The daily mass is going to get old without Francis around to ignore it with. It feels like I'm setting up camp for a king at night."

"You need light to read, Bernard. And Felician's done plenty to make this possible." They looked back at the priest leading Trotter.

"Yes, thank God for another shitting animal."

She frowned as his vulgarity. "Better than carrying it ourselves, don't you think."

"I think that I've had nothing but hard luck since I was mistaken for one of you people. Though I admit, it's unclear what all of you did to deserve it."

That evening Felician again led them in prayer while Bernard coaxed a fire. The priest ended his entreaty by thanking the Lord for the gift of another beautiful day and the plentiful water in the stream running alongside the camp.

Bernard cleared his throat. "The stream's full of water from the snow melting, Felician. There's no reason to get carried away."

"You don't see the hand of God in this life-giving water?" the priest replied, though he knew by now, and had known before they left, that the trapper was unlikely to credit their Lord with much of what transpired, in nature or otherwise.

"I don't see anything unusual about it at all," the trapper said.

"In my experience," Felician began, and Bernard bristled visibly in anticipation of his words, "most people who've survived trials like yours have a tendency to be a bit more generous to the holy will that restored them. I think it's a miracle that you're even alive."

"I don't know about miracles, but I'll grant you that certain things only happen once," Bernard retorted and left the fire to gather fallen wood though they already had plenty to last the night.

Evangeline followed him into the night, anxious to end the bickering before ill will developed. The camaraderie manufactured with the Bauers' home seemed to have been left behind with the structure, Evangeline worried. Two days of how many that lay before them? They were a long way from the river, and that still put them less than halfway to Louisiana by Bernard's uncertain estimation.

She found him not far from camp.

"I don't understand it," he said apologetically.

"The mass?" she asked.

"That's among my confusions." Bernard's voice was disembodied in the darkness, and she searched for a way to explain a part of their faith.

"The beauty of church, Bernard, is the moment facing the altar, when you stand surrounded by everyone of your acquaintance, and yet utterly alone, with less conscious thought of other people than at any other time. You and God. That is the most focused a mind can reliably be. When confronting God on His terms, even your own body falls away. There is nothing physical at all before Him. Or rather, I'm aware of my body, and I'm aware that it belongs to God. That sensation is what's so desirable. Because when you realize that your body is God's, it is a realization born of your own thoughts. Your thoughts, Bernard, not His. That's what I realize when I stand before the altar. Your thoughts are your voice echoing outside of time, with, but not of, God. You."

"What about deeds?" he asked, unconvinced but curious. "Your body is what acts. Do you see these years of pursuit as God acting on your behalf? Who is doing the walking?"

"Maybe I began too strongly. What if I said that we only control our intentions? And that your intentions will outlast even your actions, to such an extent that the actions themselves seem almost accidental side effects of what's actually within your control. Actions are but our thoughts' flawed expression, our ineffectual attempts to wrest control of time from God."

"Well, I'm as flawed as anyone else, but I don't want God's time. Thanks to you I've already got more than some would say I deserve. But I've learned to be suspicious whenever someone tries to teach me something for my own good. I don't see why you can't be satisfied with your own understanding of things and leave my thoughts to me."

Evangeline laughed. "Fair enough, Bernard. I trust you to know your mind. And I'm through trying to convince you. Felician is the one worrying for your soul. I just worry that you won't come back to camp."

After a week, the slope banked, and several days later their steps lightened as the road noticeably began to descend from the highest point of the range. Evangeline chose to credit the eleva-tion with the pace, and not the attrition of their store of dried fruit and meat.

Walking, unlike while in Baltimore, Evangeline could not avoid thoughts of what Gabriel might have found to fill his life in Louisiana. Not that she hadn't sought out news of him during the long internment, but life had held more demands when she'd had the purpose of the hospital. Even after the patients dwindled, there had been ways for her to preoccupy herself that deserted her now. They spent every waking moment inching inexorably toward Louisiana, and the slow progress left Evangeline wonder-ing, too desperate to hope that he knew, somehow, that she searched for him still.

Motivated by the ebbing of their supplies, they pitched camp outside a crude fortification, the first settlement of any kind that they'd passed in days.

They still camped outside its walls, as necessity didn't pre-vent them from minimizing the risk. "These men probably haven't seen a woman since they've been here." Bernard worried as Julian started the fire.

Felician nodded in agreement. "I'll see if they've got any food to spare."

"I'm coming with you," the trapper said. "Not every lost soul is desperate for a priest to disturb their seclusion."

Felician removed the money pouch from Trotter, and the two men entered the opening where it appeared as though a more formal gate had once stood. The walls themselves looked like they had been rebuilt recently, and several of the logs hadn't even been trimmed of their branches before being thrust into the palisade. It made the structure look like it was growing, Evangeline thought as she and the twins ate raisins and waited for their emissaries to return.

"Much as I dislike it at times, right now I wish this road ran all the way to Louisiana," Evangeline said to the twins, looking down the dark tunnel through the trees ahead. She had never seen anything like it. Most of the paths in Acadia had been fashioned by animals. Benedict had told her that there were roads in Europe that had existed for hundreds of years. This, though, was not old, or stone, it was an ensorcelling absence that reduced the trees of the surrounding forest to window trappings. It was difficult to imagine the number of men that would be required to make such a road, let alone the army that must have followed after the cutters.

"But it ends at Fort Duquesne," Jana said glumly, reiterating what they'd all learned back in Baltimore.

"Yes, but there are rivers," Evangeline said. "And we'll go even faster." It was easier to maintain her optimism free of Bernard and Felician, Evangeline thought.

"It's hard to imagine how we would have known where to go before they built it," Julian said.

"Takes a little fun out of it, though, doesn't it?" Evangeline teased.

"I usually prefer to choose my own way," Jana agreed. She cleared her throat from across the fire. "Evangeline," Jana paused after saying her name. "There's something we need to tell you. Julian and I aren't going to Louisiana."

Evangeline was speechless for a moment. She had never questioned the twins' presence, any more than she had appreciated it.

"What do you mean? Why?" she blurted, looking at Julian, who couldn't meet her eyes.

Jana could, and responded for them both. "There's no one

waiting for us down there. It's past time that we started our own lives."

The twins had always conversed apart from the others, and she'd never given much thought to what they talked about. A life apart, apparently. Evangeline had thought she was the only one with a destination.

"Where are you going to go?"

"Somewhere that's still French," Jana said. "Once we get to the Mississippi."

"The Mississippi," Evangeline said hopefully. That was a long way, yet.

"I'm sorry," Julian told her, but Evangeline was sure before he spoke that Jana had made the decision.

"How are you going to get back north when we get to the river? How will you know where to go?" Evangeline asked.

"Bernard told us that we'll be going against the current when we get there, and with just the two of us we'll need to catch on with a larger crew."

So they had already discussed their plans with the trapper, or at least Jana had, Evangeline thought, feeling more than a little betrayed. "How will you know which one?" she asked.

Jana shrugged. "He just said be careful about which boat we get on. Not everything with a flag is safe, Bernard said, but a group of uniforms should be better than those that look like him. He said that following the Mississippi north will get us to the lakes, though we may not even go so far."

"Is he going with you?" Evangeline asked.

Jana waited an excruciating length, responding only as they heard their companions approaching from the fort and whispering heatedly to each other. "He said he didn't think so," Jana whispered.

When the men emerged into the light, Evangeline saw that the sack the trapper carried was still empty.

"We're not staying the night," Felician said without preamble.

"Leave the fire burning," the trapper said as she and the twins got to their feet.

They walked past the fort in the darkness, Bernard and Julian first, with Evangeline and Julian leading Trotter behind, whispering to the horse to try to keep it quiet until the ramshackle structure vanished behind them. Invisible in the darkness, Felician trailed their party with a musket. They kept walking until dawn, though it hadn't felt to her that more than an hour had passed since they left the unused camp. Bernard led them off the road with the light.

"I'm sure we're fine," he said to Evangeline as she passed him with the horse, his eyes on Felician who was staring back down the trail in the early light. Their actions certainly suggested otherwise.

Evangeline insisted on joining Felician for the first watch, but no one fell asleep. Eventually Bernard sat up from his blanket.

"We'd probably be just as safe if we kept putting distance between ourselves and the fort."

They walked closer than usual that day, and didn't stop until the late afternoon, and then only from exhaustion.

"Do we need to follow the road?" Evangeline asked Bernard.

"For a while, but that was a risk back there that we'd be foolish to repeat."

They camped well off the road at night without fire and walked longer hours. For that at least, she was grateful. After continuing down the road for a week during which they ate only cornmeal pudding, a trail diverged, heading more directly west than the road which now ran north.

They left the road and followed the rough trail, making slow progress through days that grew increasingly long and hot, thankful that the new track rarely emerged from the shade. Early one evening they paused where the trail met a rushing stream.

"Are we going to camp here or cross?" Julian asked.

"Better to be wet at the end of the day than at the start," Bernard said.

The five of them stood on the bank, surveying the flow. Evangeline could see rocks jutting from the middle of the current and questioned their hesitation.

"It looks shallow," she said. It wasn't more than six meters across.

All three men nodded, as they usually did when she spoke. "Let's get a little weight off the horse," Felician said.

"You're leading it across," the trapper said. Evangeline wondered if he was angry because he couldn't argue with the sense of the priest's comment.

"I've led it everywhere else, haven't I?" Felician said, heatedly.

"Well it's your horse. I'd prefer we left the stinking beast here."

They all looked at Bernard, who stumped over to Trotter and untied the baggage.

"Why don't you let someone taller carry the muskets," Felician said as Bernard removed them from the animals back. "We don't want them to get wet."

Bernard ripped them loose like he intended to use one, but dropped them to the ground, took up two of the three packs, and forded the stream. The water didn't get above his waist, and they followed him across. Evangeline and Jana carried the muskets, Julian brought the other sack, and Felician dragged their reticent animal last. Evangeline hadn't held either weapon often, and she found herself strangely reluctant to part from it once they were on the other side.

Felician and Bernard wouldn't have dared the senseless exchange in front of the Bauers, Evangeline thought, and wondered how the twins' impending departure would affect their attitudes.

Following the stream the next day they reached a broad river. A large cluster of wigwams oversaw a bend in the river just upstream.

"Now this is a road," Bernard said.

"Is it safe?" Julian asked, looking toward the encampment.

"Safer than soldiers," Bernard responded. "I'll see if I can arrange for a boat."

Evangeline followed him to the water's edge where he wiped his face clean. "What should we tell them if they come by?" she asked.

"Just do what comes naturally," Bernard grinned, pleased with the chance to show off. "Tell them your chief is trading."

The trapper walked to the settlement while they unloaded their belongings off the horse. Bernard was gone for less than an hour, and came back accompanied by a baldpated sauvage who appeared particularly tall and graceful alongside the burly trapper. As the men reached them, Evangeline saw two more sauvages paddling a bateau downriver to them. It was round in the belly and looked unwieldy compared to Acadian canoes, though the design would allow for the five of them. After they beached the boat, Bernard pointed to the horse, and the three sauvages led Trotter away without a word.

Evangeline walked down to the water to look at the bateau, and Bernard came up behind her, smiling. "Now we'll make some time. I'm just sorry we have to wait for morning."

Bernard heaved the craft onto its side to inspect the bottom, and the twins joined them, while Felician waited at the edge of the woods.

"They gave us this for Trotter?" Julian sounded uncertain.

"That's right," Bernard said, hearing the tone. "I wouldn't have done it either."

"Don't they need it?" Julian asked.

Bernard snorted. "They'll make another."

When they put in the next day, though it felt like they were going the wrong way, they followed the current north, all five of them taking turns paddling two at a time, with a third on the makeshift rudder Bernard fashioned from a forked branch. Despite the trapper's expectation of speed, they would have had trouble against the current in the vessel, which seemed to plow into rather than cut through the water, but paddling at least allowed them to put different muscles to work.

"You're sure this is the way, Bernard?" Evangeline asked for the second time that morning.

"I didn't get much out of them, but those natives were able to tell me that the Ohio is just downstream."

"The Ohio?"

Bernard nodded. "The Ohio. I've heard of it, though I never got this far south myself. Augustine was on it a time or two." He spit into the water. "He said it was as big as the Saint Lawrence, but I didn't believe him."

"What about the Mississippi?" She was almost frightened to ask.

"That's at the end. The Ohio empties out this whole part of the country, and it empties into the Mississippi."

Their fourth day on the water, they passed a sprawling fort that pumped smoke into the summer sky and kept the bateau against the west bank opposite. Evangeline held her breath, and Felician crouched in the bow with a musket readied, but though it had narrowed a bit, the river was still several hundred meters across, and they passed without incident.

"Fort Duquesne, that's why Braddock built the road," Felician murmured once they were clear. "Should we try to push on tonight?" he asked Bernard.

The trapper shook his head. "My father used to say that the only things more dangerous than an unfamiliar river at night were angry women and priests." Having offended everyone but Julian, Bernard chuckled by himself as they paddled away from the fort.

"What about a baptism, Felician?" Bernard said the next morning as he steered them out from camp. The question took them all by surprise. Bernard's mood had improved since they hit the water, but it was mostly evident in the jibes directed at the priest. This question seemed sincere, however.

"You want to be baptized?" Felician rested his oar, and Evangeline did the same across from him.

"Not just me, all of us. It's an ancient custom we're bound to follow if we hope for success. A voyageur's baptism is a necessity any time you reach the headwaters of a river you've never traveled before."

"We've been paddling for days," Evangeline pointed out, hoping to forestall another argument.

Bernard shook his head. "But we've only now crossed over

to the Ohio. I've never been on it myself, but I've heard of it, and you've all noticed we're headed west." He was beaming, proud of them. "We've made the Ohio."

He passed the rudder to Julian and reached for Evangeline's paddle, which he dipped back into the stream. "Let's start with you," he said, and splashed her, much more than seemed necessary.

"Hey," she exclaimed.

Bernard laughed. "You're just lucky I didn't tip the boat like they would have done up in Canada. Say whatever you'd like to say, Felician. Jana, and Julian," he said and doused the twins, who sat, captivated by his transformation. Bernard grinned and shook a few drops over the priest's head. "You're welcome for the blessing, Father."

"You're lucky I don't hit you with my paddle," the priest responded, though his tone wasn't as sharp as the words.

Bernard handed Evangeline her paddle.

"What about you?" she asked.

He gripped the gunwale alongside her and dunked his head, coming back up sputtering through his beard. "Fair is fair," he said.

Bernard reclaimed his seat in the stern, and they went back to paddling in a spirit of camaraderie lacking since they had built the Bauers' home. Evangeline heard Bernard's coarse voice quietly humming from the stern.

Riding along the road from Rochelle city, I met three girls and all of them were pretty. It is the paddle that brings us, it is the paddle that brings us here.

They kept to the current and came to another deep bend in the river that swung them around south and they traveled down a wide uniform stretch that seemed entirely absent of habitation, camping when they found an accessible bank, or on the sandstone islands that rose from the current. Only once black clouds massing on a peak on the river's left encouraged them off the Ohio. Evangeline watched the thick water as the storm winds mounted, happy not to be braving the swells in the bateau, though she daily grew more comfortable on the water. Unlike walking from place to place, it seemed a travel lifestyle to which a person could grow accustomed. Evangeline enjoyed controlling the rudder, directing their course toward Gabriel. She quickly grew inured to the sweat of the paddling, and to the smell of the bear grease they used to ward off the insects drawn to their laboring bodies.

A week beyond Fort Duquesne they started passing copper plates blazoned with fleur-de-lis, hammered into trunks to be visible from the water. Another week's passage and the river curved back north. Approaching the bend, they found themselves before a large town, and beached their canoe on a wide bank below it.

There were more houses here than there had been when they first got to Baltimore, Evangeline thought, log-walled homes rising on both sides of the Ohio, but concentrated most heavily on the left bank around a blockhouse. A ferry fashioned of buffalo hide floated in the water to carry people across the river.

Between the buildings and the river was a camp of French-speaking white men, who interrogated them at the water's edge.

"Where are you all coming from?" one of the men asked them.

"Baltimore," Felician told him.

"Where are you going?" the same man asked.

"Louisiana," the priest said. "Where are we?"

"That is Shawnee Town," the grizzled speaker answered.

"And this," he indicated the tents at the city's margin, "is Lower Shawnee Town, which it is my pleasure to welcome you to."

There was an air of permanence in the dozen wigwams and fire rings somehow lacking from the sauvage city above, Evangeline thought, as they bedded down in a shelter several men had cordially vacated for the night.

"We should replenish our supplies before we press on," Felician said. "We could all use the rest."

The trapper scoffed. "Maybe so, but that's not why you want to stay."

"Oh, no?"

"No. You think there are souls here that need saving."

"If there are, it's my duty to help them."

"There're duties all around."

"All of the doings of my life, Bernard, and yours besides, are worthless measured against the prospect of a single soul exalting in Heaven that would otherwise be damned for eternity. A man that feels as you do can't understand what's at stake for these people."

"Well, as much trouble as it's caused me, I'm satisfied with my judgment. It seems to me that's all any of us have."

"You have God to thank for that judgment," Felician began loudly, but Bernard cut him off.

"I don't give a damn what you think." The trapper stormed from the wigwam and didn't return that night.

Felician entered the village the next morning. Evangeline and the twins left Bernard absorbing the river gossip with the French traders, while they investigated a series of mounds that led into the woods away from the habitation, following a flow that she would have thought a large river before they chanced the Ohio. The mounds rose on both sides of the tributary, nearly ten meters at their highest, and overgrown. It looked like what their dikes might in a hundred years if the bay dried up, Evangeline thought.

She walked between the twins, hoping the excursion would buoy the mood with the threat of the twins' departure looming.

"How long do you think we're going to stay here?" Jana sounded like she should, impatient to leave, anxious to part from the querulous priest and moody trapper.

"I'm not sure. You heard Felician. He won't leave before he's baptized anyone who wasn't here the last time a priest passed through. We'd better be ready to settle in for a while."

Jana headed over for a closer look at the mounds. "Why do you think they built these?" she asked.

"The mounds? It looks like a wall," Julian said without much interest.

"Maybe," Evangeline said, drawing the word out. "It's not protecting the town, though. It might be where they bury their dead."

Jana retreated from her inspection and they continued into the woods, awed into silence at the thought of bodies resting in the earth alongside them.

Jana broke the quiet after several minutes, "It looks like it goes for miles. It can't all be a grave."

"I'm sure you're right," Evangeline said. "Maybe it's a tribute to the river. In any case, this must have been a huge kingdom when they built it. Maybe the old city is somewhere ahead, and that town where the Shawnee live now used to just be the harbor."

They kept walking. Occasionally the mounds gave way, broken by young trees and creeks.

"What if your family's down in Louisiana?" Evangeline

said after a few minutes. She looked at Julian as she spoke, but Jana responded.

"If they are, I'm sure that Mama has plenty to worry about without us. But we haven't heard that they were."

"Still, you're not likely to find them out where you're headed."

"No, we're not," Jana acknowledged. "There comes a time," she was addressing her brother now, "when you just have to make a life out of what you have. And that time's long past for us. There are plenty of French towns on the way to Canada."

"What are you going to do there?"

"I guess we won't know until we arrive. But our family's always been farmers, so that's probably what we'll do. And Louisiana sounds too hot for cabbage."

Jana turned back, and after a moment, Julian followed her, leaving Evangeline to trail the twins along the mysterious mounds back to their camp.

They were all growing as sick of each other as Bernard and Felician, Evangeline thought that night. The entire trail experience was a fragile world to itself, with its own tense loyalties, fragile enough that contact with the larger world destroyed it. But the pause in their journey had left Evangeline more convinced that she needed the twins, and that she could not be left alone with the two men.

Neither had been much in evidence since they'd arrived. Bernard was repairing two traps he'd been gifted by one of the traders, swapping tales at a fire. He'd slept at one of the fires the night before, and looked about ready to resume his former ways. Felician had not come back from another day's consultation with the Shawnee leaders, although he had returned for bed the night before. Many times she would have preferred either man's company, but as they ate a large bass Julian had caught, Evangeline imagined the independence she would be afforded traveling only with Jana and Julian.

A girl ducked her head into their tent. Her hair gleamed black, swallowing the light filtering in with her from the various fires still burning about the camp.

"Good evening," she said in quiet French. "The Father told me about your journey."

"Yes, come in," Evangeline answered.

The girl lifted a buckskin bag into the tent and followed after. She was clad plainly in leather, decorated only with a scarf to match her hair. "He said that you have been seeking your husband for many years. Your story reminds me of my grand-mother, Lilianau, who my mother named me after. Many people were sick in our village when my mother was born. My grand-father died, and my grandmother grew so sick that her sister took care of my mother. Lilianau stayed in her wigwam by her-self, waiting to die, but she didn't. My grandfather's voice came to her in the night, and she said it breathed spirit back into her. Lilianau got well, and took her daughter back, but she kept hearing my grandfather's voice at night, speaking to her through the trees. One morning, she was found sleeping near the top of a walnut tree, and Lilianau's sister took my mother back. Not long after, my grandmother left the village and was never seen again. After my mother grew up, she came to this town where I was born." The girl hesitated only briefly, to gesture to the offering at her feet. "When she is able, my mother tries to help those who do not have their parents to care for them. There's ground corn, and some tobacco you can use to get what you need around the camp. My mother and I wish you safe travels and a happy end."

The girl took each of them in hand as they thanked her, and left the tent.

Jana, Julian and Evangeline returned to the mounds weeks later, to bathe in a salt spring Julian passed on a previous exploration. Bernard had traded the battered bateau that had gotten them here for a smaller canoe the twins would take downstream. Evangeline and the two men would continue in a canoe that Felician was given, a sleek, four-meter craft with holes set regularly along the gunwale decorated with red buckskin.

"We'll be lucky not to be hijacked before we're out of sight of town," Bernard had remarked on seeing the gaudy boat.

Their impending separation left them quiet in the shade of the pool. While she dressed at the water's edge, her wet skin cool in the shade, Evangeline reflected on men, and what power she might hold over them, as she watched a sparrow pick through leaves with its beak, discarding them furiously, finally hopping without anything in its beak. She wrung her hair out and they started back.

"I guess we'll never know what they're for," Evangeline said with a resigned eye on the mounds.

She had only to look once at Julian, and he stopped alongside her, and together they watched Jana disappear through the wood toward the river. He still smelled of the pond, and she leaned against him, close enough for her breasts to press into his chest, her mouth only a careless flinch from his. Her hair caught in his light beard, and she slowly disentangled it and brushed it to drape over her shoulder. Out of convenience, they'd bathed together many times over the years, but she knew the imprint of her body was fresh on his mind. Clothes made the lust, when people were as familiar as they were. Bathing together,

Evangeline believed, encouraged a sensible modesty that couldn't help but spill over into daily routine. So she kept her clothes on to seduce this man, whose neglected appreciation she would miss only when it was gone. Her power lay in his wanting, and she knew that to fulfill Julian's desire for her would be to remove her hold over him.

Julian's mouth was open, but he didn't speak as he watched her. Evangeline kept her feet in the water as she spoke. "I'm not sure what exactly has changed since we left Baltimore, but it seems that if we've come all this way together, we should finish our journey together. It's been ten years, Julian." Evangeline looked at him. "Aren't you even curious?"

"About Louisiana?"

"About Gabriel."

"You mean if he's not there?" His tone was too hopeful, by far, but it was she who suggested it.

"He's going to be there, Julian," Evangeline said firmly, then softened her tone. "But don't you want to know, after everything?"

"You've talked about choices," he began slowly. "That you realized that every day you choose to love Gabriel all over again." He drew a breath, the words causing him obvious pain. "That when it seemed like you had nothing else, that you still had the power to make that choice."

"And that for the rest of my life, whether he's with me or not, I always have the choice to love Gabriel." She couldn't even remember when she'd said it to Julian, though they were her words. Choice could not be taken from her, and she understood that the choices that she still held were the source of her strength, the strength that Felician had explained to her those years ago in Baltimore.

"Jana says you'll never love me," Julian said, without as much pain as she might have thought. "She's been saying it for years. That not even if we get to Louisiana and Gabriel's dead will you choose me. But I'd be happy to give you another chance." He looked at her hopefully for a moment, and she met his eyes, but couldn't reply. "I should go," he said.

He was right, Evangeline thought, but then remembered Bernard and Felician and the distance ahead. "You don't have to," she said.

He considered her remark, and then shook his head, sadly, and started walking back.

"Julian," she said to his back.

"I'm sorry," he called back, unwilling to turn.

Alone in the shadows, Evangeline remembered the sensation of Gabriel's fingers in the clearing when she brushed them, passing him the apple, of rubbing against him at the dance, and their hundreds of kisses. She had burned then, for Gabriel in her youth.

That was gone, when she looked at Felician, Bernard, or Julian. And thoughts of her and Gabriel reunited failed to restore her passion. She didn't love him, she couldn't until they were together. Love didn't exist at a remove, it was an accumulation of the shared experience and time they had been denied. She could begin to love him again once she found him, but now she relied on the memory of the girl she no longer was. What would that lonely boy have grown into?   She realized now that her insight into Gabriel, into men, was dependent on their presence, or rather on her presence.

It wasn't truly insight, either. Men acted as they thought she wanted when she was present. They spoke to her, considered her, watched her, no matter the company. But she understood now that the power she wielded was temporary, contingent on the force of her presence.

She had thought that she had known Gabriel, but she had merely possessed him. And now, at ten years' remove, he would have forgotten. Not the fact of her existence, or their childhood love, but the insatiable force of her presence, the reward she promised that made her compelling.

Evangeline, Felician and Bernard returned to the Ohio quietly, each of them feeling similarly abandoned while their recent companions pursued attainable happiness. It's easier to travel when you don't know exactly where you're going, Benedict used to say. Noisy in comparison, the morning was alive with Shawnees chattering to each other as they took the river. Several canoes raced them west, whooping to Felician as they swooped about them like baby birds vying for a mother's attention. Two men followed them farther than the others, coasting past in their canoe, and then sitting their paddles as they neared.

"We'd just tire out trying to keep up," Bernard cautioned as the other craft pulled ahead again, spurring them onward down the river.

They found an island and halted near midday to stretch and eat cornmeal and molasses pudding, and when they returned to the water the Shawnee were gone.

The twins had only a two-day headstart, and as the three of them paddled, Evangeline often expected to overtake them, but they didn't and she soon stopped looking for them ahead on the river. Several weeks past the Shawnee town, the three portaged around a steep falls, the first time it had been necessary since they had returned to the water. She and Felician carried the light bark, and Bernard trailed them ponderously with their two canvas sacks tied to the muskets crossed over his shoulders, a feat possible only with the quick dwindling of their provisions.

After three more days of paddling they slowed themselves in the current as they came within sight of a fort, well-positioned on a spit of land overlooking the right bank of the river. Drawing near, they saw the white on blue of the French flag waving at half-mast above the outpost.

"French," Felician said from the bow. "Should we head in?"

"It would be nice to know where we are," Bernard answered hesitantly, reluctant as always to chance human contact.

"It's getting dark," Evangeline said, looking up at the fort hopefully. "We wouldn't have to worry about a camp tonight."

As they closed on the fort they saw heavy smoke rising lazily, and a man in a blue hunting coat sat on a flat rock near two well-used canoes at the water's edge. He got to his feet slowly, his musket slung over his shoulder.

"We're French," Felician called out.

"Come ashore, then," the sentry shouted back, louder than was needed for only their ears.

They did, and the man helped them drag their canoe onshore alongside the others.

"Geoffrey Lafourge," he said, shaking hands with each of them, including Evangeline, as though she were a man. "Welcome to Fort Defiance."

"Good name, son," Felician said.

"Well, we haven't earned it, Father," the soldier said. "I never actually saw a battle myself, though this frontier has me acquainted me with death so that I forget the absence."

"Why are you still showing your colors?" Bernard asked.

"Because no one has bothered to come take them down," Geoffrey answered, "and I don't have a flag of the union to run up there for them."

Not quite the resilient garrison they had hoped, Evangeline thought, as they followed the soldier up a trail lined with the copper fleur-de-lis emblems they'd seen upriver. The earth was dry and hard as rock underfoot in the late summer, and she was sweating by the time they reached the top of the hill. They passed between two bastions and through the open gate. There was an unmanned redoubt inside the gate, several low buildings, and a sturdy-looking magazine. Two separate fires burned, though the small compound was nearly empty.

Near one, two squaws in rags of blue uniforms stooped over a pot.

"Turtle soup," Geoffrey volunteered, nudging one of the large shells almost respectfully with a moccasin. The fleshy undercarriages heaved in the boil like the flayed pelts of tiny people. The steam carried an aroma like ancient wood, moldy and moss-encrusted, dragged loose from some equatorial swamp and laid spattering atop the coals.

"It takes an awfully long time to boil the fat off a turtle." The soldier shrugged and moved toward the encampment's other fire.

Shells were scattered amid the bones of other animals throughout the interior of the stockade. Blood's tang was fresh and heavy on the air where it coalesced with the disquieting odor of the soup and gave the open courtyard an unholy smell, the reek of heedless butchery.

At the other fire was a man wearing only pants, bald but with dark hair over his chest and back. He rested on his haunches, skewering hunks of venison. The remains of the kill lay near to hand, and Evangeline was relieved to have found the source of the blood scent.

"How many of you are there?" Felician asked the man who escorted them.

"Four."

"Just the four of you?"

Felician looked back at the two women around their own fire, who might have been on a mountain across the world for the attention they paid the newcomers.

"No, there are four of us." Geoffrey pointed to the half-naked man poking sticks through meat. "There are two of them." He didn't gesture this time.

"It looks like there's plenty of meat," Bernard said, indicating the raw venison. Already a dozen pieces were stuck through and kept partly out of the dust by a log that didn't look clean itself. "Why bother with the soup?"

"Yes," the soldier at the fire chuckled. "We're better at hunting than eating, by now. But the soup's for them. We don't touch the stuff. They eat it because they think eating turtle carries the power to curse their enemies." The sitting man looked around at the three of them, but no one said anything. "And we're they're enemies," he concluded with a cackle.

"So, why let them cook it?" Evangeline couldn't restrain herself this time.

"Because, at this point, Mademoiselle, curses begin to sound more interesting than blessings."

"That's enough, gentlemen," Felician cut in worriedly. "We're your guests, and while realizing that you perhaps don't receive many, perhaps you could show more respect to weary travelers who have had little luck themselves."

"Of course, Father. Apologies, Mademoiselle," Geoffrey

said quickly. "You can perhaps understand such sentiments from men who have been inactive since the war ended, hoping only to hand over the position they vowed to defend with their lives." Their host spat into the fire. "An English ship passed by two summers ago and said they were sending a garrison to take possession of every fort east of the Mississippi. They also told us we could get return passage to France when they took the fort." Geoffrey gave a grim chuckle. "There was more official traffic on the rivers in wartime."

"And you've been waiting here ever since," Bernard said. "Where are the other two?"

"One is taking his rest out of the sun." Geoffrey paused and looked to his comrade.

"And the other has been missing since the weather got warm this spring," the soldier at the fire finished. "We haven't seen Damien for months. Hard to say if he's even alive." Neither man looked much put out, though plenty of time had passed for them to accustom themselves to the increased duties his loss must have meant, Evangeline thought.

"So you're not looking for him?" she asked.

"Madame, we cannot be certain that he wants to be found," Geoffrey replied. "But it's better for all concerned that he's no longer with us. He missed his woman the most."

"I guess you've noticed that white women are somewhat scarce in these parts." The man skewering the steaks steered the conversation back to the present without taking his eyes off his task. "It'll be a pleasure just watching you eat."

"We won't be staying past the night," Bernard said.

Evangeline hoped the near panic in the trapper's low voice wouldn't be as apparent to these men who didn't know him.

"Your way is your own," Geoffrey returned peaceably.

They spent that night in the empty magazine, a stout room with a door that barred from the inside.

"They don't want to tempt themselves," Felician said reassuringly as Bernard dropped the crossbeam into place.

"They'd have to burn the whole fort down to get at us in here," the trapper agreed.

Evangeline felt a catch in her throat over the camaraderie of the exchange, and looked at the musket resting alongside her with its bundle of shot. She had infrequently practiced since they left the Bauers in Maryland, but she felt competent enough to hit a target as large as a human from the few paces across the room. She was better prepared to defend herself as a woman, more aware of what was at stake, than when that soldier had attacked her. Unbidden, Evangeline recalled the squaws stirring the turtle soup and envisioned herself similarly captive, a victim of ambush on her way from the fort. After two years of hard travel the three of them must look like they could mount resistance enough that she wouldn't be worth the cost, especially with easier alternatives already at hand. Evangeline didn't make her bed, but propped her blanket in the corner, where she fell asleep finally, facing the low doorway through which they would have to come.

Louisiana 1768

The blossoms of passion, gay and luxuriant flowers,
are brighter and fuller of fragrance, but they beguile us,
and lead us astray, and their odor is deadly.

IT WAS ONLY MARCH, BUT ALREADY THE SPRING HAD BEEN outmuscled by summer's humidity. One lifetime wasn't enough to accustom a person to Louisiana's heat, Gabriel thought. A thin line of French soldiery, looking more attentive than usual for a speech, stood between the governor and the crowd. Gabriel stood with the masses, in town to see what Ulloa intended for them in the swamp. He was thankful as always for a reason to escape what had become a more stalwart prison than the barrier island in South Carolina. The small Spaniard was flanked by his wife and Colonel Aubry, commander of the remaining French troops and governor before Ulloa. Despite his dress regalia, the colonel appeared plain alongside the majestic couple, Ulloa in a heavy blue coat intricately stitched with gold, and his wife in a purple dress that trailed over the floor around her like a pond. They looked like a king and queen, which might have been appropriate somewhere other than New Orleans.

She was a beautiful woman, and appeared younger than Gabriel, which would make her half the governor's age. He wondered briefly what Evangeline would look like in such a dress, but couldn't reconcile the image, and imagined instead what the governess looked like underneath it. He shook his head to clear the comparison of an actual breathing woman to the fading recollection of his betrothed and looked around. Creoles made up most of the crowd, dressed in nicer clothing, but dirtier in their finery than the Acadian congregations he remembered from home. Women stuck out from the gray troops and ill-mannered merchants like diamonds in coal. Color and cleanliness, Gabriel thought, looking at his own worn dun ensemble, were the gifts that women retained while their men searched out the world's remote corners, following only when the frontier could bear them.

Gabriel saw Anna smile when he caught her eye. She had been waiting for him to see her watching him, probably while he'd pondered Ulloa's wife. Anna pointed to the back of the crowd, and he nodded. A sudden protest from the audience made him start. He'd lost track of what might have provoked the anger.

He liberated himself from the press of strangers' elbows, and Anna greeted him with a kiss on the cheek, standing up against him and craning to reach, with her hand on his shoulder, fine blond hair waving once across his face like a fan.

"So what brought you out today?" Anna asked. "I thought Lajeunesse men disdained politics. And from the sounds of this mob we're past the point of peaceful resolution anyway." Hers was the cold rationale of a woman long accustomed to disputes settled by combat.

"People are upset out our way. You know the new Acadians

are being forced up the Mississippi, instead of being allowed to sweat to death in the swamp with us. But mostly I just wanted to get away from my father for a couple of days."

She nodded. "Mine's at the speech, and they'll keep him all day, with toasts to Ulloa and colonial stability." She smiled grimly. "Loyalty does not always prove the best, nor the wisest, course."

She tucked her arm under his and they walked away from the square and turned down Chartres, leaving the clamoring behind like a conscience.

"And Alexander?" Gabriel asked.

"He went back up the river a few days ago."

"How're you holding up?"

Anna braced herself on his shoulder and threw her head back, "It's been the loneliest week of my life."

"Poor girl," he smiled.

"Forgive me, darling, you must remember not all of us possess your restraint." She smiled back as they came to a stop in front of the tall brick building Anna's father had commissioned when she and Alexander married. "I've been miserable and I need some company, so it looks like we're both in luck."

Gabriel considered her for a moment. His eyes drifted past her lips and followed the curve of her neck to her bare shoulder, and then took his hand out of hers and put it on the house with an almost audible sigh of relief. Awareness overtook him like a mugger.

"I could never live in a brick house," he said, relieved just to have spoken.

"That doesn't mean you can't come in for a while, does it?" Anna was laughing as she opened the door. "And if it burns down when the city is sacked, we'll only have to replace the floors."

She stepped over the threshold, and Gabriel looked quickly up and down Chartres Street. He saw nothing familiar or threatening, nothing that would stop him, and followed her inside.

A week later he paddled north with Antoine Thibodeaux and Michel Richard, rarely speaking, as the sun climbed, appropriate for three men strange to each other as they were. He was lucky that Philippe wasn't plying a paddle. His friend would surely have noticed something different.

Antoine Thibodeaux, Oliver's oldest grandson, and Michel Richard, paddled with him to learn how to survive in the foreign environment. The Thibodeaus had been taken to Philadelphia, where Oliver had died. Antoine and his parents were among the Acadians newly settled south of the Lajeunesse along the Teche, and neighbors of Michel, who lived with his mother and younger sister. Michel was a child when his family was deported from Beaubassin, and he'd grown up a beggar in Maryland.

They lurched up the Teche drunkenly through the afternoon heat and ate their evening meal under the deeper shade of the oaks. His companions were unable to take their eyes from an alligator sunning itself on a log. But as they chewed their dried venison, Gabriel's mind wandered quickly from the familiar danger. Old Chitimachi legend held that a chief once ascended to the headwaters of the Teche and slew the monstrous serpent there, which reduced the river from a torrent to its current lethargic flow. Gabriel thought that killing the snake would have brought more water, not less, but he wasn't raised to dwell on spiritual particulars. There was something about the stillness, though, that smelled of a violent past. He peered across at the cypress on the other bank, imagined sauvages spearing giant snakes just out of his sight, and decided to pass his superstitious fears along.

"Cannibals live in these woods, the Attakapas. Have you heard of them?" he asked, but neither answered. "Captain Bedard," he said familiarly, "says both the Spanish and the French stayed away from here until after the war." Gabriel noticed they perked up at his mention of the officer. Harsh circumstance had dictated they'd become a people who valued their warriors. "There's not many around anymore. Cannibals get diseases like everyone else."

"The English told us that the Mi'kmaq ate people, but everybody knows that's not true." Michel said.

"They aren't the Mi'kmaq. Well, Bienville saw them eating another tribe they conquered the first time he came through here. Spitted and roasted. That's why there are so many deer and beaver where we're headed. The sauvages preferred people, and left animals alone for the most part. Now that they're gone, there's no better trapping than the old Attakapas territory."

Michel raised his eyebrows, but didn't pursue it further.

"Do you always find deer?" Antoine asked.

"There are a lot of them out here," Gabriel answered. "But all skill is in vain if an angel pisses in your muskethole."

"My father says that there's no reason to go so far, he sees deer everyday."

"He was quick enough to send you off, though." Gabriel quieted the conversation.

Soon after they ate, Antoine fell asleep. Too young for the woods, Gabriel thought as he poured a sip of rum into his cup, and into Michel's when he raised it.

"To take the edge off the ground," Gabriel said. They both drank their shots, and then he put the bottle back in the pirogue and looked at Michel. "Did you know a girl named Evangeline Bellefontaine in Baltimore?"

"Sure, I did," he began.

"I was going to marry her," Gabriel said, cutting the boy off to save him embarrassment.

Michel's eyes widened. "Damn." He swallowed the jerky he was chewing to chase the liquor. "You were almost really lucky. Not that this isn't good," he amended, gesturing around with another dried strip of venison.

"This is my life." Gabriel looked out across the river. "How did you know her?"

"I didn't see her much. She worked in the hospital and I never had to go. The only good thing about getting sick in Maryland was that Evangeline Bellefontaine would take care of you."

"So you didn't see her around."

"No. I used to try though. Father Felician would feed you if you did chores around the hospital, or waited at the docks to bring news from the ships. It didn't matter what it was about, he'd still give you something to eat a couple times a week. The food wasn't great, but my family didn't have any at all sometimes." The young man wasn't despondent, just relating the commonplace. "We'd sit at this long table, old ladies bringing out oatmeal or cabbage soup, and people would almost cry at the sight. I wasn't the only one that wouldn't have eaten for a day or two. But once I got started looking at her, sitting up next to the Father at the head of the table, I couldn't swallow. She used to wear a top hat, even while she was eating. I never saw her without it." The boy turned his attention back to Gabriel from the river. "After my father died, I got his job unloading ships and I stopped going to dinners at the church. Those first years, though, I've never been so hungry."

"Our belts have been tight around here too," Gabriel responded sharply, making sure this newcomer knew that scrounging in Louisiana's backcountry hadn't been without hardship. He knew what Michel meant, though. It was a source of pride that they'd made their own way since South Carolina. Although the boy had eaten at Evangeline's table. Alms for every beggar. "So, she lived in the church?"

Michel smiled, realizing what Gabriel wanted to hear. "Yes. She didn't have any men around that I know of, and I probably would have heard. It was a topic of conversation." He laughed guiltily, and settled in his bedroll. "She left town before I did. I was half hoping to find her in New Orleans when I got off the boat."

You were not alone in that, Gabriel thought, as he sat awake listening to Michel's soft snoring, broken occasionally when a bat screeched over the Teche. He imagined Evangeline thronged by admirers in Baltimore. It seemed impossible that the boy sleeping next to him knew things about her that he didn't. But he was one among many, with nothing now to distinguish his appreciation from anyone else's. Except for their promise.

Which he had broken. Being devoured by cannibals would be appropriate, the insatiable hunger for human flesh consuming his lust for Anna. "How's that feel, Gabriel?" she'd asked after he was inside her. She was breathing fast, and looked like a stranger, and he couldn't say anything to her. He'd waited his whole life for that moment, and despite the attendant circumstances, felt mostly relief that it was past. That, at least, he was sure of. With his soul at stake, he wouldn't take back his afternoon with Anna back.

But even here in the wilderness, he was beset by reminders of his betrayal. Not of Alexander, but of Evangeline. He had proved his unworthiness. He wished he'd had Evangeline to order his life.

Thirty years old. It was a problem that Anna was Alexander's wife, but this changed nothing between him and Evangeline. If she wanted him, he would marry her. As she had said those years past, he didn't have a choice.

He hadn't had much choice with Anna, either. Philippe had Rosa pregnant before Gabriel met her. But it couldn't have been anyone. He wanted Anna, though it was beyond him whether that made matters better or worse.

"Thirty years old," he said to the sleeping boys. He might want to try it again before Evangeline found him.

After four long days with Michel and Antoine, they returned to their families downstream. After leaving the Richards, he stayed on the river until dark before he went home. He walked past his father's house without going inside and pitched his bedroll on the bare floor of his empty house.

He spent a sleepless hour on the floor of the house where he'd hoped to one day welcome Evangeline. He could only imagine her as he remembered her, a seventeen-year-old girl. That time had little in common with his life now, and he could assume with hers either. But she hadn't let circumstance keep her from searching for him.

And now she would be arriving just in time to meet Anna. The breeze blew against him, and he shivered and recalled Anna's naked legs smooth against his. He had no idea if she would keep their secret from Alexander. He thought that he could.

Evangeline was coming to his rescue a bit late. He had tried to last, but there was not enough to him. Choice, he'd thought back home, when she'd said fate and destiny. He now realized it to be mere circumstance, whimsical and pointless. They were drawn together by events beyond their control, but those events were without greater motive or purpose, no more sensible than the deportation. Hearing of her only confirmed the finality of his loss.

He didn't want his past, Gabriel thought, but it endured regardless.

"I don't want to be here," he said to the walls, his sleepless tone jarring in the barren house. Empty except for the bed. Gabriel took up his carving of Evangeline and nestled it in his mussed blankets. He didn't deserve her, but he would keep the memory. And why shouldn't he, Gabriel thought. Their courting was part of him, as real as his misdeeds, just so much longer ago.

He split the headboard and footboard with loud, laborious hatchet strokes, metal ringing off the dense cypress. The hatchet wasn't as sharp as it should be. Gabriel dragged the split halves out one at a time, and then went back for the figures. The tree with a couple delicate branches already broken off, himself, the chunk of cedar with a river and fields carved into the top on which the figures rested. Alexander, Philippe, Michael, Viktor and Alain. His father. He gathered them all up and dumped them in the fire ring.

The brown water pulsed in the firelight as he stoked the blaze with the pieces of his bed, swallowing his dreams of happiness in this foreign land, watching as the representations of his life were reduced to cinders. Neither the wedding nor the bed, Evangeline, though we hoped for them both, Gabriel thought, remembering their cautious steps toward the altar in that vanished autumn. With the crackling of the bed, the fire brightened, animating the batture, which waved alluringly in the sudden light. But the dry heat on his face soon faded, and he was sweaty and panting alone. Anything that he might have thought was his, was not.

The bed smoldered, and he was alone in the mazy darkness. Neither of their creations had fulfilled its purpose, nor him or her in the bargain. But the altar she built probably still stood in the woods outside Grand Pre, waiting with the divine patience of its maker for their footsteps to return, while his vanished into ash.

"What happened last night?" his father asked him.

"I burned the bed."

Basil regarded him glumly, plainly wishing he didn't have to lecture his grown son. "You have to stop drinking."

"I wasn't drinking." There was no comment from his father, who didn't seem to consider that enough of an answer. "I heard Evangeline was in Baltimore."

"You say *was*, son." His father turned ashen, almost reaching out to him.

"She's alive." Gabriel sat up straighter. "Just not in Baltimore."

"Where, then?"

"The last anyone saw her, she was headed west."

"That sounds like news that might have made you happy."

Gabriel exhaled, and looked away. "It got me wondering what we'll have between us when she gets here."

His father stood up angrily. "Well, you won't have a bed, anyway."

It struck Gabriel again how strange and inadequate it was

that the only person in the world who depended on him was this formidable man.

He left for New Orleans after a single quiet night in the cabin with his father and Michael, spending the four days it took him to reach the city wondering what he was going to do when he got there.

He changed his mind again as soon as he saw her in the door, smiling to see him.

"You didn't stay gone long."

Gabriel frowned, then shook his head. "I couldn't." He felt despicable.

"My father's home, we better get out of here so he doesn't mistake you for a Spaniard come for the silver."

"Whatever you say."

She closed the door tight, and kissed him as she turned. He kissed her back, and she laughed into his lips when she bumped back into the door. He roused himself from his lust, and they ran from her house like children.

They turned up Saint Peter's Street and walked more slowly now, side by side, until they came under the shadow of the purposeless wall on which Gabriel had labored during his first years in Louisiana. A graveyard was bricked off from the city, and Anna led him under the wrought iron gate and onto the large plot of raised earth, a stage from which the dead poked up tiny crosses. A large wooden cross stood alone near the center of the graveyard. Gabriel averted his eyes from it as they followed the wall around to a corner. For an instant before she turned, Gabriel tried to imagine that the woman he followed was the first he'd noticed, and that nothing existed yet between them that shouldn't.

"Take off my dress, Gabriel," she said, and he did, helping her unfasten the straps down the back so that he could slide it off where he stood holding it while she slid down her leggings. He dropped the flimsy green dress as Anna unbuckled his pants. She rested her back against the wall and extended a bare leg to him, and he took it and pulled himself up against her, where they stood over the dress, grinding it into the sodden earth beneath them.

He left that night thinking he would never return to New Orleans. Fearing that he would confess to his father, Gabriel undertook successively longer explorations of the numerous tributaries that branched off the Teche north of their small holdings. Philippe begged off after their initial venture, and alone for the first time, Gabriel stayed in the swamp for two weeks. He made huge fires from cypress logs at night, and roasted a deer he caught his third night out, eating the seared meat with his hands and spitting the charred gristle back into the fire like tobacco. The next morning he took his pirogue west without setting his traps, scouting the empty land and trying not to picture newly built shacks above the gentle bends in the shallow water. He went back to the camp that night and continued exploring the next morning. He finished the deer a week after he'd caught it, eating the haunches and even chewing on the lower legs above the hooves. He spent the hours piling fuel on the fires that he kept needlessly roaring throughout the night.

He woke one predawn alongside the embers and with the morning, pointed the pirogue for home. It had rained only sporadically during these weeks, and lightly when it came, but the early summer skies opened now, as though having waiting for his resolve to fail. The driving rain puddled in the folds of his rag shirt, leaving it hanging distended from his body like an unhealthy skin reluctant to be shed. The downpour lessened, but rain continued steadily past dark, as he stealthily made his way back to their little cove and beached his heavy pirogue next to his father's. Disregarding his disorienting hunger, he slogged to his cabin where he collapsed on his wet blanket and slept until late morning.

When he woke he waded out into the Teche to refresh himself before facing his father. But he couldn't enter the torpid water without thinking of pressing into Anna, of forcing himself inside her, descending through this soft surface easily, feeling her initial resistance give way. The warm lap of the water retained enough tension on its surface that as he broke through, he could close his eyes and remember when Anna became as submissive as the wet warmth he splashed in. He stood, sweating in the late morning heat, the water listless as a living pool of his sweat, and grew hard, thinking of Anna and how it felt to be sucked down into her depths.

"Gabriel," Basil called from the porch.

Gabriel didn't turn or respond, waiting for the thought of speaking to his father to dampen his erection. When it sullenly went its way, so did he, walking to the porch with the dull complacency of a cow. He mounted the wooden steps in silence, listening to the river water dripping off his hair onto the floorboards. Gabriel realized incongruously that his father and Michael were both smiling at him. How could the warmth on their faces be a response to his battered, mangy frame and starving soul?

"Anna's having a baby, Gabriel," Michael cheerfully declared.

"Alexander was here less than a week ago to tell us," Basil

said. "He was sorry to miss you, but he asked if you could come down to the city when you got back."

"Alexander was here?" Gabriel managed weakly.

Both men nodded enthusiastically.

"It's wonderful news," Basil said. "I know he's been hopeful."

Gabriel was unable to speak.

"You're probably hungry," Michael said. "Your father has been smoking meat for an army." He rose and led the way inside.

"Which it might be," Basil boomed as he followed Gabriel in. "Alexander also told us that the Creoles are finally going to move on Ulloa."

He walked through the house to the kitchen behind. Gabriel joined Michael at the table and thought about Anna, pregnant with his child. Three rough cornmeal cakes sat just out of reach of Michael's twitching right hand.

"This is all common enough for you, eh, Gabriel?" Basil said merrily as he bustled into the quiet room, carrying a wooden plate of sausages.

"No," Gabriel said. "I know they've wanted a child. It's," he paused desperately, but Michael interrupted him.

"I believe your father meant the rebellion against Ulloa."

"I'm sure it's all surprising," Basil said. "But you will have to step carefully down there. It sounds like our people are headed to New Orleans from the north and the west."

"Acadians are fighting?" Gabriel asked.

"Well, Alexander said he didn't expect there to be any," Basil said doubtfully. "I told him to bring Anna out here so she'd be safe while all this is going on." Gabriel looked at his father in panic. "Alexander said he'd consider it," Basil continued, "but that he's sure she'll be safe at home."

Thank Him for small favors, Gabriel thought.

"But, if they weren't expecting trouble, they wouldn't raise militias." Basil's eyes met his. "Remember that those Spaniards are going to assume that every stranger in town is an enemy." Basil went back outside. Gabriel realized that he'd emptied his plate.

Michael beamed at him from across the table. "It's good you came home, Gabriel."

Basil returned with a platter, now weighed down with the venison Michael had mentioned.

"Been a while between meals?" his father asked, noting Gabriel's condition as he reached unthinking across the table. "I would have thought you'd at least have had jerky."

His stomach was already tightening around the quantity of food, so Gabriel stood to stretch and went to the end of the table with a piece of jerky.

"I'm not going to New Orleans," he said calmly. His only certain knowledge was that he would rather die than face Alexander and Anna.

No one spoke for a moment. Michael stood into the silence. "I'm going to test the air."

The fiddler made his surefooted way outside, while inside they heard the grunt as he sat, followed by the quick rattle of old lungs drawing in breath before the sawing took a familiar pattern, and Michael's voice rose in cracked accompaniment.

Crows flapped over in twos and threes, in the pool cattle drowsed up to their knees, ha. The drawbridge fell with a surly clang, and through the dark arch a charger sprang, ha.

Inside the cabin, Gabriel and his father listened quietly, but companionably, as though he hadn't just refused his friend's request for help, and their home wasn't about to be overrun again.

Sir Launfal's raiment thin and spare was idle mail against barbed air, ha. The leper raised not the gold from the dust, saying better indeed a poor man's crust, ha. Better the blessing of the poor, though I turn away empty from the door, ha. The heart within him was ashes and dust, he broke in twain his single crust, ha.

Basil smiled. "It's hard to imagine I'd have found a place in my old heart for music. Your mother would never have believed it." Gabriel waited for his father to keep talking. "I won't tell you to mix in other's affairs. For my sake, I'd prefer you stay clear of what's about to happen down there. But your friend asked for you, Gabriel."

Basil sat. "There's something that maybe I didn't teach you as well as I might have, and living out here hasn't helped. But you can't hide from the future, son, any more than the past. I know that there are times that we seem to have done a bit of both, but if your life is to be tumult and fighting, you still need to face it. You can't choose to not live it."

But Gabriel continued his solitary journeys, spending weeks at a stretch camping along unpeopled fingers of the Teche. After one journey, Philippe was waiting at the riverside in front of his house as Gabriel piloted his pirogue back to its berth.

"Alexander's dead," Philippe said, abruptly, almost accusatorily.

Gabriel dropped the deer he'd lifted back into the boat. "What?"

"Bedard sent him upriver again to ask the Choctaw to stop raiding English ships." Gabriel looked back over the river rather than at his friend, and eventually Philippe continued. "They say it was an accident. They use canoes instead of pirogues east of the Mississippi, I know he mentioned it before." Philippe also considered the river.

"How did it happen?" Gabriel stepped onto the land gingerly, like he'd never done it before, and approached Philippe slowly.

"The Choctaw say he fell out of a canoe on their way back to the Mississippi. There were two others in another boat, but they didn't see him go under. Bedard suspects the Choctaw killed him. He saw the body, drowned, but also banged up. They say it happened when they tried to tug him off the bottom, that his sword was entangled." Philippe reached out and put his hand on Gabriel's shoulder, an unfamiliar sensation after weeks of solitude. "Your father wouldn't let Bedard in the house when he came."

"Good."

"Bedard gave me his sword. I don't want it." There were tears in Philippe's eyes. "I left it in the empty house." Philippe cleared his throat, "I don't have the first damn idea what to say to Anna."

Anna. The child. "I don't either," Gabriel said, relieved just to have said something he could be certain was true. He waited a desperate moment. The clear sky above them seemed a faded canvas stretched thinly over too drafty a hole. "The baby."

"I know. We'll take care of him."

Gabriel stood outside the house on Chartres Street for a long time, waiting, before he worked up the courage to knock on her door. He hadn't seen her since the night in the graveyard, nearly almost four months. He told himself he was sparing her his curse.

"I heard," he said, and waited. Three days reflection had brought him no further than that.

"He's dead," she confirmed.

"I know, Anna." They were silent, neither of them crying. Anna's expression was flat. Gabriel wondered what she had thought about Alexander when she was alone waiting for him. Longing? Resigned? Registering her impassive stare, Gabriel had no idea.

"What are you going to do?"

"This is as much your concern as mine, Gabriel. I'm pregnant. You're the father. And now, I'm going to be your wife."

Lacking the courage to tell his father of the engagement, Gabriel stopped at the Boiselle homestead to see Philippe. His friend greeted him on the porch, but fell silent from the strange look in Gabriel's eyes.

"I'm going to ask Anna to marry me." Liar, Gabriel thought. At least he had a friend left to lie to.

Philippe put a hand on his broadening gut and exhaled, long and loud. "That sounds uncomfortable."

"It's fast. But we're both alone, and she needs someone. The child needs a father." He choked out the last words.

"I can understand that, but I'm not sure that this is being a good friend." Philippe ignored Gabriel's dark looks and tumbled onward. "It's impossible to imagine Alexander being comfortable with this, despite his affection for the two of you." Philippe laughed mirthlessly. "Maybe someone has to be jealous in his memory."

Gabriel welcomed the scolding. Easier than doing it himself, he thought uncharitably. Certainly Alexander would have preferred that Anna not marry anyone, Gabriel included, only weeks after he was buried. I'm sorry, Gabriel said to his friend's memory.

"Have you picked a name for the child?"

"Not yet."

"Alexander might be nice, if it's a boy."

Gabriel sat on his back stoop holding the fusil Bedard had given him at the somber wedding. Gabriel preferred setting traps to hunting the deer, and usually only carried the gun as he prowled the cypress at his riverbank, or sat in a rocking chair, cradling the present like he might his son who slept inside. Alexander, his blameless heir.

Gabriel hated late fall in Louisiana, its mournful wind sweeping brittle oak leaves against their quiet house. It had been his favorite season as a child in Acadia, fishing, watching the rivers freeze. Here, he only imagined predators loose in the moonless night. Often he dozed outside in the chair until he was awakened by nearby cattle, lowing as they ate their slow way toward the riverbank. On those nights, Gabriel would put the rifle up and lie at the foot of his son's cradle until Anna woke them.

Ohio River 1768

❦

So death flooded life, and, o'erflowing its natural margin,
spread to a brackish lake the silver stream of existence.

THEY LEFT THE FORT AN HOUR AFTER DAWN. BERNARD trailed his companions, alert, but only Lafourge was awake, and the soldier watched them leave without a word, yesterday's garrulousness vanished. Now he too wore only his stained pants. He stirred the embers of the fire, eyeing them and restrained, Bernard was certain, only by their numeric superiority, instinctual as any predator. But absent other observation, they descended the wide trail marked with the hammered bronze crests and pushed off, he and Evangeline paddling, Felician scanning the receding bank with his musket propped in his lap.

They didn't talk even when safely away from the bank, preoccupied even as the Ohio yawned wide, and finally their river met the Mississippi. They crossed to river left to avoid the new water and hugged that bank the rest of the morning, suspiciously watching the brown stream rush alongside their clearer water, separate as earth and sky.

"How long do you think it's going to keep going like this?" Evangeline asked him when they stopped late that afternoon, gesturing at the still divided flow.

"I wouldn't want to guess, I've never seen anything like it before," Bernard said.

"I hate to think we're going to be paddling through that brown water."

"So do I," he answered truthfully. "But it's moving right along. We'll stay in our river a while longer, but when it mixes we'd be smart to cross to the bank opposite that fort."

"It doesn't look like it's getting any narrower," Felician said.

"No, it doesn't," Bernard admitted. "Still, I'd prefer some hard paddling over bedding down within reach of those soldiers."

"Wouldn't we have seen them following us?" Evangeline asked. "It was perfectly clear." She sounded uncertain, and Bernard's misgivings were superseded by his yearning for a chance to protect her.

"We should have," Bernard said slowly. "But they know this river a damned sight better than we do, maybe even well enough to try it at night."

"I thought you said only fools chanced rivers at night," Evangeline said. It was the strange, muddy water, not the men, that bothered her the most, Bernard saw.

"I did, but those soldiers were worse and more desperate than fools. They were men who knew for themselves they needed watching. Even a shiftless cutthroat might hesitate before raising his hand against a traveler begging bread." Bernard grimaced. "I sound like you," he called to the priest. "But we'll wait a bit before we try to cross, though I'd sleep better knowing this monster is between us and them."

"Well, let's make sure we get a full day's separation, at the least," Felician said, starting back for their canoe.

Still uncomfortable that night, they round-to behind a spit of an island, where Bernard insisted on a watch, and volunteered for the first.

"And no fire," he said. "In this current, and at night, anyone coming from the north will float right past."

"If the weather holds, we can still make Louisiana by the end of the year," Evangeline said, wishfully optimistic as she bedded down.

"We don't even know how far it is to Louisiana, but an easy end to our journey doesn't seem in keeping with what I've seen of Acadian luck. I'd imagine we still have a ways to travel," Bernard responded, his eyes on the dark river before them.

"Good that I'm paddling then, if we have so far to go. Not all of us can while away the hours bemoaning our fate," she responded.

"It's not my luck, anyhow," Bernard began defensively, but Felician interrupted him, happy to have a chance to side with Evangeline against him.

"Wiser to hope a better tomorrow will emerge regardless of how dismal today is, wouldn't you say, Bernard? Better to put your faith in our Creator's divine plan, and in the conviction that if we do our parts, we will join Him in the holy hereafter."

"Just help me carry up the canoe," Bernard said, moving on his way.

He watched Evangeline sleep until he was reminded of a Wyandot girl Augustine had bought for him years before. He felt now as he imagined that girl had as she left their wigwam in the village, one of their stops where Augustine didn't have a wife, and drunken brawling was as likely as trading.

Past thirty, and with two brushes with death already past him when he might have taken up the cross, Bernard had thought there was little left to make him feel raw and exposed. But the sinister men lurked above the rivers' meet with the fickle restraint of sated predators, and they were safer downstream no matter what they found there. Bernard wondered what his reception might have been if he had come upon the fort alone. He decided his dread would have been present whether or not Evangeline was part of the encounter with the isolated men. To ease his mind, he tried remembering instead his last drink of brandy, back in the Shawnee town sitting in the damp air around one of the trappers' fires, as the Ohio rushed past, outside the limit of the flickering light, but visible in its absence of total darkness.

An old man had shared his pouch of tobacco that last night around the fire as preamble. "That's a long way the three of you are traveling," he opined before spitting a stream of black juice between his feet. Bernard's was not a circumstance well understood by his brethren, still cleaving tight to the old ways here on the riverbank. "Must be quite a fare," the man added, his small brown eyes squinting further in scrutiny.

Bernard grunted noncommittally, "You're right on both counts, I suppose. Thanks for the leaf. I imagine I'll be doing without pretty soon."

He had drunk heavily enough then that he hadn't been tempted to open the bottle they carried with them over their weeks on the Ohio. He disliked drinking around Evangeline, not wanting to give her any reason to think him weak in comparison to Felician. But he walked down to the water's edge, broke the seal and took a slug from the bottle after pouring one into the Mississippi in hopes of safe passage.

The wind rained pine needles lightly about the camp as he returned, and he listened to their soft fall and thought about what he'd told Francis before they left Maryland. He did think he had a chance with Evangeline. Better all the time, with Julian withdrawn from the competition. But Gabriel lurked larger in his imagination now that they had reached the Mississippi. The boy might be waiting on this very river, with a homestead ready for the woman he'd never stopped thinking of as his.

Not Evangeline, but Jana might have been his, he considered. It was pointless to think of her only after she was gone, he thought, surprised he even could with the image of Evangeline, poised in the middle of the new canoe like a princess, fresh on his mind. Though they had been steadfast and good-natured companions, and though under different circumstances he might have been tempted by Jana, Bernard did not entertain the possibility of heading north with her, even if they were traveling toward more familiar country. He wouldn't leave Evangeline, even if she wanted him to.

Julian had escaped, Bernard thought, because his sister intervened to draw him away from their group, leading him north to find a home, a reasonable destination. Only he and Felician, alike in that neither had a woman to direct their paths, continued to plunge south with Evangeline. She dominated them effortlessly, wholly, without question, and maybe, though he thought it unlikely, without intent.

Evangeline had spent her life in the company of men, he realized. Whether consciously or not, she avoided women, and hadn't sought Jana out as they traveled. Bernard had assumed that Jana's resentment for Evangeline was due to Julian's obnoxious infatuation, but maybe the absent girl had other motivations. No one sought Evangeline out. One waited until she called. His destiny was bound up in the tiny space between Felician's and Evangeline's desires, complicated by the fact that Bernard thought the priest unwilling to recognize his feelings for the girl. Although, Bernard supposed, that might not be giving the man enough credit. They'd all been together in the wilderness long enough now to come to some clear understandings.

A deep bend the next afternoon brought the waters indistinguishably together, and they crossed to the west shore to make camp.

"Another fireless night," Bernard said, as they rubbed their aching arms.

Dead, limbless trunks stabbed out of the river, stuck in the mud along the bank, and they risked the deeper swifter waters of the current, pulling off early on their fourth day from the fort in a light rain that quickly let up. He was being overcautious, Bernard felt as they rested, despite the unfamiliar circumstances, but he, at least, was in no particular rush. That, perhaps, he shared with Felician.

They paddled the next day through a pale cloudless sky, the October sun bright but not warm around them. "I can't believe how wide it is," Evangeline marveled.

"The Saint Lawrence is twice as wide at the mouth, isn't it, Bernard?" Felician replied. Bernard remembered Evangeline had never seen that northern river.

"Yes, but the fleuve doesn't stay that way long," he answered.

Ahead of him in the boat, Felician and Evangeline paddled infrequently as he steered, the day's steady wind substituting effectively for muscle, Bernard thought, checking the sky again. The current followed a bend back to the east, and Bernard let it carry them along as he looked at Evangeline sitting before him with her slender, chestnut fingers trailing through the opaque water.

As though lured from the depths by her hand, a sawyer surfaced in the river before them, and like a whale breaching, crashed down in a sudden wave that rocked the canoe starboard, where Bernard leaned watching Evangeline's delicate movements. He spilled out, flipping the canoe as his weight passed over the lip.

He plunged into the river headfirst, and came back up easily, almost like he'd wanted the dip. Evangeline struggled, clinging to a paddle, while Felician floated downstream faster, thankfully clinging to the upturned side of their canoe. He swam to Evangeline and held her up by the elbow as they treaded water together in the current. "Are you all right?" he asked.

"What happened?"

She must be fine, Bernard thought.

"I tipped us. I'm sorry. Let's get the canoe."

They swam after Felician who kicked his legs and kept hold of the craft. "Thanks for the expertise back there," the priest remarked as they joined him at its side, panting from the exertion.

Bernard was silent. He could say that he'd been distracted, wondering what would have happened if he had taken up with the twins instead of Evangeline and the priest. That maybe it wasn't too late to see if Jana would make a good wife. After he recovered his strength for a moment he ducked his head back underwater and resurfaced beneath the upturned canoe. "Let go," he called out. Bernard braced his palms against a gunwale, kicked his legs and thrust the boat out of the water, finding it as light as he'd hoped. From the water, he kept his weight on one side while Felician climbed in and then helped Evangeline in from the other. He lifted himself easily back in, not even minding the swim, until he saw what the others had already noticed. One of the canvas sacks had come undone, and flopped empty against the birchbark, half their provisions given as offering to the mighty river.

The heavy silt of the water muddied their clothes and sloshed dangerously in the canoe, the wobbling more disquieting than the swimming, Bernard thought as they paddled delicately for the near shore. Felician spotted two planted trunks leaning against the high bank and they bumped to rest against them. Evangeline took the natural bridge to land and Felician passed out the sack with its cornmeal, their wet blankets and muskets while Bernard tied them off on the trunks. Thankful for the dryness of the day, Bernard had a fire burning quickly, and they spread out their clothes and blankets to dry in the chill afternoon sun.

"We need to replenish our food, and it will be easier before it gets cold. I can find us meat."

"Are you sure that we should stop?" Felician asked the question Bernard might have himself.

"I don't like it anymore than you do, but we need food," Bernard growled. "Unless you think you can pray some up."

"It would be unseemly to ask the Lord to gift us what we threw away," Felician replied smoothly.

"Happy you're enjoying this, priest. Why don't you and Evangeline see if you can get a few fish, and I'll have a look around."

"How far?" Evangeline asked. "Shouldn't we all just fish?"

No one trusted him to take care of himself, or them, Bernard thought.

"Just keep the muskets at hand, and I'll see if I can find something more substantive. We'll head out tomorrow after everything dries out." He put on his damp breeches and shirt and left Evangeline and Felician at the fire.

Bernard found the woods quiet, and didn't hunt long before returning empty-handed to find Felician alone in camp.

"Where's Evangeline?"

"Where's the deer?" Felician replied, and then saw Bernard's scowl, "She's at the river."

"Why did you leave her?"

"I came back to stoke the fire so these clothes dry out."

"You left her alone? You trust too much, Felician."

"I don't know about that. She seems to look after herself well enough, praise God Who grants her the fortitude. A virtue beyond the pale of a man so desperate with lust that he dumped us in the river."

"At least I stand by my claim," Bernard hissed. "More than you can say." He pitched his voice lower to make sure Evangeline didn't hear him, "I'll bet she had a good-looking mother about your age, Felician. Were you acquainted with Madame Bellefontaine?"

"No, cur, I never knew her. Anna Bellefontaine died when Evangeline was young."

Bernard was happy to have found a sore spot. "That's a shame, a woman you might have gotten along with about your own age."

"I'm not going to hear you mock the woman's memory," Felician snarled.

"What would you like to do about it, Felician?" Both men considered the musket Bernard had left resting peacefully near the fire.

The priest looked back at him as they heard Evangeline's return. "I'm going to pray that the Lord forgives your transgressions," he said quietly, before pitching his voice to carry farther. "What were you asking about Evangeline's mother?"

The trapper felt like a child, and like one he moved to strike the irritating man, but Felician didn't flinch, and Bernard left him at the fire, brushing shoulders with Evangeline as she returned to the camp.

Only a few angry steps from the camp he saw human eyes flash in the evening, just before he was leapt upon. Fixing on the wild eyes, his hand found the man's throat under his mangy beard, which he caught between the thumb and fingers of his right hand as they fell tangled together. Bernard landed on top of the man, howling with pain as his contortions twisted the knife that he found in his stomach. He didn't know when exactly he'd been stabbed, before or after they'd fallen, but he ignored it, and brought his left hand to the other's throat. The man's hands closed over Bernard's wrists, but couldn't dislodge them. The trapper bore down on the man's windpipe as he squirmed beneath him, legs flailing. The man viciously kneed Bernard in the groin, but the pain only made him squeeze harder, and he jerked the man by the neck and off the ground. The man's head lolled sickeningly, and Bernard rolled from his limp victim, coming to rest alongside him. The knife had dislodged itself in the struggle, and he closed the wound as best he could with his fingers. The attack hadn't lasted more than ten unthinking seconds.

Bernard was fortunate to have been so furious leaving the camp. His anger had sharpened his reflexes and heightened his ferocity and kept him alive, at least temporarily. What had the man wanted? What they all wanted. He must have been following her back to the fire, when Bernard accidentally crashed into him. He and Felician might have had their throats slit in their sleep, wounds they couldn't have closed with their fingers.

Bernard heard his name called, but was unsure of the direction or source and didn't respond. He turned his head to regard the dead man, motionless in his woolen blue rags. After several breaths, the trapper felt a chill descend on the clearing, as the corpse cooled beside him and the heat of the struggle receded, but his belly burned. He kept his left hand tight around the ragged edges of his skin. The blood flowed through his fingers down his side to soak into the torn blue breeches of his attacker. The first man that Bernard had killed.

Another moth consumed by Evangeline's flame. He was no more than the window, crushing not out of intention, but merely with his presence.

Bernard held his breath like the body next to his, locked in its inhalation. Was something ascending heavenward from the attacker? If anything, it seemed more that the ground sapped the man's vitality, reducing the corpse to insensate carrion. Bernard's blood continued trickling onto the dead man. It was possible for a moment to imagine his living blood reinvigorating the renegade. He let his breath out heavily, and choked.

Death conquered life, it didn't begin another existence. So long as he kept the blood inside him, he might stave it off awhile longer, he thought as he became aware of Evangeline and Felician crouching over him, replacing his hands with their own.

"Is this the other soldier?" Evangeline asked.

"We didn't do much talking," Bernard croaked.

She smiled weakly at him.

"How does it look?" he asked. To have her hands on his body one time without prodding a wound, was all he wanted. He started chuckling at the thought of them lying together in peace, low-pitched bubbles of laughter that sounded hysterical even in his own ears.

"Bernard?" She slapped him lightly on the cheek. "You're laughing." Even as faint as he had grown the concern was plain on her voice.

"One time," he responded dreamily, and closed his eyes, ignoring the indecipherable words above him as he basked in the remembered warmth of the corpse.

Mississippi River 1768

The stars, the thoughts of God in the Heavens,
shone on the eyes of men, who had ceased to marvel
and worship save when a blazing comet was seen.

FELICIAN TOOK A MUSKET AND LEFT TO SCOUT THE TRAIL ahead while Evangeline waited with the wounded trapper. Past where the men had fought, the way narrowed, and he ducked warily under the bare limbs, listening for human sound in the forest other than the heaving of his own breath. He heard nothing, and the deer trail widened as it emerged onto a tributary ten meters wide that they'd yet to pass. Downstream, the posts of an old stockade grew out of the bank almost as naturally as the trees they'd once been, and a single roof peaked from within.

He slipped back into the woods and approached from another angle through the fallen leaves, smelling a recent fire under the musty dampness clinging to the walls. He found a gap between posts and peered at the mission town inside. There were two longhouses near his vantage, and a small church at the center of the halfmoon enclosure. The stockade protected the bank, but was open to the water, which was empty save for two posts of an abandoned pier, looking like trees ravaged by beaver. The roofs of both longhouses had caved in, but the primitive church's still held. He entered the silent stockade with his musket ready. The church was empty except for a musty heap of cornshucks on the dirt floor. Outside it, Felician paused next to a fire ring. The burnt stones lay where his little house would have stood if the structure in front of him had been Saint Charles, and the priest regarded the church anew, as though all of their traveling had only served to return them to an even more desolate Grand Pre than the one they'd been forced to abandon a dozen years before.

He walked a sentry's slow circle around the perimeter and then returned to his companions.

"It looks like Bernard finished off the defenders," Felician said when he returned to Evangeline.

"At least we've found another church," Evangeline said.

He grimaced at Bernard's weight as he lifted under the trapper's arms while Evangeline took his legs.

"Pretty stout," Felician said.

"I pride myself on it," Bernard returned weakly.

They returned through the hole in the wall where the gate had been and laid Bernard on the hard packed earth inside the church. Felician rested his gun next to the trapper, and he and Evangeline returned to reclaim their canoe from the unused camp on the Mississippi.

"Maybe there's something to eat in the longhouses," Evangeline said. She gathered their provisions into the sailcloth, grown light since Shawnee Town.

Felician shook his head and gestured her into the bow. "Picked clean."

They worked their way down the west bank for nearly an hour until they saw the tributary, and let the flow steer them further to midstream, where they turned and fought the strong current upriver until they reached the stockade.

They ate a little jerky, and Evangeline replaced the moss covering the hole in Bernard's stomach like a green scab. "I'm sorry we don't have the salve Felician made back in Grand Pre."

"Maybe you should try staunching it with my hair. All that stuff ought to be good for something." The trapper seemed cheerful in spite of the pain. Having surrendered his body to them again, he apparently felt more free to speak as he wished.

"Prayer might shield you from these recurring grievous injuries," Felician chided Bernard. "Daily mass has kept me from ever having been stabbed or shot."

"That's a pretty direct relationship you're describing."

"It is."

"Well, it didn't work too well for that soldier back in the clearing."

"How do you mean?"

"Well, you said you found a small fire ring outside the mission, so, the man I killed was sheltering here, hoping for protection from the same walls and spirits that we're counting on."

"Rest easy then that you have come upon this place in the company of a priest. It is a blessed circumstance."

"Again, that seems to depend on your perspective. Prayers didn't suit in Acadia. Your medicine has kept me alive, Felician, your skill with infection, not your intercessions."

"I'm going to look for something else to close that wound," Evangeline said.

"How old are you Bernard?" Felician asked after she'd gone.

"Thirty-two."

"Assuming I keep you breathing until we get to Louisiana, what are you going to do?"

"I've never seen much use in wild speculation. Maybe's that why I'm uncomfortable with all your talk about life after death."

"There's nothing speculative about eternity. God will reclaim your sliver of the divine consciousness, and He will judge you."

"Well, I'm sure that no matter where I go in this life or another, there's going to be somebody there disagreeing with me too."

"Doesn't that suggest something?"

"Yes. There's no place for me in the world, or at least around other people. That message I've gotten loud and clear."

"Well."

The trapper picked at the moss dressing over his stomach. "It's not even bleeding anymore."

"She knows what she's doing."

"I'll say. That makes her the opposite, then, of the two of us."

"I know what I'm doing with myself, Bernard. I'm not wandering just to do it."

"You've got God telling you where to go."

Felician scowled. "He does direct me, but it's left to me to interpret that direction. I'm here to rescue souls from the all-consuming darkness."

"Well then, it's more of a shame so many of these villages are abandoned."

They gathered thatch from the fallen roofs of the longhouses and made pallets in three corners of the church, leaving the place unbalanced, Felician thought as they huddled around a small fire as the wind howled outside, blowing leaves against the walls like the arrows of an invading army.

The next day, they collected wood and failed to catch any fish, their breath frosting as they cast out from the bank.

"Tomorrow, I'll shoot a deer," Felician assured Evangeline as they warmed themselves by the fire before retiring to their corners.

He set out with the light the next morning, wrapped in his wool blanket against the cold, and walked laboriously upstream until he found a creek. He turned up this smaller flow and followed it until he found a clearing across the stream. Felician situated himself behind an oak tree overlooking the clearing, pulled the blanket up over his fur hat and prayed for something to come looking for a drink. It was cloudy enough that the sun's rising brought scarce warmth, and Felician had to periodically massage his hands to make certain he'd be able to fire, though he worried he might frighten off his prey. He was blowing into his cupped hands when he saw a sauvage coming up the bank toward him.

Felician struggled off the frozen ground as the man walked toward him with hands raised to the priest to show that they were empty. His hair was shaved except for one lock on top of his head, and a long braided strand, like a tail, running down his back. There was a crimson streak running up from his forehead, meeting a white circle around the scalp lock. He made no move toward the musket on his back, and Felician silently thanked his gracious Lord.

"English?" The sauvage asked his question in English.

Felician shook his head, and smiled at the man. "French," he said in French. The priest traced a cross in the air and pointed to himself.

The man nodded at the information and pointed to himself.

"Quapow." The name meant nothing to Felician, but he nodded to show that he understood. They sized each other up silently, and after a moment, the sauvage rummaged in a pouch at his belt and extended a piece of jerky. Felician bowed his head in thanks after accepting the morsel. He only had the patience to chew it briefly before swallowing the tough meat.

"Pox?" the sauvage asked, pressing his finger against a leathery cheek.

"No," Felician shook his head emphatically.

The sauvage regarded Felician gravely, and then set off the way he'd come, leaving Felician to stumble wearily behind.

The village they reached consisted of numerous wigwams clustered around two longhouses similar to those in the stockade. There were no animals around, not even dogs, that the priest could see or hear.

He was ushered inside one of the longhouses, where four men sat smoking a thin pipe. Felician collapsed without being asked to sit, as his guide spoke rapidly to the men. He couldn't pretend that he wasn't ravenous any more than he could pretend that he wasn't nearly fifty. He was too weak even to be angry with himself.

One of the men offered the pipe, but Felician coughed and shook his head.

"Food," he said. The men nodded and one said something to the guide, and the man withdrew. Felician's eyes closed helplessly in the warm darkness of the room, and he dozed.

He woke up as a gourd filled with cold water was thrust into his hands. He drank deeply. The four men sat, still smoking or smoking again. He had no sense for how much time had passed.

After he drank, one of the four came over to sit beside him, and the guide returned with a bowl of rice.

"Thank you," Felician said. He remembered to bless the food this time, and ate the rice with his fingers as no utensil was offered.

"The French." The man who'd left the circle spoke to him after he finished eating, pointing to the wooden bowl. Felician held up the rough vessel quizzically, but the man shook his head and pointed inside. "The rice."

Felician nodded. "Thank you," he said again.

The sauvage led him to one of the longhouse's shadowy corners, where two buffalo skulls held fat candles, illuminating a steel sword, a stone-tipped spear, and tiny figurines carved variously of clay and wood. A crucifix and a plain cross hung together on the wall behind the treasures. He wasn't the first missionary to these untrammeled parts, apparently.

"The French?" Felician asked.

"Yes," the man nodded. He picked up the spear. "This killed the river God," he said, and set it down again.

Felician nodded. He pointed at the crucifix again. "The French? When do they come?" He shrugged his shoulders and looked pointedly around the room.

"Spring," the sauvage said after a moment.

The priest didn't have that long to wait. He returned to the bowl, and mimed putting something in it. The man watched him, and then Felician tried a word, "Take food?" Again he demonstrated putting food in the bowl, before walking with it toward the door. He returned to his host. "Can I take food to my friends?" he asked.

After a cornbread breakfast the next morning, the same sauvage who found him freezing in the woods led Felician back to the derelict mission carrying a deerskin loaded with potatoes and jerky. They arrived just before sunset, and Evangeline met them in the open gate, where it seemed to the priest's feverish imagination that she recognized him well before she lowered the musket.

Their silent guest should feel perfectly at ease in their company, Felician thought ruefully as they ate potatoes pulled warm from the fire. After the meal, Evangeline left for a moment, leaving the three men staring at each other in silence. She returned quickly, carrying an armload of the dried cornshucks from the longhouses that they'd scrounged for pallets in the church. She dropped the bundle and returned to the night. Felician followed her into the longhouse.

"You don't have to bother with that," he said.

"That man brought us food, Father, the least we can do is give him a bed."

"That's not what I meant." He exhaled. "There's no reason to make an extra pallet, we can share one for the night."

"I'd rather not."

"We have plenty of times before."

"There's no reason to," she said, passing him with the next load. "There's plenty of stuffing to go around."

He waited outside the church for her to return. "Are you afraid of what this man will think?"

She stopped before she reached the roofless structure and turned back to him glowering.

Felician pressed on despite her look of warning, and helplessly named his fear. "You're not afraid of what Bernard will think?"

"I don't want to share a bed, Felician." There was no mistaking the anger on her voice.

"I know that you offered yourself to Julian," he said quietly.

Evangeline advanced on him, and he withdrew from the sudden menace on her face.

"What do you know?"

"I know that you tried to seduce him. Jana told me." He said it angrily, aware that every word was a mistake.

She regarded him for a moment. "And what do you want to do about it? Do you want me to strip off my clothes for you?"

He opened his mouth, but couldn't think of how to respond. "No," he finally managed, though he missed the chance to mean it.

"Good," she said. "Do not forget that you chose your fate, whereas I have grudgingly accepted mine. And if I do not bemoan it more frequently, do not mistake that living as a spinster does come accompanied with its portion of bitterness. With Julian," Evangeline said hesitantly, "I did as I felt I had to."

Felician looked mutely back at her. He didn't choose to hear God, so much as realize and accept that God was what he heard. They had rarely spoken of his childhood, but she knew that he was raised in the seminary. She knew his blood burned. Yet the holy restraint kept his mind pure, or at least closer to pure, and the words came to him at last.

"I realize that I've become a burden to you," he said, guilty, but including her in his blame. "I see how it might not have been so, but now the Lord is loud in my ear. I will remain here."

"What?" she said. Faintly in the moonlight he saw her hair shake back and forth.

Felician continued, recklessly charting a future where he might be further removed from daily sin. "I will stay and rebuild the mission, and it and I will serve the wanderers of this benighted land. You are a proud woman, Evangeline, and you don't need me any longer." If you ever did, the priest thought.

She reached out to him, and his hand took hers, as reflexively as his eyelids closing for sleep, he thought. "No, Felician, I have need of you still."

Evangeline took her hand out of his after a moment, and went back into the longhouse. She didn't look at him when she carried out the load of cornshucks, and she didn't come back out of the church.

Felician stared into the dark water. Forgive me, he said, and waded out a few steps. It was warm compared to the air, compared to her tongue. If he let that water close over his head, she might forgive him the confrontation. The priest shook it off. The girl still had plenty need of a guardian, best that he began again fulfilling his responsibility. Forgive me, he said again, though he didn't know who he was asking.

His Quapow guide left the next morning, and so did Evangeline, without a word as to where she was going. Felician briefly searched the woods close to the stockade before returning to pace the interior of the church. Unable to sit up fully without aggravating the stomach wound, the trapper watched suspiciously as Felician took up his Bible. The holy book he'd carried since Baltimore wasn't faring much better than the trapper, waterlogged, and completely illegible past Maccabees.

"Where's Evangeline?" Bernard asked.

"She went for a walk."

The trapper looked at him, trying to glean information from his silence, and then put his head back down on the floor.

"What about a reading," Felician said, not expecting a response from Bernard as he opened the book without reflection to Isaiah. He looked down the page to God's impending judgment on the earth, and read the words aloud in French so that the trapper could understand them.

The earth shall be utterly laid waste and utterly despoiled for the Lord has spoken this word. The earth dries up and withers, the world languishes and withers, the Heavens languish and wither with the earth. The earth lies polluted under its inhabitants for they have transgressed laws, violated the statues, broken the everlasting covenant. Therefore a curse devours the earth and its inhabitants suffer for their guilt, therefore the inhabitants of the earth dwindled, and few people are left. Felician stopped reading, and recited from memory. *Terror, and the pit, and the snare are upon you, inhabitant of the earth, and its transgressions lie heavy upon it, and it will not rise again.*

He looked down at Bernard on the floor. "This war was foretold. The Lord has made the world desolate, and left us here to run through the benighted lands, seeking solace in His blasted churches."

The trapper watched him closely, paralyzed like a waiting sacrifice on the floor, the dry blood validating his words.

"Why do you think that churches are all that's left standing? As a mark of the everlasting life we have turned our backs on, in pursuit of sin and violence. Perhaps you were prescient, Bernard, to not preoccupy yourself with the afterlife, as man has brought Hell unto the earth, and we dangle in the fire like so many rabbits."

Felician crossed the room to his bed and laid the Bible down on his robe.

"But there have been other wars, and some will survive this one, though whether we are among them is the will of the Lord. And He punishes those who make war, and serve its ends. What is war's commandment, Bernard? Take or be taken. Kill or be killed. Rape or be raped. Where is its root? In the man who says, serve yourself, if you would be well-served." He looked to the door, wishing that Evangeline listened as well. "This is not the voice of the Lord, Our Shining Light, Who commands that you serve Him and Him alone. And how? By toiling in the service of others, and extending holy charity. Yet we have killed, Bernard, though you are no more accountable than I. And both of us less, maybe, than she who you acted to protect."

Louisiana 1769

⁓

And when the echoes had ceased,
like a sense of pain was the silence.

"IT'S BEEN A QUIET WINTER BETWEEN YOU AND FELICIAN," Bernard said. Felician was gone now, hunting for a deer to smoke before they left. Since apologizing to her, he'd often found reason to keep away.

"He feels that I've jilted him. No one but me left Baltimore actually wanting to reach Louisiana." She looked at Bernard squarely, implicating him as well, and then waved her arm to the wind. "This is how he's handling it."

She waited for affirmation, but it seemed more honesty than the usually forthright man wanted. He poked a finger in his dressing like a child.

"Stop that." She knelt at his side and took the trapper's hand away from the bandages and held it. Something in Bernard's look as Evangeline met his eyes gave her pause.

"We're not to Louisiana yet," she said quietly.

"No," he replied. Her comment might have encouraged his

hopes, she saw. She needed to be clearer.

Evangeline kept holding his heavy hand as she spoke, looking into his eyes. "I know what you want Bernard, but you can't have me. I need you to take me to Gabriel." He frowned instinctively at the name. She sat back. "Because that's where I'm going. To Gabriel. And I'm certain that he knows."

"That you're alive?"

"That I'm coming for him."

"It might have been the other way around," he said.

"Not with us, Bernard, but that says nothing against Gabriel. I know him well enough to know he's more inclined to accept a situation that I might be." She took a heavy breath. "I've never seen fit to explain. We don't, I don't talk about Gabriel at all.

"What I'm saying is that he's known tragedy in his life before, worse in some ways than what the English did to us, because he suffered it alone." Bernard regarded her intently, waiting for her to continue. "He had three older brothers, and they drowned, with his mother, when he was thirteen. I sometimes wonder if he thinks about me now like he used to think about them. Or if everything we've both suffered in the years since has shaken him at all. A person feels only so much in life before they stop feeling anything, though they might carry on afterward. Even years ago, it took more to move Gabriel than anyone else I knew. And I loved him for it. I wanted to protect and comfort and cherish him so that his vulnerable moments were happy ones. And they were, mostly, when we were together. I can do that for him again."

She continued speaking as gently as she could. "You love me, and it's kept me alive, brought us all so far. But I'm never going to love you."

He took his hand away, and she paused at the anger in his eyes, as sudden and overwhelming as his desire moments before.

"I'm telling you this out of respect, Bernard."

He didn't look like he felt respected. "I'm only here because you saved my life."

"I want you to know what's waiting down the river. I need you to be able to face it. Be honest with yourself, you don't want my body. I need you to take me to Gabriel. I know that you don't want to hear this, but please know that I only say it because I admire you and appreciate everything that you've done for me." She smiled at him as she finished. "So now you know where I stand."

"I always have," he responded quietly.

Felician came home with a doe two days later. By the time they smoked the meat, Bernard pronounced himself fit to paddle, and they returned to the Mississippi.

Spring had a different feel in the timeless southern warmth, noticeable in a heavier musk rising off the river as life blossomed in its depths. They dug in diligently, without ability now to turn aside from what they'd started so long ago. Despite their speed, they didn't pass a settlement for several days, and were forced to slow their pace to pick berries and fish to supplement the jerky. They camped on a wide island cut out of the Mississippi's west bank, and Felician shot a deer unlucky enough to try to share it with them. They woke the next morning to a fog that hung thickly over the island for three days, which they passed cooking venison crusted with cornmeal and keeping near the fire to ward off the dampness. Night and day collided under the heavy mist, and when the sun finally returned to the valley, it seemed an unsustainable aberration.

After weeks on the water they spotted smoke dancing over the cypress. Though it was visible from late morning, the clear sky made the fire appear closer than it was, and they sculled down the west bank of the river toward it through the afternoon. They skirted a densely wooded island where a little tributary met the main flow, and found a rough homestead in its lee. Bernard beached the canoe, and the two men waited with the canoe while she crossed the slick mud to the small house, realizing as she approached that the smoke they'd seen from the river was actually coming from behind the home, which had no chimney.

A man with a black beard and a musket stood in his open door, marking her approach, but he lowered the weapon as she drew near.

"Howdy," he called, not extending much warmth with the greeting.

"Good afternoon, Monsieur." There was no porch, just two steps up to where the cabin rested on fat stumps.

"Passing through?" It sounded like there had been few opportunities for the man to practice his French recently.

"Yes we are," she said as Felician and Bernard joined her. "We're headed for Louisiana."

The man gave a gruff chuckle. "Well, I guess that's what this is."

She took in the wide familiar river and lonely house again. From the look of the man and his farm, there might be some distance yet to travel before they could expect to see anything resembling what they had heard of New Orleans.

"What can I do for you?" Having given them time to process the new information, he returned to his suspicions.

She smiled. "We might say our supplies are running low. Or

we might say that we haven't eaten since yesterday, and that it wasn't much."

The man nodded as though her answer wasn't as bad as he feared, but rather than inviting them in, he joined them in front of his house.

"Let's go tell the wife."

They circled the house, and found a haggard woman baking in an outdoor oven. Evangeline counted six children, caked in dirt, who stayed away from them, either out of politeness or fear, whispering in German.

Scraggly corn was the dominate crop in the field past the outdoor cookstove, with dozens of trees felled to allow for light, and maybe future expansion to the modest holding.

"We've got three for dinner, Martha," the man said after a moment, and went inside.

The woman returned to her fire.

A dispirited, unfulfilling union was easier to imagine here in Louisiana's swampy margins. Though she would probably have been the one doing the ordering, with Gabriel as her begrudging companion as they raised their children to toilsome lives apart from society.

They left the family and after three days' paddle moored along a wide beach where a tributary churned west into the sunset. Evangeline stood at the water's edge in the rising light, picturing Gabriel, gliding between the cypress in a canoe as the cranes flapped lazily overhead.

As though conjured by her vision, a raft appeared bobbing up the sluggish branch like a phantom, and she waited at the edge of the water for the solitary traveler. The man was a colorful splash on the muddy raft, his blue coat and red pants were shot through with silver thread, and he wore a wide straw hat.

"Andre Foret, at your service," he said as he came to rest next to their canoe. It was the most cheerfully she'd heard anything said in as long as she could recall.

"Evangeline Bellefontaine." She smiled back. "Do you travel much on the Mississippi?"

"Well, I traveled from the lakes to New Orleans during the war, but I've learned more about the river hereabouts ferrying rice in the years since."

"You're a rice merchant?" she asked, seeing only dyed clothing and a couple tanned deerskins.

He shrugged away her scrutiny. "Partly. I can also fix anything you have that's broken. And I'll take most things most places. My friends say I have a daring heart," he said with a wink. "Where might you be from, Madame?"

"We're," she stopped herself. "I'm an Acadian, and we've come from Baltimore."

He looked skeptically at their canoe. "You've paddled from Baltimore?"

She nodded. "Much of the way. Actually, I'm looking for someone in particular, a man, about thirty, Gabriel Lajeunesse."

"Gabriel Lajeunesse." He thought for a moment. "Yes, I know him. I used to serve under his wife's father."

"His wife's father?"

"Yes, Captain Bedard. He took his money and sailed back to France last year after they deposed Ulloa." He saw her face. "I said something I shouldn't have. Too much, I guess, for a simple creature like me to imagine why a woman traveling with two men might be looking for another."

Evangeline looked over her shoulder at Felician and Bernard. "Do you know where he lives?" she asked quietly, not wanting to be overheard, not willing yet to claim this Gabriel with his name. People were forever mistaken, and it could be this wanderer as easily as she.

"He's been trapping out west for years. It's good that you asked me, because you were about to paddle right past this here." He indicated up the tributary. "The Atchafalaya will take you out there, no reason to go down to New Orleans. It sounds like you've come far enough to not need any warnings from me, but that's still a big swamp you have to cross. But you'll only find your own people once you get out there." He splashed off of his raft, carrying his tierope. "Stop when you see a place to camp, they're rarer than jugglers' fingers. Don't worry. Those that come to Louisiana to look for a husband don't have to look long."

She walked back to Felician and Bernard. "This is the Atchafalaya," she said flatly. "It will take us out to where Gabriel lives." She couldn't continue, and they sat around their breakfast fire, watching silently as she tried not to break down.

"So the man knows Gabriel?" Felician asked. Evangeline nodded.

"What's wrong?" Bernard asked. She saw hope in the trapper's eyes and hated him for it.

"Gabriel has a wife."

Like ghosts retracing lives already lived, they paddled up the still Atchafalaya. A grim week passed, toiling through the aisles of cypress trailing their moss around them like old ladies' hair. She kept watch from the bow for alligators, but quickly lost her initial fear of the monsters, and even risked brushing one spiny backside lightly with her paddle as it glided past the canoe.

"I hate those creatures," Bernard said one evening as they watched an alligator catching the last of the filtered sunlight from a fallen log out in the water. They were the first words spoken in hours.

"I'd rather take my chances with a bear," Felician agreed.

The two men hadn't exchanged a cross word since she'd told them the news. And, though the end was already known, neither of her companions raised the possibility of turning aside. Evangeline marveled at their steadfastness, for she wanted nothing but to turn from the unimaginable confrontation before her. She realized now how small the long way they had come would seem when faced with an obscure future. But there seemed no recourse other than to follow the murky river.

Felician looked at her across the fire. "It's not Gabriel that's sustained you these years, Evangeline."

She looked at him, uncertain of his meaning.

"Your dream of Gabriel, not the man himself, has been the source of your comfort during our journey. Your feelings have not been in vain, for you have made purpose for yourself in turmoil."

"Thank you, Felician, but hope for our future together was my comfort, and that salve is gone."

"I think it is what we do in service of lost causes that proves our mettle," Bernard said.

Later, as her companions slept, Evangeline considered the effort that had been expended in her search, the many years that others had devoted to her. Did they have the same sense of failure and frustration as she? These men had accompanied her to Louisiana against their own preference, out of affection and respect and love for her. But there was no insinuation now of their desire for her, or the chance that they might take up what another had disregarded. Perhaps her quest was fundamental to her attraction, Evangeline thought, before she remembered Gabriel, and his feelings toward her as a boy in Grand Pre.

That night, she dreamt that she paddled up the Atchafalaya, alone in the moonlight, and unafraid. She became aware, suddenly, that she watched herself, and with the knowledge, the figure in the boat became Gabriel, and the moon a sun that set, and Gabriel vanished with it across the horizon. She woke in the humid darkness, breathing fast, fighting the urge to call out. She put her head between her knees and sobbed, grasping the mud with both hands as though her convulsions had the power to tear her from the earth.

Felician steered them softly to rest against the pier, Evangeline sitting with her paddle braced upright, watching Bernard scowl fiercely at the foreign shore, unhappy as ever at the prospect of civilization. The long canoe met rotted cypress as they came to rest with a cluster of flat-bottomed boats and a raft big enough for a dozen people tugging at its moorings in the deceptive current.

"Here we are." She stood in the empty echo of her words, their years-long journey down to its final stroke. Here they were at Gabriel's home on the Teche. Two old men, one unmistakably Gabriel's father, sat on stumps near the water's edge as though they'd been there for hours. Basil Lajeunesse, in the wrinkled flesh, an uncomfortable reminder of how much Gabriel must also have aged.

Two low houses rose with the cypress above the muddy bank behind them, the thatched roofs and porches not much different from those in Grand Pre, except for the outdoor stove, which gave the whole enclave the feel of a temporary necessity. Here they were.

Basil raised himself wearily and came down to the water to meet them as they disembarked, leaving his companion behind, staring sightlessly, Evangeline now realized, in their direction.

"Felician Abadie?" Basil called out in disbelief as the priest stepped to the bank. "I'm grateful to have the chance to welcome you as a friend." The man extended a huge knobby hand to the priest and drew him onto the pier.

"Have you been waiting for us?" Felician asked, looking to where the blind man still sat, listening to the reunion.

"Not exactly. But I hoped that someone might be coming down the river today."

"Basil, it's no surprise to see you've survived. Now why don't you let a younger man pass? We've come a long way in search of Acadian hospitality." Felician took the sacks in turn from Bernard, the two men working smoothly together after the years on the trail. Next, the priest reached for Evangeline, while the trapper stayed in the boat, steadying it for her as she stepped out. Bernard remained in the canoe as though he didn't like what he smelled on shore. Felician moved past with their belongings, and Basil extended his arms toward her, cracked eyes brimming, though hers were not.

"Evangeline, you can certainly travel." She stepped into his embrace feeling as if she walked into a trap, with Basil's old sweat the castoreum.

"Your father?" he asked expectantly.

"Buried in Grand Pre. I know about Gabriel." She said it evenly, as though one of the children she'd never had disappointed her slightly. "I still want to talk to him."

"Evangeline." Basil looked at Felician while he composed himself. "He waited as long as he could," he said, as though admitting a terrible failure.

She said nothing, the words plainly insufficient when addressed to one who waited still.

"Where is he?" she finally asked.

"He's been gone longer and longer, trapping. Weeks sometimes."

"He's gone," she said. "Do you know where he goes? Can you take us?" Evangeline now spoke quickly. She couldn't accept that he wasn't there, that she couldn't even see him at the end of it all.

"No," Basil said grimly. "I haven't been out with him in years. He left a few days ago. Philippe might know. He's a friend."

"Well, let's ask him. Where's Gabriel's house?"

"I'm so sorry, Evangeline. For you both." She was barely listening, imagining the impossibility of Gabriel's wife being a woman other than she, a woman she would be speaking to in moments. She recoiled from the thought and Basil reached out to her, but she brushed past his hands and looked back and forth between the houses.

"Which one is his?"

Basil pointed out the one on the right with a visibly trembling hand, and followed her across the marshy ground. She was conscious of the movements of the men behind her, and the smell of the deer skins hanging outside the house she approached. The porch might have been the one they'd have sat on together, two sturdy chairs and a rocker, all with clean, hide seats, and a pipe lying on one, maybe Gabriel's, though he hadn't been smoking when she imagined his life here.

She walked up the steps with long strides, but paused on the porch. Basil and Felician hung back, neither man wanting any part of what was inside the house, for her or themselves. She was the one that should be mournful over this twisted outcome to her hopes, Evangeline thought. Her anger finally propelled her through the door.

Inside, a woman sat at a table, a letter before her. She looked up at her without recognition or surprise. A baby whined from his corner. Evangeline took two slow steps into the room, her eyes fixed on the woman, approaching as she might a cornered animal. It might have been the first time yet in her life when someone else should have led the way, but the men lagged back at the door.

"Do you know who I am?" Evangeline asked.

"Yes," Anna answered.

"I'm looking for Gabriel."

"Well, you won't find him here."

"His father told me he's in the swamp."

"He's always in the swamp."

"This is his child?"

Anna nodded. Evangeline walked to the crib, but resisted the temptation to take the baby into her arms.

"I'm going to find him."

Gabriel's wife shook her blonde hair and nearly smiled, though her eyes were furious.

"You're arriving a bit late," she said. "Gabriel doesn't want to be found." The woman's little blue eyes got sharper, and she addressed Basil who now stood in the doorway. "But take him his son."

Finally, Basil entered the room, probably not the first time he'd waited until bidden to enter this home, Evangeline thought.

"I'll take care of him," Basil said firmly, and then scooped the boy up in gigantic arms and shushed his crying. "We'll bring Gabriel home, Anna." Evangeline had hoped not to hear her name.

"I don't care where he goes," Anna said.

Anna shuddered as Basil departed with his grandson, a tremor that stopped at her face as she turned to Evangeline. Evangeline stared back for a moment, and then followed out the door.

Evangeline and Bernard passed the afternoon on the stumps where they had found the old men that morning. The blind man fiddled from the porch of Basil's house. Basil and Felician returned after several hours, trailed by a pirogue carrying three bearded men. Their guides stood in the water after arriving, as though afraid to step onto the land. One finally came toward them and shook hands around.

"Philippe Boiselle," he said to Evangeline, "Gabriel's friend." He looked at her and then back toward the house where Anna remained. Evangeline wondered who the other men were, if not Gabriel's friends, but did not ask.

"Evangeline Bellefontaine," she said.

Philippe nodded slowly, as though this confirmation dashed an unlikely hope.

"How far do you think he's gone?" she asked.

"Not too far, I imagine." Philippe ventured a look at Basil. "Gabriel would sometimes sleep outside just to do it, you know?" He spat back toward the water. "We'll find him directly. I just wish I wasn't leading the ambush."

"He'll want to see her," Basil said.

"Of course he does," Philippe said, and spat again. "Well, Madame, I suppose you've waited long enough."

They would have had so many stories to share, she realized. Under different circumstances, the man before her would have become a part of her life. But instead, he knew Gabriel's mind, a thing that she now only guessed at.

Evangeline, Felician and Bernard climbed into Basil's pirogue, leaving their own canoe behind to allow them more clearance on the Teche's shallow tributaries. Evangeline disliked leaving the canoe, if only because it meant that they would be forced to return here. She did not know what she would say to him when she saw him. It wasn't a message she brought, but the promise of a life they could no longer fulfill.

They followed Philippe's boat, paddling through the late autumn for the two hours remaining before dusk, passing few homesteads. The closeness of the air and low visibility made it seem as if they made little progress. They camped late amid stubby palmetto sprouting from the firmer ground, and the light failed before they had the fire started. Philippe offered around brandy, and she and Felician declined before the other men accepted.

"It's been a long time between drinks," Bernard said appreciatively.

"Well, I'll be damned if this isn't the night for it," Philippe replied, and drank until his neck bulged. He looked around more calmly. "We'll likely find him tomorrow."

"How long has he been gone this time?" Evangeline asked.

Philippe shook his head. "Probably two weeks. Maybe a little longer."

"And he's just one day away?" she asked.

Philippe took another long drink before looking at her. "Gabriel doesn't spend much time at home."

Evangeline dared hope at the words, but, either seeing her expression, or perhaps sensing her thoughts, Philippe mollified his comment. "He will, though, once that boy gets a little older."

The men drank without more talk of Gabriel, and before the bottle was empty, Philippe passed out sitting next to the fire.

"I remember you," one of the others addressed her. "I'm Michel Richard, from Baltimore." He looked disappointed when she remained expressionless at the name. This man would have only been a boy in Baltimore. How could he expect her to remember him, when her whole past had been washed clean since the conversation with the tinker? The years in the hospital seemed irreconcilable with the ineffectual toiling that had followed.

"I'm sorry," she said, finally, and they sat quietly looking into the fire.

"He asked me about you," Michel said finally.

"What did you tell him?"

"I told him you weren't married," Michel said defensively.

Evangeline waited quietly for a moment before changing the subject. "Did you trap with him?"

Michel nodded. "He showed me around when I got down here."

"Did he enjoy doing this?"

Michel shrugged. "He hasn't opened up much to me. But he knows this country as well as anyone."

Evangeline tried to feel proud. Instead, she thought about what Gabriel might be searching for in the oblivion of the swamp. It was impossible to imagine him happy anywhere but at her side, and certainly not out alone in this thick blackness. But happy or not, Gabriel was close at hand. She watched the fire burn down before her and imagined him doing the same in his solitary camp. Though she thought that it wouldn't, eventually sleep claimed her.

The next morning, they explored a branch leaking west from the Teche, the water stiller than any they had seen en route, a stagnant brown stain befouling the green carpet of the swamp.

Sometimes hemmed in by trees so that they could hold hands with the men in the other pirogue, the flow mostly resembled some forgotten lake, though never so deep as to prevent trees from shading the entire route. Birds flapped through the low canopy just over their heads, and more than once in her tension, Evangeline mistook their echoing calls for screams. When the tributary widened, they followed opposite banks, like hunters scouting the shore for signs of their quarry, and as they made their way deeper into the unceasing lowlands, she resisted the urge to scream his name and shatter the quiet of the swamp.

They came upon the boat before noon. She looked quickly over the pirogue, halfway pulled up on shore as though its owner intended to leave suddenly. Fallen leaves lay thick about the traps and musket inside. They all smelled a fire, though she couldn't see the smoke. Evangeline looked to the other pirogue, where the men turned toward them from their own explorations.

"Give me a moment alone with him," she implored her companions.

No one followed as she jumped into the ankle-deep water and forged up the bank, her muddy skirts weighted as if they carried the river with her. What would she say, Evangeline wondered? How could you? Didn't you believe I was coming?

Up a slight rise the cypress parted their waving branches in a clearing, and there, before a cold fire, in a trench cleared of the oak and cypress leaves, she saw a form, curled up and facing away from her.

"Gabriel," she screamed, the sound bursting forth like a child. Here he was. She had found him.

He rolled to face her, and his mouth gaped silently in response, exposing a tongue black and swollen and hanging like a tiny, gangrenous limb, or the tail of a black snake that gnawed his heart. She approached slowly, her feet dragging against her will as her mind forced her to understand what lay before her, lips repeating his name as he inaudibly gasped hers from the swamp floor.

Gabriel was shirtless, deeply tanned, and unrecognizably muscular, lying in what would soon have been his shallow grave. She dropped to her knees in front of him, and he shook his head wildly. The skin she touched was sticky with old sweat, and his back was serrated with fresh welts from thrashing about on the ground.

Sitting by that fire he had made and fed until his strength failed, she gathered his head in her lap and stroked his hair, the only part of him unchanged, she thought distantly. His gums and teeth were awash in blood, which she wiped away with her dress.

"No, no, sweetheart," she wept as he weakly squirmed, trying to shift his unresponsive body away from her. "Don't worry, Gabriel. Let me hold you."

He looked up into her eyes then, for the first time since she entered the clearing, and he stopped struggling. The sweetness she remembered better than her name flooded them, and he looked at her without panic, mouthing her name again, so that she thought she heard it at last.

"No, no," she repeated softly, her tears dripping onto his face. "Oh, Gabriel. I found you, sweetheart." She kissed where the hair met his forehead. "And we're together now."

She heard another voice call out but paid it no mind. Evangeline sat, savoring his name as she repeated it, over and over, into those beautiful brown eyes. She kept saying it until the brown faded to a paler color she couldn't name.

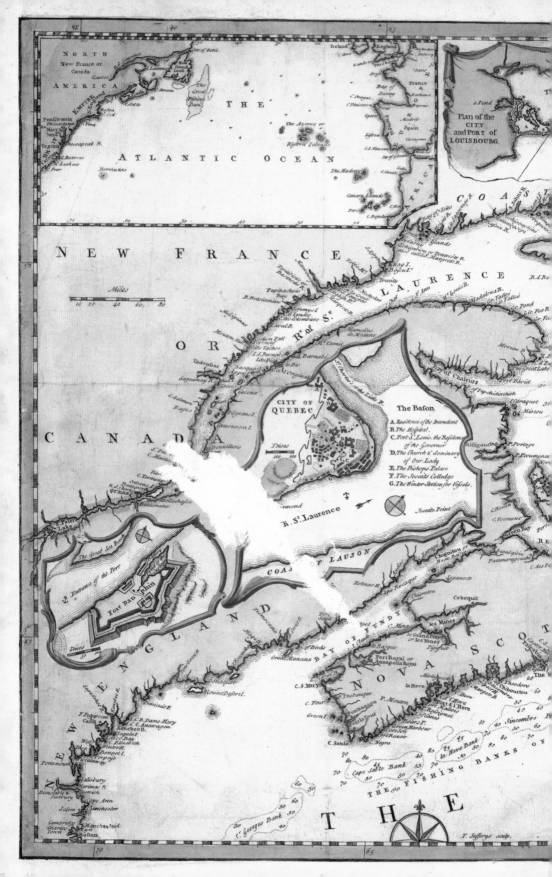